A
RESTLESS
TRUTH

By Freya Marske

The Last Binding trilogy
A Marvellous Light
A Restless Truth

A

RESTLESS

TRUTH

FREYA MARSKE

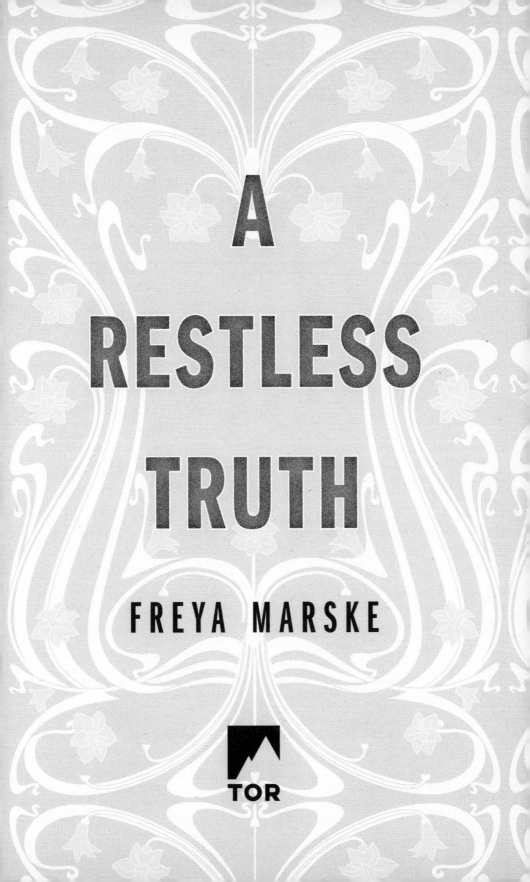

TOR

First published 2022 by Tom Doherty Associates

First published in the UK 2022 by Tor
an imprint of Pan Macmillan
The Smithson, 6 Briset Street, London EC1M 5NR
EU representative: Macmillan Publishers Ireland Ltd, 1st Floor,
The Liffey Trust Centre, 117–126 Sheriff Street Upper,
Dublin 1, D01 YC43
Associated companies throughout the world
www.panmacmillan.com

ISBN 978-1-5290-8093-3

1 3 5 7 9 8 6 4 2

A CIP catalogue record for this book is available from the British Library.

Printed and bound by CPI Group (UK) Ltd, Croydon, CR0 4YY

Visit **www.panmacmillan.com** to read more about all our books
and to buy them. You will also find features, author interviews and
news of any author events, and you can sign up for e-newsletters
so that you're always first to hear about our new releases.

*For everyone, everywhere, who's been stuck at home
and dreaming of adventure*

A
RESTLESS
TRUTH

1

Elizabeth Navenby was known for three things: needlework, talking to the dead, and an ill temper at the best of times.

These were not the best of times. Seasickness had taken rough shears to the edges of that temper. And being subjected to well-meaning jabber about the stateroom's furnishings, and how the handkerchief-waving crowds lining the New York docks as the *Lyric* pulled away looked *exactly* like a flock of doves—didn't she agree?—had hardly helped.

So Elizabeth had ordered the talkative Miss Blyth, who had truly disgusting amounts of energy for a girl her age, off to explore the ship.

"Finally," said Elizabeth to the empty interior of the cabin. "I could do with some quiet."

It was not truly quiet. But the buzz of the ship's engines was no more difficult to ignore than the normal noise of a Manhattan afternoon. And the stateroom's furnishings, now that she turned her attention to them, were . . . adequately luxurious. If rather modern. Green glass lamps like mildewed snowdrops hung from the brass arms of the chandelier. The chairs were upholstered in a paler green. Dorian's cage sat upon a low bureau whose drawers had inlaid patterns of tulips with long, looping stems.

"I suppose you'd approve of *that*, Flora," said Elizabeth. "You always did like your outdoors to decorate your indoors."

Another wave of nausea was joined by a dull ache like something had taken her knee between blunt-toothed jaws. Elizabeth had serviceable dry-land knees. They weren't used to exerting themselves to steady a body against the sea.

She wobbled to sit in the nearest chair and cradled a warmth-spell. The yellow light of it shimmered dimly, reflected in the polished wood of the bureau, then vanished as she applied the magic to her knee. Heat seeped into her bedevilled old joint.

"And I won't hear a *word* about how I should be using a stick," she said.

One of the senior stewards had descended simperingly upon them as soon as they set foot off the gangplank. She'd suspected him of wanting to make calf's eyes at Miss Blyth, but instead he'd given Elizabeth some damned condescending twaddle about how difficult the crossing could be for the elderly and infirm, and how the White Star Line prided itself on its little comforts for first-class passengers, and if she had any need of extra pillows—some warm broth or ginger tea to soothe her stomach—a walking stick—

At which point Elizabeth had called him an imposing busy-body and strode past, leaving Miss Blyth making apologies in her wake. Pointless. Men would never learn to behave if you apologised at them.

"Infirm!" she muttered now. "The *cheek*."

"*Cheek,*" said Dorian.

Though it sounded more like *cheat,* which Elizabeth had taught him to say after she caught that boring old fart Hudson Renner trying to wear wooden rings at her poker table. There was no excuse for using illusions at a civilised gambling party, no matter how much of your fortune you'd frittered away on investments that anyone could have told you were foolhardy bordering on idiotic.

Elizabeth creaked to her feet. Her knee felt better. Her stomach did not.

"I simply didn't expect to be making voyages in this stage of my life. Though I will allow"—grudgingly—"the last time I crossed the Atlantic, I remember the seasickness being even worse."

The last time had been in the other direction, when she and her husband left England behind in search of a different life in America. That ship had been far smaller. Nothing like this enormous liner.

Elizabeth snorted in reminiscence. "Poor Ralph. He spent the first day rubbing my back and emptying basins before I was well enough to remember that I had packed one of Sera's stomach-calming tonics, and that dried chamomile from your garden—"

Grief's jaws were not blunt of tooth. They snapped shut like a poacher's trap.

Elizabeth stood with her hand clenched around her silver locket and kept painfully behind her teeth the urge to curse the dead for dying. She wanted to hurl magic at those green lamps for the pleasure of watching something shatter. Memory plagued her, gutted her, snarled at her heels. Flora had wrapped magic like gossamer around her chamomile as it grew. She'd whispered to it until even the flowers' subtle scent on the edge of a breeze was a soporific charm, like fingers laid on the eyelids.

Slowly Elizabeth's grip on the locket loosened. She checked her palm, as if she might have pressed the pattern of sunflowers into her skin.

Surely the size of this pain was out of proportion to all reason. She and Flora had spent the latter halves of their lives on different continents. They were old enough that death might well be expected to come knocking.

None of that made any difference to the way Elizabeth had been scooped out, left desolate and raging, when Miss Blyth had first shifted her feet on the carpet and blurted out the news of Flora's death.

Their age made it *worse*. It was absurd. Elizabeth was too old to go around avenging murders.

She would do it anyway, of course. Even if her bones felt too brittle to hold the anger that drove her forward.

"I know, I know," she muttered. "As long as I've life, I can choose what to do with it."

Elizabeth Navenby talked to the dead not in the general, but in the particular.

More than that, she had talked to her *particular* dead person since long before the descriptor applied. Ever since leaving England, she'd talked as if Flora Sutton were there—as if the locket linked them in more ways than the metaphorical. As if they'd found a way to overcome the limitations of magic at vast distances, and any words she spoke would truly be carried back across the ocean and into Flora's ears.

She'd refrained in front of Miss Blyth. Her tongue felt crammed full of things that had been building up unsaid. Now that she could let them out in peace, the weightiest ones were rolling forward.

"I thought I would know the exact moment," said Elizabeth Navenby to her absent dead. "I truly did. I thought—oh, I'd sit up in bed with my heart aflutter. Be stopped in the street by a moment of dread. No—I had to be told to my face, *months* after you were in the ground. Had to sit there gaping like a fish, and realise that even after—even—nobody thought I might appreciate a damned *telegram*—"

Another surge of angry grief. As if sensing it, Dorian gave a long croak of a sigh.

No. The wretched bird was not empathetic, merely passive-aggressive; he resorted to the pathos of croaking as a hint that he wanted attention. Or lunch.

Elizabeth removed the bowl from his cage and filled it with fresh water. Hopefully Miss Blyth would remember, during her exploration, to ask the stewards about food for him. Unlikely. The girl was magpie-brained. They'd be lucky if she remembered her way back to the cabin.

"If you were here, you'd be telling me not to trust the girl at all." A laugh tried to huff its way out. "You always were a paranoid creature, Flora. Never fear. Not a word has passed my lips about my piece of the contract. We don't tell—not until there are no other options. We promised."

She replaced the brimming bowl. Dorian nipped her finger in approval as she withdrew.

They'd promised. And yet the paranoid Flora herself had by all accounts given her part of the contract to her unmagical great-nephew—had laid secret-bind on him, sent him to his death, and taken her own life in turn to keep from betraying it—because there were *no other options*.

Because after all these decades of keeping the Last Contract safe, keeping its three pieces separate and unable to be wrought into a weapon that would pull power from every magician in Britain, a net was closing on the Forsythia Club. On the women who'd been arrogant and curious enough to drag that weapon into the light in the first place.

"Hubris," said Elizabeth, as if the word were a charm. It tasted bitter on her lips.

She shook herself. Never any point dwelling. Look to the next thing.

Something to quell this nausea, perhaps. She'd sewn a helpful charm into a shawl for a niece suffering a difficult pregnancy—couldn't recall the exact spell she'd used, now, but piecing it together would be a distraction.

Her sewing kit was in one of the trunks. On her way to rummage, the ship gave a particularly queasy shift. Elizabeth gritted her teeth.

After a few moments she admitted the futility of trying to beat sickness with stubbornness, and went to retch unpleasantly over a basin in the stateroom's small bathroom.

Someone chose that idyllic moment to knock on the cabin door.

Elizabeth gripped the basin edge and refused to answer. Let them think her asleep. She would not be coddled by stewards. She'd conjure a nest of thorns and hurl herself into it before she accepted an offer of *broth*. She would deal with this herself.

Once her stomach stopped trying to clamber up the inside of her lower ribs.

The lock clicked. The main door creaked gently open. Miss Blyth, then, already bored with exploring. Elizabeth scowled at the porcelain and waited fatalistically for the flood of bright chatter to resume.

Nothing.

And into the nothing, footsteps. Too heavy to be Miss Blyth's. Too slow. *Cautious.*

Alarm flooded in. It managed to shove aside some of the nausea. Elizabeth straightened. The bathroom door, swung ajar, hid her from the main room.

The stunning-spell she prepared was one of Flora's, built with a single hand and a firm will—leaving the other hand free to hoist a nice solid candlestick, they used to jest, in case the spell missed. Magic filled her palm like snow.

Elizabeth took a deep breath.

She shoved at the bathroom door with her free hand. The damn thing *creaked,* robbing her of a chance at surprise. A curse slid between her teeth. She had only a brief glimpse—a man, lifting his head sharply from where he was bent over the dresser, pawing through her effects—before she flung the spell at him.

The creak had been enough warning. He dodged. And—oh, hell, he was cradling himself, now. A magician.

She had to try again. Another spell, fast. *Blast* her stiff old hands. She could hear Flora telling her, as if finally picking up her half of the conversation: *You still rely too much on those cradles, Beth, I've always said so.*

Flora was right. Damn her, Flora was always right. But Elizabeth was bound by her own weaknesses now. The spell struggled to form between her shaking fingers.

I'm sorry, Flora. I did so want to kill them for you.

Her heart shook even more, bounding half out of her chest with fear and fury. It rendered her light-headed and shaken even before the moment when hot-smelling magic sprang from the man's hands and engulfed her senses like the crash of lightning.

I'm sorry.

2

Maud knew Mrs. Navenby was dead as soon as she opened the door.

She wasn't sure how she knew, precisely. She'd never been in the same room as a corpse before. It was not a situation that a baronet's daughter might frequently expect to encounter in the course of her life.

Nevertheless, certainty hit her like a pail of flung water.

Mrs. Navenby lay sprawled on the floor. Her eyes were open and the look on her waxy, unmoving face was not something that Maud wanted to look at for more than a few seconds.

"Oh my *heavens*," Maud heard herself squeak, and sagged back against the door.

She felt a ludicrous pang of disappointment. Firstly, that she had *squeaked*. Secondly, that she hadn't seized the opportunity to say *Fuck*. She'd never been game enough on any lesser occasion, and surely this was the most obscenity-deserving situation she would ever find herself in.

"*Whaaaat?*" said Dorian.

A giggle like a mouthful of vinegared wine spilled from Maud.

"My thoughts exactly," she told the parrot, and that broke the cold bind that held her paralysed against the door.

Maud flung herself across the room. She promptly tripped and caught herself on one knee as the floor shrugged and one shoe caught in her skirt. Her sea legs hadn't returned yet, and the captain had told them to expect a choppy start to the voyage.

She felt for a pulse. She had no idea if she was feeling in the correct place. There were no marks on the visible skin, and no blood—Maud winced, feeling gingerly at the back of the dead woman's head—in the hair. She could have died of a sudden apoplexy. Her heart could have given out.

But a few hours ago, Mrs. Navenby had been hale and well. And magic didn't have to leave marks when it killed.

At a Suffragette meeting in London, Maud had once met a Miss Harlow, who was studying medicine at the Sorbonne and who told vivid tales of gory injuries and learning anatomy from examining the dead. Maud, much as she longed to attend university, did not think her stomach was lined with the exact sort of grit required of a physician. Miss Harlow had passed around a human skull. Maud had run her fingers along the sockets of the eyes and wondered what colour those eyes had been in life, and then she'd felt queasy and passed the skull on to Liza.

And when her parents died, it was in a motorcar accident. There had been no question of Maud being asked to identify the bodies. Robin had done that, while Maud shut herself in her bedroom so that nobody would see her failing to cry. All their lives Robin had done the unpleasant things so that Maud didn't have to worry about them. All their lives he'd protected her and had never failed her.

And now she'd failed him, at the one enormous vital thing she'd sworn to him that she could handle.

Mrs. Navenby was dead, and that meant someone on this ship knew that Mrs. Navenby had an object of immense and dangerous potential power in her possession, and they wanted it.

The old woman had refused to tell Maud which of her belongings was her piece of the spell-made-solid known as the Last Contract. *Safer that way,* she'd said, in her snappish no-argument tones.

And now Maud had a corpse at her feet and a full six days of the Atlantic crossing ahead of her, trapped on a boat with at least one magician willing to kill, when Maud had no magic of her own and no idea what she was protecting, or even if it had already been taken—

Maud rubbed her hands over her face. *Stupid, stupid.*

She made herself focus as she looked around the room. She'd partly unpacked Mrs. Navenby's luggage while they were still in the harbour. The room didn't look as though it had been searched, but enough things stood half-open that it would be hard to tell.

Maud inspected the dresser through a pinkly acidic pulse of panic. Boxes of brooches and rings. Knickknacks. What was missing? Anything? There was a parlour game: one stared at a tray of objects before it was taken away, adjusted, and placed back in front of one's eyes. Some things added. Some things removed.

Robin was excellent at that game. Maud was . . . not.

But she'd set everything out on the dresser that very day, and then spent a good quarter hour adjusting things according to the old woman's finicky taste, and—

The mirror. There had been a silver hand mirror in a matching set with a hairbrush, both heavy and ornate. *They* were missing.

Recognition calmed Maud's heartbeat. She managed to pick out some more missing things: a bangle of beaten silver featuring elephants in an Indian design. A small silver bottle like a gentleman's hip flask, which contained one of Mrs. Navenby's favoured scents.

Silver. Silver. The first piece of the contract to be recovered— and then lost—by Robin and his partner, Edwin, had been three silver rings that became a single silver coin. Maud hadn't asked if the cup, Mrs. Navenby's piece, was made of the same substance.

Silver.

A single glance confirmed what had prickled at the back of Maud's mind when she was lifting the corpse's head to feel for blood. The locket was gone. Heavy and oval-shaped with a design of sunflowers on the front, Maud had never seen Mrs. Navenby without it hanging on a chain from her neck. She had noted the woman's attachment to it and had already begun to form some private suspicions.

So. A few silver items missing, and plenty of valuable jewels left in plain sight.

It was murder, and by someone who knew precisely what they were looking for.

"Fuck," said Maud.

"*Fuck,*" agreed Dorian.

"Are you sure we can't fetch you some water, Miss Cutler?" asked the master-at-arms. "Or a cup of tea?"

"No, thank you, Mr. Berry." Maud smiled weakly. "But it's so kind of you to offer."

The head of security for the *Lyric* had a sturdy figure and a kind face with a reddish moustache that was doing its best to engulf his upper lip, as though he'd inherited it from a larger relative and was waiting to grow into it. He eyed Maud with the familiar alarm of a man unsure if the girl in front of him was about to burst into tears.

He decided to err on the side of assuming that Maud was too upset and too feminine to know what she needed, and directed the nearest steward to bring a cup of tea at once.

Maud concentrated on keeping her expression neutral. "What will happen to her now?"

"I dare say it may seem morbid to a young thing like you, Miss Cutler, but the White Star Line is well prepared for tragic occurrences of this nature. This isn't the first time one of our elderly guests has passed out of the mortal world and into a better one during the course of the voyage." Mr. Berry touched the point between his collarbones where a cross might sit on a chain beneath his shirt and uniform jacket. "We'll see to it she's treated with respect, and kept where she won't—forgive me—spoil."

"Oh, goodness. I hadn't thought of that." Maud bit her tongue on asking if they had a secondary ice room set aside specifically for dead bodies, and if not, if the first-class passengers were aware that the ice used for their desserts was also being turned to such a purpose. Mrs. Navenby would have found that amusing.

"Was her passing . . . very unexpected?"

As a matter of principle, Maud hated to lie. She was aware that to a young woman currently travelling under an assumed name and about to embark on an undercover detective investigation, this principle was as much use as a pincushion in a boxing ring.

Nevertheless. The truth was a flexible reed of a thing. One could weave it into all sorts of shapes, depending on what one needed it to be.

What Maud needed was for nobody *else* to be conducting a murder-robbery investigation in any official capacity. That would stir up alarm and get in her way and put Maud's enemies— who at this moment were likely congratulating themselves on their success—on their guard.

Besides: Maud read detective stories. She had discovered the body; if there was a whiff of foul play in the air, she would be questioned, and she was, after all, travelling under an assumed name. If someone started doing inconvenient things like telegraphing back to New York or on to London with enquiries, there was a risk of said someone discovering that Mrs. Navenby's distant and impoverished cousin, Miss Maud Cutler, was a complete fabrication.

"Mrs. Navenby was . . . very aware of her age. She wanted to come home, to England, as a matter of some urgency."

Mr. Berry nodded. He'd seen *illness* in the shape of those sentences, and it suited him.

"Even so." He patted Maud's shoulder. "No matter how expected, losing those close to us is always a blow."

Maud's eyes filled with hot tears. It was a waste. It was a

bloody stupid *waste,* and she had *failed her brother,* and Mrs. Navenby *should* be alive. People should not be allowed to kill other people simply because they got in their way, as if they were no more than *things.*

The master-at-arms opened his mouth and was interrupted by an outraged squawk. The returning steward had bumped Dorian's cage in passing. Everyone present winced. Dorian gave another squawk, this one softer, and went to the floor of the cage to plunge his head indignantly into his water bowl.

"Mrs. Navenby was very attached to her bird," said Maud in apology.

"Charming creature, I'm sure," said Mr. Berry. "Now, perhaps you'd like to retire to your own room and have a lie-down. I'm sure we can arrange—ah, there we are, the tea. Rogers, send word to the kitchens that Miss Cutler will take her meals in her cabin for the next few days."

"No," said Maud quickly.

Eyebrows rose. To cover, Maud took a fortifying sip of the tea. Now she needed to truth-weave her way out of any expectation that she would stay languishing in her room when what she needed was to be out looking for answers. And murderers. And the stolen piece of the Last Contract.

"That is—thank you for your concern, but I think some bright, cheerful company will do me good. Distract me. I must confess, Mr. Berry, I didn't know Mrs. Navenby very well. I'd spent only a short time as her companion, and she was not the easiest of employers." Maud gazed down into the saucer, where some tea had sloshed. She called up not Mrs. Navenby's short temper and acerbic tongue, but a memory of her own mother. Whose tongue had never been anything but sweet, even as the words that dripped from it settled in your mind and choked there.

Maud said, "You must think me awfully callous."

"Not at all," said Mr. Berry at once, and the hovering steward made a distressed noise of assent. Maud peeked up at him from beneath her lashes. Rogers was not much older than herself, with a prominent neck and a spotted chin, and he turned pink when he met her eyes.

"Thank you both so much," she said meekly. "I *shall* go and lie down until dinner."

Her adjoining room was smaller than the main chamber, with a narrow bed tucked against the wall and less distinguished furnishings. Many of the staterooms had such arrangements, for families with children or those travelling with personal servants. Maud's own role of companion was a step up from servant, but not by much.

She closed the door between the rooms and leaned against it. In the sudden quiet, the lack of eyes upon her, the sway of the ship found her again. This time Maud planted her shoes and imagined herself an anchor lodged in the sand of the seabed, among the weeds.

She had failed. She was alone. But she would *not* return home to her brother, in six days' time, and have that be the story she told him.

Maud went to her trunk and retrieved the notebook from where it was wedged between two books near the bottom. She flicked through the pages scattered with short paragraphs in Robin's careless writing, with occasional annotations in Edwin's neater hand. At the centre of the book was a sketch of a woman's face: a long nose and a decided chin, the fairness of her hair obvious in the dearth of pencil lines in the top half of the page.

There were some advantages when one's older brother had visions of the future.

Maud grasped her anchorness. She would make things right. She would find the magician—or magicians—on this ship and discover which of them had killed Mrs. Navenby. She would get those stolen objects back, every one of them. She would find those people who didn't yet know that they were her allies, and she would enlist their help.

And she would step off the ship in Southampton in *triumph*, and Robin would be proud of her, and it would be the first important and worthwhile thing that Maud Blyth, baronet's daughter and baronet's sister, would have done in her entire short useless life.

3

Bright and cheerful the company was indeed as Maud entered the first-class dining saloon for dinner that evening. The huge room was abuzz with people. One long edge of the saloon had doors leading out to a deck promenade, and at this dark hour of night the windows were nothing but a canvas reflecting the brightness within. Electric lights and table candles fought one another for prominence, illuminating the greens and reds of the carpet and the darker green upholstery of the chairs.

A few groups of richly dressed people still lingered standing, like clusters of jewels hung from a woman's throat, but most were seated. The steward who'd opened the door for Maud cleared his throat meaningfully.

Maud had meant to be early, and now she was late. She was not accustomed to dressing for formal dinners without the assistance of a maid, and some of the buttons on her evening gown had proven fiddly. The dress had won the battle with Maud's shortening temper; one button had come off entirely in the struggle. She'd thrown a wrap around her shoulders to disguise it.

"Shall I sit . . . ?"

"Wherever you fancy, miss. Only the captain's table requires an invitation." The steward nodded across the room to where the gilt trim of the captain's hat caught the light as brightly as the polished glasses and silver place settings.

Maud skimmed her eyes over the throng. There were empty seats scattered at various tables. She'd never attended a dinner where her place at table was not predetermined. She'd never been asked to *choose*. She was filled with the sudden conviction that if she chose wrongly, the hubbub of conversation would turn at once to a stony silence and every eye would find her.

Maud clutched the strings of her evening bag tightly in one gloved hand, willing that hand not to shake, and turned her head in unthinking response to a laugh too loud for propriety.

At a nearby table sat a woman with simply dressed yellow hair and a dark-blue gown cradling the creamy skin of her shoulders, which shook with the aftermath of that laugh. She was taking a gulp of champagne. To her right, a middle-aged woman was staring at her with a look of mixed horror and pleading, which manifested as a mouth clenched tight enough to crack walnuts.

To her left was an empty seat. Maud realised this in the same moment that the blond woman lowered the glass from her lips, revealing the firm and striking profile that adorned the middle pages of Robin's notebook.

Maud's heart gave a pound.

The next moment, she was on the move. She trod without shame on the foot of a portly gentleman with a monocle, who had clearly espied the blond woman and was just as eager to fill the empty seat, and slid herself triumphantly to lay a hand on the chair's back.

"Good evening." She dimpled at the table at large. "Is this seat spoken for, or may I intrude?"

Seven pairs of eyes landed on her. The first person to speak was one of the only two men at the table, seated directly across from Maud's purloined chair. He looked around Robin's age, with heavy brows and brown hair pomaded back but beginning to curl rebelliously behind the ears, and a serious but not unkind expression.

"By all means." The North sang baritone in his words. "I'm sure we'd be glad of your company."

Maud deposited herself in the seat before anyone could gainsay this welcome. As if it had been a signal, another steward appeared and poured a shallow inch of champagne into her glass, and suddenly there was a flock of the men, like magpies in a flower garden, beginning the dinner service.

Maud shrugged off the wrap. Her back was to one of the pillars; she could probably risk it. The air was close and warm and alive, the scent of food mingling with the perfumes of hundreds of ladies.

Well. No time like the present to begin an investigation.

Before her gloves were even removed, Maud discovered through polite questioning that the Northern gentleman was called Mr. Chapman, and the majestic pile of furs and diamonds seated beside him was a Mrs. Moretti. To Maud's left were two women with the same nose: a pair of married sisters from Boston who left their husbands at home and did this trip every year, to go to London and Paris for the fashions. Maud murmured her admiration of the sumptuous beading of Mrs. Babcock's dress and the drip of emeralds from Mrs. Endicott's ears, after which the sisters turned back to each other and ignored her entirely.

Maud inhaled a determined breath to ask the blond woman if she was travelling alone, and was struck with the conviction that Champagne would bolster her courage. She took a quick gulp from her glass.

Unfortunately, she'd forgotten that she was still inhaling.

It was entirely typical of how this day was going, Maud thought in wheezing despair, that her first encounter with the mysterious blond woman from Robin's visions—who was almost *certainly* meant to help her in this dangerous and magical adventure—was said woman handing Maud a fresh napkin to dab at the now-soaked front of her dress while Maud coughed around a flurry of cold bubbles in her nose. Maud was probably bright red too. She always went red when she coughed.

"All right?" American, cool and bemused.

"Yes." Wheeze, splutter. Maud wanted to die. "Th-Thank you. Goodness. I'm so sorry."

"Not in the least. I like a suitably dramatic opening number.

Have you considered taking to the stage? I could introduce you to all the least reputable producers in New York."

"*Violet*," wailed the walnut-mouthed woman. "*Please*, my dear."

"But that would require me to know your name," the woman prompted Maud.

"Oh! Maud. Maud Cutler."

"There. Violet Debenham." She turned in her seat and held her hand mannishly out to Maud. Yet more self-conscious heat filled Maud's cheeks as she shook. Miss Debenham had a firm grip. Her eyes were a pleasant grey, and they sparkled.

Miss Debenham was travelling with Mrs. Caroline Blackwood—fair, fussily dressed, and with a figure that put Maud unfortunately in mind of chicken bones—and this lady's son, Clarence, a young man desperately in need of a portion more chin. Clarence nodded at Maud with his eyes fixed somewhere below her neckline.

"And what brings you to England, Miss Debenham?" Maud asked.

"Money," said Miss Debenham.

A pained noise escaped Mrs. Blackwood. Miss Debenham's eyes gained even more sparkle, as though the attention of the table were a spotlight and she wished to relish its illumination.

"A distant relative of ours recently passed away and named me as her heir. A *rich* relative. So my dear, *concerned* aunt and cousin took it upon themselves to come to New York and deliver me from treading the boards in that pit of dissolution known as the Bowery, and restore me to the bosom of my loving family. I am eternally in their debt. Or so"—with a rich laugh—"they hope."

Mrs. Blackwood gave a small twitch at the word *debt*.

"Don't speak rot, Violet," said the young Mr. Blackwood. "Practically had to drag you out of that place by the hair."

"*Clarence*," snapped his mother.

"Clarence, you couldn't drag a kitten out of a bag," said Miss Debenham. "The money did the dragging."

"Violet," her aunt assured the table, "is an English gentleman's daughter—"

"He has five of us, I doubt he missed one."

"A *gentleman's daughter,* brought up in comfort and propriety—"

"And now upon the stages of the Bowery?" Mrs. Moretti looked to have scented blood. "That must have been quite the scandal."

"Indeed it was."

"*Violet,*" moaned Mrs. Blackwood.

"It was three years ago. I fancied a change of scenery, and so"—a shrug of those fine shoulders, where a simple necklace of gold filigree sat draped over her collarbones—"I packed up and got on a ship."

"All on your own?" said Maud, who felt rather as if she were observing an energetic game of badminton.

"On my own." Miss Debenham smiled. Her accent was stronger than Maud would have expected for someone who had only divorced herself from her native shores for a handful of years. It wasn't the genteel tones of the Boston sisters either. It was a smoky, brash twang that Maud had heard often enough on the streets of New York but never in its parlours.

"So you are an actress, Miss Debenham?" Thrilled questions jumbled themselves up in Maud's mind. In her parents' circles, any woman on the stage could be assumed to have the loosest of morals.

Maud had voiced her intention of becoming such a woman, once, when she was sixteen. Her mother had flashed a look of heated poison with those green eyes—so exactly like Maud's own—and Maud had gloried in a moment of attention. Then Lady Blyth had given one of her mild, buttery company-laughs, and said, "What strange fancies you do get into your head, Maud."

And removed her attention, again.

"I am a performer." Miss Debenham sparkled even harder. "Most of what appears on a concert-hall stage isn't exactly Shakespeare, you know."

"Did you ever do any magic?"

The pause was not long. Maud kept her expression innocently hopeful; Miss Debenham's didn't change, but there was another subdued twitch from her relatives. *Ah.* Good.

"Magic?" said Miss Debenham.

"Isn't stage magic popular in America? It's all the rage in London. My friend's brother took us to see Mr. Houdini perform once, and before he came on there was a mentalist who named every single member of a woman's family, and another man who made objects disappear. Mr. Houdini is an American, isn't he? Though perhaps," Maud mused, diverted, "he came to England because the Americans care less to see that sort of thing."

Miss Debenham's expressive mouth was twitching. Maud noted it with the part of her mind that wasn't now busy wondering if Mr. Houdini *was* in fact a magician. She felt vaguely cheated by the idea.

"My theatre did engage some stage magicians, yes." Miss Debenham hadn't moved her glittering grey eyes from Maud's.

"*Sadly,* there are some frauds in this world who call themselves mentalists and spiritualists in order to fleece a gullible public," said Mrs. Moretti. "It does nothing but make life difficult for those of us who are *truly* gifted in that regard."

The spotlight of the attention's table turned. Maud's stomach rumbled and she realised that she had been neglecting her dinner. She hastily took the opportunity to get down a few large mouthfuls of herbed carrots and fish in white sauce.

"Indeed, ma'am?" said Mr. Chapman.

"Oh, yes." Mrs. Moretti stroked her fur. "Amongst my own circles I am a famed medium, and I was consulted in New York by such ladies as—well, I shall respect their privacy," she said impressively, "but rest assured you would gasp if I named them. I am *extremely* sensitive to the spirits of the departed. In fact . . ." She leaned forward. A corner of the fur began to collect gravy. "Did you hear that a passenger on board the *Lyric* has already died? Oh, yes. Barely out of port. I heard some of the

stewards discussing it, but of course I already suspected something of that nature had happened. My senses are so attuned.
Oh, don't be afraid, my dear." She directed her impressive look
at Maud, who was attempting valiantly not to laugh around
a piece of carrot. "There is no negative or malevolent energy
aboard. Quite the opposite. I'm sure the saintly departed will
be watching over us and ensuring our safety throughout this
voyage."

"How reassuring," said Mrs. Endicott faintly.

For a ludicrous moment Maud wondered if she could get
away with pretending the death had nothing to do with her.
But sooner or later someone at the table was going to ask what
brought *Maud* back to England, and then it would look suspicious that she hadn't spoken up now.

So she swallowed her carrot and said, "It was Mrs. Navenby
who died. The woman I was travelling with."

General gasps and murmurs. Mrs. Moretti looked displeased
to have lost the spotlight. Maud kept her eyes open for reac-
tions as she gave a slightly expanded version of the explanation
she'd given the master-at-arms. This one contained the necessary falsehood that she was a distant cousin of Mrs. Navenby's,
and had obeyed the summons to America to act as the snappish
old woman's companion because she had no prospects in England and felt herself a burden on her brother.

"My family is not as well off as we once were," she finished,
which had the advantage of being true.

"And now the old lady's died, I suppose you're holding out
expectation of being left something in the will, for your pains?"
Mr. Blackwood laughed at her. Maud, who had been mocked
by experts, felt only the mildest sting and brushed it away like
an ant at a picnic.

She lowered her eyes to her plate. "No. I have no such expectation."

"At least you had the chance to cross the Atlantic. Twice!
Look on it as an adventure, then," said Miss Debenham. "Clarence, I know you can't help being such a toad, but perhaps the

next time the urge strikes you to open your mouth, you could shove some bread into it."

Mr. Blackwood did in fact open his mouth. Then he jerked, shot a look at his mother, and closed it again.

"Your dress appears to be of a remarkably fine make, Miss Cutler," said Mrs. Endicott.

"Thank you," said Maud, "I—"

"Yes, I had one just like it made up for my daughter." A sweep of unimpressed gaze down Maud's body and back up again. "*Several* years ago."

Maud having now been mentally filed in the role of *poor cousin*, the majority of the table seemed content to ignore her. She chewed over this problem, along with a slice of rare roast beef, while Miss Debenham gestured for more champagne and then flirted outrageously with the serving steward, to her relatives' rigid discomfort. It didn't matter what anyone thought of Miss Maud Cutler, who didn't exist, except that Maud needed people to *talk* to her. She needed information.

During the dessert course the captain of the *Lyric* gave a short speech of formal welcome. This first night's dinner was a special affair included in the price of first-class passage; most nights, as with the luncheon service, the dining saloon would function as a restaurant. The captain explained that the final night before they arrived in Southampton would again be a formal event of this nature, but closer to a ball, with an early dinner and a lottery followed by an orchestra performance and dancing.

The captain then introduced the musical entertainment for the evening: the celebrated mezzo-soprano Miss Elle Broadley, fresh from an opera company in New York City, who had been engaged to perform on the *Lyric* during her own relocation to England to seek further fame and fortune in the Old World.

Miss Broadley was a Black woman with a stunning set of jewels winking at her ears and a red dress with darker layers of gauze and beads. Her white satin gloves shone against the dark hue of her skin. Her posture was immaculate as she gestured her readiness to the accompanist at the grand piano in the corner.

And for the next quarter of an hour, Maud forgot that she'd choked on champagne; forgot that Mrs. Navenby was dead and the contract piece gone; forgot that any magic existed except this. The opera singer had a voice like running one's hand first the wrong way and then the right across an expanse of velvet. The music carried the throb of yearning and the twist of agony, and something hotter and darker, which sat low in Maud's body.

When the music ended, Miss Broadley bowed low to applause and made her sedate way out of the saloon. A disharmony of spoons on plates filled her absence.

"You enjoyed the music, Miss Cutler," said Mr. Chapman.

Maud, still struggling up from the warm depths of her enjoyment, simply nodded.

"She's superb," said Miss Debenham. "I bet she's being paid a third of what she's worth."

"Perhaps Miss Debenham could contribute to the ship's entertainment budget by donating *her* services for an evening," said Mrs. Endicott.

"Splendid idea," said Miss Debenham. "There's a trouser act I did last year that would do nicely, though I suspect some of the lyrics would— Aunt Caroline, kicking *Clarence* beneath the table may shut him up, but I'm not afraid of a few bruised shins."

Mr. Chapman hastily volunteered that he saw no shame in money coming from hard work, and that his own family's wealth was in cotton mills. He had been to America to learn more about the state of the cotton industry there, and to consider the purchase of some modern machines for his father's factories.

"There certainly is some *very* new money aboard." Mrs. Babcock appeared to decide that if everyone else planned to indulge in the vulgarity of this conversational topic, she wasn't going to be left out. "Did you see that red-faced gentleman at the captain's table? And that woman beside him wearing a prince's ransom in rubies? That's Mr. and Mrs. Frank Bernard. He's an industrialist. They've two daughters with them— clearly hoping to marry them off in England. Fancy themselves grandparents to a duke or a viscount, I'm sure. England's full of gentry families who act like they've just come from tea with the king but haven't two pennies to rub together."

Maud briefly imagined Robin's face if she befriended and brought home an heiress for her brother to marry. The entire table was now engaged in attempting not to look like they were staring in the direction of the captain's table, while staring as hard as they could.

"Looks like they've begun on the right foot," said Mrs. Moretti. "Someone told me that young gingery one is the son of a marquess. And Mrs. Bernard's simpering at that other gentleman, so he must be worth something."

There was a pillar in Maud's line of sight. All she could make out was one shorter head—gingery, yes—and one taller one, dark.

"I say, mater," said Mr. Blackwood suddenly, "isn't that—"

Another invisible kick was delivered. For some reason, both Blackwoods now looked at Miss Debenham as though she were a barrel of gunpowder rolled perilously close to a flame.

"Vi," said Mr. Blackwood, too loudly. "Tell us more about—"

But Violet Debenham's eyes had widened.

"Oh, *look*. It's dear Hawthorn."

Maud clenched a hand in her napkin. "Lord Hawthorn?"

"Are you acquainted?" asked Mrs. Blackwood, sharp. The whole family now watched Maud with the same wary interest as they had when she'd mentioned magic.

"No, not for myself. I believe a friend of my brother's knows him slightly."

"At one time, he and I were very close indeed," said Miss Debenham.

Maud wondered if Mrs. Blackwood was going to wear out the toes of her shoes.

"Violet, my dear," the woman said between her teeth. "I believe Clarence was asking you—"

But Miss Debenham pitched her performer's voice effortlessly above the interruption. "What my aunt and cousin are so desperate for me not to mention, Miss Cutler, is that before scandalously ruining myself by running off to become a concert-hall performer in New York, I first ruined myself in a much more conventional way." A broad, leonine smile. "With Lord Hawthorn's able and *thorough* assistance."

One of the Boston sisters choked. Maud blushed, incredulous, and then found her eyes trying to simultaneously swivel to inspect Lord Hawthorn and to remain where they were, pinned to the satisfied mouth of the woman who'd just dropped that explosive little fact at a table full of strangers.

"I still think of him fondly. In fact, perhaps I'll see if he has any interest in renewing our acquaintance. It would be only polite to greet such an old friend."

"*Violet!*"

The girl pushed back her chair, collected her wineglass as an afterthought, and was on the move: a tall, slim figure like a dash of blue ink on the page, golden head erect as she shimmered across to the captain's table.

The Blackwoods were now matching shades of mortified puce. The Boston sisters had their heads together, whispering in scandalised cadences.

Maud waited for the blush to settle in her cheeks. She had never met anyone like Violet Debenham. How did one attain that kind of confidence, and that ability to not so much prod one's relatives with sticks as hurl an entire armful of javelins in their direction?

Why had *Maud* never found the courage to ruin herself and run off to a New York concert-hall?

"Miss Cutler?" Mr. Chapman was doing the polite thing and turning the conversation elsewhere. Maud sidestepped some queries about her life in England by chattering vaguely about the sights she'd enjoyed in New York, but her attention kept leaping across the way.

Lord Hawthorn. So Robin's visions had been entirely correct on that score.

Maud made her excuses and left the dining saloon before any of the captain's party rose from the table. She made her way quickly to her own cabin, where she retrieved an item from her trunk and then left again, trying to walk as Miss Debenham had walked: head high, with purpose. As if anyone questioning her would be made to think themselves a fool.

And so the truthful Maud Blyth, brought up in comfort and propriety if not much love, made her way in the dangerous hour of the evening to baldly lie her way into Lord Hawthorn's bedchamber.

4

The steward who escorted Maud to Lord Hawthorn's cabin was not, alas, the young and impressionable Rogers. Instead he was a cool-mannered man called Jamison, with sleek hair and overlarge teeth, who pocketed Maud's American dollars with alacrity. He thawed somewhat on the journey as Maud asked breathless questions about the ship, most of which she already knew the answers to from her exploring earlier in the day.

Some of it proved useful though: once he had the money in hand, Jamison informed her of the presence of a directory, displayed in the first-class elevator foyers, which would save her the bother of asking after an acquaintance's room number in the future.

"Is there a similar list for the second and third classes?" Maud asked.

A full list of her suspects and their cabin locations *would* be something. Although it still wouldn't include the ship's staff, would it? On the other hand, did she really believe that a murderous magician would go to the trouble of gaining employment as a deckhand or steward?

Well—*she* was playing at being in service, of a sort. No reason to think someone else wouldn't. And they might have better access—

"A full passenger manifest?" Jamison interrupted Maud's thoughts. "Not on display. I suppose the chief officer would have one. Begging your pardon, but why would you want to see such a thing?"

Maud hastily dropped that line of questioning and moved on

to showing an interest in Jamison's own career with the White Star Line. A new frisson of nervousness had alighted upon her, alone in his company, now that she'd moved the entire crew of the *Lyric* into the category of "possible killer."

"You're near as bad as that journalist we have on board, miss," said Jamison after a while. "Here we are. His lordship's expecting you, you said?"

"He's a family friend." Maud deployed her dimples. "I had hoped to surprise him."

Knocking produced no answer, and Jamison shrugged an apology. "He mustn't be back from dinner. The gentlemen often retire to the smoking lounge at this hour."

Maud had been counting on the fact that Lord Hawthorn might be that sort of gentleman. "Then I shall wait for his lordship in more comfort than this corridor is currently affording. Open the door, please."

A blink. "I can't do that."

"Nonsense," said Maud briskly. "Of course you can."

He frowned. "If you're a friend of the family, why don't you—"

"Oh, dear." Maud put a hand to her mouth and gave a silent laugh. "Look, perhaps I wasn't quite honest about why I'm here. You see, someone told me the most *intriguing* story about Lord Hawthorn at dinner. And I would *very* much like to find out for myself if that story was true." Maud's tongue wanted to rattle on, loose with nerves, but she forced herself to bite down on it and give what she hoped was a suggestive smile.

She'd have been the last person to call herself a believable coquette. But Jamison's eyebrows shot up, and for a moment he looked almost *paternal,* as if he were going to demand that she produce a relative or chaperone who could hustle her away from this potential den of sin.

Maud thought of what Robin would say if he saw her in this situation and swallowed a hysterical gurgle of laughter.

"Do you think his lordship will object to finding me in his

room, under these circumstances?" she added. "More to the point, do you think I could possibly do him any *harm*?"

Jamison's face admitted that he thought this doubtful, but he shook his head.

"More than my job's worth, letting anyone into the parlour suites who shouldn't be there."

Maud didn't want to stand here arguing while the other occupants of this hallway began trickling back from dinner. She tugged the earrings from her ears. Each long teardrop pearl fell from a cluster of smaller ones set in gold. They were Mrs. Navenby's, and she felt sure the old woman would have approved of the use to which they were now being put.

"Please," she said, and held them out.

Jamison's eyes locked onto the lustre of gold and cream.

"If his lordship objects," said Maud, "and makes a report to ship security, I'll say it was someone else who helped me. Is there someone you'd like me to name? Some unpleasant bully among the ship's staff, perhaps?"

A different light entered Jamison's face. "Galloway. Service supervisor. He's lazy and a drunk, and he always blames the new hires when his sloppy work's discovered." He looked startled to have said it, and eyed Maud warily, as if she'd done a magic trick.

She hadn't, of course. There was always a bully.

"There you are, then." She jiggled the earrings in her palm. "And if you're prepared to give up half the fee for the satisfaction of seeing Mr. Galloway dismissed, you could always plant one of the pearls in his belongings, and it'll be more evidence that he accepted it from me."

Jamison's mouth opened, then closed. "And what if, as you say, his lordship doesn't object?"

"Then pretend another passenger reported the pearls missing," Maud said impatiently—really, did she have to do everything herself? "Or, if you'd prefer, steal it back again. Now, do you think we might hurry this along?"

Jamison let her into the cabin. Maud threw her most approving smile at him through the closing door.

Lord Hawthorn's parlour suite had a large sitting room, with a view through an open doorway to the smaller room containing the bed, another door that probably led to the bathroom, and—Maud drifted over, delighted—the round porthole was set in a door leading out to a piece of private deck enclosed by glass, like a pretty little patio. The sitting room contained a proper plush set of sofa and chaise longue and armchair set around a low table, a writing desk tucked next to a credenza with gorgeous marquetry, and a higher table with two sleek, narrow-backed chairs. In the centre of this table stood a brassy vase of which the twin handles were diving women, their arms outstretched.

All in all, it was far grander than the stateroom allocated to Mrs. Navenby and Maud. Luxury was to be expected: the man was the only son of the Earl of Cheetham, and bore a courtesy title of his own. He had a dead sister, an uneasy relationship with his parents, and an even uneasier one with the society of magicians within which he'd been raised. And he had lost all of his own magic, as far as anyone knew.

Those were the plain facts within the briefing on the Baron Hawthorn that Edwin Courcey had given Maud before she left London. The more colourful facts boiled down to this: Lord Hawthorn, in Edwin's firm opinion, was an arrogant, insulting, self-absorbed bastard.

Robin, who'd only met the man once, had agreed with this assessment.

"Though at least," he'd added, "he's the kind of bastard who wears it on his sleeve."

The Blyth siblings had exchanged a look of perfect understanding. Honest unpleasantness was to be chosen, every time, over hypocrites and liars.

Thanks to his visions, Robin had been certain that Maud would encounter Lord Hawthorn on one of her voyages. Most likely the return one, as Hawthorn had been in America since the previous autumn. For his part, Edwin had reluctantly admitted to enough faith in Hawthorn's character that he could be trusted not to be on the side of the murderous villains.

"Go to him if you're in trouble," Robin had told Maud. "He might not have magic, but he knows it, and he has more than enough of the ordinary kinds of power."

"It sounds as if he's likely to laugh in my face and tell me to go away."

"Probably," Edwin agreed.

"Maudie," said Robin, with a grin for his sister, "can be *remarkably* persistent when the mood takes her."

Maud ran her fingers over the polished blond wood of a chair's back. Yes. She could. Now that she was alone and in the quiet, the bubbling energy of improvisation that had carried her through the conversation with Jamison was ebbing.

Voices sounded on the other side of the door, and there was the first clack of key in lock. Maud took a deep breath, preparing herself, and then froze. Voices. Plural.

She'd planned to have a private conversation with Lord Hawthorn and refuse to leave until he agreed to help her investigate Mrs. Navenby's murder. She had not planned for anyone else to be present.

There were no large, Maud-friendly wardrobes in this room; nor was there a convenient floor-length tablecloth. The quickest route of escape was through the doorway and into the bedroom. She took it, just as the cabin door began to open.

"How impressive," said the non-Hawthorn voice, female and abruptly clear. "Does it come complete with someone to fan you with palm fronds, as well?"

Maud bit very hard into her lip, leaned against the tiny space of wall available between the doorway and the boxy frame of the bed, and shook with laughter. The manic energy was back, as if she'd reached out to metal after walking on wool.

It was Miss Debenham. Of *course* it was.

Lord Hawthorn, when he spoke, had a deep voice that didn't

sound as though it had ever been excited about anything in its life. One dressed it immediately in broad shoulders and a slight sneer.

"Keep it up if you must," he said, "but is there a reason you're insisting on that ghastly accent, Violet? Or do you simply enjoy tormenting my ears?"

Violet Debenham laughed. When she spoke again, *her* voice was entirely different. Now she sounded like the English lady her aunt had desperately described her as, though with vowels that had passed under the flattening iron of America.

"It wasn't you it was supposed to torment."

"Delighted to hear it. I'm having a drink."

A spike of panic hit Maud until she remembered that she'd seen the decanter atop the credenza, not in here with her. Glass clinked on glass.

"Oh," said Miss Debenham.

"Did you want something?" said Hawthorn.

"I don't remember you being so obtuse, your lordship. When an old friend goes to the trouble of practically groping you at the dinner table and then asks if you'd like company for the evening, it's not exactly a subtle signal."

"We are not friends." Not quite hostile, but an audible warning. "And I'd no idea if you planned anything more than leaving the dining room visibly attached to my arm. You may help yourself to my sitting room. Leave after whatever you think is a suitable time period. For my sake, you might make it at least half an hour."

"I thought we could amuse each other."

"What did you have in mind? Chess?"

"I hate chess." She paused. Maud hoped that Miss Debenham would take the man's amused disinterest as a cue to leave *now*, but instead she added, curious: "If you didn't think I was offering to go to bed with you, why did you let me in?"

"Have I hurt your pride? I thought you were here because you had none."

"Oh, up your *arse*, Hawthorn."

Now it was Hawthorn who laughed: a short gunshot of a *hah!* that reminded Maud for a painful moment of Mrs. Navenby. "I agreed for the same reason I agreed three years ago."

"Three years ago," said Miss Debenham, "you told me that you don't fuck virgins or people who don't know what they're asking for."

There was a girl whose first adventure into obscenity had definitely not been mere hours earlier. Maud mouthed the word to herself, trying to make it comfortable, like doing determined circuits of the house in a pair of overstiff new boots. *Fuck.* Her teeth caught in her lower lip, satisfyingly, at the start of it.

"Yes. And you didn't," said Hawthorn. "But I added, if I recall, that I had no objection to being used as a pair of sharp scissors if you were so desperate to shred your reputation. And *that*, Miss Debenham—it is still Miss, I'm assuming?— still stands."

There was a longish pause. A slight rustle of fabric. Maud bit her lip again, not in service of any words this time.

"Though I admit," Hawthorn went on, "I'm curious whether any pieces of your reputation remain intact enough that you're once again in need of my services."

"I'm not, really," said Miss Debenham. "Well, the prospect nearly gave Aunt Caroline a fit of apoplexy—that's something. But *I'm* curious about what I missed out on by being too virginal and too naive for your tastes. I approached you because of your reputation, after all. And I have several points of comparison now."

Another untranslatable near-silence. Maud had the twin longings to be anywhere else in the world, and to be one of the flying bats she'd heard of when attending a lecture on natural history: they could send out invisible bursts of sound and know, from sensing their return, the exact shape of what was happening in front of them, even if they couldn't see it.

Perhaps there was a spell that allowed that to happen. She'd have to ask Edwin.

Hawthorn sounded even lower and more amused now. "I haven't any pride either, girl, so you needn't go trying to pique it. Just ask, if you're going to."

"Oh, for God's—" Miss Debenham sighed. "Lord Hawthorn. I'm bored and intrigued, you are an extremely attractive man, and I wish—for my own reasons—to cause as much scandal as possible. So I'd consider it a favour if you would fuck me."

Maud wondered morbidly if there were a limit on how many times one could blush in a day. Perhaps at a certain point it would become permanent.

Miss Debenham was still talking, as if making a list for a shopping expedition. "Nothing that could get me pregnant, and I'd prefer to avoid any diseases. Other than that, I'm game for whatever you fancy."

"I very much doubt that," said Hawthorn. "But we won't dwell on it. You set sensible conditions. I see this is how you've gathered these points of comparison without finding yourself in trouble."

"I can't say I avoided *every* kind of trouble." Miss Debenham's laugh was almost too light, as if it took effort. "But yes." A beat. "That, and fucking women more often than men."

Maud's cheeks overflowed; the heat rushed into every far crevice of her, to the end of each finger, to where her feet now felt in their shoes as though they would ignite if she moved them.

Robin had described how it felt to have one of his visions imposed on him from nowhere. Something like this, Maud thought. She didn't have her brother's clairvoyant gift, nor his artistic imagination. But her mind was a train hurtling down tracks without her consent, insisting that she consider Miss Debenham's words and attempt to put images to them.

It was not enormously successful. Maud's knowledge of sexual acts was purely academic. She felt like a musician trying to reproduce a sonata by ear, when it had been heard only once, underwater.

Now she could hear soft, breathy sounds from the adjoining room, as well as the rustle of fabric. Oh *God*. Miss Debenham had asked, and Lord Hawthorn had obliged. Sooner or later they would move proceedings to the bed—surely?—and as Maud was not a magician and could not turn herself invisible, she had a vanishing window to put a stop to this herself before she ended up looking like not only a sneak-thief but also like . . . the sort of perverted voyeur she *clearly was*.

The sooner the better, she told herself. *Just do it.*

She screwed her eyes half-shut, pushed herself away from the wall and around through the doorway in one awkward motion, and came to a stumbling halt in front of a tableau that was—even viewed through her trembling lashes and the haze of mortified nerves—not academic in the slightest.

5

Violet had learned at an early age that there were different levels of scandal that it was possible for a young woman to achieve.

Among the Debenham sisters, these levels had been measured by how many inches their father could be induced to lower the newspaper at the breakfast table, and how high their mother's voice rose as she related whatever gossip she was anxious for her daughters to imbibe as a cautionary tale.

Running off unmarried to ruin oneself with the Earl of Cheetham's dissolute son was already teetering at the end of the scale that might lead the newspaper to be begrudgingly laid entirely aside. Violet often wished she'd been present to hear how shrill her mother's bewailments had been, when their too-tall, too-difficult middle daughter had so thoroughly exploded their little world and left its dust to settle without her.

Writing her first and last letter to Alice from New York City, informing the family that she was alive, tolerably well, and had now found employment in a *theatre*, had been no more than gilding the lily. The screeches of dismay must have been heard halfway across the county. Violet had kept herself warm with the thought of that, all through her first New York winter in a tiny, damp room in a tiny, damp boardinghouse, grimly learning to cradle warmth-spells with enough precision that she could manage them with the magic left over at the end of the day.

Violet might have to invent a whole new section of the scandal-scale for being caught with her dress and petticoat tugged up above her waist, and with the dissolute and obliging

Lord Hawthorn's hand both inside her drawers and then two knuckles deep inside *her*.

"I'm sorry, I'm sorry, *stop*," said the young woman standing in front of them. She'd flung one hand across her eyes. The parts of her face visible below that were a radiant blushing red.

The dress of sunset-hued taffeta and the nut-brown hair, however, identified her immediately as Miss Maud Cutler.

Violet wasn't easy to embarrass. She nonetheless felt herself turning a matching shade of scarlet. It was the embarrassment radiating off Miss Cutler that did it, as if the girl had brought enough to spare for the whole room.

Hawthorn slid his fingers out of Violet in an unhurried motion that sent a last flurry of sparks down her legs. Her body hadn't caught up to the situation yet. It had been building its leisurely way towards one of the better orgasms of the last twelve months, and now it hung suspended and confused between pleasure and its opposite.

"We have," said Hawthorn, in a voice dripping authoritative ice, "stopped. You may remove your hand from your eyes. And then, whomever you are, you may expect to be removed from this room."

The girl dropped her hand. Her defiant and mortified gaze flicked from Hawthorn to Violet and then back. There was certainly a lot of Hawthorn to look at. Even apart from the harshly handsome features and the solid bulk of his thighs, Violet appreciated a man who could exceed her in height. The Bowery hadn't exactly been swimming with them. Something to look forward to, in returning to the bosom of the well-nourished English gentry.

"Her name's Miss Cutler. We met tonight at dinner." Violet wrestled petticoat and dress back down over her hips. "She's a magician."

"Actually, no." Maud Cutler's hands formed decisive fists at her sides. She was staring right at Hawthorn. "I'm not a magician. And my name is Maud Blyth. I'm a friend of Edwin Courcey's."

The name rang only the faintest bell of familiarity for Violet. Hawthorn's expression darkened further, scorn deepening the crease between those brilliant blue eyes.

"Christ," he said. "Halfway across the bloody ocean and I still can't escape his persistent fucking prying. If you're hoping to impress him, I can inform you with some authority that Courcey is never going to marry you. *Or* fuck you. Or are you here because you've worked that out, and you, too, wish to avail yourself of my apparently well-publicised prowess?"

It was an attack; and with that mercilessly cold tone wielded as a weapon, it was a vicious one. Most well-born girls would have dissolved beneath it.

Miss Cutler—Miss *Blyth*—solidified instead. Her rosebud mouth, which would have had her cast as everything from Juliet to Innocent Shepherdess, gained a look of absolute stubbornness.

"Edwin came to see you with my brother, Sir Robert. Perhaps you remember, my lord? He had"—she gestured to her own gloved forearm—"a curse."

Hawthorn stood in silence a moment longer. Then he looked at his fingers, muttered a colourful oath, and wiped them on his trousers. Violet bit her lip. Hawthorn crossed to the decanter to refill his glass with a generous dose of amber spirits, drank off half of it, and then looked between the two of them with thunderclouds in his face.

"Sit," he ordered Miss Blyth, pointing to a chair, and she did so. "Violet—"

"Stay," said Miss Blyth quickly. "Please."

"Appearances notwithstanding, Miss Blyth," said Hawthorn, "I am not going to beat you or ravish you if left unsupervised."

"I want Miss Debenham to stay."

"Miss Debenham," said Violet, "will make up her own mind on the matter, thank you very much."

Violet's body had given up all hope of an orgasm. It had chosen instead to burn with curiosity as to what this girl was doing aboard the *Lyric,* under a name not her own, accompanying a woman who had just died, and speaking of magic as if she knew it.

Violet went and poured a drink of her own. Then she sat. She gave Hawthorn a look that inquired whether he intended to beat *her.* He returned it witheringly and turned back to Miss Blyth.

"So. You've gone to the extreme of chasing me down mid-Atlantic, and I can see that unless I throw you overboard—*don't* tempt me—I'll have no peace at all. Talk."

"I will." Miss Blyth dug in her beaded bag and pulled out a small candle. "Once I'm sure I can trust you. Do you have a lighter? Oh, and a penknife or a razor?"

"Explain," directed Hawthorn.

"This is a truth-candle. Edwin explained it—something about an imbuement on the wax, and then another used to soak the wick. He's trying to find a way to power it *without* requiring the participant's blood, but no luck so far."

"It detects the truth?" said Violet. "I've never heard of anything like that."

"Edwin is *very* clever." Said with pride. "Will you go first, Miss Debenham?"

It was testament to the increasingly bizarre momentum of this evening, and also to Miss Blyth's brisk and dimpled charisma, that Violet came within a hair's breadth of agreeing. Then good sense slapped her back.

"I'm not putting blood into a spell I don't know."

Miss Blyth set down the candle and removed her evening gloves. "I'll do it first. If you haven't a lighter, how about a matchbook?"

"I can give you a light, but not a finger-prick." Violet didn't trust her control over the knife-spell she knew. She'd only wielded that particular spell once, and she swallowed a wash of nausea at the memory.

Hawthorn did have a knife, sharp and well kept. Violet cradled a flame and lit the candle. Miss Blyth clutched it in one hand and held out the other for Hawthorn to nick the side of her finger, then let a drop of her blood mingle with the small pool of melted wax already forming at the wick's base.

At once the flame rose eerily high and turned a vivid green.

"My name is Maud Blyth and I really do need help, and I'm going to tell you the truth about why," Miss Blyth said rapidly. It was burning down faster than a candle should. "And, er, I'm wearing a purple hat."

The candle responded to that last with a fierce leap of the wavering flame, which turned bloodred. Miss Blyth blew the candle out and looked at Violet.

Curiosity won out. Violet removed her gloves. She was wearing Jerry's wooden rings on her thumbs beneath them, both habit and reminder. She closed her eyes rather than watch her blood join the wax, and the flame nipped at her finger.

Miss Blyth said, "Miss Debenham. Were you responsible for Elizabeth Navenby's death?"

"No." The flame stayed steady and green.

"Are you associated, in any way, with Walter Courcey and the group of people trying to find the last contract in order to use it?"

"I—no."

Green. Miss Blyth extinguished the candle again.

"Walter Courcey?" said Hawthorn.

"Yes." Miss Blyth held out the candle to him. "I *will* explain."

Hawthorn impatiently answered the same questions in the negative, after which only half the candle remained. Miss Blyth tucked it away in her bag.

"The ingredients are expensive, and it burns down fast. Especially if you lie."

And then, as promised, Miss Blyth explained. It took nearly enough time for a normal candle to burn down; time enough that Violet finished her drink, and then wanted another, and then forgot to want another.

Maud Blyth's equally unmagical brother, Robin, had been

unbusheled last year by accident, and cursed by men who thought he was working against them. The curse had been removed—with no help from Lord Hawthorn—by the man called Edwin Courcey. Between them, Edwin and Robin had uncovered what their enemies were seeking: three items that had been discovered and removed from a church, midway through the previous century, by a group of lady magicians who called themselves the Forsythia Club. The unofficial leader of whom had been a woman called Flora Sutton, who had been killed for her part in hiding one of these items. And whose diaries, in code, Edwin had inherited.

By the time Edwin's brother, Walter Courcey, appeared in the narrative, Violet had managed to brush the mental dust from the name Courcey itself. A magical family, more powerful than her own, though not as wellborn by the standards of unmagical English society.

The items themselves—coin, cup, and knife—had long ago been separated and disguised and hidden again by the women who found them. Because they were the physical symbols of the Last Contract, the bargain made centuries ago between the departing fae and the magicians of Britain, that magic would be left in the hands of humans in exchange for their stewardship of the land.

"*What*," said Hawthorn flatly.

Miss Blyth, whose bright voice was beginning to fatigue, waved a yes-I-know sort of hand and sped them onward.

As magic was contract, any magician from the bloodline of the families who had made that bargain could now have their magic drawn upon, used without their direct consent, if the contract was manipulated in the correct way. Walter Courcey was part of a group of magicians who wanted to do just that. Who had begun their search for the contract with the blessings of the British Magical Assembly, but who were now almost certainly operating by their own rules.

At some point, Miss Blyth herself had become involved in this adventure. When Edwin's efforts to trace the other members

of the Forsythia Club had led them to the émigré Elizabeth
Navenby, Miss Blyth had travelled to warn the old woman that
there were people trying to recover the contract, and to use it,
in the way that the Forsythians had decided it should never
and could never be used.

On hearing of Flora Sutton's death, Elizabeth Navenby had
dressed herself in impeccable mourning, packed her bags, and
informed Miss Blyth that she would be returning to England
to see this business through. She had kept her own piece of the
contract a secret still.

"Why didn't she leave it in America?" Violet asked. It was
by no means the least of her questions, but the first she'd managed to shoehorn into Miss Blyth's rapid narrative.

"Edwin says the people on the other side are learning to locate the pieces through magic. We don't know if they could
find it in America, but it's possible. And if she'd left it, she
wouldn't be there to protect it."

Though she wasn't there to protect it now. Or to steal it
back, as it had apparently been stolen from her room aboard
the *Lyric*. There was only Miss Blyth.

And, Miss Blyth hoped, the two of them. Violet and Hawthorn. One theatre magician, trained largely in tricks and
splendour; and one ill-tempered aristocrat whose own magic
had deserted him years ago, under circumstances that Violet
had heard only the worst rumours about.

"There are three hundred first-class passengers on the
Lyric," Miss Blyth added. "Just over one hundred and fifty
in second class. A *thousand* in third class. And three hundred
crew." She might have been reciting from a pamphlet. "I can't
investigate them all on my own, let alone get Mrs. Navenby's
piece of the contract back again."

"You want our assistance to identify, from within these hundreds of people, a dangerous magician who *may* have killed
someone, and recover from them some stolen items," Hawthorn said. "One of which *may* be a physical representation
of the Last Contract, which is a story for children." His soft,

ruthless tones were as much a pushing-away as his initial descent into obscenity had been—and had the same lack of effect on the dauntless Miss Blyth.

"Yes. This children's story has killed several people already. It nearly killed my brother."

The Last Contract.

Before Violet's father had resigned himself to a lack of sons and was still prepared to humour his horde of girls, he'd told them stories of a magic far less tame than that used in their household: of fairies, of magicians in the wild times, of quests and bargains and spells large enough to alter the world. Violet had absorbed them like a parched lawn and retold them over and over for her sisters.

Then, when her father's wellspring had run dry, she began to invent her own. She did the low voices of forest spirits and the regal one of the fae queen, and performed the squabbling of the three sisters who founded the Three Families, until Alice and Julia fell across the bed laughing, and Ellen and Meg nudged each other in the doorway, where they hovered pretending to be too old for stories.

Violet had never been too old. She had sought stories, always. The Debenhams had been invited exactly once to Cheetham Hall, the seat of Hawthorn's father: a grand old place where magic stuck to the skin like cobwebs and made you shiver, and where Violet had felt uneasy throughout the whole gathering. Afterwards she had kept her sisters awake with stories of ghosts, and of Lady Elsie Alston, who'd gone mad and leapt from the roof.

She'd felt bad about that, later, when she was old enough to know about the pressures that could be put on a girl. And the shapes that a girl could turn beneath those pressures.

Did *she* believe all of this? And regardless of the tale behind it—did she really think Miss Blyth was going to have the slightest amount of luck finding her needles in this ocean-bound haystack?

Perhaps not. But the story of the Three Families and the

Last Contract was one of those that had captured young Violet's imagination. Even a hint of it being real was like opening a door, newly discovered in a familiar house, to find boxes of treasure and a map to more.

She said, "Count me in, Miss Blyth. I'll help."

"Why?" said Hawthorn, cutting over the start of Miss Blyth's delighted thanks.

"As I told you, my lord Hawthorn, I'm bored and intrigued. And a pretty girl is offering me something more exciting than six days' worth of quoits and promenades and musical performances."

"A wild goose chase with a side order of possibly being apprehended for theft."

"Or, apparently, murdered," said Violet. "Doesn't it sound a lark?"

It rather did. The open door of wonder was a motive that she could keep tucked away for herself. This would cost no money and demanded no investment of emotion, and Maud Blyth—for all she was young and painfully naive—captured attention like the *once upon a time* of a fairy tale.

Violet wanted, quite simply, to see what would happen next.

"Lord Hawthorn?" Miss Blyth's hands were clutched together on her knee. A piece of her hair had escaped its pin during her long explanation, and lay against the side of her neck like an errant duck's feather.

"No," said Hawthorn. "I don't do things for a lark. If the two of you wish to race around the *Lyric* flouting locked doors and courting danger, you have my blessing. But not my help."

"These people are a threat to all the magicians in Britain. They want to steal power, and they've killed to advance their aims. Don't you care even a *little*?"

Hawthorn stilled. His face flickered, tongue moving against closed lips as if he were trying to rid his mouth of a bad taste. For a moment it seemed as if Miss Blyth had aimed correctly.

But then he shrugged. "People kill. Sometimes they have good reasons and sometimes they don't. It does not mean I will be dragged into a treasure-hunting conspiracy because Edwin Courcey has dragged *you* into it and seems to think I can be relied upon for chivalry. I cannot."

Miss Blyth raised her chin. Violet wanted abruptly to reach out and curl that lock of errant brown hair around her own finger, which still stung at the tip from Hawthorn's knife. She wanted to *pull*.

"No. What Edwin said was that you'd do your best to hurt me, to make me go away, and that your best would be very good indeed. But you're what I have, my lord. I refuse to be killed before I can get this piece of the contract back. I will do this for my brother, who you didn't care to save, and for Edwin, who *did* save him. And for Mrs. Navenby. And for all the magicians of Britain, because *I* care about what's right, even if you don't."

The girl would have her audacious belief in the mythical goodness of people ruined eventually. Hawthorn was doing a fine job of ripping it to shreds tonight. But Violet, looking at the fire in Maud Blyth's eyes, didn't want Lord Hawthorn to have it all his own way. His lordship's masterful nature might send thrills down Violet's spine under sexual circumstances, but it was becoming tiresome now.

She said, "Do you really want the girl's death on your conscience if things go wrong, Hawthorn?"

"This ball of righteousness," said Hawthorn, "is not my wife, my ward, or my sister." And Violet remembered all over again, with a sensation in her stomach like a coin dropped into a dark well, that Hawthorn had *had* a sister; and remembered what happened to her. "She is not my responsibility. If she were to die through her own rash misadventure, I would sleep no better or worse than I currently do."

"You might have trouble sleeping if her brother finds out you let her come to harm and comes to kick your door down. What did you say his name was, Miss Blyth?"

"Sir Robert Blyth."

"Easy enough to track down in the event of your demise, I should think."

There was a pregnant silence in which they turned their eyes to Hawthorn.

"Your move, my lord," said Miss Blyth.

"I don't respond well to blackmail either." But a treacherous corner of his mouth had begun to look amused. Miss Blyth clearly noticed it; she pounced.

"At least tell me if you become aware of any other magicians on board. You have a better chance of recognising them. I won't ask you to go poking around and breaking into rooms—I'm sure I can manage that, if I have Miss Debenham's help. But I want to know we can call on you if we find ourselves in trouble."

"Further trouble," said Hawthorn.

Miss Blyth looked around the parlour room. Her gaze landed on the chess board atop the credenza. "I'll play you for it, if you like."

"I beg your pardon?"

"If I win, you agree to help. If I lose, I'll leave you alone."

"You're prepared to sit here in my room, all night, and play chess for my cooperation? Without knowing anything about my level of skill?" Hawthorn paused. "Or is this more intelligence from Courcey?"

"No," said Miss Blyth. "It's not. But you don't know my level of skill either."

The two of them gazed at each other for a beat.

"So, yes," added Miss Blyth. "I'm prepared to play you for it. But if you'd prefer something quicker . . ." She was out of her seat. In a drawer of the writing desk was a packet of playing cards. The light shone off their glossy backs, red stamped with the white star of the ocean line. Miss Blyth handed the pack to Violet, who obligingly took up shuffling duties. The cards had the crisp edges of newness.

"Poker?" inquired Violet, enjoying herself.

"Even simpler," said Miss Blyth. "We each draw a single card. Highest wins."

Hawthorn rubbed a hand over his face and came to the edge of his chair. He looked, for the first time, tired. Violet didn't

blame him. Being in an enclosed space with the buoyant energy contained in the skin of Maud Blyth was like standing
uncomfortably close to a fire.

Violet fanned the cards. Hawthorn plucked one out: the ten
of hearts.

Miss Blyth chose her own card and flicked it to lie on the
table.

Queen of spades.

"And what," said Hawthorn, "would you have tried next, if
you'd lost?"

"Goodness knows." Miss Blyth had pleased colour in her
cheeks. "I might have tackled you around the knees, I suppose."

Hawthorn gave one of his whip-crack laughs. "You really
are Blyth's sister, aren't you? He was barely holding himself
back from popping me one the entire ten minutes of our acquaintance. Very well. You win, Miss Blyth. You may call on
me if required. Now, if business is concluded, you will both
leave my room."

That dark amusement was back. At the door, he even lifted
Miss Blyth's hand and kissed it in mocking farewell. Violet's
fingertips he kissed more lingeringly, which she recognised as
revenge. She was clearly not going to find out what she'd missed,
now.

"Oh, I am sorry," said Miss Blyth, looking at Violet's fingers
resting in Hawthorn's larger ones. "I ruined your plans for the
evening, didn't I?"

Violet took her hand back, and her regrets with it. "I'm sure
there are plenty of people aboard who'd be happy to oblige
me. And if not, I do have a few helpful devices in one of my
trunks."

"Devices?" inquired Miss Blyth.

There was a short and fascinating silence. Violet burst out
laughing, mostly at the look on Hawthorn's face.

"I am not," said his lordship the Baron Hawthorn, "explaining the concept of bedroom aides to a pugnacious baronet's

sister. Or perhaps I *will* start doing so, if it will get you out of here faster."

Still giggling, Violet linked her arm through Miss Blyth's and marched them grandly out into the corridor.

"Thank you, my lord," she called through the closing door. "We will consider your kind offer."

A collective inhalation alerted her to the presence of other people. A gaggle of middle-aged women like well-dressed water-fowl had halted nearby.

Miss Blyth's arm went rigid where it was tucked through Violet's. Violet made eye contact with the frontmost woman, a rake-thin creature in unfortunate purple, and gave a deliberate wink. The woman flinched as if Violet were some sort of dis-eased street cat.

"Good evening, ladies. Don't let us interrupt you. Come on, Maud, my dear girl," said Violet. "I find myself *quite* worn out, don't you?"

Miss Blyth murmured something as the gaggle edged past them with many backwards glances and a crescendo of shocked muttering. Violet laughed and looked down at Miss Blyth, who was gripping her gloves and her bag, pink-cheeked.

"Well," said Miss Blyth gamely. "The scandal part of your evening's gone to plan, anyway. That'll be all round first class by the end of breakfast tomorrow."

6

My dear Violet,

I write this note in a moment of impulse. Perhaps I will change my mind. Perhaps in a fortnight or a decade I will consign this to the fire and amend my will and you will never read these words. But my best decisions have been made impulsively, and I have regretted none of them.

Let us assume the matter stands unaltered. Therefore: if you read this, then I am dead, and I am leaving Spinet House and all my worldly goods to you.

The more tedious members of this family will never believe that I am acting out of anything but petty spite. If any lawyers are engaged to contest the issue, on the basis that far closer blood relatives than you exist, you may wave this letter in their faces, but the fact remains that I have sealed the latest version of my will with runes and with wax, and imbued the ink with my intent. The house will recognise you when you come to it.

They will be correct, of course, about the spite.

This society of ours is obsessed with blood, and magicians are worse than most. Yes—by blood our connection is very thin. But I have always considered us kindred of the spirit, and hearing of your recent bold escape to the Americas has only confirmed this. I would like to think that I would have named you my heir even if there was nothing of blood to link us at all.

So. The money is yours. Save it. Waste it. Invest it.

*Devour it. Use it to live your life only and exactly on
your own terms, as I was fortunate enough to be able
to do.*

Your fond cousin,
Mrs. James Taverner

The first time Violet had opened the letter, breaking the
seal with a fingernail and a nudge of an opening-spell, the
paper had been blank but for a small inked star in one corner.
Memory had come flooding back: afternoons spent visiting
her eccentric elderly cousin in the even more eccentric Spinet
House, which was full of hidden nooks and secret passage-
ways and puzzles of magic responding to music before all
else.

Violet had hummed the tune a few times to be sure she had
it, then sung the final verse of Dufay's rhyme. *Old paths we
walk anew—The near ones and the far—Burning bright as
stars—To pay the dusk its due.*

The fluid handwriting had appeared beneath her gaze.

By now she'd read it enough times that she could recite it.
She read it again this morning, sitting with knees curled up on
her bed aboard the *Lyric,* as one read the script in the interval
on closing night: for comfort more than necessity.

Violet carefully put the letter away. Her body clung both
to theatre hours and to the unaccustomed softness of the bed;
she'd slept through breakfast, and still had a little time before
her planned meeting with Miss Blyth. She washed her face,
threw a dressing gown over her nightdress, and was interrupted
by Aunt Caroline. Her aunt rapped anxiously on the door to
Violet's cabin and, when admitted, proved to have been drinking from the fountain of Violet's rejuvenated scandal while taking breakfast in the dining saloon.

Miss Blyth had been right. The story had gone from one end
of first class to the other and was now making its leisurely way
back again, growing new details like daisies. The notorious

Lord Hawthorn had entertained both Miss Violet Debenham and Miss Maud Cutler in his stateroom last night.

"I can't see why you insist on making things *worse*." Aunt Caroline's eyes were even more prominent than usual, and she vibrated like a struck fork. "You've been away from England long enough that the initial—incident—"

"Ruination," said Violet obligingly.

"Had begun to fade from memory! This was your chance to turn over a new leaf! To show yourself a reformed character, a truly refined lady—"

"Or at least one with enough money to buy good reviews if I perform like one?"

Aunt Caroline made a face. Violet thought longingly of coffee. She was sick of having this conversation.

The door was rapped at again, and Clarence opened it before Violet could answer. He looked irritated and was holding his mother's shawl.

"Clarence!" cried Violet, edging sideways on her chair to better display herself to the open doorway. "I'm not decent!"

Her cousin scowled and shut the door hastily behind him.

Violet was waiting, with a sort of dreary fatalism, for Clarence to propose marriage to her. Or rather, to her money. The only question was on which day of the voyage Aunt Caroline's unsubtle bullying of her only son would triumph over Clarence's tendency to eye Violet as though she were a particularly unattractive vegetable that had uprooted itself from the garden and learned to talk.

Given that Clarence bore more than a passing resemblance to a weedy parsnip himself, this was equal parts relieving and insulting. It wasn't as though he was incapable of normal human lust, or of recognising an attractive woman when he saw one. He'd cast more than enough yearning looks at Maud Blyth's breasts last night.

"I say, Vi, you're really taking this too far." Clarence had been hit by the scandal fountain, too, then. "One fellow asked me if my cousin's likely to be open to disgracing herself with *anyone,* or only with titles."

"Clarence, I'm going to dress," said Violet. "You may stand facing the corner and lecture me from there."

He did. Violet tuned him out after the first two sentences. Over underthings, stockings, corset, and petticoat went one of the new outfits she'd bought with the money that Aunt Caroline, reluctantly, had handed over as an advance on Violet's inheritance, so that Violet wouldn't disgrace them on the voyage. It was a travelling suit: a dark-pink-and-white-striped skirt, with a jacket of the same pink that opened to show the exuberant layers of her shirtwaist's bodice. The fabric was heavy with quality.

Violet dug out her ring pouch and went through her morning routine. Glass was good for combining the elements: she could cradle a warm steam and run her hands down the length of her jacket and skirt, removing any creases.

Then she replaced the glass ring on her finger with the precious ivory one bought from an old man who sold out of his top-floor Brooklyn apartment and took only spells in barter, not dollars.

Ivory held memory. Violet had dressed her hair over and over again, wearing this ring, sinking her magic into it, singing to it, because Claudette swore by song and half the Bowery was in love with Claudette. Everyone sang to their rings eventually.

Now Violet cradled a spell that shone as yellow pinpricks in her cupped hands, then swept those hands up the nape of her neck, gathering the nighttime plait of her hair. When she straightened, her hair was in its neat everyday style, piled atop her head with no need for hair pads to create its rounded shape or pins to keep it in place.

Aunt Caroline sniffed her disapproval of this untidy, un-English way of doing magic. Violet thought of the ring boxes kept in the manager's lockbox at the Penumbra, carried backstage each night and guarded with superstitious fervour by every performer and stagehand.

The wooden rings went on her thumbs, again, and stayed there. One maple and one pine. Wood enhanced illusion, which was Violet's primary skill. And . . . Jerry had turned these rings for her. She wore them so that every time she even *thought* about letting her guard down, she could give one of them a twist, and remember.

Clarence, unbelievably, was still talking.

"Thank you, Clarence," said Violet, pulling on her gloves. "Shall we pause the lecture there? I'm sure you have better things to do on this fine day. I certainly do. I'm meeting my new partner in sin at the Café Marseille."

On impulse she cradled a single illusion, a cluster of fresh violets nestled at the band of the trim straw hat that she set atop her hair with two large pins. She felt frothy and satisfied. If everyone was going to stare at you anyway, you damn well gave them something to stare at.

Clarence turned around. No appreciation for the suit or the hat, of course. Just a look of constipated misery.

"*Why* do you insist on being so outrageous? What do you possibly have to gain, apart from making us all a laughingstock and yourself a pariah?"

Because if I try hard enough, Clarence, you might not propose to me at all.

She didn't say it. It was only a quarter of the truth; and besides, he'd never understand. He wasn't born a girl, let alone one of five. He'd never grown out of childhood feeling himself get taller and taller as the life expected of him grew smaller and smaller, until he could barely breathe for the confines of it.

"I am doing it," said Violet, "in honour of Mrs. Taverner."

"Is that what that letter said?" Clarence shot back. "Do show us, then. I'm agog to see where Lady Enid asked you to tread the family's reputation into the mud."

He held out his hand as if he thought she would produce it on his demand. Almost tempting. She could use her finger to underline the words *petty spite.*

But—"Mrs. Taverner's words," Violet said sweetly, "are for my eyes alone."

The name was a bit of needling. Clarence and Aunt Caroline insisted on referring to their deceased relative only by her title, as if by doing so they could reverse the years and pretend that the young Lady Enid Blackwood had never disgraced her birth by eloping with a tradesman-magician.

No magician could turn back time. History and death were absolutes unconquered by magic.

Besides: if Lady Enid hadn't married James Taverner, then the fortune he earned would never have led her impoverished family to come trickling hopefully back into her life. And the fortune would never have landed in Violet's hands.

Violet kept her head high, playing at Cleopatra, as she made her way through the ship. At one point she slipped into the confident stride of one of her trouser roles, and nearly tripped over climbing into the elevator when that persona came into conflict with her fashionably narrow skirt.

The Café Marseille was set along the edge of the ship on C Deck. Walking into it made Violet blink hard against the glare. It was extremely *white*. White wall panels, white patterned plasterwork on the ceiling, and white wooden trellises through which real ivy climbed from blue-glazed pots. The wicker chairs had been painted white as well. Lace curtains framed the huge windows along one wall, which looked directly out onto the expanse of the sea and a sky dusted with cottony clouds.

The café smelled of coffee and butter—and was that chocolate? Violet was starving—and the throb of the *Lyric*'s engines played counterpoint to high musical notes of glass and china and conversation. The waitstaff danced between tables, trays held aloft, dodging newspapers and elbows and parasols and the stuck-out legs of small bored boys trying to cause a traffic accident.

Maud Blyth was drinking coffee at a corner table. She looked as though, like the sky, she'd sent down to inquire about the décor and then chosen her outfit to match. Her own white shirtwaist was ruched, with an amber brooch settled in the front of the high lace collar, and instead of a jacket she wore a warm brown waistcoat buttoned snugly around her corseted waist. Her skirt was blue with white trim and her hat matched it, a wide brim of blue-dyed straw trimmed with white feathers and white silk flowers.

When she lifted her face to greet Violet, those extraordinary large eyes turned the exact colour of the sea outside the window and shone just as beautifully in the May sunlight.

Remember, murmured the hot core of Violet's body, *how we didn't get what we wanted last night?*

Violet told her body to be quiet and remember the existence of bedroom aides. She softened Cleopatra into something friendlier as she seated herself at the table and ordered coffee and toast. With her back to the wall, she was aware of the occasional glance thrown in their direction; the occasional head bent and murmuring.

"You were right about the speed of gossip. We are officially the first-class strumpets, it would seem."

"Yes." Miss Blyth added a lump of sugar to her coffee and stirred for longer than necessary. Her manner was polite and subdued compared to the previous evening.

Ah.

"We can let it be known that it was only *me* being debauched," Violet said. "Perhaps you were only in the stateroom because you were trying to rescue me from my own folly, by giving myself and Lord Hawthorn an earnest lecture on morality."

"Oh, can you *imagine?*" Miss Blyth broke into giggles. "He really would have dragged me out by the ear. No, I'm simply— not accustomed to being stared at. But I'm sure I'll adapt."

"Truly? We could stage a great disagreement right now, if you wished." Violet gestured around the café. "You could break into a storm of angry weeping for the state of my selfish soul, and—oh, thank you. Yes, with milk."

The coffee smelled rich and good, and the toast came with a

selection of jams and marmalades in tiny pots. Violet ate two slices immediately and then moved another two onto her plate while she debated luxuriously between more of the fig jam or cracking open the blackberry. When she looked up, Miss Blyth was watching her over the rim of her coffee cup, sea-green eyes creased in amusement.

"Help yourself, Miss—Cutler. There's enough here for an army."

The girl shook her head. "You called me Maud, last night."

"Did I? I needn't, if you'd prefer us to be businesslike."

"No, I meant, I didn't mind." She coloured.

"Oh, *good*. I didn't think you were stuffy." Violet brushed crumbs from her cuff and held out her hand. "Violet."

Two dimples tucked themselves into Maud's cheeks. They shook solemnly over the jams.

"I don't know if I could carry off a storm of angry weeping anyway," said Maud. "I haven't spent years in a theatre, like you. It does sound wonderful. Did you miss England at all while you were there? Your family?"

It must have been some trick of those eyes, green like the truth-candle's flame, which brought an unexpected lump to Violet's throat; and a half-started admission with it. She firmly swallowed them both. The worldly and scandalous Miss Debenham had brushed her girlhood from her skirts like crumbs, with no regrets.

She donned one of her most uncaring smiles.

"I missed the English weather during my first summer—I thought I would absolutely *dissolve*." Violet launched into some anecdotes about the summer of 1907, when the magicians of the Penumbra had celebrated the successful opening of a new show by climbing onto the roof of the building and going to ludicrous lengths to cool themselves down in a heat that clung to the limbs like wet fabric, slathering them in the grime of city sweat. Maud laughed when Violet described Claudette's ice-spell that would follow a person around, seeking the gaps in their clothes, and how Thom had yowled so loudly when struck with it that stray cats in the alley beneath had raised their voices in harmony.

Maud poured more coffee for them both. In between stories Violet sampled all the jams on the table and had a brief, passionate affair with the ginger marmalade.

"So," she said when she was pleasantly full. "What's your plan of attack for today?"

"I've been thinking about that for hours already." Maud drummed her fingers absently against the tablecloth. "In the detective stories in the *Strand,* the murderers always have the decency to leave a clue at the scene. And the detectives use the identity of the victim himself—or herself—to discover the possible *why,* and that leads to the *who,* but the problem is . . . I *know* the why, and it doesn't seem likely to help."

"Not given the vast pool of possible *whos,*" Violet agreed.

"I don't suppose you know any convenient magical ways to identify other magicians in a large crowd?"

Violet shook her head. Outnumbered as they were, it was second nature for magicians to keep themselves hidden. There were ways of testing the water one-on-one, and subtle signals that could be sent. American magicians might wear rings of substances other than metal, but it was a practice more of the working classes than the sort of society likely to be found among the *Lyric*'s first-class passengers.

It was a marvellous coincidence that Maud had found herself at dinner with Violet and the Blackwoods, honestly. And if they hadn't shared a connection in Lord Hawthorn, then Maud might have spent the voyage entirely ignorant of Violet's own magical nature.

"Given all that," said Maud, "I think the best way to start narrowing down *who* might be sorting out the *where.*" She pulled some paper from a deep pocket of her skirt and unfolded it between them, nudging the empty toast rack aside. "This is the only map of the *Lyric* I could find—there's a stand of them in one of the foyers—and it's not very large, or thorough."

Violet leaned over and inspected the pamphlet, which contained a cramped representation of every level, from the sun deck down to the cargo hold and boiler rooms on E Deck. It was clearly designed for first-class passengers; it focused on proclaiming the many attractions available to them, such as the Turkish baths and the Grand Reception. Plenty of the aftmost regions of B and C Decks, and almost all of D Deck, were simply white spaces. Not worth bothering with, or labelling. Areas of the ship clearly allotted to the lower classes.

"We'll need the second- and third-class versions of this," Violet said. "If they exist."

"Whomever killed Mrs. Navenby both knew where to find her and had access to the first-class staterooms." Maud's finger indicated what must be the cabin in question, close to the foot of the Grand Staircase on C Deck.

"First-class passenger or crew, then?" Violet raised her eyebrows.

"Most likely. But I think we should start by finding out more about who can go where, exactly, and who might see them doing it."

"There are plenty of security officers wandering around."

Maud brightened. "Good thought. I'm sure one of them would be happy to talk to us. And"—with another flick of her fingertips over the map—"keep your eyes peeled for anything that would look like a good hiding place, if you had some stolen items you wanted to keep hidden away until arriving back in England."

An ocean liner was nothing *except* hiding places. This wasn't a haystack—it was a small floating town. But the hook of interest was lodged fatally within Violet. She loved secrets, loved being in on the trick, loved moving in a crowd working to a purpose that they didn't know. She loved the *backstage* of things.

She said only, "This is a very large ship, Maud."

"I know." Maud gathered her map and stood. "We'd better get started, hadn't we?"

7

They began at the top and worked down.

Last night, Violet had barely noticed the Grand Reception's transparent ceiling, a rounded dome of glass that pushed up into the sun deck. This morning the sky poured daylight down into the carpeted area that spread out from the top of the Grand Staircase.

The huge double doors to the dining saloon were closed now, awaiting the lunch service. Nevertheless, the Reception was busy. Corridors curled backwards from it to the A-Deck parlour suites, and two more well-trafficked exits led out to the promenades, which ran the full length of that deck.

"Aha," said Maud with satisfaction. She tugged Violet with her to a corner of the Reception, where a clump of security officers stood near a wood-topped bar that had served cocktails the previous evening. "Excuse me?"

"Yes, ma'am. Miss. Misses." The man who turned to Maud's greeting looked harassed but mustered a polite smile. "I can assure you that we are doing everything we can, and if in the meantime you wish to deliver any valuables to the ship's safe, then the master-at-arms . . ." He trailed off, realising that neither of them was following. "Er. Begging your pardon, was there something I could help you with?"

"You're doing everything you can about *what*, exactly?" Violet asked.

The officer looked like he wished he could swallow back the last few seconds. "A few of the passengers have reported that they returned from dinner last night to find valuables missing from their rooms."

Maud went still. Violet pressed a showy hand to her own chest and gasped, "Valuables?"

"Jewels," he admitted.

Violet was ready to perform some minor anxious hysterics, but it wasn't necessary. Maud widened her eyes and leapt into a plaintive, fussy interrogation of the officer ("Ferris, miss") about whether the lower-class passengers had the *run* of the *ship*, and how she was supposed to *sleep* when there could be ruffians stalking the corridors in the *night*.

Ferris looked taken aback when Maud pulled out the map and a pencil, but he pointed out all the firm barriers on B, C, and D Decks that separated the second- and third-class areas from the first-class cabins and amenities. No, holders of lesser tickets could not pass through those hatches or access these elevators. Yes, they had security officers posted there as needed.

Violet couldn't resist another gasp. "Does that mean you are looking for the culprit among the *first-class* passengers? A gentleman thief?"

Ferris hesitated, visibly torn between casting aspersions on the quality of first-class passengers and admitting to possible flaws in security.

"If you're curious about these areas, miss"—indicating the blank spaces on Maud's map—"there's a framed blueprint in the library. It may be more technical than you care for, but . . ."

But please leave me alone now, dangled unsaid.

"Oh, *thank* you," Maud said, with a final deployment of dimples.

Violet's gloved palm floated on the gleaming wooden banister as they descended the staircase. "Maud. If there's a real thief aboard, could *they* have stolen Mrs. Navenby's silver? What if they simply surprised her? Old women's hearts can just stop, you know."

"A thief would have taken more of the real valuables. No. Her death was about the contract. I'm sure of it."

"In that case . . ." Violet hesitated to burst Maud's investigatory bubble further, but it had to be said. "Any moderately creative magician can slip into an unmagical place where they aren't allowed. I doubt there's any sort of warding here."

"Yes." Maud frowned. "We can't narrow the suspects to first class yet. So it's even more important for us to know every part of the ship."

Violet bit her tongue on wondering if traffic was allowed in the widdershins direction. She had a rapidly enlarging confidence in Maud's ability to charm her way past obstacles.

As well as the Café Marseille, the fore half of B Deck held the bulk of the first-class cabins, and the first-class library and smoking lounge. The single occupant of the library was a man with a prodigious grey moustache snoring in an armchair, newspaper draped over his chest, the tidal swell of his belly straining against his braces. The room smelled of leather and wood polish.

Maud ignored the shelves of books and located the blueprint of the *Lyric,* hung on the wall. The amount of detail made Violet squint, but Maud gamely covered her pamphlet in notes and subdivisions and scribbles.

The second-class staircase, quite aft, went between B and D Decks only. Ferris had assured them that third-class passengers were largely confined to the cabins and social areas on D Deck, though they could take a direct elevator to B Deck to access the main promenade there.

"I saw this yesterday," Maud said, tapping a small square. "The Grand Staircase stops in the foyer on C Deck. So there's this small staircase from the foyer down to D and E, to give access to the squash court and the Turkish baths. It looks like it might go all the way to the cargo hold! Shall we find out?"

The Grand Foyer was even busier and more opulent than the Reception. Crystal dripped around electric lights in the enormous chandelier, and every surface was polished to a glossy shine. The grandeur of it all felt like a theatre, just as the good new clothes Violet wore felt like a costume. And she was enjoying today's role. It was always fun to match the energy of a generous partner.

The first-class elevators were full of people equipped with parasols and shawls and boaters, clearly on their way up to the sun deck. Maud and Violet took the narrow doorway in the corner of the foyer and proceeded down a staircase that was serviceable rather than opulent. The first landing on D Deck had a sign pointing the way to the squash court—if Violet strained her hearing, she could faintly hear the solid thwacks and breathless calls. The engines were louder down here.

Another sign announced that the entrance fee to the Turkish baths was two shillings—"I'm afraid ladies' hour has already passed for today," the hovering attendant said when Maud and Violet approached. "You're welcome to come back tomorrow."

The glass panes in the doors were clouded with steam and etched with a stylised white pattern. One door swung open, emitting a young man with damp hair wearing only a thin undershirt with his trousers. His already pink face pinkened further when he saw Maud and Violet, and he stopped in the doorway to scramble into the sweater he held.

Violet took advantage of this to peer shamelessly around him. Fronds of ferns and walls tiled in turquoise blue were visible through the steam beyond. Like a gasping beast, the baths had emitted a puff of damp, fragrant air into the space where they stood. The sweet, deep scent caught at a memory for Violet. Before she could chase it down and match it to a place or time, the door closed and the scent faded.

The staircase they'd taken did continue downwards, narrower and dimmer. Two men with dirty coveralls and soft caps, which they touched absently when Violet glanced over, came up through the stairwell flipping through a sheaf of paper and conversing in low voices. Maud's best wide-eyed curiosity was met, this time, with a firmly courteous *no* at the prospect of peeking into the cargo hold.

"What next?" Violet asked as they ascended to the foyer. So far this exploration had produced a great deal of ship and nothing in the way of clues. *She* didn't much care—she was more than adequately entertained—but Maud was looking deflated.

"I said last night you'll be able to help me break into cabins to look for Mrs. Navenby's silver. Will you? Can you?"

"Let's find out," said Violet cheerfully.

They began with Violet's own stateroom on B Deck. Violet had an opening-spell in her repertoire but discovered quickly that it didn't take well to the slippery keyholes of the cabin doors. Or perhaps she was remembering the cradles wrong.

Maud pretended to adjust Violet's hatpins in case someone walked past, and Violet moved her fingers through the remembered motions. The spell was like a puff of mist. It kept fizzling to nothing when Violet tried to coax it against the keyhole of the nearest door. Which of her rings would help here? Perhaps the leather—

"I say," said Maud, "these flowers aren't real. My fingers go right through them."

"The violets? No, they're illusion."

"And you've held it this long? Doesn't that take a lot of concentration?"

"The spell's anchored to the straw. I put in enough magic to hold it for a day, I thought. Are they fading?" She let the unsuccessful cradle drop and looked at Maud. For the first time it occurred to her to ask: "Maud, how many magicians do you actually know? Is it just Edwin Courcey?"

"More or less," said Maud. "Oh, and Kitty Kaur, but I haven't seen as much of her since she—" A subtle gesture to her midsection. "Edwin says illusion needs a visual imagination, and that you have to keep your focus, to sustain it."

"For something large or complex, yes. But there are shortcuts. Ways to self-sustain. Most of the magic of the Penumbra was illusion."

"Edwin's going to *love* you. I hope you're prepared to be sat down and treated like an encyclopaedia. He was so excited that I was going to America. He wanted me to take notes. He would have gone himself, but he and Robin are—watched."

Violet skipped directly over the assumption that she would ever come face-to-face with the other members of Maud's little conspiracy, and returned her focus to the opening-spell. She breathed smoothly and held each intermediate form of the cradle in a way that Claudette would have laughed at, and this time the mist was thicker and slid gracefully onto the lock.

It clicked.

"There." Violet opened the door a demonstrative crack, then closed it. "I'll have to practice that one. I—"

She was interrupted by a high, weird drone of sound. It coughed into nothing. Then came again. It had the echo of distance but was quite distinct.

"What is *that*?" Maud was already moving in the direction of the noise. They followed it aft, past knots of people also craning to discover the source, and came out on a smaller deck. As they stepped into the open air, the noise battered exuberantly at the ears. Shrill wails, punctuated by drums, stopped and started in bursts. Several young men in military dress, including kilts, were forming themselves into lines for rehearsal. Half of them carried bagpipes tucked under their arms like unruly children.

With some shouting, Violet managed to establish from an elderly gentleman nearby that this was the Pipes and Drums of the London Scottish Regiment, who had been to America to perform a demonstration and were now returning home.

The nearest piper paused in his red-faced puffing to send a shy grin in Maud's direction. The noise was sounding closer to music now. Violet could feel the crisp rattle of the drums in her breastbone. It was awful and glorious at the same time.

"Oh, *drat*," said Maud suddenly. She turned to half yell in Violet's ear. "The parrot! Mrs. Navenby told me as soon as we were aboard to send to the kitchens for Dorian's feed, but it kept slipping my mind, what with—well, everything!"

Maud located a steward and asked the way to the kitchens. She required, she said, to beg some fruit and nuts for her employer's parrot.

"I'm sure I can arrange for whatever you need," the steward

said, in tones that meant the young ladies would be very much in the way.

"How *kind*," said Maud. "But it's such a tedious list of things that he will and won't eat. Just point us in the right direction, and I'll speak to the cooks myself."

The steward hesitated, but Maud had gathered around herself the impervious confidence of someone who wasn't used to being refused and was going to be obstinately unable to comprehend anything that sounded like refusal. Violet wasn't surprised when the steward gave up and escorted them to the first-class galley. The supervising chef reacted with startling irritation to Maud's request.

"I give up!" he snapped. "First I am told to provide for monkeys, and *tigers,* and the good Lord only knows what else! Now I am to also feed birds that do *not* appear on the list!"

Feelings thus expressed, the man stalked off to the other side of the hot, noisy space. An aproned woman took his place and, once the situation was explained, put together a basket of discarded nuts and bits of fruit that were on the turn.

"I do appreciate it," Maud said. "Might I know your name? Have you been with the White Star Line long? And before that—oh, in Piccadilly? I've not been there myself, but I know the name—"

Violet's aunt was of that category of women who considered it a sign of poor breeding to pay much attention to the help, beyond making sure they weren't shirking or stealing. It no longer surprised Violet that Maud, for all she was a baronet's daughter, was alive to how much the unseen class of people might see, and hear, and be able to tell you. Maud quickly extracted from the bemused woman some details about conditions in the *Lyric*'s staff quarters, and the existence of staff hatches and corridors to allow for easy movement through the ship.

Apparently Maud's mention of the *Strand*'s detective fiction had been apt. Violet considered the narrator of those Sherlock Holmes stories: a man dragged into following his chaotic genius of a roommate, first out of boredom and then appreciation.

She could sympathise.

"I should feed Dorian directly," Maud said as they left. "When he's hungry he makes noises like those bagpipes, truly—it's why I remembered him in the first place."

"Perhaps you should donate him to the regiment as a mascot."

"Monkeys and tigers," said Maud. "I wonder what he meant?"

"Monkeys—? Oh. Mr. Bernard's menagerie, I expect."

"Menagerie?"

Violet opened her mouth with an explanation, and an idea slid into her mind.

"Now, *that* might be a way for you to see the cargo bay," she said. "Come along, Maud, my dear, and bring your basket. I'm going to introduce you to some Americans."

8

They found the Bernard family taking the air on the first-class promenade, which took up much of the sun deck. It was a fine, calm day. On most of the lower decks, one could forget entirely that the *Lyric* was anything but a hotel. That the hundreds of souls aboard her were suspended above the chilling depths of the ocean.

One remembered, up here. The breeze was brisk, and it parted the lips for the flirtation of salt. It plucked at loose hair and sent hat ribbons and feathers and wispy lace flapping. Groups and couples strolled past the canvas-covered lifeboats or sat in the elongated deck chairs and watched the unchanging view of the ocean.

Violet led Maud towards a small cluster of deck chairs, where Mrs. Bernard and her daughters were sitting. The younger one, Helen, eyed a nearby game of shuffleboard with restless longing.

"Good morning!" called Violet.

Mrs. Bernard's eyebrows rose, but she lifted a hand in acknowledgement. Violet had taken her measure at dinner last night: a mixture of resentful knowledge that she and her daughters would never be considered the best society, and smugness that her husband's money would go a long way to allowing people to overlook that.

Of all the people she'd met at the captain's table, Violet calculated that the Bernards were the most likely to either not have heard about the strumpet business, or to be prepared to pretend they hadn't.

Violet introduced Maud to Misses Rose and Helen Bernard. Rose sheltered beneath a parasol in addition to her wide-brimmed hat. She shook hands with Maud and then returned to low conversation with her mother. Helen, who couldn't be eighteen yet, had a sprinkling of freckles and a friendly smile, and shifted on her deck chair so that Violet and Maud could sit along one side.

"We've been to the kitchens." Violet indicated Maud's basket. "Maud has taken ownership of her employer's hungry parrot."

Helen had spent fifteen minutes last night peppering the ship's captain with questions about the varieties of monkeys he'd encountered when he sailed for a merchant trading company. She lit up at once.

"What sort of parrot? I don't suppose he's a macaw? I'm dying to see one."

"A grey one," said Maud. "Perhaps this big?"

"An African Grey, most likely." Helen wasn't beautiful—neither of the Bernard girls were—but money and taste had dressed her to make the best of her reddish hair and slim figure, and she had an intense, lively manner that reminded Violet of her sister Alice. "Queen Victoria had one. They're supposed to be *very* clever at speaking. We have two white cockatoos in the aviary, but I haven't managed to teach them anything."

"Is it true, then? Violet told me that your father has a whole menagerie aboard!"

"Yes—it was to go ahead of us, but there was some delay with the paperwork, so most of the animals are also coming across on the *Lyric*."

"I'm glad I only have one parrot to feed," said Maud, and explained about the chef's *monkeys and tigers* complaint.

Helen laughed. "Mr. Hewitt, Papa's chief keeper, had to give them a list of how many pounds of meat would be required per day. There's probably an entire extra ice room full of supplies for the animals. He feeds the whole lot of them at one o'clock. Would you— I don't suppose you'd like to come with me and watch?" It was offered with shy eagerness, and Violet swallowed a crow of triumph. Maud hadn't even had to raise the idea herself.

"In the cargo hold? Are we permitted down there?"

"Mr. Hewitt knows I'm interested in the animals. He'll take us along."

After they bid the Americans farewell, Maud and Violet strolled towards the aftmost portion of the deck, where the railing allowed them to lean out and admire the *Lyric*'s churning white wake. You could throw a stone down to the deck below, more thickly crowded with people, the main open-air space available to second and third class. Violet could see three card games, with men smoking and laughing as they tossed cards onto the pile, and an incipient hair-pulling fight among several children who were arguing over a single ragged kite.

The breeze was brisk. Violet inhaled deeply.

"I wanted to ask . . ." said Maud.

Violet waited. No more emerged. With the basket dangling from one arm, Maud's hands were clasped together on the railing, tightly enough that the knuckles beneath must have been as white as the gloves.

"Yes?"

"Last night, you said that you fucked women more than men." Maud's voice dropped so low on the word *fucked* that it was nearly inaudible.

Violet put a hand to her hat to check its security, then took a moment. She had no fear that she was about to be lectured about morality.

"Yes," she said eventually. "And you didn't know such a thing was possible."

"I'm sure you think me frightfully naive. But it hadn't occurred to me. I know that there are some men who—prefer the company of other men."

Violet nodded. It had shone between Maud's words whenever she talked about her brother, Robin, and Edwin Courcey.

Maud said decidedly, "So. You prefer women? But . . . Lord Hawthorn."

Violet's cunt gave a wistful squeeze around phantom fingers. Ah, Lord Hawthorn.

"Some people have no preference either way." Including Lord Hawthorn. But that wasn't Violet's to give away, if Maud didn't know.

"How did you . . . realise?"

Well, it wasn't as if Violet hadn't guessed where this was going. She swallowed a burst of hilarity that she of all people was being put in the position of *mentor*. Her own first encounter with another woman had been one of tipsy and enthusiastic mutual discovery with a girl called Florence, whose family owned the pawnshop two doors down from the Penumbra. By that time, Violet had been in the Bowery long enough for her eyes to be opened to the wide range of the things that people might enjoy doing with and to one another. She hadn't needed to be walked carefully up to the idea like a skittish horse.

She shrugged. "All the things you think of when you look at a man—how you might want to reach out and touch him, or have him touch *you*. Do you ever have those thoughts about women?"

Maud's brow puckered and she turned back to the horizon. "I don't know. I mean—I do *know* how things work. Between a man and a woman, that is. And it's not as though there are educational tracts on the subject." She sounded put out. "Society never wants girls to learn anything *real*."

"Well," Violet said lightly, "in some ways it's easier for women inclined to their own sex than it is for men, because women can be *companions*. Or *dear friends*, who never marry and choose to share a house. Affection is expected of girls. Nobody will blink if I take your arm, like this." She did so. "Or slide an arm around your waist, like this. And kiss your cheek."

It was an impulsive tease of a kiss. The skin of Maud's cheek smelled of honey, and her breath hitched as Violet drew back. Her pupils were dark. Her body swayed against Violet, who had kept her arm in place.

With no effort, Violet could move her hand down a few

inches onto the warm curve of Maud's hip. Maud's face was uplifted to hers and it was, Violet thought abruptly, like something from a story. A perfect sprite encountered by a questing hero, temptation made flesh, ready to melt into nectar against the lips and leave the arms empty and coldly aching.

Violet pulled her arm back. "I don't think the Bernards are magical, if you were wondering."

Maud took the change of direction with grace. "And I can't imagine them killing anyone, either, but— Oh, this is hopeless." She slapped her hands against the railing. "Nobody marches around *looking* like a murderer, do they? We're no closer to narrowing things down than we were. We'll have to search every cabin at this rate. I wish . . . I wish Robin were here to tell me what to do. He'd find that very amusing. I spend so much time informing him that he *can't* tell me what to do."

"At least you have a gift for getting information out of people," Violet said.

She'd meant it as encouragement of sorts. And a warning to herself. To her surprise, Maud's expression clouded.

"It's not a gift. It's something I learned from watching my mother. I—I *haven't* lied, not to anyone." Said like someone defiantly waving a banner. And when Violet thought about it, she was right. Maud had asked questions, widened her eyes, wheedled and worried. Not a single untruth had actually passed her lips. "My mother would. She'd do anything to get what she wanted out of someone. Flatter, if they'd respond to it, and lie if they wouldn't. Spread a story about them, to weaken their standing in society, and then swoop in while they were at their lowest, all commiserations and promises to help."

"Charming."

"Oh, yes," said Maud bitterly. "She was."

Violet had met women like that. In her experience, they couldn't help but shape their children in their own image. She wondered what sort of odd familial crucible had created instead this shining moral stubbornness. Maud had sat there in Hawthorn's room and said *I care about what's right,* and she hadn't needed a candle. The truth of it had burned in every inch of her.

It didn't make her safe, Violet thought, looking down at the deck. The opposite, in fact.

Artlessness loosened tongues as effectively as the colder forms of manipulation, and Violet hated the sensation of being loosened. She could tease Maud and open locks for her—and even talk her through some light self-discovery—but she wouldn't be enticed into more. Violet wasn't a mystery to be solved by deadly truthfulness and beautiful, seeking eyes.

"Maud," she said suddenly. "Look down there. That's Lord Albert."

"Who? Where?"

Violet pointed. "I met him at dinner last night. His back's to us, and he's walking, but watch his shoulder—there." A quick twitch, the left shoulder giving a jerky shrug. It had happened a few times the previous night, though everyone at the captain's table had been far too polite to either comment or stare. A group of small children down on the deck felt no such constraints; one of them began to ape the motion before he was dragged aside and delivered a smack by his father.

"Is he the marquess's son? What's *he* doing down there?" said Maud. As Violet had hoped, the clouds in her face had cleared at the prospect of some officially suspicious behaviour to investigate.

"Shall we ask him?"

Maud turned in a whirl and stepped promptly into the path of someone not much taller than herself. When they'd extricated themselves, the other party turned out to be an olive-skinned young man with the kind of soulfully flawless good looks that made one want to rake one's fingernails across his cheek. He was Romeo. He was the helpful young page who in the third act would be proved a prince in disguise.

He was also holding a notebook and was dressed down compared to most of the gentlemen on the deck: trousers shiny with wear, the strap of a messenger bag crossing his waistcoat and shirtsleeves, and a soft cap atop his black curls.

"I do apologise," Maud was saying. "My fault, I'm sure."

The young man didn't hasten to claim responsibility. He flicked a razor gaze back and forth between Maud and Violet that calculated, Violet was quite sure, the cost of their ornaments and the cadence of Maud's speech. Only then did he smile and touch his cap. A pencil appeared from behind his ear.

"Ladies, I'm sorry to trouble you. Alan Ross. I've been employed by the White Star Line to work on their next set of advertisements. Might I ask you some questions about how you're finding the voyage so far?"

It was a London clerk's voice: literate, but not lofty. Maud breathlessly expressed her admiration of the *Lyric*'s amenities, with special mention made of the Café Marseille and Miss Broadley's performance at dinner. Ross's pencil moved busily.

"But *you* must be able to go anywhere on board, Mr. Ross," Maud added, as if it had just occurred to her. "What are the dining rooms like in second and third class? Oh, have you seen the *engines*?"

Mr. Ross admitted that he had not thought to go and inspect the *Lyric*'s engines.

Violet caught the man's eye, pretended to stretch her gloved fingers, and rapidly formed an obvious cradle for fire. There were various ways by which a magician could make themselves known to any other magicians in company. The easiest and commonest, for those trained in any of the traditions either British or British-derived, was to perform a well-known cradle without putting any magic into it.

Ross didn't react. Not even a flicker of his eyelids.

Maud dimpled. "The run of the entire ship and a license to ask questions? Perhaps we should be applying to *you* for the latest gossip."

Ross tucked his pencil back behind his ear, where the inky curls swallowed most of it. "I'm also writing an article on the voyage for a London society magazine. Can't give away all the best gossip for free. I suppose you know that there was a death on board yesterday?"

"And we have a jewel thief," said Violet.

Fingers twitched towards the pencil again. "I did hear that. Can you tell me anything more? I hope neither of you were among the unlucky victims."

"Goodness, no. Does a thief count as an amenity?" mused Maud. "I suppose it does add to the excitement."

"I don't imagine the theft of its passengers' jewels is quite what will best advertise the White Star Line to the public," said Violet.

"I'll leave it out of the copy." Ross touched his cap again in farewell and took his notebook off to accost a middle-aged couple nearby.

"All the society gossip," sighed Maud. "What do you suppose he was writing? *Miss Cutler, at first glance, doesn't look like the kind of fast young woman one associates with debauchery—*"

Violet laughed and tucked Maud's arm through her own. "But you're not really Miss Cutler, so that's all right. Besides— nobody's the kind of person they look like at first glance."

9

They ate lunch in the dining saloon. Maud chewed over the morning along with her cold pie and tried to convince herself that she had anything approaching a narrower list of suspects. The crew could move as they wished—so could Alan Ross. So could magicians, as Violet had pointed out.

Could she rule out the Americans on board? Even magician-Americans surely had little reason to be involved in a conspiracy of English magic.

Although . . . Edwin had pointed out that they had no proof of what the bloodlines of the Three Families would *mean,* when it came to the impact of the contract on the magicians of Britain today. What of those magicians who'd emigrated, like Mrs. Navenby, or whose parents or grandparents had done so? Distance governed the strength of magic; what of distance when measured in terms of oceans? Or time and generations?

That was usually the point in the proceedings at which Edwin would slam his research book shut and then immediately lay his palm on the cover in silent apology. After which Robin would go to haul his beloved forcibly out of his seat and insist on a brisk walk in the fresh air.

No. All told, it was far likelier that—as Maud's bubbling pool of guilt suggested—an English magician had been secretly watching Maud as well as Robin and Edwin, had followed her to New York, and found Mrs. Navenby that way. Maud was supposed to warn her, and instead Mrs. Navenby might have died *because* of her. It was unbearable to think about. All she could do was work harder to solve this.

Her excitement at having Violet on her side had carried her through the morning. The sobering reality—this vast ship carrying hundreds of people, none of whom were conveniently presenting themselves as magicians or murderers—had now taken hold of Maud's lungs and was gently, thoughtfully kneading them into a loaf of dread.

Asking Violet to magically unlock one door at a time wasn't going to work. A new approach would be needed. Several new approaches.

"Maud?"

Maud looked up at Violet's prompting. A steward inquired if she wanted a spoonful of the lemon pudding being offered as the dessert course.

"No, thank you." Her appetite had vanished.

Still, she couldn't help but watch as Violet's lips closed with relish over a spoonful of pudding. Part of Maud had been lighting up whenever that mouth curved into a full, pleased smile. Or quirked at the side with a smaller and more sarcastic one.

You want to reach out and touch him, Violet had said. *Or have him touch you.*

Maud drained her water glass with glum resignation. The problem was that Violet assumed Maud *had* had such thoughts about men.

Maud had been waiting for most of her nineteen years for these thoughts to appear. She'd met friends of Robin's, and Liza's brother Paul, and spent time with several young men whose parents *her* parents had approved. Many of them had been perfectly nice. Some of them she might have enjoyed talking to, if she hadn't been so determined to feel the exact opposite of what her mother wanted her to feel.

Robin had expressed his concern that one day she'd run off with a chimney sweep, just for the pleasure of writing the letter informing Sir Robert and Lady Blyth what their daughter had done—that this particular scrap of their manipulated existence had insisted on acting as though she were a full and separate human being.

"It wouldn't work," Maud had said, sighing. "I'd end up sneaking back to look through the window at their faces as they read it, or there'd be no point. And I'd be using the poor chimney sweep just as much as *they* use people."

And Robin had kissed her hair and made himself particularly agreeable, particularly obliging, so that Maud could slip out to a Women's Society meeting while their parents were arranging their only son's life for him.

Maud held on to the image. *That* was why she was here: for Mrs. Navenby, yes, but also for Robin. To make up for her failure and set things right. Not to sit mooning after a sophisticated scandal-trap of a girl, no matter how attractive her mouth.

She parted ways with Violet at the end of lunch and went to meet Helen Bernard. Violet had volunteered to question Lord Albert, and Maud herself was unlikely to get another good excuse to visit the cargo hold.

And . . . there was something she hadn't shared with Violet yet. One of Robin's possibly-ship-based visions had included wild animals. She'd be silly to pass up the opportunity to learn more about this menagerie.

"Miss Cutler!"

Maud smiled, shoved the enormity of her worry aside, and relaxed into Helen's chatter. Helen Bernard had lived all her life in upstate New York, and wanted more than *anything* to travel to Africa and see giraffes and lions and zebras and elephants and all the other things that her father's explorer friends told stories about or brought home remnants of: tusks and tails and skins.

"And photographs," said Helen, as they took the staircase to D Deck. "Papa's promised me a camera for Christmas, and I plan to become a lady photographer of great renown, so that publishers and magazines and collectors will ask me to go to Africa to take pictures of all the animals."

"I hope you do!"

"I had thought of becoming a naturalist, but I suppose you need to study at a university to be taken seriously by the Royal

Society. Do you suppose there are any unmarried dukes or viscounts in England who might be interested in also becoming intrepid explorers?" she asked hopefully. "Good day, Mr. Hewitt! How's the porcupine?"

The Bernards' menagerie keeper was waiting for them at the head of the stairs leading down into the hold. He was in the same category as Ross, Maud thought—someone whose occupation meant he could move wherever he needed to be.

"Stopped bringing up her guts, at least. Can't say she looks her best, miss, but if she'll take some water and keep it down, she should see out the voyage."

Hewitt wore a leather apron over his clothes and had a wide reddish nose, thick grey brows, and a flavour of American to his accent that was unfamiliar to Maud. He was clearly fond of Helen, and just as clearly resigned to a further five days full of seasick porcupines.

Maud and Helen followed him down the stairs, through a large open hatch and into dimness. The cargo hold was a huge space, with bare electrical lights set at intervals casting a greyish-gold glow. It was more low-ceilinged than Maud had expected. Piles of crates, large trunks, bandboxes: all were huddled beneath canvas and tied securely down to metal bolt-loops in the floor. There were even several motorcars, their headlamps reflecting a gleam like sleepy eyes.

You could hide anything down here, Maud thought with a renewed squeeze of despair.

The ground purred beneath her feet with the proximity of the ship's great engines. The air smelled damper, warmer, tinged with leather and straw and petrol and a densely animal odour that grew stronger as Hewitt led the way to one corner of the hold. As they approached, the general rumble of noise split and became several distinct noises all chattering, growling, complaining at once. The menagerie.

It was a small, grubby zoo: an assembly of thick wooden crates with gaps in the slats, through which the moving shapes of animals could be glimpsed. There were several metal cages, including an aviary Maud's height and nearly as wide as it was tall, within which several birds of various sizes hopped from perch to ring to seed-scattered ground. Could you magically train an *animal* to seek magical items, like pigs with truffles?

"Were you wanting to help with the feeding, miss?"

"Thank you," said Maud, giving the answer she was fairly sure he wanted, "but I haven't so many outfits that I can afford to get this one covered in . . ."

"Fish." Hewitt hoisted a bucket. "For the otters. And the bear."

Helen launched into an enthusiastic monologue about bears. Maud stood respectfully back as Hewitt opened cages or prised up the lids of crates in order to feed the inhabitants. Fish for the bear. Raw meat, coolly dripping, for the cheetahs, who blinked their cat's eyes at Maud and stretched their graceful, spindly limbs. Parrots, finches; monkeys, porcupine. A kangaroo. An enormous snake, coiled like bulging rope in the corner of its crate, that had apparently eaten before being loaded up and would live off it until they reached England.

"He looks terrifying," said Helen, "but he's not really dangerous to people unless he's starving or scared. We could open the crate and he'd probably do nothing at all. Perhaps he'd go poking around in search of a better corner to curl up in, where he could feel the warmth of the engines."

"You're already halfway to being a naturalist," said Maud. "You know, you could go to university in England, if your parents were willing. There are colleges just for girls at Oxford and Cambridge. I plan to study there," she added.

"Do you really? How *thrilling*. What will you study?"

"I don't know." Maud watched the snake. Which, if released, might do nothing at all with the freedom thus offered except exchange one dark corner for another. "I don't know if I'm even clever enough for it."

"I'm *sure* you are."

Maud smiled. She wasn't used to feeling like the most grown-up person in a conversation. And she also hadn't expected to say what she'd said: the secret fear she'd so far kept even from Robin. The quiet, niggling worry that her dream of university, for all that it had proven solid and persistent, had nothing to do with Maud herself being made in an academic mould, but was in fact the career equivalent of a chimney sweep.

"If I am, or if I'm not, I'd still like to find out for myself. When the— I mean, if we can afford it." She'd bitten back the word *estate*. Miss Maud Cutler's brother did not administer an estate. Was not grimly engaged in dragging said estate back into being a profitable holding, when he wasn't working at the Home Office as the civil service liaison to the Magical Assembly, or reporting to the Assembly about his visions of the future. Or furtively investigating a magical conspiracy.

The feeding over, Maud and Helen went back up to the sun deck and settled on a pair of chairs. Maud watched the wandering passengers for anyone who might be watching *her*—though she supposed any glances were just as likely to be due to Miss Cutler's scandalous ways.

"Where will you keep all the animals, in England?" she asked Helen.

"The house Papa's bought has enormous grounds. And he's already got men there building a proper set of enclosures and sheds. The weather will be different to what the animals are used to. I'm sure they'll all get used to it soon enough."

The slight shake in the girl's voice was easy enough to diagnose. Maud thought of Violet saying brightly, *I missed the weather.*

"Are you sad to leave America?"

"Not for the most part." Helen's smile resurrected itself. "It's not quite exploring the wilderness or the jungle, but it's still an adventure. I'm mostly sad to leave my friends. My bosom friend Anne and I have known each other practically since we were born. We've promised to write every week, but I know I'm going to miss her horribly."

"Writing does help," said Maud. "I have a friend who—well, she didn't move across the ocean." She laughed. "Though sometimes it feels that way. She was married last November. She doesn't have as much time to spend with me. It's only natural."

She kept her voice brisk. That was another set of feelings she hadn't wanted to trouble Robin with; she barely allowed them to trouble herself, these days. They were stupid feelings anyway. Maud's heart had no right to feel so bruised and raw, seeing Liza glowing and spending her time with her husband instead of dragging Maud to book clubs and parties and Suffragette meetings.

Girls grew up and were married; friends grew up and grew distant. Maud had never expected that it would be herself and Liza Sinclair, each being the other's favourite person, forever.

Except that a dumb animal part of her clearly had.

"Oh," said Maud blankly.

"Oh?" Helen looked at her.

Maud felt like she'd been handed a jigsaw puzzle: one made for children, with large, obvious pieces. One of the pieces was the way her body had turned to a slow bonfire of curiosity beneath Violet Debenham's hand, and her inability to stop thinking of Violet's lips. The other was the last time she'd felt anything even close to that, when she and Liza lay giggling on Liza's bed with their arms linked, breathlessly reliving the jokes of the pantomime performance they'd just seen. Maud buoyant with unquestioned joy at her friend's attention; Maud feeling as though she'd been punctured by a knife when Liza drew away and promised her laughter to someone else.

The pieces slotted together and formed a picture. Maud felt even more of a fool than usual. Clever enough for university? She was barely clever enough to know herself.

I wonder, she thought, *if it runs in the family. Like magic.*

"Maud?"

"Oh. Nothing," she said to Helen. "Nothing important."
It both was, and wasn't, a lie.

Lord Albert, son of the Marquess of Welmotte, was not in his cabin. Violet interrupted his valet in the midst of some very important shoe-polishing and trouser-brushing, from the look of the apron tied around the man's waist. They'd been at sea only a day; how much damage could one aristocrat do to his clothing in that time?

The valet gave Violet a look of deep ambivalence when she introduced herself. All domestic staff that Violet knew were expert gossips, so no doubt her strumpet status had reached him as well. He offered with lukewarm professionalism to take a message for his lordship, but something about his tone suggested that the message would be forgotten as soon as Violet was out of sight.

Lord Albert himself had the misfortune to settle the matter by appearing. His gingery hair stuck to his sweaty forehead, and he was clad in what looked like tennis flannels. He stopped a few feet away.

"Sir," said the valet.

"Lord Albert!" said Violet.

"Miss Debenham," said his lordship. His shoulder twitched.

"I was hoping to beg a moment of your time, my lord." Violet looked meaningfully past the valet's shoulder into the parlour suite. "In private."

Lord Albert coughed. "Er. I'm not sure that would be . . ."

"Proper?" suggested Violet happily, when the man proved unequal to the task. "Or I suppose you could buy me a cup of tea in one of the *public* dining rooms."

Lord Albert caved to the inevitable. Violet liked that in a man.

The valet retired to the adjoining room and closed the door with a snobbish *snick*. Lord Albert showed every sign of intending to seat Violet on the settee and then hover as far away from her as possible, so she gave her best smile and crowded herself into the man's space. He was a good few inches shorter than Violet, who had long ago decided to favour heeled shoes despite her height, out of what Jerry had called her innate damned contrariness.

Violet performed the fire-cradle she'd used with Ross, this time with her magic held barely in check. She was investigating a possible killer, after all. At the slightest hint of guilt or even recognition, she would set the man's white flannels aflame and make her escape.

Lord Albert didn't do anything but continue to eye Violet as though she were a bull and he was regretting his lack of red rags.

"Miss Debenham. I r-really think that—"

"My dear man." Violet let her hands fall. "You seem very pleasant, I'm sure. But do you really think I would waltz out of Lord Hawthorn's bed and immediately try to find my way into *yours*?"

A pause. "That was an awfully r-rude thing to say." The stammer, unlike the twitch, had been less obvious at dinner last night. Only a hesitation before certain words, and a forceful way of attacking them.

Violet gazed into the uncertain face with its trim red moustache. So he wasn't a magician; he just had a secret. She could sweep her way out of the cabin and pretend all of this had never happened.

But she'd joined Maud's endeavour because she *liked* secrets. At least, when they belonged to other people.

"Yes, it was," she said. "I'm sorry."

"If you're not here to seek out a lower grade of product," he said, with a sudden dash of ironic spirit, "then what the dickens do you want?"

Violet couldn't help herself. "Perhaps I'm looking for someone who's prepared to offer me a more formal arrangement than Lord Hawthorn will."

Lord Albert laughed. It transformed his face; his eyes creased and true good humour shone out of him. "Miss Debenham, I r-regret to inform you that my affections are engaged elsewhere."

Violet retreated to the truth. "I saw you down on the lower-class deck, in the sort of hat you might have borrowed from your stableboy. I know you're hiding something, Lord Albert. I want to know what it is."

This time his jaw twitched along with his shoulder. He was at least unselfconscious about a weakness that had probably seen him teased mercilessly at school, unless it had developed in adulthood. But the way he covered for the stutter spoke of careful speech lessons.

He said stiffly, "Were you hoping that blackmail might turn a tidier profit than marriage?"

"It would certainly be *ruder,* wouldn't it?" said Violet. "No. I have more than enough money, my lord, or at least I will shortly. I'm just insatiably curious."

He sighed. "Suppose it'll be easiest if . . . Come with me." He offered her his arm.

A small stab of conscience hit Violet. She was surprised that she recognised it.

"You know I'm being talked about. My asking after you can be explained as promiscuity or shameless fortune-hunting, but if you now escort me halfway across the ship, it'll look like you decided to take me up on *one* of those two options."

A bemused look stole onto Lord Albert's face. "That's all r-right. Might even be helpful."

And *that* was a hook so intriguing that Violet took his arm without another thought.

In the elevator down to C Deck, Violet exerted herself to make some small talk about the Pipes and Drums, and discovered that Lord Albert had both an older brother in one of the royal regiments and a keen interest in classical music. Violet, in possession of one sister who'd married a soldier and a comprehensive knowledge of music-hall songs from the childish to the outright filthy, carried them through the next few minutes in amiable conversation.

His lordship was extolling the wonders of Bizet when they reached a hatch that led into a small, irregularly shaped space off which branched several boxy rooms. Violet couldn't recall what this had been on Maud's map.

For a moment Violet thought that Lord Albert's description of opera had caused her to imagine the sound of incoherently harmonic strings. Then she realised that these were music practice rooms, or at least had been claimed as such. Through the circular glass pane in one thick door Violet could see the cramped-looking ship's orchestra, each man trying not to elbow his neighbour in the viola. Another held a quartet, who appeared to be having an argument.

Lord Albert opened the only other closed door and led Violet through it. The sound of a melody painstakingly picked out on a piano stopped at once. Miss Broadley stood up as Violet and Lord Albert entered.

The mezzo-soprano was dressed for practice rather than performance, in a plain green dress with white piping and a severe line of lace at the waist, but no other trim. She was smaller than she'd seemed when she was singing. Her dark eyes moved between the two of them and she gave a small curtsy that had something of the stage to it. One expected roses to come flying and gather at her feet.

"My lord," she said cautiously.

Lord Albert pulled the door shut. "It's all r-right. Elle, this is Miss Violet Debenham. Met her at the captain's table last night."

Affections otherwise engaged. So the man had a Black opera singer for a mistress, and was following her to England. Or vice versa.

"Miss Debenham," he said, warm with pride, "meet Lady Albert Barton. My wife."

Oh.

Lady Albert Barton rolled her eyes and sat down heavily on the piano stool.

"Bertie," she said, "do we have different definitions of a *secret* marriage?"

"*Oh*," said Violet, weak with delight.

"She saw me poking around the lower deck this morning, after I'd visited you." Lord Albert crossed to his wife's side and took her hand to pat it apologetically.

"And you couldn't think of a single good lie?"

"You know I'm no good at it."

"I, however, am *excellent* at secrets," said Violet. "You've nothing to fear from me, Lady Albert."

"You should call me Miss Broadley. In case you slip in public. And . . ." A low chuckle, hinting at the richness of her voice. "I still don't know how I feel about wearing Bertie's Christian name as well as the other."

"Tradition," Lord Albert said. "Sorry, m'dear."

"Why is it secret at all?" Violet asked. "Do you have another engagement to break off first, in England?"

"Frank, aren't you?" said Lady Albert, amused.

Violet shrugged. "He's not the first lord to marry someone plucked off the stage."

"Didn't *pluck* her. She's staying on the stage. She's too good to waste off it. And it shan't stay secret," said Lord Albert. "It's my father. Don't want anyone *else* telling him. If it's sprung on him as gossip, he'll fly into a r-rage and not speak to me for a year. Need time, is all. I'll be able to bring the old boy around to the idea. Especially when he's met her."

He sent his wife a besotted look. Hers, in return, was more muted, and contained clear doubt as to whether Lord Welmotte would be as swayed by her charms as his son had been.

Did it contain love? Did it matter? People used one another. People made partnerships, romantic and otherwise, for every reason under the sun. Did it make a difference if he was being played, as long as they were both getting what they wanted out of it? At least she'd have to stay with him, to take advantage of what he could offer.

Violet flexed her wood-ringed thumbs, swallowed the tired

rage that was trying to make itself known in her throat, and smiled at the couple. "Should we leave, my lord? Any of the orchestra could look in here and see us."

"Not to worry. If anyone asks what we were talking about, Miss Debenham wants to give you some money, Elle."

"*Do* I," said Violet.

"Veteran of the stage. Recently inherited a fortune. You're interested in becoming a patron of Elle's new company."

"*Is* she?" said Lady Albert, with much more scepticism.

So this was why Lord Albert had gone to the trouble of bringing Violet down here, when he could have explained the situation and begged for her discretion in less than a minute.

"I warn you, I'm officially ruined and very disreputable; I'll be rubbish for clout. You'll want a few patrons with good names too."

"I intend to start a coloured opera company, Miss Debenham. I'll take anyone's dollars to begin with," said Lady Albert dryly. "Which stages are you a veteran of?"

"The Penumbra," said Violet. "Bowery establishment."

Lady Albert blinked. Her look took in Violet's entire outfit, shoes to hat.

"My feathers and fishnets are in my trunk," said Violet.

That got her another chuckle. Violet agreed that Lord Albert could tell anyone he wanted that he was paying serious attention to a shameless newly monied girl fresh from the Baron Hawthorn's sheets; if *that* rumour reached the Marquess of Welmotte's ears, Lord Albert pointed out, brightening, then being presented with a fully respectable wife might seem a positive boon.

They left Lady Albert to her rehearsing, and Lord Albert handed Violet personally back to her own corridor, where he left her with a grateful smile. Violet planned to freshen up; it had been warm and stuffy in that practice room. Then perhaps she'd have a nap before she started room-breaking. Maud was off feeding tigers and monkeys. They would reconvene for drinks before dinner.

She stepped on the folded piece of paper that lay just inside the door. On the White Star stationery found in every desk in the ship was a message in an unfamiliar hand, informing her that Lord Hawthorn wished to entertain Miss Violet Debenham (and Miss Maud Cutler) to tea in his suite. He would receive them at their earliest convenience.

The word *earliest* was underlined with a bold, irritable dash.

Violet, because of her innate damned contrariness, took her time and refreshed herself anyway. She splashed her face in the bathroom and reapplied some scent. Then she took herself back up to A Deck and rapped on Lord Hawthorn's parlour-suite door.

Hawthorn himself opened it at once, pulled Violet in with a grip on her forearm—she bit down on a squawk of protest—and closed it behind her again.

Maud was in the room already. She was on her knees on the rug, next to the credenza, and she was bent anxiously over the motionless body of a man.

"What on earth . . . ?" said Violet.

"As I told Miss Blyth," said Hawthorn, "this appears to be part of *your* mess, ladies. So you may have the pleasure of dealing with it."

10

Alan Ross the advertising-copy man looked younger when he was unconscious. The sharpness and the smile were both smoothed from his face, and his curls were rough where the cap had come askew when he fell. He looked like a painting by . . . oh, one of those artists who were obsessed with light and shadow. Robin would have been able to name them at once.

Maud held the face of her pocket watch in front of Ross's lips again. The glass still fogged. Maud exhaled in relief.

She had thought he was dead at first. It fit the pattern of her luck, as though the universe had looked at Maud's morning of menageries and new hunger and new friends, and sent her a second corpse as punishment. As if to say: *Remember that you failed, and that other people are paying for it.*

"He's not dead," Hawthorn had said in response to whatever had appeared on Maud's face when she first entered his cabin. He said it again now, to Violet. "He is, however, the second person to have broken into my room in two days. I can't help suspecting"—dry as powder—"that the two events may be related."

Violet came to peer down at the unmoving Ross.

"Fuck," she said, as easily as if the word were *frog* or *fancy.* "It's that man with the notebook."

"Alan Ross." Maud looked at Hawthorn, who was lifting the unstoppered decanter of whisky cautiously to his nose. "You're sure you don't recognise him?"

A brief, considering dart of those blue eyes. "No. But I don't know every magician in the country, Miss Blyth. Especially not the *writing* ones."

The working ones, who wore flat caps instead of stiff hats.

"Not dead. Is he asleep?" asked Violet.

"He *looks* asleep," said Maud. "But he won't wake."

"Are you sure? Stab him with a hatpin."

Hawthorn said, "I tried shaking him when I found him. But I've no objections if you want to stab him as well."

"*I* object!" said Maud, getting to her feet.

"As to what's wrong with him." Hawthorn replaced the stopper in the decanter and set it back in place. "Going by the available evidence, I think he's been poisoned."

"That's . . . something of a leap," said Violet.

"There was a glass tipped over, with the dregs of spirits in it." Maud nodded to where she'd set the glass upright and aside. "Some of it had tipped out onto the carpet. I could smell it."

Hawthorn said, "Can you handle a basic detection-spell, Violet? One with an imbuement focus, if possible."

Violet stripped off her gloves. "You'll have to show me the cradles for that focus. My detection-spells run mostly to making sure nobody's placed any charms in my corner of the dressing room."

Maud wanted to ask *What kinds of charms?* and get another of Violet's anecdotes about theatre life, but she swallowed it. She'd only seen a few people perform magic. Edwin's technique was, by his own admission, an increasing muddle of the classic English tradition—and he had so little power that he had to use a string to guide his cradles, ensuring the finger positions were exact—and the new one-handed system of magic he was piecing together from Flora Sutton's research notes.

Catherine Kaur, sister to their friend Adelaide Morrissey, also practiced something out of the ordinary: what she called, dryly, a colonial patchwork of her father's English techniques and her Punjabi mother's tendency to combine finger movements with spoken words. "Cradling with the tongue," Kitty

called it, when she wanted Edwin to turn pink with the effort
of repressing his endless questions.

Hawthorn demonstrated the detection-spell, slowly, and Violet copied his motions. Each of them drew their palms together
and then apart, fingers bending and weaving.

"No, you've picked up the American drawl," said Hawthorn. "This one's highly contractual, you can't drop the middle. Sharpen up."

Violet shot him an unfriendly look, but the motion of her
fingers became more precise and angular. "How does the focus
clause—oh, I see."

The spell was visible now. It was dusty grey, as if Violet
had dragged her fingers through the ash of an unswept hearth,
speckled with tiny flecks that caught the light and glowed. Violet closed the fingers of her right hand around this diamond
dust of power, unstoppered the decanter, and made a sharp
flicking gesture that deposited the spell into the liquid itself.

The grey vanished at once. Instead the whisky began to twin-
kle with those same flecks, like a night sky done in burnished
amber.

"Magic, not poison. That settles that question," said Hawthorn. "Or part of it."

"He imbued your whisky and then drank it himself?" Violet
frowned. "That doesn't seem right. Unless he took a sip as a
test and it was stronger than he thought."

"Or," said Hawthorn, "he's a common thief who got himself
caught in a trap meant for me, and is in fact the *third* person to
have broken into my room in two days. I should be charging
an entry fee."

Hawthorn's face was closed-off and hostile. He shook out
his right hand as if it had spasmed. Maud wondered what it
meant to him, to have abandoned magic years ago and now to
be pulled back into performing the empty motions of it, like a
chorister reduced to mouthing along with the soaring notes of
the chorus.

Maud averted her gaze before he could catch it with his own. She knew when someone was looking for an excuse to strike out.

"You heard about the jewel thief?"

"I had a look through that while I was waiting for you." Hawthorn indicated something hanging over the back of a chair: Ross's leather bag. He pulled from his own pocket two small objects, which winked like the stars of the detection-spell. Gold cufflinks, set with what Maud was prepared to wager were diamonds. "These are mine. They were in one of the inner pockets."

Maud opened the bag herself, heart aflutter. It seemed far too much to hope that the objects stolen from Mrs. Navenby's room would be inside it. Indeed, most of the bag's contents seemed to be small pamphlets or slim bound books. Maud pulled out a few. None of the authors or titles were familiar to her. She opened one at random and skimmed her eyes down the page.

Then went back to the top of the page and read more slowly.

"Ah, Miss Blyth—" said Hawthorn belatedly.

"*Goodness.*" Maud read several more lines. She opened another of the booklets and read a portion: more of the same, although this one seemed to involve several more participants. When she looked up, Hawthorn had an expression of resigned amusement on his face.

"What is it?" asked Violet. She came and read over Maud's shoulder: "—*that my rod once again swelled, in glorious ecstasy, as I buried my face in her dripping—*oh," and gave a gale of laughter. "If you're out for whatever you can steal, why would you steal dirty books? They're not worth half as much as the number of precious knickknacks you could fit in the same space."

Much as she wanted to keep flicking and reading, Maud gingerly slid the booklets back into the bag.

Hawthorn knelt by Ross's side and delivered a painful-looking pinch to the webbing of the man's thumb. Nothing. "Well, at least magic can be reversed."

"Can it?" said Violet. "Without knowing what kind of imbuement it was in the first place? Enlighten us, my lord."

"Miss Blyth. Go and get that candle of yours. I want answers when he wakes up, and I want to know they're true."

That made sense. Maud did as she was asked.

By the time she returned to Hawthorn's suite, the others had pushed the furniture back to create more space around Ross's unconscious form. Violet knelt at Ross's head and was pouring greenish-gold oil from a small stoppered bottle into an empty whisky glass. Hawthorn stood from the writing desk when Maud entered. He held another piece of notepaper with the White Star letterhead, on which he had drawn several odd-looking symbols.

"Have you worked out how to reverse it?" Maud asked.

Violet made a face. "Not really. This will be the magical equivalent of hurling a bucket of paint blindfolded at a wall and hoping enough of it lands on the individual brick in question. Power in place of precision."

Maud knew that one; or rather, knew its opposite. Edwin relied on precision to achieve as much as possible with his limited power. A bucketload of magic could afford to be sloppier.

She asked for the details of the spell so that she could write them down for Edwin. Violet explained that olive oil, like other plant oils, took imbuement directly—unlike water or most alcohols, which needed to be steeped with preimbued substances.

"And that?" Maud indicated the sheet of paper.

"I've never learned to work with runes," said Violet. "Apparently, they're a family speciality for his lordship here."

Runes. Looking at the dark symbols caused a shiver of memory to dive down Maud's spine. Robin had borne a rune-curse on his arm, and it had nearly killed him.

Hawthorn brusquely explained his side of the workings. Runes were simply a way of representing the clause or clauses of a spell. You could make them *become* the whole spell—as with curses, Maud assumed—or use them to hold a complex clause in your mind and reinforce it while you worked on cradling the rest of the spell.

"I still don't know if it'll be enough," warned Hawthorn. "Depends on your strength, Violet."

Violet brushed a curl back from Ross's forehead, separating a few thin black strands from the others. She wound these around one finger then jerked it away to pull the hairs out at the roots; Maud winced in sympathy, but Ross didn't respond any more than he had to Hawthorn's pinch.

Violet wound the hairs twice more around her finger, creating a loose ring. "It might add something. I've seen some specialists use hair as a focus for spells affecting the body. What on earth is that look for? If you can pick America from my cradles, you can't be surprised at the rings."

Hawthorn didn't deign to answer. He disappeared into the adjoining bedroom.

Maud was shaping an Edwin-worthy question about the use of rings in magic, but before she could ask it of Violet, Hawthorn emerged from the bedroom holding an *actual handgun*.

Maud jerked back. Hawthorn held the gun out, grip-first, in her direction.

"What? Me?"

"Unless *you* want to be the one showing Miss Debenham how to perform a general negation suitable to imbue an organic oil. In which case, I'll be more than happy to hold our unwelcome visitor at gunpoint when—God bloody willing—he wakes up."

Maud flushed. Hawthorn fit the revolver into her hands. It was certainly meant for someone much larger; her fingertip only just touched the trigger.

"What if it goes off by accident?" Maud asked.

Hawthorn gave her a look that spoke eloquently about how little skin off *his* nose it would be if someone like Mr. Ross was hit by a bullet or two. Maud's hand, usually very well behaved, felt on the verge of giving an involuntary twitch.

"It's not loaded," said Hawthorn.

"Oh," said Maud. "Good."

As with the detection-spell, Hawthorn demonstrated and Violet copied. She practiced it several times, each repetition more fluid, until she could do it without watching her fingers. Then she cradled it with true magic, and with her eyes fixed on the sheet of runes. This spell was a red glow. It slipped over the surface of the olive oil, then sank in.

Hawthorn lifted Ross's head to lie on his knee and opened the man's mouth so that Violet could tip a portion of the oil inside. Some dribbled out of the corner of Ross's lips, but Hawthorn pinched them closed and stroked his thumb down the front of Ross's throat.

Maud was holding her breath. She let it out slowly, the gun an odd weight in her hands, her eyes on Ross's closed lids.

Nothing.

"I did it correctly," said Violet, somewhat defensively.

"You did. It should have worked. Hm. Bloodstream's more drastic, but if that's what it takes . . ." Hawthorn lowered Ross and fetched his knife, then coated the blade in the imbued oil.

Violet paled. She looked to the side as Hawthorn made a shallow cut on the back of Ross's hand that sent bright blood welling to the skin.

"Violet," said Maud quickly. "Do you theatre magicians put any sorts of imbuement on greasepaint?"

Violet looked at her and resurrected a smile. "You could, but most of the effect would be— *Christ!*"

Alan Ross's uncut hand had flung out and struck her. His whole body jerked and shook. At the end of it his eyes flew open and he rolled to one side, coughing as if to expel grubby fog from his lungs.

Hawthorn stood and stepped over him in a single motion, took the gun from Maud's unresisting grip, and pointed it down at the now-wheezing Ross with nothing but a flat, bored expression on his face. As if he'd pointed hundreds of guns at hundreds of people. Maud didn't blame Ross when he looked skittishly among them all and paused like a frozen field mouse as his gaze met Hawthorn's.

"Welcome back, sir," Hawthorn said. "You've another count of ten to catch your breath, and then you will start talking."

11

Violet agreed with her late cousin Lady Enid on many points, including this: magicians put far too much stock in blood. Both the perceived strength of it as purveyor of magic within a family's line, and the use of it in spells.

It *was* important for the latter. That was the horrid thing.

And Lord Hawthorn, one remembered belatedly, had been in the military for several years. He was clearly just as handy with a blade as he was with the ivory-handled contraption he aimed at Mr. Ross's face. Nothing about his manner suggested that it was unloaded, or that he'd hesitate to use it.

Ross coughed once more and raised himself on his elbows, brown eyes fixed on the gun. He said, far more witheringly than Violet suspected she'd have been able to manage in similar circumstances: "And what would *sir* like me to talk about?"

His accent was rougher than it had been when he was conducting interviews, as if coming up against Hawthorn's cut-glass aristocracy had bounced him reactively a few rungs down the ladder.

"I think answering questions should suffice. Candle, Miss Blyth," Hawthorn ordered.

Thankfully, no further cuts were needed. Maud took advantage of the existing wound on Ross's hand. Ross gave a short noise of alarm when he saw it, but Maud smiled at him from close quarters as she smeared some blood onto the candle's business end, and he subsided.

"Hold this for me, please, Mr. Ross," said Maud.

Ross's hand obeyed, seemingly without recourse to his brain.

Perhaps it was the dimples. They were practically a coercive charm all on their own.

Violet cradled a light for the candle and revelled in the way Ross's eyes bulged. She was used to performing magic for the unbusheled, but usually they were expecting it and thought it was no more than a particularly clever trick.

Aside from the blood, this was better than a matinée.

"What the *fuckin'ell*," said Ross. It came out rather high. He sat cross-legged, and his gaze flicked between the gun and the green flame of the candle as though he wasn't sure which of them would explode first. The flame was sluggish and smaller than previously, and gave the occasional hiccup of yellow within the green.

"Nothing will happen to you if you tell the truth," Maud assured him.

Hawthorn snorted. Ross's scoff came out in unison.

"Like hell I'll believe *that*," said Ross.

"I'm not lying," said Maud, frowning.

Hawthorn said only, "Your name. Now."

"Julius sodding Caesar."

The candle flared high and red. Ross swore and dropped it; Violet jerked back, but the flame showed no sign of catching on the rug. The candle lay on its side, burning green, and Ross scooped it warily up.

"Try again," said Hawthorn.

"Alan Ross."

Again the candle seemed both weak and indecisive. A flare of red showed, then settled. Then another.

"That's interesting." Maud leaned in. "Is it partly true?"

"Is it?" said Hawthorn. "We'll have the name your mother gave you, I think."

By now the wariness had hardened like toffee into a glare of absolute dislike. "Alanzo Cesare Rossi. But I write under the other, so it's true enough. Again—*what* the *fucking hell* is going on?"

"Caesar. Quite. You broke into my room and drank my whisky, Alanzo Cesare Rossi." Hawthorn lowered the gun. "Why?"

Ross looked at the candle. "What *is* this? Witchcraft? Magic?"

"Yes," said Maud.

Ross looked at the candle some more.

Then a strangled laugh emerged from him. "If devils and angels and all the saints are real as well, my ma will faint from joy when I start attending Mass again."

"Do we strike you as particularly angelic?" said Violet, amused.

"No, nor saintly neither." Ross's eyes drew back to Hawthorn. "You, I'd believe a devil."

The corner of Hawthorn's mouth twitched. "Stop stalling."

"I broke into your room because I figured there'd be something in here worth stealing, all right?"

Green flame.

"And you drank some of my whisky because . . ."

"I fancied a swig of the good stuff. And it was there."

"I'd rather not use up the candle," said Maud. "Mr. Ross. One more question. Are you involved in the conspiracy to find the Last Contract, or the death of Elizabeth Navenby?"

"What?"

"Yes or no, please," said Maud.

Ross sputtered a negative. Maud blew out the green-glowing candle and took it from him.

"So you're the thief," said Violet. "Not an advertising man. Or writing an article for a magazine."

"Yes, I am," said Ross indignantly. "Both. I wouldn't be allowed up in the first-class areas asking all the rich folk to gush about their *Jugendstil furnishings* and that *darling French café*, otherwise. But writing doesn't pay much. Can't blame a man for keeping an eye out for other opportunities."

"And the pornography?" said Hawthorn. "You're a purveyor, aren't you? Quite the multifaceted businessman."

Ross's hand went to his chest, searching for the strap of his bag. Some fear crept in around the edges of his expression. There was still so much hostility there that it couldn't get far.

"Fuck you."

"The correct address would be: fuck you, my lord." Very dry. "Violet, I assume you've lethe-mint. Go and fetch it."

"*No.*" Maud had been kneeling next to Ross on the rug. Now she stood, putting herself between Ross and Hawthorn, at whom she glared. "No lethe-mint. We're not stealing *any-one's* memory. He was just dosed with a magically poisoned drink, and now you want to do it again?"

"Maud," said Violet. "I know it seems unfair, but it's—"

"But nothing. It's what Edwin's hateful sister and her friends tried to do to me."

"And should have been allowed to succeed," said Hawthorn. "I don't know what Courcey was thinking."

Maud's glare redoubled. "They could have, so they should have? That's the kind of thinking, my lord Hawthorn, that leads to trying to steal other people's power for yourself. Which is what we are trying to *prevent*. To fight against."

There was that unshiftable core again. Violet could feel it tugging seductively at her own conviction. She envied Haw-thorn, who appeared unmoved.

"You're very free with that pronoun, Miss Blyth. I am not part of your army, or your *we*."

"Oh, you—" Maud looked as though she was contemplat-ing her threat to tackle Hawthorn around the knees. "Even without Violet's magic, you have all the advantages of rank and wealth. Using it to trample all over human dignity, against a person's will, is *not* what power is for."

"It's the only thing power is for."

It was Ross who'd spoken. The young man climbed to his feet. "If you think otherwise, you're a fool. Even without—sodding *magic*"—with a whirl of his index finger—"that's the way the world works. Powerful people are out for more power. And they don't care who they tread on, on the way."

"I'm trying to *help* you, Mr. Ross," said Maud indignantly.

"I didn't ask for your bloody help." Ross brushed his hair back from his brow. Several curls made a mockery of the motion at once. "In fact, you're inflicting it on me against my will. An insult to my human dignity, that."

Hawthorn snorted again. Ross directed an obscene gesture at him. Maud practically stamped her foot.

"Would you rather have your memory of today wiped clean like a chalkboard?" she demanded.

"It's not up to him, Miss Blyth," said Hawthorn. "Charming as they are, these morals of yours are becoming tiresome. Violet?"

Violet opened her mouth. Ross deserted Barricade Maud and put himself where he could glare directly at Hawthorn from a more convenient distance. Violet closed her mouth. She wasn't selfish as a performer, even if she was cheerfully so in all other parts of life. She knew when someone else was about to be far more entertaining.

"Bloody naive or not, at least she's got the excuse of being able to *afford* morals," Ross spat at Hawthorn. "Most of us fucking can't. I know how much this suite costs for the voyage, right down to the penny. Your *lordship* should spend some time in third class. You might find out how much of a difference it would make, to anyone sleeping six to a cabin in wooden bunks, if they had even a *tenth* of the amount you laid down for—what? So you wouldn't endanger your delicate toff's constitution with anything less than an embroidered bedspread and a full range of liquors?"

Hawthorn's expression warred between leftover amusement and icy temper. "And you'll take their hard-earned pennies off them in exchange for dirty stories? Those of them who can even read."

Ross's neck and lower cheeks darkened. His hands formed fists. "The man who cleans windows deserves a bit of pleasure in his life just as much as the man who owns them."

"Indeed," said Hawthorn, "and I suppose you'd say he can

thereby experience being fucked by the aristocracy in more ways than one." He closed his mouth sharply. He didn't look uncertain, but wary, as if he'd let out something he shouldn't.

Ross's glance sharpened in return. He glanced at the bag full of erotica and then back at Hawthorn. Something hostile and alive, like a firecracker loosed from a careless boy's hand, writhed alight in the air between them.

Maud cleared her throat. "Mr. Ross—"

Hawthorn said, not moving his eyes from Ross, "I'm not saying I disagree with your description of the world. But this particular power isn't yours to see or write about. And if Miss Blyth here knows anything about her brother's position at the Home Office, she knows I'm telling the truth."

Ross said, "I don't know what you—"

"*Mr. Ross!*" shouted Maud. She put a hand on his arm and yanked him around to face her again. "I am trying to *recruit* you."

Violet lost her battle with an incredulous burst of laughter at that point. She was in dire need of an unpoisoned drink. It was late afternoon; surely someone on this bloody ship was pouring gin somewhere.

"We've a lot of ground to search in the next few days and there's only . . . two and a half of us," said Maud, sparing an unimpressed look for Hawthorn. "You clearly possess the skills for breaking and entering. And have the perfect excuse to be almost anywhere."

"Breaking and entering?" Ross raised his eyebrows. "What am I being recruited for? I didn't think you'd be the sort to head up a criminal gang, given that little speech about dignity and abuse of power. But perhaps"—very sarcastic—"you only steal from those who deserve it."

"We're not stealing," said Maud.

"Well," said Violet. "We are."

"We are *retrieving* stolen items from the person who took them from Mrs. Navenby," said Maud. "And also killed her."

The word *killed* shook Ross for a moment. He looked to

Hawthorn, then Violet—she gave him a speaking shrug—and then back to Maud.

"You'd better tell me the whole story, then," he said.

"Off the record," said Maud seriously.

Ross slapped a hand over his heart.

Maud told him the whole story.

It took some time, during which Hawthorn and Violet exchanged several glances. Violet tried to convey that *she* had no intention of honouring Maud's rash declaration about lethemint if Ross showed even the slightest sign of following the normal human urge to blab the existence of magic to half of his acquaintance, let alone *publish* anything about it.

Hawthorn's answering look was hard to read. Knowing him, he was trying to convey his own willingness to permanently solve the problem of a talkative writer. Possibly via the gun.

"So you want me to keep an eye out for these silver things," said Ross finally, "during the course of my own activities. The— what did you say? Flower locket, hand mirror, other knick-knacks."

"Yes," said Maud. "Beginning with first class. Violet will do some cabins as well; it'd be best to compare notes and divide up the decks, so that you can cover more ground." She frowned thoughtfully. "Perhaps if you teach me to pick locks, Mr. Ross, then I can do some myself. Lord Hawthorn . . ."

"Did not agree to any of that," said Lord Hawthorn. "You won my help in emergencies, Miss Blyth, not my active engagement in criminal activity."

Ross snorted. "Don't see why not. You're the one most able to buy your way out of it if you're caught in the act. And speaking of money—not to be crass, but what do I get, for my assistance?"

"What do you *get*?" said Maud.

"Can't afford to work for free."

Hawthorn stirred. "Miss Blyth tells me you're being paid twice over to write about this voyage, you're selling pornography

for what I can only assume is a commission, and you're sup-
plementing it with jewel theft. Do you expect to be paid *more*?
How's this, Mr. Ross. As payment for your assistance, I won't
turn you in to the master-at-arms with the suggestion that he
search your own cabin for the jewels already reported missing.
And to keep Miss Blyth happy, I will not erase your memory.
However. The slightest hint that you've talked about magic, to
anyone, and I will have Miss Debenham put a secret-bind on
your tongue. A *painful* one."

Maud said, "*Lord Hawthorn.*"

Ross let his tongue run thoughtfully over his lower lip. He
and Hawthorn continued to eye each other like prizefighters
sizing up their opponent before trying to knock them into the
ground.

"No deal." But it didn't sound final. It sounded like the first
movement in a dance.

Hawthorn caught it. "Are you trying to *negotiate*?"

"What if I am? Murderers, Miss Blyth said. Magic ones. I
should be paid for the danger, if I'm throwing my hat in with
you lot."

"I'll buy your pornography," said Maud.

"I—" Ross stopped. Turned back to her. "You'll what?"

"Help us for the rest of the voyage, and I'll compensate you
for taking your time away from—salesmanship." Maud waved
a hand at the bag. "I'll take all of it."

"I've more," said Ross at once.

"Then I'll take that too. Bring it to my . . ." Maud visibly
reconsidered. "Bring it here, after dinner, and I'll buy it all.
And"—her eyes sparkling with inspiration—"Violet will give
you a scandal for your society papers."

"I will?" Violet felt rather tide-swept, but wouldn't have
tried to put her feet down and anchor in the sandy ground if
she'd been paid. This was far too much fun.

"You want to make as loud a splash as possible, to annoy
your relatives," said Maud. "You can give Mr. Ross an exclusive
interview, with all the shocking details. It's a very good story.

Debauchment of a well-bred maiden by a rakish peer. Life on the stage. Triumphant and unapologetic return of the ruined girl, enriched by an unexpected inheritance." Pause. "Further debauchment, on the high seas."

"I can't put *sordid* details in that sort of article." Ross grinned at Violet. It was a crooked, wicked smile—far more sincere than the polished one he'd pulled out earlier in the day. "But you should tell me all of them anyway. I'll dress it up in stuffy and scandalised language and tell the magazine it's an exclusive."

"Violet," growled Hawthorn, "you don't *know* any sordid details."

"Don't I?" said Violet. "I think I know enough to . . . extrapolate."

"Perfect," said Maud brightly. "Mr. Ross? That's my final offer." She extended her hand, and Ross shook.

The pinched lines on Hawthorn's forehead vanished as he laughed. "Christ. What a waste of a woman you are, Miss Blyth."

"What's that supposed to mean?" demanded Maud.

"It means there are some specimens of supposed officer material in the Royal Army who could learn a lesson from you about motivating the troops."

"Bribing the troops," said Violet, "to be fair."

Maud shot Hawthorn a look full of Suffragette fire, but ended up laughing herself. "You *are* part of my army, my lord. And I am requisitioning your suite as our base of operations. After dinner?"

"After dinner," Ross agreed. "With all the pornography I can carry."

12

The question, Hawthorn pointed out before their growing army of counter-conspirators broke up to prepare for dinner, was this: why had someone imbued his whisky with a sleeping charm in the first place?

Was it simply a matter of getting him out of the way, given that he was a well-known magician—*ex*-magician—now publicly linked with Maud and presumably, in the eyes of Mrs. Navenby's murderer, recruited to her side? Had they expected him to take a sip of whisky that night and then sleep through the entire voyage?

"Why not kill me, in that case?" Hawthorn said. "If they've shown willingness to do so."

"A dead earl's son in the prime of his life might attract a lot more attention than a dead old woman," said Maud.

"And an unbreakable sleep wouldn't?" Violet pointed out.

"The point being," said Hawthorn, "someone got into my suite and left me an unwelcome surprise. Who's to say they haven't done the same to you?"

So Violet found herself accompanying Maud back to her own cabin, after having demonstrated a general detection charm until Hawthorn was satisfied it should catch most kinds of charms and imbued objects. She hoped she had enough magic left. She'd grown used to gauging the limits of her power using the spells that she'd practiced over and over in the Penumbra, keeping some spare for self-protection and small comforts in her boardinghouse before she collapsed into sleep a few hours before dawn.

In Maud and Mrs. Navenby's cabin she kept the physical parameters of the detection strict: to the bounds of the two connected rooms, and no further.

"Will it sparkle?" Maud asked. "Like the whisky?"

"It should be visible, if there's anything," said Violet. "I didn't have a lot to put into it, so it might fade quickly. Search fast."

Maud nodded. "I'll take my room; you take this one."

Violet's brisk circuit of the space was halted almost immediately at an exclamation from Maud.

"Here! Is this something?"

A line no wider than a hair ribbon glowed acid green on the floor, like a trip wire laid across the doorway leading from the main room into the smaller one.

"It's something," Violet agreed. *Maud!*

Maud retrieved her hand, with a guilty look, from where she'd waved her fingers in the air above the green line. "If the whole doorway was the trap, wouldn't all of it be green? Besides, I feel perfectly well."

"And what if it's something delayed?" Violet's heart had given a hard, unpleasant pound. She knelt to inspect the line, which was already fainter in hue as her spell's effect began to fade. The carpet glistened oddly and the scent of peppermint rose to her nose. "I think this is an imbued oil."

"Like the olive oil you used to wake Ross?" Maud picked up her skirt and took a firm step over the green line. Violet's heart gave another curious thud, then subsided, as if to tell her that there was no use to it reacting every time Maud Blyth did something rash.

"Be careful," she said anyway.

"If it's in the oil, perhaps I need to touch it. Besides, all of my clothes are in here, and I need to dress for dinner."

"Dinner!" came a loud, harsh voice from behind Violet. She jumped what felt like a foot, and nearly fell herself onto the green line.

"Bloody hell," she gasped.

"Bloody hell."

"Oh, Dorian," said Maud. "You still have fruit in your cage, you silly bird, I can see it from here. And I refilled your water bowl."

"Dinner. Hello, shut up. Cheat! Go away."

"Charming vocabulary," said Violet.

"Maybe I *should* give him to the—oh!" Maud beamed. "I wonder if Helen Bernard would like him, as a gift?"

Violet cradled a more everyday negation than the one that Hawthorn had shown her for the whisky. This was the kind cast to cause a blackout at the end of an act, when several different light charms or illusions were going at once. She was pleasantly surprised when the green line winked into nothing. Though now she did feel the worn-thin sensation, like coming to the end of a lungful of air, that meant she didn't have a lot of magic left.

They quickly searched the rest of the space, in case more than one surprise had been left, but nothing else showed up. Maud even searched her luggage. Her shoulders relaxed when she tugged a slim, black-covered volume, like a cheap notebook, from the depths of the trunk.

"What's that?" Violet asked.

"Nothing. Or rather—it's Robin's. I can't lose it." Maud replaced it hastily. "Shall I have to ask you to cast that detection-spell every time I return to the cabin, now? I hate the idea of wasting your magic like that."

So did Violet. She looked down at the gleam of oil—now harmless—along the door line.

"I've an idea," she said.

Several times she'd been with her friend Thom to his family's workshop in Queens, a poky space accessed through a mirror in a drugstore. His parents wore rings of polished coral—hard to come by, but ideal for imbuement. The workshop smelled of dried plants and pure organic oils: rose and olive, sesame and mint. And also the sweet, intense fragrance of Indian sandalwood, which took beautifully to charms for warding. Thom used it in minuscule amounts to keep moths and rats from the Penumbra's costume storage.

Violet had smelled sandalwood earlier that day. That was why the memory was close to hand.

"What is it?"

"I can't promise it'll work, but there's something I can try, if I can get my hands on some sandalwood oil from the Turkish baths. Perhaps Mr. Ross can steal it for us."

Violet left Maud to dress for dinner and returned to her own stateroom to do the same. There, the detection charm showed nothing except the imbuements that Violet knew existed on her own belongings.

The dining saloon was a little over half-full, and Mr. Bernard was already applying himself with a single-minded air to his wine when Violet sat down. Hawthorn was bookended by Rose and Mrs. Bernard, who were fluttering attention upon him.

"Good evening, Mr. Chapman!" called Maud.

The young cotton-mill man was strolling hesitantly between tables and had slowed to a hopeful crawl as he passed them. He returned Maud's smile.

"Good evening, Miss Cutler. I trust you're enjoying the voyage so far."

"Very much. We've a seat free, if you'd care to join us. Unless you're waiting on someone else, ma'am?" she appealed to Mrs. Bernard. "No? There, that's settled."

"Very kind of you," said Chapman, and sat.

The string quartet was playing unobtrusively in the corner near the grand piano. Violet ordered the duck and watched Mr. Chapman attempt to impress Maud. At least he was asking her questions, instead of assuming that his own opinion would be fascinating to any woman. And he'd shown no sign of being turned off by Maud's burgeoning involvement in scandal; though perhaps, given he was travelling unattached, the gossip machine of the ship simply hadn't reached him.

Violet made an attempt at conversation with Rose, was

bored to tears by the first insipid answer, and gave up. The duck was dark and tender beneath a port-wine sauce. The wine was even better. And Mrs. Bernard, champion entertainer that she was, was back singing her favourite tune. The chorus went: *Has Your Lordship Ever Considered Marriage?*

"I'm afraid I've never been tempted," said Hawthorn. "After all, what are the benefits for a man in my position?"

"You know," said Violet, "I'm sure I heard a song on that very topic once. What was it called? The Benefits of—oh, something."

Mr. Bernard coughed on a mouthful of veal and turned a shade redder. Violet applied herself angelically to her buttered parsnips. The song's title was "The Benefits of the Marriage Bed." It had eight verses. The last two had been banned from public performance in even the most disreputable of establishments; at the Penumbra they were pulled out only at rooftop parties, when they were drunkenly shouted into the noise of the El rattling overhead.

"Companionship," said Mrs. Bernard. "Surely."

"I prefer my peace and quiet," said Hawthorn.

"Someone to manage your household for you."

"I am self-managing, ma'am." An ironic bow of his head. "And I employ an excellent housekeeper."

"What about children, my lord?" Violet asked sweetly. "The continuation of your ancient line? Don't you want a young future earl of your own, to dandle on your knee?"

"I have cousins," said Hawthorn, exactly as one flattened a fly with a newspaper.

"Well, that's stumped me." An imp of spiteful mischief had been knocked to Violet's surface by this topic of conversation. She let her pine-wood ring click against the gilt edge of her dinner plate, then ran her fingertips down her neck and toyed with the trim at the neckline of her gown, which dipped generously low. "I can't think of *any* other reasons one might want to marry."

"What about love?"

Maud had spoken quietly, but it carried. The table recentred itself around her lifted chin and the way she left the word dangling there like a gauntlet for Hawthorn to pick up.

"Exactly, Miss Cutler," said Mrs. Bernard. "But perhaps Lord Hawthorn thinks the concept old-fashioned."

"Modern, I'd say," said Hawthorn. "Or no more than a pretty fantasy."

"A fairy tale?" said Maud at once. "I know a few fairy tales with truth in them. But I happen to disagree with you entirely, my lord, and I have evidence in my favour."

"Oh, are you in love, Miss Cutler?" said Hawthorn, in his most coolly disinterested tones.

Maud's cheeks flamed. She took a long gulp of her wine. Mr. Chapman and both Bernard sisters now looked at Lord Hawthorn with dislike. To anyone assuming that Hawthorn had extended his favours of debauchery to Maud the previous night, this would look like a cruel and humiliating set-down.

Maud said heatedly, "No. I'm not. But I know what it looks like, companionship with love. I've seen it. I've lived in the same house with it."

"How lucky you were," said that imp in Violet, "to have such paragons for parents."

Maud looked at her. Maud, who didn't like lying, and who Violet knew had not been thinking of her parents when she spoke.

"My parents *did* have a happy marriage. Their personalities and principles were in harmony." Maud paused. "It's just a pity those personalities and principles were so *bloody awful*."

Helen Bernard gave a startled hiccup of laughter. Everyone else looked politely blank.

Maud swayed in her seat. She pressed a hand to her flushed forehead and let out a startled giggle, a beat after Helen's.

"Let's talk of something else, Miss Cutler," said Mr. Chapman, with a hard look at Hawthorn. "You were telling me about when Mrs. Navenby took you to Central Park, and—"

"Maud," said Violet. "Are you all right?"

"A little warm." Maud giggled again. "No, I'm fine, really." Her eyes looked odd. How much wine had she had? How much wine was she accustomed to having?

"You do look very flushed," Violet said. "I think you need some sea air. Lord Hawthorn, will you assist us?"

Hawthorn levelled a long, considering look at Maud and thankfully didn't fall back into his usual rudeness. He pushed back his chair.

"You needn't trouble yourself, my lord," said Chapman with another look of dislike. "I'm sure I can escort Miss Cutler—"

Hawthorn ignored him. He scooped a firm arm under Maud's and helped her to stand. She swayed away from him.

"I'm well," she said peevishly. Then, as she swayed back— "Oh. No, perhaps I'm not. Is the ship going through a storm? A—what do they call it? A swell?"

"Miss Cutler, we're taking you out on deck," said Hawthorn. "Ladies, enjoy your evening. Chapman. Bernard."

Mr. Bernard waved a spoon at them as they left. Chapman was still half out of his chair. Violet cast a longing look at the dessert trolley as she followed Hawthorn and Maud out onto the promenade that ran alongside the dining saloon.

The ship was not going through a storm, or a swell. The air was breathtakingly crisp, and quiet after the music and chatter of indoors. Early stars shone on satin-blue patches of sky between the masking clouds, and the dark expanse of the sea melted into an uncertain horizon.

Hawthorn steered Maud to the railing and placed her hands on it until they gripped. His starched shirtfront was very pale against the black of his dinner tailcoat and his dark hair.

"If you fall overboard, I will let you swim to Southampton," he said.

"I never learned to swim," Maud told him.

Hawthorn sighed. "How do you feel?"

"*Never* become a physician." Maud giggled tiredly. "I haven't told you the story of what Mrs. Navenby said when we were in Central Park, have I?"

"She's only drunk," said Violet.

Hawthorn's mouth was set. "Are you sure?"

Violet thought suddenly of the green line, and Maud waving her hand across it.

"No. But I can't manage another of those negations. I'm drained for the day."

Hawthorn swore. He took Maud by the shoulder and slapped her cheek, not hard.

"Miss Blyth," he said. "Maud. Look at me. At least we can try emptying your stomach."

"Oh, that. I can do that. I did it when I was ten, to ruin one of Mother's parties." A grin broke out on Maud's face. "All over the tiger-skin rug they'd just laid down in the parlour. She was furious."

Maud demonstrated her skills over the edge of the ship. No doubt that piece of railing had played host to plenty of people emptying their guts. Violet shivered. She'd not bothered with a wrap, and the wind nipped at her bare upper arms.

"Ugh." Maud made a fastidious face when she was finished. She took Hawthorn's proffered handkerchief and wiped her mouth on the monogrammed *J.F.C.A.* "That was strong wine. I feel so silly for drinking it that fast. I'm sorry I ruined your dinners."

"Nothing was ruined. Hawthorn was probably an inch away from insulting one of the Bernard girls to their face," said Violet. "I like being a scandal, but I'd rather we didn't drive away *everyone* else on this ship. It's only the second night, after all."

"And it's not over yet," said Hawthorn. "Or am I expected to take delivery of your shipment of pornography myself?"

13

Lord Hawthorn and Maud played chess while they waited for Ross. Violet had flung herself onto the chaise longue with the only book that Hawthorn had in his possession, a biography of Alexander the Great.

Maud espied an opening for her knight that was possibly a trap. She took it anyway, lifting her fingers decisively as soon as the knight touched down. *Your game falls apart when you start second-guessing*, Edwin had told her.

Maud had never quite picked up the knack of conversation with Edwin Courcey. She loved him for how happy he made her brother, but he had a way of looking at you as though he saw all your worst qualities and was waiting to have them turned onto himself like knives.

He played a beautiful game of chess, though.

Maud considered the Baron Hawthorn as he considered the board. She thought of the easy, drawling way he'd declaimed the idea of romance. She thought of his hand disappearing beneath Violet's clothes.

Robin didn't lie to Maud, but he did on occasion let truths slide by unmentioned if he was trying to protect her; or to protect Edwin. And Edwin's bitterness towards Lord Hawthorn, along with the edge to Robin's manner whenever the man was mentioned, spoke volumes.

Hawthorn reached for his queen. Maud opened her mouth to ask the Edwin question at the most distracting moment possible, but they were both forestalled by a knock on the door.

Ross had said he had more pornography than the messenger bag. He had, in fact, an entire small suitcase.

"Oh, my," said Violet, abandoning Alexander without a qualm.

Maud turned to Hawthorn. "Will you give me an estimate of its value? I want to make sure I'm paying a fair price."

"Not being outrageously fleeced, you mean." Hawthorn took the suitcase and emptied an extensive amount of books and pamphlets onto the table. Violet dived for one and flicked through it as Hawthorn counted and sorted.

"Well, what did you intend to demand?" Hawthorn asked when he'd looked over the whole lot.

Ross named a price. Maud winced. Hawthorn named a much lower one. Ross called Hawthorn an inbred skinflint arsehole, pointed out that he was including the suitcase, and lowered his own price by an infinitesimal margin. Hawthorn, wearing the same expression he'd directed at the chessboard, called Ross a bloodsucking Mediterranean gutter-rat.

A few minutes later, they'd come to an agreement. Hawthorn fetched his chequebook.

"Wait," said Maud. "I'm the one making the purchase."

"Don't be silly. There's no point in you spending that much on material you've no interest in," said Hawthorn. "And I'm sure I can afford the sum more easily than you can."

"I *can* afford it!" snapped Maud. She couldn't justify using another of Mrs. Navenby's jewels on this, but she had a little money of her own. "I'm the one who made Mr. Ross the offer. It's very rude of you to try to pip me at the post. Though I will," she added after a moment of consideration, "need to appeal to you for a loan, until we reach London and I can pay you back."

Hawthorn slapped the chequebook onto the table. "You won't let me buy it, and now you insist that I finance you? Spreading baseless rumours for the hell of it is one thing, but this does count as corrupting an innocent girl."

"No," said Maud. "I'm corrupting myself. You're merely giving me a gentlemanly loan. It's none of your business if I spend it on—educational tracts." She turned her shoulder on him. "Mr. Ross. Talk me through my purchases."

"Don't even think about it," growled Hawthorn.

"Most of it *is* aimed at an audience of men, Miss Blyth. Perhaps you should let Lord Arsehole here buy it instead."

"Nonsense," said Maud. "I'm not completely ignorant of the—the mechanics of the thing. Mrs. Sinclair let me sit in when she talked to Liza about what to expect on her wedding night, because she said I don't have a mother to do it for me when my turn comes."

"I'm not sure that counts as useful information," said Violet, laughing at her. "Two awkward minutes on lying back and thinking of England, and not whimpering too much?"

Maud glared. She felt covered in bristles that poked out painfully through the shell of her cheerfulness. Her enemies had nearly poisoned Hawthorn and had been in her cabin laying nasty charms to do God-knew-what, which made her skin crawl whenever she remembered it. She'd made a fool of herself with a single glass of wine. She was a silly girl, only pretending to know what she was doing.

But she wouldn't be *patronised*.

"Pornographic literature is no sort of practical education either," said Hawthorn. "It's titillation. It's not supposed to be accurate."

"Isn't it?" Ross reached for a purple-covered booklet and skimmed it, then read aloud. "*At the touch of his hand upon my bare thigh I could not have moved even if the ropes that held me had melted into nothing. I was just as much a prisoner to the hot rasp of my own breath and the quiver of need that sang along my nerves, and the more I wanted the more I was set ablaze in the shame of the wanting. If he removed his hand I would die. If he moved it I would die. I was no longer a man, only desire encased in flesh.*"

Maud forced herself to loosen her hand, which had clawed

around her skirt. She had felt each word of that like—like music. Her breath *was* hot. All of her was hot.

"You've never felt like that, your lordship? You must be doing it wrong." Ross tossed the book back onto the pile. "Or choosing your partners poorly."

Maud wondered at his choosing that particular book to needle Hawthorn. A preference for other men could be a dangerous accusation both to make and to receive. Was there some sort of *signal*? She'd never asked Robin how he knew, with Edwin.

"Well." She thought of what Edwin would do in this situation. "Let's have a variety of texts, or I can't say I've done a comprehensive survey."

She gathered up a selection and took it over to settle herself on the chaise longue, where she opened the first that came to hand. The title page read *Memoirs of a Fallen Lady*. That seemed promising.

"I had little inkling of what awaited me, that fateful night in April when I first came across the house with the red door."

Hawthorn, when he realised that Maud also intended to read aloud from her purchases, rubbed a hand over his face and collapsed in an armchair. He cast a longing glance at the tainted whisky.

Contrary to Violet's assumption, Mrs. Sinclair had given a version of the wedding-night talk, which had leaned hard on the idea that women deserved pleasure just as much as men, and that a sensible modern girl might do a bit of experimentation to see what caused *herself* pleasure before she let her husband anywhere near the anatomy in question. Liza had spent the entire time moaning *"Mother!"* while holding a cushion over her face.

Maud had taken mental notes.

She wasn't sure how much of what she'd learned lined up with her new collection. There seemed to be a lot of swooning and hysterical sobbing in these stories, which sounded unpleasant. There was also a tendency to refer to a certain part of a woman's anatomy as the *red hawthorn berry*, which made Violet wheeze with laughter.

The purple booklet was entitled *In the Dark Duke's Dungeon. By a Roman*. A few paragraphs into that one Maud's voice thinned into nothing and she had to put it down; she couldn't stop thinking about Robin and Edwin, which was frankly horrifying. *Mysteries of the Red Dew* purported to be a vision-dream that the narrator had experienced after consuming a potion.

"Before I'd travelled much further on the emerald road, I came across a tall oak tree, with a ravishing nymph entangled in vines which held her fast to the trunk. 'What manner of creature are you?' I inquired."

Violet stood, snatched a white silk scarf from where it was draped over a chair, and flung it around her neck. She adjusted her posture and became, quite suddenly and despite her lavender gown, *mannish*.

"What manner of creature are you?" Her voice was no over-gruff impression of a man but a silken, ambiguous rasp that matched the new cant of her hips and the arrogant angle of her jaw.

Maud's thighs clenched together hard. A shiver rose from the middle of her spine. She wanted to slide onto the rug and rub her bare skin against it. She wanted—

"Maud," said Violet, a prompting whisper.

"Yes. Ah— *The nymph turned upon me a pair of limpid eyes. I felt Priapus stir at the sight of her skin, barely contained within the meagre rags which strained across the curve of her hips. 'Oh, sir!' she cried. 'Will you not help me?'"*

Silence. Violet looked about her.

"Oh, *sir*. Will you not help me?"

Maud nearly dropped the book.

Alanzo Cesare Rossi had leapt onto the stage. He was a less accomplished actor than Violet, and didn't manage to transform himself into a nymph merely by shifting his posture. He tangled his ankle around a chair leg and batted his eyelashes in her direction.

"Dear God," said Hawthorn.

Maud managed to continue. There was some dialogue laden with innuendo—some of which Maud caught, and some of which she could only guess at based on the leering faces that Violet made—before the narrator agreed to unfasten the nymph from the tree in exchange for the favours of her nubile body.

The action carried Violet and Ross closer to Maud's chaise longue, where they teetered in something only vaguely resembling a passionate embrace. Ross's shoulders shook as he fought against laughter.

Maud was close to bursting herself. *"As I held her fast, there emerged from the nearby wood an imposing figure. He had the head of a bull and the body of a man, and his erect member was of such girth as to make the nymph in my arms gasp in lusty anticipation and fear."*

The room turned, as one, to the Baron Hawthorn.

Hawthorn raised a single eyebrow. A breathless silence hung over them.

"You can all go and fuck yourselves," he said.

Violet released Ross and collapsed across Maud's legs, howling with laughter. Maud heard herself shriek out the dregs of her own embarrassment. Ross sank to the ground, where he drew up his knees and buried his face in them. His curls were unruly, his face stained with tears of mirth when he lifted it.

"You're all mad," he groaned. "And I must be too. Utter Bedlam, this place is."

Maud gasped for air. Violet emitted a pleading moan—"Maud, please, I can't *stop*"—and continued to laugh herself silly.

Hawthorn's mouth twitched. He glanced at the walls. For the first time Maud realised that the racket they were making was likely to be audible.

"My reputation as a master of orgies would appear to be complete," he said. "Miss Blyth. Give your unfortunate troops their marching orders for tomorrow. And then be so good as to march them out of my cabin."

Maud wouldn't sleep for hours if she lay down now. Her heart skipped with laughter and with a restlessness that she'd only just begun to recognise; a melody stuck in her head, to which she'd just been handed the words.

A whole suitcase full of words.

"Come on," she said, gripping the suitcase more tightly, and Violet followed her out onto the dark and star-spangled stage of the small deck where the Pipes and Drums had rehearsed.

It was one of the best things about Violet. Even Robin had a tendency to humour Maud's enthusiasms in a way that said he was sure they would burn themselves out. It had taken weeks before he'd agreed to let her go to America.

Violet never told Maud not to do something. She followed cheerfully along and laughed at the consequences.

Violet had stolen Hawthorn's white scarf. It glowed in two slim columns down the front of her gown, pearlescent in the meagre moonlight and few electric lights that turned the deck into a chessboard of shadows. The moonlight silvered her hair. Maud wanted to take it down, pin by pin, and watch it fall around Violet's shoulders.

"Ohhh." Maud leaned against the wall, facing the open sea, and inhaled the fresh night air. "I do love this. I could spend my whole life on boats, couldn't you?"

"No. There are only so many games of quoits and shuffle-board I'm prepared to play in a week, no matter how nice the view."

"It's not . . ." Maud struggled to pull the words together. "We're not in one place or another. We could be going anywhere, in the darkness. The sun could rise tomorrow and we could be in—Alexandria, or Venice, or among the islands of Japan."

"*That* would take more magic than I've ever heard of."

"It's *liminal*," said Maud, pleased. The word was one of Edwin's favourites; he used it a lot when discussing Flora Sutton's system of magic.

"Liminal," said Violet, as if tasting it. It wasn't quite the rasp of a voice she'd used when playacting, but it was close, and the restlessness in Maud whirled all at once into a near-hurricane of incoherent want. She really would burst. She would rend at the seams like something poorly stitched.

If she opened her mouth she just *knew* she would babble more nonsense about boats.

She set down the suitcase and reached out to catch Violet's wrist, and used it to tug her closer. Fabric slid on fabric, glove on glove, but Maud held fast. Violet looked down at her, amused and questioning, and Maud seized a desperate burst of courage and moved her hands to rest on either side of Violet's waist.

Maud's back was on solid wood. They were in shadow. The deck was empty and the stars were kind, and glittering, and very far away.

"Maud?" said Violet softly. "What are you doing?"

"Looking," said Maud, above the din of her heart, "for a more practical education."

Violet said nothing. Moved nothing. Her expression was difficult to make out, lit only on one side by the dim glow of electric light. Beneath Maud's hands were layers of fabric and an elusive heat; she couldn't feel whalebone or metal. Perhaps Violet wore softer corsetry. Perhaps *nothing,* just camisole and combinations and skin, skin, soft, tasting of all the things that skin might taste of.

Violet let out a slow breath. Their faces were close enough that the very end of it caught at Maud's lips, which tingled as if bruised. Images from the suitcase's selection flooded through her mind and down into her body.

She heard herself make a tiny, lost sound. If Violet kissed her, she would die. If Violet didn't kiss her, she would die. She was filled with a great deal of sympathy for the young man in the Dark Duke's dungeon, even if he *had* brought his fate upon himself by sneaking into a mansion owned by someone called the Dark Duke—

Maud tried to rope her flyaway thoughts. She could smell Violet's nearness, her scent. She was burning with it.

Violet pulled back, out of Maud's grasp.

"I'm sorry, Maud. But I don't think that's a good idea."

Why? screamed Maud's body—every nerve in every limb. She wanted to argue. She was good at arguing.

But she had just enough sense left to realise that to ask for the answer would be to demand a bed of knives and then fling herself upon it.

"No. *I'm* sorry." She heard a shaky laugh come out. "I shouldn't have—I apologise if I made you feel uncomfortable."

Violet's own laugh was pure relief. "We're friendly, aren't we, Maud? Let's leave it there."

Which was the answer, really. Violet, by her own admission, had no problem going to bed with all sorts of people. So the issue was with Maud: an inexperienced girl must not be what Violet looked for in a partner. Maud could hardly blame her.

"Yes, let's."

"I'll see you tomorrow," said Violet, and squeezed Maud's arm before she left.

Maud stood there a minute longer, alone on a deck that was suddenly empty and cold and dark. She took the suitcase and made her way back to her own cabin, and once she was there she took a long time to fall asleep.

14

After breakfast the next morning Violet was stopped in her tracks, on her way across the first-class parlour on B Deck, by the word *magic*.

"—that for those of us truly gifted with the Sight, the word *spiritualism* sets us apart from cheap stage tricks and charlatans peddling love potions."

Mrs. Moretti was holding court nearby. The self-proclaimed medium was somehow wearing more furs every time Violet saw her. Perhaps the things were mating.

"You really have seen ghosts, then?" asked an eager woman.

"The Sight does not refer to what we perceive with the eyes. Spirits are ephemeral. They are a presence, a will. What use have they for an earthly form, having been separated from their coarse flesh?"

This was accurate enough that Violet drifted closer. She had a morning of sneaking and room-searching ahead of her. Ross would do the same in between continuing his interviews. Maud would deliver Dorian to Helen Bernard, who'd delightedly accepted the offer of a talkative African Grey, and then intended to visit the Turkish baths during ladies' hour to try charming a sample of sandalwood oil out of the attendants.

Hawthorn had not volunteered his plans for the day.

"In that case, how does one know of their presence?" asked another of Mrs. Moretti's audience. This woman was dressed in mourning.

"There are various signs, to those of us with sensitivity," said Mrs. Moretti impressively.

Cats, Violet was tempted to say, but she kept her mouth shut.

It was commonly agreed that there was at least one ghost in the Penumbra, given how the theatre's cats behaved, and that its preferred haunts were the prompt side wings and the storage space beneath the stage. In the absence of true mediums, who were rare, there *was* no way of communicating with ghosts, so the company had bandied about competing stories as to who the unfortunate person had been and how they'd died.

Henri had worked at the Paris Opéra, before being dismissed for stealing, and claimed that theatres were often riddled with ghosts. He had a whole theory, which he'd deliver with increasing volume and decreasing coherence over half a bottle of bourbon, that it had something to do with music and vibrations in the air. He'd even known an unmagical journalist who became interested enough in the Paris Opéra's ghosts that he planned to write a novel about it.

Mrs. Moretti was now explaining to her enraptured circle that she had been aware of her gifts since girlhood: sometimes a cold sensation on the skin or a stirring of her hair, sometimes a whisper in her ear, asking her to give voice to the voiceless departed. Why, her own dear husband, who passed five years ago . . .

It all sounded like absolute bollocks. But then, the Penumbra had functioned by presenting real magic in the guise of handmade spectacle. Magicians made all sorts of choices as to how they wanted to exist in a world ignorant of their true nature. And New York's magicians were self-policing; no official body existed like the Coopers did in England, to chase down and suppress—and punish, if necessary—anyone endangering the secrecy of magical society.

Perhaps Mrs. Moretti *was* a magician, and a cunning one. Or even a true medium, camouflaging herself with the trappings of nonsense.

Either way. Violet went and consulted the directory, and then broke into the woman's cabin on general principles. The opening-spell came more fluidly to her fingers today.

She searched quickly for any of the silver items that had been taken from Mrs. Navenby's belongings. There was plenty of jewellery; most of it, Violet judged after careful inspection, was paste.

More furs, though none new, and none with a maker's label still present, only holes where they'd been unpicked and removed. Theft? Careful shopping in secondhand stores?

The most useful discovery was a nondescript black case, which Violet pulled from the back corner of the wardrobe. It contained—*ah*. Fishing line, wound on a wheel. Metal wires and bent hooks. Folded gauze. A small bottle of fluorescent paint with a spattered label. Notebooks.

Only a professional fraud would need these props. Perhaps the woman had fleeced one of her oh-so-rich and influential clients of a little too much money, and was making the hasty move to London to impose herself on a new set of suckers.

Violet had the sudden urge to throw the black case at the mirror and watch it smash.

Instead she put it back in place, let herself out into the corridor, and stood there, breathing the anger down. She was *not* going to think of Jerry, the deceitful smiling prick, except to be savagely glad for the lesson he'd taught her.

The maple and the pine were smooth as satin against her skin. Wood, for illusion.

Learn the lesson, Violet. Trust is a luxury.

Before she'd completed the thought, Violet was walking, with her confident Cleopatra stalk. People stepped out of her way; men touched their hats. The disapproving looks and gleeful whispers were still there, but Violet had every right to be aboard the *Lyric* and to walk wherever she wanted.

She used the opening-spell on Maud's cabin and let herself in.

Violet refused to feel guilty. It was past time she did some digging. So far, there had been little of storybook fae-wonder in this—what had Hawthorn called it? *A wild goose chase with a side order of possibly being apprehended for theft.* It had been entertaining, and promised to continue to be so, but Violet wasn't sticking her neck out further without all the facts.

Truth-candles were one thing. Maud Blyth was able to talk perfect wide-eyed truth, lace-making around the gaps in the information, to get what she wanted. A morning watching her at work had been very instructive. Violet had begun, yesterday, to listen for the gaps.

It's Robin's wasn't an answer to the question *What is that?* even if it was true.

Black cases, black notebooks. Everyone was hiding something.

Violet went into the adjoining room, where Maud's own belongings were. The bed was neatly made but there was still a faint impression on the feather pillow, a dimpling of fabric that sent heat throbbing through Violet's body as she remembered how Maud's hands had felt on her waist the previous night.

She didn't honestly think that Maud had propositioned her out of anything more than an impulse of the moment, born out of newly recognising that women could *do* that sort of thing with other women, and having compounded the problem by reading pornography all evening.

The problem was how much Violet wanted to be seduced. How easily she could have taken Maud up on her offer. She could have pressed the girl back against the wall and kissed her, filled her hands with Maud's body and then opened Maud's rosebud mouth with her own, taught her to bring all that blazing awakened hunger into a kiss, taught her what other purposes mouths could be turned to, taught her to *crave* it—

Violet bit down hard on the inside of her cheek. She knew better. She was too canny to let herself fall into temptation without thinking.

She knelt by the largest trunk and felt between layers of clothes and paper-wrapped packages, taking care to leave things more or less in position.

The notebook was in a bottom corner. Violet drew it out and sat on the edge of the bed.

Not every page was written on, and most pages weren't full. Each held a few paragraphs, sometimes less. There were occasional sketches in black ink or soft grey pencil. There were no dates such as one would expect with a diary. The hand was strong and loose. Violet read an entry at random.

> An interior view down a long corridor, carpeted in dark green, lit with electric. Two young men (unfamiliar) dressed in sporting jackets flung themselves back against the wall, as if to make themselves small. They were staring to their right and one was speaking.
>
> A group of animals dashed past them. Most of the animals moved too fast for me to make them out, but they were of various sizes, and all moved in different ways. Not just dogs or cats. One was definitely a monkey—it came last, more slowly, but didn't stop as it passed the young men. I could not shift the vision to see where the animals came from or where they were going.
>
> (Note: I cannot be sure of this one being aboard a ship, but the corridor matches another of those featuring Hawthorn.)

Violet turned to a different page.

> Harriet was seated in an armchair. Her palms were pressed together in front of her, and she gestured with them as she spoke. Something about the way she moved made me think she couldn't move her hands apart.* She looked like she was arguing heatedly. A man stepped in front of the chair—I could only see the back of him, fair hair and dark braces over white shirt—and swung his arm, very hard. I think he hit her across the face.
>
> (Note: I was pushing hard to return to this one, and you know Edwin has theories about that. Possibility and probability. For God's sake BE CAREFUL, Maudie.)

---

*This is a spell called priez-vous or Dumb Prayer. The Coopers often use it to disarm a magician for questioning.—EC

Violet turned a few more pages. The notebook fell open naturally, as if at a page that had been returned to over and over. It was a pencil sketch of a woman's face nearly in profile, spread across both pages. Violet turned it sideways to right the image.

Cold water pooled in the gaps between Violet's bones. It stayed there, freezing her, for a few heartbeats. Then it began to warm itself at the brazier of her mounting anger.

She traced with one fingertip down the severe straight line of the nose. The artist was not an expert. The forehead was lopsided and the hair sketched in hurriedly. In contrast, some of the pencil lines showing the shape of the chin and lips had been many times erased and redone, as if the artist were painstakingly trying to get them correct.

It was still, recognisably, a sketch of Violet herself, drawn by someone who had studied her face well enough to reproduce it.

Beneath the drawing was the name *Harriet,* in the same handwriting as the other entries.

Violet kept flicking. Now she knew what she was looking for, her eyes were pulled to it on page after page.

Harriet, on a poorly lit night, opening the door of a motorcar and climbing in. No other details. Glimpsed only briefly in between two others when I lost control momentarily.

Harriet at an evening party, crowded. Definitely aboard the ship this time—I could see the portholes along one wall. She wore a dark blue gown and was shaking the hand of a blond man in a red coat.

Violet closed the notebook and looked around. For the first time, it occurred to her to be afraid.

Or not to *be* afraid—there was little room for that, what with the size of the anger and a grand swooping sense of vindication: she'd been *right* to go snooping, *right* not to trust anything as sweetly offered as Maud Blyth and her adventure—but to wonder if she *should* be afraid.

The anger was what carried her to where she knew Maud would be.

Violet paid the two-shilling entry fee and took the robe and towels she was handed by the bath attendant. She had tight hold of herself now. She did not charge into the fray fully dressed and heedless. She changed as directed and entered the perfumed mist of the Turkish baths with only the rough, pale robe and the wooden rings on her fingers. And the notebook in her hands.

A small handful of women, most of them elderly, were taking advantage of the ladies' hour. One sat alone in the dry-heat room, another lay under the newfangled electric heat lamps, and a group of three chatted quietly in the temperate room.

Maud was the sole occupant of the steam room.

In here the mosaic pattern on the pillars and walls was picked out in purples and blues, the light scattered into a grid of shadows by the Moorish wooden screens placed across each of the portholes. Wooden benches of a similar design dotted the room. The tiles were smooth as pearls underfoot, alternating white feathery flourishes and black. The *Lyric*'s baths were like nowhere Violet had ever been before.

She was not in any sort of mood to enjoy them.

Maud was making a circuit of a pillar in one corner, her fingers curiously tracing the mosaic. She looked over at Violet's entry, and a smile lit her expression.

Violet should have worn nacre. Nacre was for blunt strength.

"Good news! I have some of that oil for you, though I did have to pay for . . ." Maud faltered. Her eyes searched Violet's face. "Violet? What is it?"

Violet didn't speak. Maud's gaze dropped to the notebook. The cynical part of Violet had time to snidely marvel at another, smaller part, which even then whispered: *It's all a silly misunderstanding. She'll laugh, and explain.*

Maud didn't laugh. Guilt flooded her extraordinary windowpane of a face and made a vulnerable confection out of her mouth.

Violet did not want to kiss it. Oh, she did. She wanted to *bite*.

She thought suddenly and with a wrench of awful nausea of the single time she had used the knife-spell, and the way blood had soaked her gloves as if she'd dipped them in a warm basin—she thought of the morning after Jerry left, when she'd imagined chasing him down and using that same spell on him. She'd imagined it until she could almost taste the hot red copper of fresh blood, and had ended up on her knees retching over a pot, emptying her stomach as if her body were trying to turn itself inside out to be beaten like a carpetbag.

"Violet—" Maud began.

Violet flung the notebook onto a bench and a smile onto her face. She didn't stop to work out which smile from her repertoire it was. The curtain-spell pulsed like a heartbeat in her hands and she threw it wide—Maud flinched—muffling this corner of the room to both sight and sound. Nobody would disturb them. Violet could shout, if she wanted.

Instead she used her height to crowd Maud back against the beautiful pillar, until Maud couldn't step back any farther and couldn't move forward unless she wanted to shove Violet aside. Violet dearly wished she'd try.

But no—nacre rings would have added nothing. Maud sagged easily, bonelessly, with unshed tears glimmering in her eyes. Real? Manipulation? Violet didn't care.

"Maud. *Maud,* my dear girl."

Maud flinched again. Violet kept smiling.

"Who's Harriet?"

"You. You are," said Maud.

Despite the heat, despite the steam rising with faint floral hisses from the grates set along the side of the room, a chill chased over Maud's skin. For a single moment, before the performance flicked on, Violet's face had been entirely hard; entirely angry. Even now, no light sparkled in those grey eyes at all. Maud's heart gave a great rabbity whimper of fear in her chest, followed by a completely unreasonable clench of desire. Her nerves were so confused.

"Am I," said Violet.

She was so close that she must be able to hear the race of Maud's heart. Maud had messed this up so very, very badly. Of *course* she had. How had she ever fooled herself she knew what she was doing?

"Please. Please let me—Violet—I'll explain everything, it's not—it doesn't *change* anything."

Wrong thing to say. Again. *Stupid.*

Violet gave her a look of stifled violence. Then she stepped back, sat on the bench, and arranged the robe around herself, a queen settling on a throne. Her eyes were still hard as marble.

"All right," she said. "Explain."

Maud eased away from the pillar and glanced at the notebook. Violet pulled it into her lap. The pages would curl with damp if they stayed here long.

Truth, then. All of it.

"I told you Robin has foresight," Maud said, sitting next to Violet. "He's been writing his visions down since they started. All he gets is tiny glimpses, but he knew something would happen to me on board a ship. He kept seeing Lord Hawthorn too."

This queenly version of Violet had a dignity that defied even the strands of yellow hair unpeeling themselves from her hairline and sticking to the side of her neck. "So I imagine you weren't too worried about picking the right card from the pack."

"Yes. No," Maud said. "I knew he'd be involved, one way or another. But I didn't think he'd react well to being told he was *destined* to help. Given, er, his personality."

"And you thought I'd react well to being lied to?"

"I didn't—"

"No, you just *withheld*."

Maud looked down at her own pale ankles and flushed toes

where they emerged from the robe. Set against the cool tiles, the soles of her feet might have existed in a different world to the rest of her, which glowed with warmth.

"I was going to tell you soon. I'm sorry. I honestly am. I wasn't sure what to *do*," she said desperately. "Should I have told you at once, as a near-perfect stranger, that my brother had seen enough visions of you to draw you from memory? *I* never liked being told that I had no choice what to do with my life. I was afraid if I told you or Hawthorn about Robin's visions, you wouldn't listen to anything else. You might have refused to help me out of sheer contrariness." She swallowed. "It's what I'd have done."

Violet was silent. Water sloshed on the edge of hearing: the baritone beat of the sea against the side of the ship, with a louder treble of water being poured into itself somewhere else in the baths.

After a while Violet said, "I'm a fool. You trusted me on no acquaintance at all, and I barely questioned it." Her eyes narrowed. "You sat next to me at dinner. You even asked if I'd done magic. You *knew* me."

"I knew what you looked like, and that you were probably a magician. Nothing else. Robin called you Harriet as a joke, because he couldn't keep calling you *the blond woman*. And I didn't trust you until I used the truth-candle."

"For a few specific questions!" said Violet. "I could have been any sort of person!"

Real exasperation escaped past her anger, and a tiny fleck of hope rose in Maud. Sometimes truth was the most devastating when you delivered it unadorned.

"I like the sort of person you are. I liked you from the moment I heard you laugh. And I trust my first impressions."

That wiped some more of the performance away. Violet's fingers clenched and unclenched around Robin's notebook. She took half an age to answer.

"I hadn't ever thought about it as something personal. Foresight. It's almost as much of a story as the Three Families and the Last Contract, and—yes, I do hate the idea of my life being inevitable, and someone else being able to see it. Like flicking ahead to the end of a novel when I have to live it one page at a time. That's not fair."

"If it helps, Robin is the best person in the world to have this sort of ability. He'd never do anything awful with it, or anything to take advantage. He's—*good*." It felt, for the first time, like an inadequate word. It held within it the huge, warm symphony that was everything Maud saw in her brother and loved beyond her own untutored ability to describe.

Violet had collected her face again. She did not comment on Robin's goodness or otherwise. "He's flicked to the end of the book for you and told you all about it. Written it down, in fact."

"Only bits and pieces. He can't control what he sees," Maud said. "The most certain visions are those that arrive on their own, when he doesn't try to force their direction at all, and often they're useless."

Another long pause. "Would you ask him to tell you? If he could see how your entire life falls out?"

Maud had asked herself this question. Who wouldn't? She'd asked herself a few others too. If Robin saw disaster—if he saw his own death, or Maud's—would he tell her? She didn't think so. He would *withhold,* which was a different beast of a verb to *lie,* and he'd do it out of love.

And out of love, she hadn't asked him. If she did, he would tell her the truth.

The cold was climbing Maud's legs. She rolled her feet forward so that the only part in contact with the tiles was her toenails. Now that she'd calmed a little, she recognised the occasional shimmer of air that surrounded them as a curtain-spell. She hadn't realised how much she'd wanted to talk about this. Even before Liza's marriage, Maud had been sworn to secrecy about magic, and had hated having that secret between them along with everything else.

"I don't know," Maud said. "It would be a relief to know that there is one thing out there that I'm supposed to do with my life, so I can finally stop worrying about choosing the *wrong* one. But then I think, what if I *want* to keep doing a lot of things? And then I think, well, that's *selfish*, what if my interest keeps leaping on to the next thing, just as it always has, because I'm scared of missing out on something, and I end up doing that forever? And then turn around one day and discover I've never done anything truly worthwhile? What if I die in a motor accident like Mother and Father, and I've not even managed to do as much with my life as *they* did?"

She wasn't explaining this well. It was as much of a muddle on her tongue as it was when it throbbed behind her eyes at night and kept her from sleeping.

She pushed down on her largest toe until it ached.

Violet said, "And what did they do?"

It was becoming clear what this was. Violet was demanding recompense in the form of disclosure before she would let them move on.

So Maud told Violet about the charity work: the donations, the auctions, the dinner parties. The endless hunger that her parents had for praise and attention. Her father's careless disregard for how the conditions for tenant farmers at Thornley Hill worsened and worsened with every year, as all the money from the estate went to London and bought another flattering magazine article or another expensive piece of art to be hung on the wall and forgotten.

Lady Blyth's gift for sparkling and laughing and charming what she wanted out of people, keeping up a perfect performance in front of those whose weaknesses she exploited and whose human foibles she laughed over in private.

"Personalities and principles in harmony," said Violet dryly.

It took Maud a moment to remember what she'd said about her parents at dinner, when the wine was starting to work on her.

"They were . . . very happy. They probably died happy. They didn't *deserve* to." She winced at her own words, then looked hesitantly at Violet. "What about your parents? Is their marriage—harmonious?"

"At least you can be sure your parents would be very *unhappy* if they knew that you were spending your money on a comprehensive collection of erotic literature. I bet you anything there's at least one scene in a Turkish bath somewhere in those pamphlets. All bare skin and slipping towels and perfumed massage oils."

Maud opened her mouth to repeat her question, but the image that Violet had conjured sprang into her mind and overtook her previous thoughts.

She was being distracted.

If that was how Violet wanted to move her pieces, Maud would meet her play.

"I have no doubt that *men* are allowed to wander these baths wearing only towels. And are allowed the use of the shampooing stalls and massage tables, perfumed oils and all." Maud loosened the tie at her waist. "As usual, we women are expected to content ourselves with a lesser experience. Mrs. Sinclair would say that someone should stage an act of protest."

"Maud, when it comes to the Suffragette agenda, I'm sure . . ."

Violet's voice stuttered. Maud tilted her head to one side, enjoying the caress of air on bare skin. She'd only let her robe fall to an inch below the angle of her shoulders. Her collarbones were exposed, and the very tops of her breasts.

Women in modern evening gowns exposed more skin than this in public. Even so: the scandalous and experienced Violet Debenham had stopped talking at the sight of her. A thrill of triumph washed over Maud, and it turned to an outright rush of dizziness as she looked Violet in the face. Violet's brow had a small furrow, and her lips were parted. There was a flutter in the hollow of her throat where drops of sweat had collected.

For a few seconds Maud, too, forgot how one formed entire English words.

Then she blurted, "So it's *not* that you don't think I'm—I mean, that you find me—"

Not much better.

Violet lifted a restless hand and rubbed at the back of her own neck, as if something there had bothered her. The weight of her gaze on Maud's skin was like stepping into sunlight from shadow.

"You're completely lovely and someone should have taught you it's rude to fish for compliments," said Violet, flat.

"They did," said Maud. "I ignored them. Do you . . ." She fumbled her own tongue, again. So much for her promising first attempt at flirtation; *how* did half the ship believe her to be a loose woman, honestly? Her brain kept mechanically repeating words like *oil* and *skin,* or else trying to throw up more images from those erotic pamphlets. "Do you . . ."

It was just a word. Violet could say it. A *parrot* could say it. Maud could too.

"Do you want to fuck me?"

She wondered if Violet would lie about this, when those grey eyes were so hot and revealing. She wondered if she would ever forgive Violet if she did.

But Violet said, in that voice of smoke: "Yes. I do."

"Then why did you turn me down?"

"It's a bad idea. I told you."

"*You,*" said Maud fiercely, "Miss Debauchery and Scandal— *you* are the last person to tell me I shouldn't pursue what I want. Bad idea or otherwise."

Violet tugged Maud's robe back up atop her shoulders. Her thumbs brushed against Maud's skin as she did so. The drag of fabric felt like the kindling of fire. The roof of Maud's mouth ached; she felt knocked stupid by the way her joints went buttery and lax. Oh, God, *everything* made this worse.

"And you're the last person to be telling me how much of myself I should trust you with, right now," said Violet, remorseless. "Besides—so far, Maud Cutler is being gossiped about, but it's all just hearsay. And Maud Blyth is still a respectable girl. I know you want to have fun, but you shouldn't rush into something you can't take back."

"*You* did."

"My situation was different."

"Oh?" Maud raised her eyebrows, inviting. But Violet didn't volunteer anything more, and Maud found herself swinging straight from breathless with want to buzzing with anger. She'd opened herself up at Violet's request. She'd exposed parts of her grubby personal tapestry that only Robin had ever seen. And here Violet was, brushing off the smallest of return questions.

There was a high, firm wall beneath the constant performance that was Violet Debenham. She was the opposite to Edwin; his walls were all up front, the warmth there beneath them if you had the patience to wait to be granted entry.

Violet's warmth was on the outside. Sweets spread temptingly out on a blanket. Pause and let yourself accept the entertainment, the offering, and you might not notice the wall at all.

Maud's mother had been like that. But Lady Blyth had had a mocking emptiness at her centre; Violet, behind the barrier of her pretence, had more than that. Maud was sure of it.

"Very well," Maud said. "You told Lord Hawthorn that there are other people on board who would oblige you. I'm sure the same holds true for me."

"Plenty of *women*?"

"Or men," said Maud, needling.

"Don't be a fool out of bad temper," Violet snapped. "There's no guarantee any man will care a whit for your pleasure, or stop before you get in trouble."

"Thank you for the advice. But as you've declined to participate, Miss Debenham, I can't see that it's any of your business."

"You—" Violet looked away. She rubbed again at the back of her neck. A hint of red showed beneath her fingertips.

"Have you hurt yourself?"

"It's nothing. An itch."

"I can see blood there, Violet." Maud stood and brushed Violet's fingers away. The red mark was just below the hairline, where it would be covered by a collar. It wasn't a bloody scratch, or a welt. It looked as if someone had taken a red-inked pen to Violet's skin and made a strange shape there.

"Have I nicked myself with my own nails?"

"It looks . . ." Maud swallowed. "It looks like a rune."

The muscles of Violet's neck stiffened. As Maud watched, the red mark deepened to crimson and then, swiftly, faded to nothing.

"Tell me exactly what it is."

"I don't know if I could draw it," Maud said. "It's gone now. It was only there a moment." Violet looked pale as her robe. Maud, thinking of the curse on Robin's arm, didn't blame her. "Runes. We should ask Lord Hawthorn."

Violet's expression darkened. Her fingertips lingered at the nape of her neck.

"Yes," she said. "Yes, I would very much like to ask Hawthorn about this."

15

Violet's chance to confront Lord Hawthorn wasn't far off. That afternoon they'd arranged for Ross to interview Violet for his article and use the opportunity for him to report back about his day's findings. Maud sent one of the stewards with an invitation for Lord Hawthorn to join herself and Miss Debenham for a friendly game of quoits on the upper deck.

"Quoits," said Hawthorn flatly, when he appeared.

Maud passed him one of the stiff rope rings. "Nice healthy exercise in the fresh air."

The Pipes and Drums were giving a performance the next day. The faint wails and rattles of their distant rehearsal could be heard like a battle taking place on the other side of a mountain. But the air was, inarguably, fresh.

"A ride on a horse or a good session of singlestick would be exercise."

"When I locate the *Lyric*'s stables, Lord Hawthorn, I shall let you know."

He tossed a quoit with a careless flick of his hand. To Maud's annoyance, it landed directly on the pole. Ross and Violet broke from their conversation and turned to watch.

"Behold," said Hawthorn. "I am participating. Now: what emergency has arisen that requires my help?"

Maud explained the itch of Violet's neck and the red rune that had been visible and then vanished again.

"And it occurred to me," said Violet, eyes hard on Hawthorn, "that I *do* know a magician, from a family expert in runes, who has had a recent opportunity to lay his hands on me."

There was a long pause. Maud worried at the inside of her lip.

"I am not a magician," said Hawthorn.

Violet laughed. "Of course you are. Even if you—"

"I am not. A magician." Each word was quietly and deliberately placed. "Or do you suppose I've been lying about the absence of my own power for the past fourteen years?"

"I don't know." Violet leaned back to rest her elbows on the railing. The breeze played with the feathers of her hat. "Have you?"

Hawthorn smiled at her. It was a smile searching for bruises with the intent of pressing down. Maud found her hand clenched tight around her last quoit, the roughness of it digging into her palm.

"Naturally," he said. "Because *you* abandoned your family and the society that raised you for no reason other than childish petulance, I'm sure nobody else could have a real reason to do so."

Colour slashed across Violet's cheeks.

"Violet," said Maud hastily. "You can't truly think Lord Hawthorn is one of the villains of this piece. The truth-candle, remember?"

Violet's hand went protectively to her neck. "This might not have anything to do with your contract."

"What, then?" Hawthorn dripped aristocratic disdain. "There's nothing I want from you, Miss Debenham. And if I did, I wouldn't need magic to get it."

"Oh, *fuck* you," snarled Violet.

"No, thank you."

Ross gave a cough. His eyes shone with amusement. It was time to intervene before this disorder amongst Maud's troops got out of hand.

She said, "These people rune-cursed my brother. I'm willing to assume they're employing the same tricks now. Lord Hawthorn, I believe that you didn't put any sort of rune on Violet, but can you think of what it might be designed to do?"

Hawthorn picked up another quoit and tossed it. Something about the motion suggested he was relieving his feelings by imagining an act of more satisfying personal violence. This one, too, landed with a perfect wobble and thump atop the pole.

"If it's not there now, I can't tell you anything," he said. "Fetch me if it appears again. The circumstances, if that occurs, may give you more information. It sounds like it may only be visible when it's activated."

"*Activated?*" Violet's voice rose.

Hawthorn looked hard at Maud. "Your game's starting to become more real, isn't it? A sleeping charm in my whisky. A rune laid on Violet with God-knows-what purpose."

"It started with a dead body," Maud said with more firmness than she felt. "It was never a game. I'm not . . ." No, that would have been a lie. "I *am* afraid, but that doesn't matter. I'm not giving up."

For all that was worth. Maud was the most useless member of her own group. Hawthorn had knowledge and experience; Ross had lockpicks; Violet was the only one with magic. And their enemies, whomever they were, clearly knew it.

She forced herself to say: "I'm sorry, Violet. I can't insist that you keep putting yourself in danger."

Violet let her hand fall from her neck. "If this *is* to do with whoever killed Mrs. Navenby, then it sounds like my best option is still to help you find them. So we can make them remove it."

Too late, in other words. Maud let herself feel miserable with guilt for two heartbeats, then squared her shoulders. Violet was right. The only way to fix this was to see it through.

"Do I get to nobly refuse to desert my post as well? Or does the offer only apply to the officer class?"

All eyes turned to Ross. Fairness warred with desperation in Maud. She needed all the help she could muster. But the writer had even less chance of defending himself against magicians than Maud did.

"A pity. One really can't find good staff these days," murmured Hawthorn, so diamond-posh that he was clearly doing it on purpose.

"Up your arse," said Ross, not looking at him. "I didn't say I was turning tail. You think I've never been in danger before? Besides—you've paid me. I don't give refunds. And I keep my end of a bargain, which is more than I expect from . . ." A wave of his hand in Hawthorn's direction.

"Thank you, Mr. Ross. I assume you didn't find anything this morning?" Maud asked him.

"Might have done." Smugness crept in at the side of his expression. He looked like a particular cherub in a painting that Maud had always hated. She'd been very glad when Robin sold it, when they moved into a smaller townhouse; that cherub had always made her want to poke her finger through the canvas.

Now, she could have seized Alan Ross by the curls and planted a kiss on his angelic forehead for the eager leap of hope beneath her breastbone.

"You did? You found something?"

"One of the things on your list of silver was a dressing set. Hairbrush and mirror? Matching, with twirly bits on the back? I saw those. Didn't see any of the other things you mentioned in the same room, though." The smugness spread across his mouth. "Just some lovely pearls rolled up in a scarf and tucked away in a drawer. *Asking* to be nicked, in such a shoddy hiding place."

"Where? Whose cabin? Tell me the number—no, you'll have to show me, I can't get in on my own. Or—Violet?" Maud turned her eyes hopefully.

"There's probably more than one silver brush and mirror set on this ship, Maud," said Violet. "And would your murderer really leave it out on display? *Use* it?"

"It was a woman's cabin," said Ross. "Travelling alone, I'd guess. There weren't any men's clothes."

"Women can be murderers," said Maud. Mrs. Sinclair would have been proud of such a bluestocking proclamation. "Come along, Mr. Ross. No time like the present. I'd know Mrs. Naven-by's set if I saw it again, so you'd better let me into this cabin to check."

Ross did so. The cabin was on B Deck. Maud had a cover story prepared about gathering names and donations for a widows-and-children charity event in London—she could slip into the language of philanthropy as easily as Adelaide Mor-rissey lapsed into Punjabi when annoyed—but there was no response when she knocked on the door.

Then they had to wait a few minutes for the corridor to clear entirely, during which Ross wielded his notebook and asked Maud a series of earnest questions about how she would ad-vise the White Star Line to improve the *Lyric*'s accommoda-tions. Perhaps there should be a small selection of books in each cabin, to save the lazy traveller the walk to the first-class library?

Maud agreed this would be a charming addition, and—"All clear," she said, feeling thrillingly like a street gang's lookout in a penny dreadful.

Ross tucked notebook and pen away, pulled lockpicks from the pocket of his waistcoat, and turned to open the door. Maud imagined him ducking in and out of cabins like this all day, ca-sually letting himself into places he wasn't allowed. Roaming first class with jewels stuffed into his messenger bag, ready to touch his cap and ask for a quote—and all the while know-ing he was worth less, in the eyes of the security officers, than one of the lapdogs carried around by first-class passengers. No wonder he'd scoffed at the idea of quitting. He was probably carved from sheer solid daring.

As soon as the door clicked he stepped away, gave Maud a mocking little bow, and strolled off. If Maud were caught, it'd be best if nobody was given an excuse to search Alan Ross's belongings.

Maud slipped inside the cabin and closed the door behind her. Her heart beat faster. She could be daring too.

There was a mustily floral smell in the air, lavender layered with mothballs and shoe polish and soap, that reminded Maud of Mrs. Navenby's bedchamber back in New York. Perhaps her cabin would have smelled like this, too, if Mrs. Navenby had lived past the first day on board.

The thought shook Maud into action. The silver hairbrush and mirror set lay in plain view on the dresser, surrounded by a profusion of bottles and jars. Some looked likely to hold medicines; some scent; some various creams and unguents. Each label held rows of tiny black writing. The cabin's occupant was either a nervous health fiend or extraordinarily anxious about her complexion.

But was she a magician? Or a killer? Or—the thought struck Maud like a raindrop in a puddle—had the real killer gone to the trouble of scattering the stolen items among the belongings of others to avoid suspicion?

No. That was daft. Strange accessories suddenly appearing in one's cabin would cause just as much confusion and comment as theft, surely.

Unless they believed them to be a gift of the White Star Line. Complimentary for use, like the chess sets and playing cards.

The puddle of her mind was alive with idea-drops now, its surface roiling with them. Maud gave her head a quick shake. *Concentrate, Maudie.*

At first glance the hairbrush and mirror did look extraordinarily like the stolen ones. They were the right size, the right heaviness, the brush's dark bristles a similar length and tangled lightly with greying hair.

Maud's heart sank as she turned the mirror in her hand. Twirly bits on the back, as advertised. But the pattern was, while similar, not the correct one. Maud was certain of it. This was a false lead.

It was still worth pursuing, she told herself firmly, letting herself out of the cabin again. It was—

She stopped, her hand on the doorknob. Perhaps four yards away stood a man, heavyset and wearing workman's clothes. The corridor was empty but for the two of them. He was star-

ing right at Maud, arrested as she was halfway out of a cabin
that wasn't her own, and just as Maud began to haul her best
baronet's-daughter, of-course-I-belong-here smile onto her
mouth . . . the man's hands moved against one another, cradling
faster than she'd ever seen anyone do it before.

Maud had barely time to inhale before he dragged the brimming spell over his own face, which—*melted*.

Maud's stomach lurched with the sheer wrongness of it.
Instead of a face the man now had a swirling, no-coloured mist,
the outline of his head only just visible as if viewed in a mirror
in a steam-filled room.

She knew what this was. Robin had described illusion-
masks to her; Walter Courcey had used one, as had the men
who attacked Robin and cursed him when he first took over
the liaison job.

But it wasn't only this that caused Maud's hand to tighten
on the door handle. It was how the man's eyes had looked in
the moment before the mask obscured them: wide with surprise, and then narrow. And absolutely devoid of anything that
Maud would call human emotion.

Fear rose in Maud like hot water, soaking her from toes to
teeth.

The man turned on his heels and ran.

Maud made an abortive move after him, then stopped,
thinking furiously about her map. If she gambled that the man
was hoping to reach a service staircase—if she assumed he'd be
avoiding the main areas, with his face so magically hidden—if
she wanted to get there *ahead* of him, or at least stay close
enough that she could see where he went—

Maud turned, gathering all her energy to dash in the opposite direction to the masked man.

She collided at once, painfully, with someone else.

"Pardon me!" Maud gasped, extricating herself. "Oh, I do
beg your pardon, ma'am, I . . ."

The woman was no taller than Maud, round as a currant bun
in both body and face. She looked so perfect and comfortable

an old lady that she should be in advertisement for something—
boiled sweets, perhaps, or slippers. She also looked startled, as
well she might, and she pressed a wrinkled hand to her old-
fashioned bodice as she looked from Maud to . . . oh, dear. The
half-open door to the cabin.

The old woman took an enormous, quavering breath.

"*Thief!*" she warbled, with substantial volume for her age.
"*Thief! Help!*"

"I'm not—" Maud said desperately, but she didn't have time
for this. Not if she was going to have any hope of staying on
the masked man's trail.

She dodged a blow from a brocade bag large enough to hold
three knitting projects and an embroidery hoop, stammered
another apology, and took off for the end of the corridor with
the old woman's yells still rising behind her.

"*Thief! Over here! Someone stop that girl!*"

16

This time, Mr. Berry the master-at-arms did not offer Maud a cup of tea. Maud could see the instinctive desire to do so warring with his sense of professional duty. On the one hand, there was a gently bred young lady seated in a chair across from him, looking upset.

On the other hand, the young lady had been caught red-handed in the cabin of a complete stranger, and instead of staying to explain her innocence had promptly fled the scene.

The *Lyric*'s security staff were taking the presence of a jewel thief on board as a personal insult. They had—of course—come running at speed on hearing the cry of *Thief!*

Maud had dashed nearly into the arms of a uniformed man whom she recognised, with a sinking heart, as Ferris. The officer she'd pestered about the ship's security, and how one might move through it without being apprehended.

That seemed in keeping with her current run of luck.

Insulted zeal had overcome Ferris's hesitation in laying hands on a lady; Maud had been marched, by a polite but firm grip on her arm, to the master-at-arms's office.

She clasped her hands in her lap and straightened her spine. Maud Cutler, she reminded herself, did not have the smile of a baronet's daughter. Maud Cutler was the hired companion to her (deceased) elderly relative. Maud Cutler had, unfortunately, spent two days treading on her own reputation and allowing herself to be seduced by barons and concert-hall performers. But Maud Cutler was *not* a jewel thief, and was *appalled* to be accused of criminal behaviour.

It was a lot to keep straight in one's mind. No doubt Violet would have known exactly the right way to behave.

"If you are not the thief, Miss Cutler," said Mr. Berry, "then would you care to explain what you were doing in Mrs. Vaughn's stateroom?"

Maud had had time to think about this one. An outright lie would be required.

"I saw the door to the room was ajar as I passed," she said. "I thought one of the maids might be cleaning, and I stepped inside. I wanted to ask for fresh towels to be delivered to my own cabin. But there was nobody inside. I assumed perhaps the door had been improperly closed."

"Mrs. Vaughn is certain she closed and locked the cabin door behind her, when she left."

Maud felt awful about it, but she gave the sort of delicate, telling shrug her mother had been expert in. It said: *We're both far too kind to comment on the failures of memory that might plague a woman of a certain age, but we are aware of them, aren't we? Such a pity.* "I can't explain that, Mr. Berry. I can only tell you what I saw."

"She has also reported a string of valuable pearls missing."

Of course she had. They were in Ross's possession. Maud aimed for polite but exasperated.

"If I'd taken these pearls, they would still be on me, would they not? You have my word of honour, there are no pearls anywhere on my person! In fact, you may search me, if you believe otherwise."

Mr. Berry's moustache twitched. "I intend to." He nodded at the doorway. "Thank you—?"

"Agnes, sir." A girl in a maid's uniform shot a curious glance at Maud.

"Thank you, Agnes. If this is a misunderstanding, Miss Cutler," the man said stiffly, "then naturally I apologise for the imposition. But there is a thief aboard, and my position—the very reputation of the White Star Line—requires certainty. I cannot take your word for it. You understand."

"If you think it necessary," said Maud. She was rather taken aback. But where Miss Blyth could frostily protest the liberties taken by laying a single hand upon her person, such an argument would hold less water coming from the lowly Miss Cutler. And it did seem like the quickest way to prove her innocence.

All the men stepped out of the office. The maid patted Maud carefully down, layer by layer. The girl's face flamed and she avoided eye contact with Maud. Nowhere in her contract of employment, Maud wagered, did it mention that her duties might involve searching disreputable jewel thieves for evidence of their ill-gotten gains.

The complete lack of pearls was duly reported to Mr. Berry, whose face staged a battle of relief against frustration. Maud smiled hopefully at the man, but before she could speak, the door opened to reveal yet another member of the *Lyric*'s staff.

"Ah, Jamison," said Mr. Berry. "Is this the young lady in question?"

Jamison gazed upon Maud. Maud gazed upon the slick, dark hair and calm face of the steward upon whom she had pressed Mrs. Navenby's pearl earrings.

"I couldn't say, Mr. Berry. Name of Miss Cutler?" At Mr. Berry's impatient nod, Jamison went on: "I haven't met her, myself. But Mr. Galloway told me when he was"—he coughed—"indisposed, that he took a bribe from a Miss Cutler to let her into a lord's cabin. He'll deny it if you ask now, sir," he added, lavishly decorating this confection of lies, "but I'd wager anything if you search his locker you'll find the bribe. A pearl earring, he said."

"Pearls again, hey?" Mr. Berry raised his eyebrows at Maud as if he'd moved his bishop to threaten her king.

Maud glared speechlessly at Jamison. They'd been *allies*. She'd *bought* him. But clearly he'd planted the earring in his drunkard of a supervisor's belongings, as Maud suggested, and was now seizing a second opportunity to get the man dismissed. The truth of the situation brimmed at Maud's lips, but she forced herself to think. It was her word against Jamison's, and she was not, at present, in a position of strength. And if she kept quiet and protected him, he'd be in her debt.

"That's right," she said sweetly. "And if this is the only other piece of evidence against me, then we can clear this up in no time. The man whose cabin I was trying to enter is Lord Hawthorn. If you ask him to join us, Mr. Berry, then I'm sure everything will become clear."

Mr. Berry looked nonplussed. He did, however, send Jamison in search of Lord Hawthorn. Maud spent the awkward interim making earnest conversation with Mr. Berry about how much she was enjoying the voyage so far, and how *helpful* Ferris had been in pointing out all the amenities and attractions on board the ship.

If she got out of this, she vowed to herself, she was going to triple her efforts. She would come up with new, brilliant ideas. She would make up for her ongoing failure. She would not only find out who that fog-masked man was, and if he'd killed Mrs. Navenby, and what form the contract piece took. She would also—somehow—find out *how* these people intended to use the Last Contract to steal power. Not even Edwin had managed to deduce that yet.

Maud was stuck on board a ship with these people. All right. They were stuck on board with *her.*

When Lord Hawthorn appeared in the office, he seemed to instantly highlight its cramped size simply by existing. Maud sprang to her feet and sent him an adoring look, and—

His name. What on Earth was Lord Hawthorn's Christian name? Maud's mind, already sorely tried by circumstance, was utterly blank.

Well. The man was heir to an earldom. Surely even lovers would use his title.

"*Hawthorn,* darling," Maud gushed, and took two steps to fling herself into his arms. Or rather: at his midsection. She buried her face in his chest and tried to psychically glare her need for his cooperation into the buttons of his sports jacket.

After a few moments, Hawthorn's hand settled on her back. "Maud. May I gather that you're in some manner of trouble?"

Maud was as revived by this as, she imagined, the fast Miss Cutler would have been to find herself in the strong arms of her protector. She raised her face to him and explained the situation—*so unfortunate*—and the subsequent testimony of Jamison.

"You can tell them the truth. I asked to be let into your cabin to surprise you," she appealed.

Hawthorn exchanged a look with Mr. Berry.

"Miss Cutler is, indeed," said Hawthorn, "a surprising young woman."

"And I don't need to *steal* things, do I? When you've promised to buy me all the pretty things I want?"

She kept her fingertips lightly on Hawthorn's front, and hoped her eyes were huge and trusting. It helped to imagine Robin, whom she missed horribly; to imagine herself full of faith that this man would move the world for her.

Hawthorn, thus revealed as the sort of cad who might rashly promise luxurious gifts to a girl he had no intention of keeping upon their return to England, looked down at her. It was a look that somehow managed to communicate how dearly he wished he'd never set foot out of bed this morning.

"That's right, sweetheart," he said, in a low, dark drawl. "I'll see to it you have everything you deserve."

Maud's hands were blocked from the master-at-arms's view where they rested on Hawthorn's chest. She pinched him. Hawthorn's mouth twitched and he took her hands prisoner in his own.

"It does seem to be a misunderstanding, sir," he said, directing the full force of his cold lordliness at Mr. Berry. "May I assume that Miss Cutler is free to go?"

Miss Cutler was free to go.

Violet had been neglecting her strumpetly duties when it came to Lord Albert. She had no idea how really promiscuous women kept strings of lovers all at one time. Surely one would need vast organisational skills, or a secretary.

"I've been interviewed by that reporter, Mr. Ross, for an article in one of the society magazines," she said. "Perhaps I should go back to him and make some pointed comments about how much I've enjoyed meeting you, and how much time I hope we can spend together in London?"

"Good plan. Appreciate the thought," said Lord Albert.

They stood in the Grand Reception, smoking a pre-dinner cigarette and being officially *seen*. Violet associated cigarettes with end-of-run parties and theatre dark nights. There was something thrillingly theatrical about accepting one from a gentleman's silver case and smoking beneath a glassy ceiling of night sky while the glittering throngs of the *Lyric*'s first-class passengers made their way up the staircase.

Lord Albert gestured to a steward, who hastily brought over a sand-filled brass ashtray on a tall stand, and they went in for dinner. Violet had agreed to eat with her aunt and cousin, and invited along their lordships Albert and Hawthorn. And Maud, who was—as usual—late, having neither a lady's maid, a helpful aunt, nor magic to assist her with dressing.

Maud smiled at the table as the men rose, then took her seat beside Hawthorn. Her dress was a deep, pearly grey, with loops of black beads forming little cap sleeves. Falling from the waist was an overlay of dark gauze with tiny embroidered roses in pink and green. She wore a thin headband with matching silk-ribbon roses along its length. The contrast of flowers against the syrupy turbulence of the grey silk, along with the way Maud's eyes picked up the green of the embroidery, was devastating.

Clarence's face fell into one of abject wistfulness. Violet felt almost friendly towards her cousin, who if nothing else seemed to share exactly Violet's taste in women. The friendliness was tried almost at once when he leapt in to plaintively scold her for not paying more attention to her aunt.

"I was looking for you earlier, Vi," he said. "And you were— where were you?"

"Here and there," said Violet. "It's a large ship, Clarence. I'm sure there are people aboard it whose company will suit you better than mine."

"There was a musical variety performance," said Clarence. "We thought you might enjoy it. That's all."

Aunt Caroline sent Violet an unusually fierce version of her disapproving moue. Clarence did appear to be presenting her with some kind of olive branch. Violet couldn't bring herself to apologise, but she managed a grudging nod.

"I didn't think that would be your sort of thing," she said.

"Well, you don't know much about me, do you?" Clarence collected his tone. "You act as though you and Lady Enid were the only people in the family to care a fig for music, but it's not true."

Violet bit her tongue on telling him that he exuded an aura of being so uninteresting that it was bizarre to think of him having interests. But it was true that she'd never bothered to ask.

"Was your relative a patron of the arts, Miss Debenham?" asked Lord Albert.

"Of a sort," Violet said. "Her husband was a carpenter by trade. When they married he owned only two workshops. He had a good eye for an investment, it turned out, and he ended up part of a successful shipping concern. But he kept expanding the carpentry business and also began to specialise it." She shot a smile at Lord Albert. "His passion was always musical instruments. He sent apprentices to Germany and Austria to learn from the master violin-makers there."

"There's a harpsichord in our London house which Taverner made himself, when he was young," said Aunt Caroline unexpectedly. "The lid is made of different sorts of wood, all cunningly inlaid. He made it as a special order for Lady Enid's sister. It was how he and Lady Enid met."

"I didn't know that," said Violet. "Seems rather ungrateful of them to then refuse to see their daughter in company, for the mortal sin of marrying a tradesman, doesn't it?"

"How wonderfully romantic," said Maud.

"To answer your question, Lord Albert—yes. Mr. and Mrs. Taverner, once they'd made their fortune, spent rather a lot of it on music. I believe they endowed the first chair of a chamber orchestra somewhere."

In fact, James Taverner had come from a family of working magician-craftsmen, and through sheer hard work became one of the only thaumoluthiers in the Western world since the days of the Tieffenbrucker family. His workshop's instruments were not just musical but magical; wood and catgut both held magic beautifully, and could be used to produce harmonies that were close to spells of their own. And the orchestra in question was the English Magicians' Chamber Group, which had once caused a freak spring snowstorm when a performance interacted poorly with a difficult rain-spell being attempted by a family of magician-farmers nearby.

After they'd eaten, Lord Albert invited the other gentlemen to the first-class smoking lounge for drinks and cards. He looked so hopeful that Violet felt sorry for the man when Hawthorn declined.

"Happily, my lord, Clarence was telling me earlier how much he was itching for a good game of écarté," said Violet. "And you share an interest in music, it seems."

Clarence gave Violet a suspicious look, then a kicked-shin jerk. His mother wasn't about to risk him missing an opportunity to be on friendly terms with a marquess's son.

Violet was punished for having put a hankering for écarté into Lord Hawthorn's head by being forced to play against him in his suite while they waited for Ross. Maud, who'd never played the game herself—"My parents preferred whist or bridge, if they had to play anything at all. More people at a table to gossip with."—kept track of the points.

Violet herself hadn't played it for years. She and her sisters had learned all the card games they could, from an old rule-book of their father's, and she'd learned several more—most with variants involving alcohol, cheats both magical and unmagical, and filthy nicknames for the face cards—in New York.

Hawthorn played very fast, with his usual demeanour of bored superiority. He had a fiendish memory for trumps. Violet lost a hypothetical fortune to him while laughing at Maud's description of the master-at-arms's face when he was trying to arrest Miss Maud Cutler as a jewel thief. A good portion of Violet's annoyance with Maud had eased when she wasn't looking; and it sounded like Maud's afternoon had been punishment in itself.

The actual jewel thief, when he arrived, was disgruntled.

"They've stepped up security," Ross said. "It was already getting tighter before you embarrassed them, Miss B. Now you can't sneeze in the first-class corridors without a chorus of *bless-you-sirs* from keen thugs in uniform." He peered over Hawthorn's shoulder and raised his eyebrows at his lordship's hand. "I'll have to retire the jewel arm of the business for the rest of the voyage."

"I'm sure you've stolen enough to be getting on with," said Maud. "And even though that wasn't the dressing set we're looking for, it did get me face-to-face with a magician, and the important thing is that he clearly recognised *me*." She briefly outlined the events preceding her arrest for Ross's benefit. "Coming across me unexpectedly must have rattled him," she finished. "If he'd had more presence of mind, he could simply have walked right past, and I'd not have thought anything of it."

"What'd he look like?" Ross asked. "Before the—" He waved a hand in front of his face. Alan Ross appeared to be treating magic as something akin to polo or trap-shooting: yet another eccentricity of the upper classes, with little bearing upon his own life given that he could not personally turn a profit from it.

"I didn't get a good look. Fairish hair, heavy build. And I didn't like his eyes. He looked as if he'd throw you overboard if you were between him and something he wanted."

"Not exactly enough for a sketch," said Violet. "So where does this leave us? More security is going to make searching difficult."

"I know. And it's a useless approach anyway." Maud sat back in her chair. "It's too large a problem. We need a better strategy to find these items."

"I don't know any tracking-spells that seem like they'd help," said Violet. "And—didn't you mention something about that, when you were telling us how your brother and Edwin found the coin?"

Maud nodded. "Edwin says the components of the Last Contract are magically inert to most spells seeking objects of power. They found the last piece of the coin with a fossicking-spell seeking silver, but they only had to search a single room. There'd be far too much silver on the *Lyric* for that to be at all useful."

"Tell me again what the stolen items were," said Hawthorn. "A bracelet, a locket . . ."

"And a scent flask, and the hairbrush and mirror set."

"Hair." He looked at Violet. "Do you remember your lock ceremony?"

"Barely," said Violet. She remembered Alice's and Julia's, which took place closer together than their ages would have dictated; Alice was slow to show her magic, to the extent that their parents had begun to wonder if she had any at all.

"What's that?" asked Ross.

"When a child in Britain first shows magic, a lock of their hair is cut," said Violet. "It's sent to the Barrel, in London, and their full name is registered there as a magician."

"Like a christening?" said Ross. "Right. What's the point of it?"

Violet had never questioned the point. There were a lot of pointless ceremonies in life. She looked a query at Hawthorn, who said, "The safety of magical society. In theory. If a magician is in danger, or missing, a map-spell can be cast using their hair to locate them, if they're within the bounds of Great Britain."

"Mother of Christ," said Ross. "*That* sounds piss-easy to use for ill purposes."

"Robin and—" began Maud, and then shut her mouth.

"Maud," said Hawthorn sharply, when she didn't seem likely to continue.

"It's rather a secret."

"If you don't trust us with your secrets, then what are we doing here?" said Hawthorn.

"Excellent question," murmured Violet.

Maud shot her an uneasy look. "Kitty Kaur let Robin into the Lockroom and did the map-spell for him, when Edwin was missing. She used to work with the Coopers, so she knows how the process works."

"You're saying we should be able to—do it in reverse? Locate the hair in Mrs. Navenby's hairbrush?" Violet asked Hawthorn.

"Possibly," he said. "I know a few map-spells. The one in the Lockroom can search all of Britain because the map itself is charmed to high heaven. There's enough magic in that room alone to blow up the Barrel. But we have a map of the *Lyric,* do we not?"

"We do! I do!" Maud was transformed with the scent of potential success.

"Hold on." Ross had pulled up a chair and was sitting backwards on it, chin resting on hands folded on its back. "So there's a spell that can find a person, using their hair. What are we using to find the hair in a brush, then?"

"More hair should do it," said Hawthorn.

"Hats!" said Maud. "I'm sure we can find a few strands

caught in the bands of Mrs. Navenby's hats. And I can look in her spare combs as well."

Hawthorn shook his head. "I doubt you'll be able to get enough that way. We'll need as large a lock as possible, to strengthen the sympathy."

"Then . . ." Maud trailed off into a thoughtful silence, which remained intact while they considered the implications. Violet was the one to break it.

"Ah . . . where is Mrs. Navenby now, Maud?"

"In the ice room," said Maud. "Mr. Ross, I doubt the security there is very tight, especially if they're focusing all their efforts on the first-class corridors."

Ross straightened and stared at Maud. "You want me to break into an ice storage room and bring you a lock of hair from the *frozen corpse* of a dead lady?"

"How much extra will that cost me? I can—"

But Ross gave a rippling gurgle of a laugh that shook his shoulders. "Not even my brother and sisters would've come up with that one, and we used to dare each other to go into graveyards at midnight and touch someone's tomb. I'll do it for nothing. So long as his lordship here will come and yank *me* out of trouble if need be."

"You're welcome to claim to be another of his mistresses," said Maud, now outright sparkling with glee. "Though I'm not sure what the master-at-arms will think."

"Nobody will accuse you of jewel theft in an ice room, Ross," said Hawthorn. "As a matter of fact, you could very easily ask to see the place for your advertisements. Something about the amount of eggs and milk needed to feed the passengers, and how they're kept fresh for the voyage, surely?"

"All right," said Violet. "Say we get the hair, Hawthorn teaches me the map-spell, and we use it to locate *more* hair, thus showing us where on the ship the hairbrush is. We still have to break into that cabin. If it's even in a cabin. And the problem of ship security still stands."

"What we will need," said Maud impressively, "is a diversion." She beamed at them, hands clasped together as if she were holding herself back from running out and seizing the opportunity right this very moment. "And I have an idea for one of those."

17

Once the planning session was complete, Violet walked back to Maud's cabin to check the hairlock charm she'd created earlier that day. Her skill didn't run to a really strong warding, but a hairlock—two strands of Maud's hair, coated in the sandalwood oil that Maud had bought and Violet had done her best to imbue—was a poor man's warning system, tied to Maud's identity.

It was intact. Even better, it fell promptly from the wall when Violet herself entered the cabin, which meant it was working.

The hour wasn't late—certainly not by Violet's standards—but she found herself stifling a yawn on the bare back of her hand. She'd stuffed her gloves into her evening bag.

"How can you be tired?" Maud flitted around the stateroom like a butterfly in a ballet. The embroidered gauze layer of her gown floated and swayed, a bar behind the melody of her body. "I swear I won't sleep for hours, I'm too nervous for tomorrow. Having a real plan is such a *relief.*" She butterflied into the adjoining room, out of sight, and Violet could hear rustling fabric as Maud began the process of changing into her nightgown.

"Do you need any help?" Violet called. "Hairpins, buttons, corset strings?"

"Thank you—no, I'm much handier than I was."

Violet was fingering the back of her neck again. She forced her hand down to her side. Dwelling on it wouldn't help. The only way to get the bloody rune off was to track down this illusion-masked man.

"I wanted to apologise again for dragging you into this," said

Maud, as if she'd sensed the thread of Violet's thoughts. Her voice was muffled. "I won't let you get hurt, Violet. I promise."

Nobody could make such a promise. But Violet didn't want to puncture the sweet, fierce confidence in Maud's tone by pointing that out. Instead she smiled and ran her fingers over the back of the nearest chair, seeking the hints of dust in the crevices of the well-turned wood, thinking about Lady Enid and James Taverner.

"At least I'm not bored. It was going to be a tedious week, brightened only by the prospect of giving Aunt Caroline the vapours at every opportunity."

"Do you mean you don't regret it? Good," said Maud. "Because I'm sorry you might be in danger, but I can't say I wish it had never happened. I'm not sorry you were the one in Robin's visions. I'm not sorry I met you."

Violet's mouth, open to admit that she wasn't sorry to have met Maud either, dried up entirely when Maud reappeared in the doorway.

Maud hadn't been changing into her nightgown. Or rather, she'd begun the process, and paused it halfway. She'd removed gown and petticoat, camisole and corset, and the stockings of her evening outfit. What remained was only a pair of drawers and a short chemise: a single lace-edged layer of ivory silk through which Violet could glimpse the outline of dark pink nipples.

Maud's hair was pin-free and wild with it, a mass of fluffy waves still unwinding as if it were exhaling all on its own. It drew the eyes down to the expanses of skin. Violet was used to seeing half-dressed women; used to seeing their nipples, even. There wasn't much mystery or modesty between the members of a theatre company.

She'd thought it was bad when Maud let the robe slip from her shoulders in the baths. Now she could see Maud's *knees,* and it felt practically obscene.

"What are you doing?" She heard the echo, her own words in her own dry mouth, from last night out under the stars. As then, it wasn't a real question. It was a line thrown in to buy time.

As then, Maud was working off a different script.

Maud said, "Asking again."

"*Maud.*"

"I'm very persistent," said Maud. "It's one of my worst qualities. And your argument about Miss Cutler's rumoured depravity being hypothetical was rather ruined by what I did today in order to *not* be arrested as a thief, and I *still* haven't had a chance to do anything that I'm supposed to have done." Some strain escaped into her voice. She was within touching distance now. The green of her eyes was dark as wet leaves. "And I might as well be hanged for a penny. So. I'm giving you another chance to say no."

The sheer courage that took, to ask again after being twice turned aside; to put oneself out there to be thrice denied. There was something ritualistic about it. It called to the storyteller in Violet: three princes setting out to make their fortune, three families entrusted with fae magic, three days to guess someone's name.

Here they were on the third night of the voyage, and Maud was asking again, standing there flushed amongst those airy waves of brown hair like a stubborn bird in a ravaged nest. Her hands rubbed fretfully at her own bare arms.

Violet did remember how it felt, in those first days and weeks after you finally woke up to what the bloody fuss was about—how this was a hunger that could distract you during the day and keep you awake at night, your whole body a cymbal set ringing, a quilt of needy inhalations, a hollow throb right in the core.

Now Violet's own body gave the same throb. How could it not? How could *anyone* with eyes avoid feeling like this, looking at Maud with her bitten lip and soft curves? Her toes, bare on the floor. The pink-and-white of her skin straining against the creamy silk and lace.

"Violet?" Maud said, uncertain.

"I'm not . . . saying no."

"But you haven't," said Maud, "said—"

And stopped, because Violet's fingers were on her lips.

If Violet had taught herself anything, clung to any principle when it came to partners and pleasure, it was that no single act was an agreement to any others. A kiss was a kiss alone, until the next kiss was bestowed. Asking a man for his mouth on you didn't mean you'd agreed to have his cock inside you next, no matter what some might think.

Touching Maud's mouth was not a statement that anything else would happen. It could just be this: the pink, perfect bow slightly parted, and parting further with the press of Violet's thumb in its centre.

At any point, Violet could stop. At any point, she could resurrect the bones of her reservations from where they were crumbling to dust.

Maud took a very small step forward. Violet's thumb slipped into her mouth.

Violet's heart beat once, hung thrilled and heavy in her ribs for a soft forever—then beat again, the pulse in her thumb enormous where it sat against the inside of Maud's lip. Maud's chest rose and fell. She smelled like sugar.

Violet took her hand back. Maud's mouth stayed open, as if in complaint. As if Violet could plunge her fingers in again, or her tongue, and ruin it like a windfall plum lying bruised in sunshine heat. God, Violet could *taste* it. She swallowed, hard, and reminded herself that she'd done this before. This was what she did. Violet knew how to be exactly what a person wanted her to be, between the sheets.

And these were classic, well-worn roles. The blushing in-génue and the rake willing to debauch her. Pleasure was pleasure. Violet didn't have to trust Maud entirely to do this. In fact she should *keep* the dregs of her anger, coat herself in it, like licking one's fingers before extinguishing a candle flame.

She drew a smile onto her face and made sure it was exactly the one she intended it to be.

"What do you want?"

"Anything you'll show me," said Maud at once.

"Anything *anyone* would show you, it seems." She put her fingers at Maud's jaw and tilted the girl's face up, then let those fingers drag down the side of Maud's neck, to the lace-edged silk of her chemise. Goose pimples sprang up beneath her touch. The pink of Maud's cheeks deepened further.

"No," Maud said. "You. Violet."

"Why me?" Violet, appalled that she'd let that question escape, immediately pulled on a further defence: the arch laughter of a woman sure of the answer. "Because I'm beautiful?"

"No."

Maud, who didn't lie, punctured the archness with a word. But she was thoughtful rather than insulting. She looked at Violet as if trying to recognise her. It was clear she was disagreeing with the specific word only because she wanted to find a better.

"No," Maud said again. She lifted a hand and flattened Violet's where it lay, over silk—over skin—over the uppermost part of Maud's beating heart. Now Violet couldn't tell whose pulse was whose. "Because when you're in a room I don't want to look anywhere else."

Violet's free hand moved before she could tell it to. It scooped up the back of Maud's neck, all that heavy brown hair, and dragged Maud close, her hot body flush against Violet's, so that Violet could kiss that open mouth.

Maud's gasp sounded like triumph soaked in need like sponge cake in syrup; and tasted sweeter even than that.

Maud had witnessed exactly four kisses over the course of her life.

The first had been between her grandparents during a visit to Thornley Hill when Maud was very young. She remembered the drizzle of rain on the windows, and the servants running around with dishes to catch the drips. She remembered thick

layers of petticoats about her own legs and the smell of hum-
bugs on her grandmother's breath.

The kiss in question had been a brief, absent press of lips
as the old baronet bid his wife farewell, departing for a visit
to London. Maud's mother had made a face as if someone had
dropped a teacup.

The second had been on the stage. Mrs. Sinclair had taken
Liza and Maud to see Henry Irving and Ellen Terry in *The
Merchant of Venice* at the Lyceum. Maud remembered the elusive music of the spoken word, the magnetic energy of Terry as
both the frustrated Portia and the eloquent Balthazar, and the
passionate embrace between Portia and her new husband once
she had thrown off her disguise. A stage kiss. Its emotion both
false and compellingly real.

The third, Maud's parents. In company, Sir Robert and
Lady Blyth were physically affectionate only in proper ways:
the slide of a hand beneath an arm, or the press of a shoulder.
They cared about the look of things.

It was sheer luck that Maud had been sneaking back from
a late-night trip to the kitchens—using the servants' stairs,
where she wouldn't be seen—and caught a glimpse of them
through the door of Lady Blyth's bedchamber. They were
standing close together, fully dressed. They looked caught up
in each other, as if nobody else in the world existed; and even
if they did, such people could *never* be as fascinating and beautiful and real as the two of them, and therefore were not worth
looking at in the first place.

The final kiss was one that Maud had been deliberately allowed to see. Robin, laughing at something Edwin said, then
crossing the room to bend down and lower the top edge of Edwin's book—and to kiss him while smiling, with the ease that
said he'd done it a hundred times before, and the confidence
that said he wasn't ashamed.

There had been more emotion in the brief press of Edwin's
fingertips to Robin's jaw, his sharp blue eyes falling closed,
than in an operatic aria.

Based on these four examples and the extensive descriptions in Ross's suitcase, Maud had attempted to formulate a guess as to how it would feel to kiss Violet Debenham.

She'd been halfway right, and halfway wrong.

Wrong because she'd thought it would be natural, effortless. For her body to want something so much, it should know what to do once it had it, like shaping one's voice to the pitch of a note. But she was not sure if her mouth was doing what it should; the same for her free hand, which clutched inelegantly at Violet's shoulder. Or if she was breathing in the right places. Or at all.

She'd been right because even with this evidence of her inexperience, it still sent Maud's blood singing. She'd be happy to stand here for another hour—two hours—kissing until her lips turned numb, learning every taste of Violet's mouth.

Violet's hand was crushed against Maud's chest between them, a lid for the noisy pipes and drums of Maud's heart. The ring on Violet's other thumb caught in Maud's hair as she tugged, using the grip to break the kiss and create some distance between them.

Maud licked her lips. Caught her breath.

"Three times really is the charm, it seems," Violet said.

Before Maud could ask what she'd meant, Violet leaned in. She kissed one corner of Maud's mouth, then the other. Each kiss dragged Maud's breath with it when she pulled away, like a ribbon reel unspooling. Maud barely realised that Violet had taken her hands back until those hands untucked Maud's chemise and landed on the naked skin of her waist.

"Oh," Maud said, "*yes,*" and got herself closer.

Violet was still entirely dressed. Maud had a picture of them, clear as one of Robin's visions: Violet in her ink-blue gown, and Maud pressed up against her in nothing but her rapidly crumpling underthings. The image seared her mind and shook her legs.

One of Violet's hands was in the centre of her back now, and the other slid up to cup one of Maud's breasts. Her thumb moved over a nipple. Maud tipped her face forward into the crook of Violet's neck and made a small noise.

"All right?" Violet said.

"Very all right. Exceedingly all right. That feels—*ah*," as Violet bent and took the nipple, silk and all, into her mouth.

Several of the women in the erotic stories had screamed when their nipples were thus treated. Maud didn't particularly want to scream, even though pleasant shivers were skating down her arms and burrowing into her flesh. She *did* want to know what expression Violet would make when someone did the same to her, and what it felt like to have the softness of a nipple turn stiff and wanting between your lips, and what it would take to make Violet scream.

Maud had a moment of hysterical kinship with Edwin Courcey, who would approve of her experimental approach, and then banished him entirely from her mind.

"*Please* can we take your clothes off now?" she said.

They did. Undressing another girl when you knew that what was beneath was for *you* was probably the best thing in the world, Maud thought. Like unwrapping a present. She'd been right: Violet wore a soft corset, nothing rigidly boned. Her evening underthings were cotton instead of silk. She had narrow legs, and a reddish birthmark in the small of her back, and a long, thin scar along the inside of her left upper arm, which Maud hadn't noticed before now.

"Have you ever frigged yourself?" Violet asked.

The blunt word was like the flick of a finger between Maud's thighs, a place that already felt heavy and hot.

Maud nodded. "But I couldn't quite—get it to work."

"You didn't like it?"

"It felt . . . like I was walking *around* something but couldn't find the path *through* it."

Violet stepped back. Instead of removing pins from her hair, she cradled a brief spell and swept her palms up over her forehead and back. Her hair fell from its arrangement at once, in long blond hanks with only the hint of wave at the ends. She looked younger with her hair down.

"I thought," said Violet, "I could show you what *I* like, and you could try it on yourself and see whether you like it too."

That sounded like taking things slowly, sensibly, and Maud felt rather like a steam train devouring an open stretch of rail. She didn't *want* to slow down. But she also didn't want to reject anything that Violet was prepared to offer.

Violet moved with a swagger to her hips and the sparkle back in her eyes. She removed her drawers and sat back against pillows at the top of the grand bed in the main room, one knee straight and the other crooked to the side; and Maud sat across from her, and copied.

Violet, frank and fearless as ever, told Maud to suck her own fingers to wet them, and that there was nothing wrong with using oil to ease the way if one's body was sluggish. She indicated that the *red hawthorn berry*—"No, for God's sake, let's just call it a *clit*"—was the seat of pleasure in most women, though not all. That Violet herself had found it uncomfortable to pay that spot too much attention when she was first being introduced to bedroom activities, and Maud might want to come back to it when everything else was—warmed up, as it were.

She'd slipped into the smoky registers of her voice. Maud would have been happy to sit with her eyes closed and her hand in her drawers while Violet recited—oh, *anything*, Shakespeare or filthy poetry or French verbs or the railway schedule.

But with her eyes closed, she'd have missed the sight of Violet: her skin gaining its own peachy flush, her knuckles glistening in the light of the electrics as she pressed two fingers into herself, then pulled them out, then pressed in again. The motion was assured in a way that Maud would give anything to mimic, and that compelling performer's face was upturned to her audience as if already hearing the applause.

Maud's fingers slid between her own folds. She didn't know how it was supposed to feel. But she felt *good*: grown-up and free, and enjoyably wicked.

She appreciated Violet's lesson. The attention to her own pleasure, just as Mrs. Sinclair had recommended. But what Maud had wanted all along was *Violet*.

Maud undid the small top button of her chemise, then the second. Her fingers were sticky. That, of all things, made heat fill her cheeks again.

"Maud?"

"Oh, carry on," said Maud, as innocently as she could manage. "Don't mind me."

Violet did so. Her grey gaze was tangible like the tip of a feather as Maud removed the rest of her clothes. It slid across Maud's breasts when they were bared, and down to Maud's hips and the place between Maud's legs.

Maud, kneeling on the bed, squeezed her thighs together to quell the quiver of sensation. Then she settled herself right next to Violet, propped up on one elbow. A new scent filled the air: not quite vinegar, not quite salt. It mingled with the scent of lavender from the pillows.

Maud's courage had taken her this far, but it gave out when her right hand touched Violet's. Now Maud was almost touching Violet's—*cunt*. The word curled in the mind with a satisfying crudity. Her fingers lay over Violet's own as if resting on the keys of a piano, not yet daring to press down and hear the chord.

"Can I—?" she whispered.

In answer Violet moved her own hand quick as a cradling, swapping their positions. Now Maud's fingers were held between Violet's own and the hot, so-slick flesh, and now the lesson began in earnest. Violet abandoned performance: she chased her pleasure with short sharp motions, demanding, and she used Maud's hand to do it, and Maud boiled with desire and delight until she thought she might burst. Her mouth was open against the tip of Violet's shoulder. She could feel it when Violet's body arched, Violet's rib cage heaved, and the breath shuddered out of Violet as if being hauled over rocks.

Violet released Maud's hand. Maud kept her fingers where

they were, marvelling. Violet's now-soaking cunt gave tiny shivers beneath her fingertips.

"R . . . Right." Violet sounded a little slurred. "Fuck, I needed that. *Now.*"

And with a burst of movement that Maud had not been expecting—some of the pamphlets had made it seem as if achieving release melted one's muscles entirely—Violet turned, and rolled, and all of a sudden Maud was flat on her back with Violet sitting astride her hips, Violet's hands on her shoulders, Violet's chemise gaping as she leaned down.

Every sensation in Maud's body went from pleasant moderato to urgent allegro. It felt—close to fear, but nothing like fear. She was aware of things that she hadn't noticed until now. The puckered stitching of the bedcover beneath her palms, and the prickle of her own hair against her back. The distant voice of the ship's engines, heard in Maud's bones.

This time when Violet kissed her it was looser, dreamier. It seemed only natural for Maud to open her mouth to the press of Violet's tongue, and to explore with her own for the brief glorious minutes that the kiss lasted.

"Now then, Miss Blyth," said Violet, sparkling grandly. "Full marks for participation, so far. But for the next lesson, I only require you to lie still."

"What was it you said? Lie back, think of England, and don't whimper too much?"

Violet grinned. "Whimpering is *encouraged.*"

Maud bit back a gulp of mingled anxiety and anticipation. She could see the tip of Violet's tongue.

And then she could feel it go to work. Violet mouthed all the way down Maud's body. She scraped her nails through the curls between Maud's legs, then shifted lower, and touched—so gently that Maud wanted to yell at her to get *on*—where Maud was wet and hot and wanting.

Violet looked up to meet Maud's gaze. She swept her own hair elegantly to one side of her neck, and then ruined the effect with one of the most wicked smiles Maud had ever seen.

In that moment she was the Dark Duke, and the grinning sa-tyr, and the bold courtesan, and every figure of fantasy ever invented.

Maud knew what Violet intended to do. Some of the pamphlets had been extremely fixated on it. None of them, however, prepared her for how it actually felt to have Violet's fingers and tongue working in harmony upon her.

It made all the difference not to know what would happen next, *not* to be the one directing the action. Maud had nothing to do but . . . lie there. To focus helplessly on the drip of pleasure down her legs and the hectic crawl of it beneath her skin, and the tightening of some low, unseen muscle, like a mousetrap pulled back and held.

Violet sucked hard on the sensitive nub of her clit. Maud thought deliriously, *hawthorn berry.* One of her legs jerked, hard. Violet lifted her face only enough to laugh; Maud felt the puff of breath on unbearably sensitive folds.

"Sorry," Maud panted.

"Give me a black eye and I'll take it as a compliment," said Violet, sounding very New York for a moment.

"Oh—please, can you—*please—*"

Maud didn't know what she was begging for, only that she wanted to greedily gather all that her body could take. She wanted the steam train.

"I've got you, darling," Violet murmured, still with the city clinging to her consonants. And bent back to her task.

After a few more timeless ebbs and flows of pleasure, Maud became aware of a slow, new pressure. She tried to push her hips into it, encouraging. Only then did her lust-fogged mind realise that Violet had put a finger there, all the way to the base.

Violet is inside me, Maud thought, her whole body making a bewildered fist of itself around the sentence. And then—as if the words had called it into being—all the tension spilled over at once.

An inelegant sound flew out between her lips. She stared at a spot on the underside of the bed's canopy as hot waves of sensation grabbed and released everything beneath her navel, rhythmic as kneading dough.

"Fuck," she whispered, when she'd recovered.

The word was getting easier. And nothing else seemed strong enough for the occasion.

"That's the spirit," said Violet, sounding very satisfied indeed, and wiped her mouth on her hand.

It took some industrious wriggling and tugging to get them both beneath the covers. Maud couldn't stop looking at Violet's mouth, parted with her slowing breath. She wondered what Violet's first time had been like. Or her last time, before Maud.

Well. The last time had been Hawthorn, in a way.

"What's it like, to do it with a man?" Maud asked.

A curious blankness spread over Violet's face. It was replaced almost at once when she let out a howl of laughter and buried her face in a pillow.

Blood flew to Maud's cheeks. She wondered it had the energy.

"*Maud,*" said Violet, muffled. "Having completed an enjoyable sexual encounter with someone, it's *not* the thing to immediately start wondering aloud about someone else."

"I wasn't—I only meant—oh, bother, that *was* awfully rude, wasn't it?"

Violet removed her face from the pillow. "Everything I just did to you would be the same if it were a man doing it." She paused. "Perhaps scratchier, if he'd a moustache."

That was not what Maud had meant. She didn't *want* to do this with any man; at least, if she was scrupulous about it, not with any man that she'd met so far in her life.

But she had no intention of digging herself any deeper by trying to explain.

"It was wonderful." She smiled, and then smiled harder when Violet poked a finger teasingly into one of her dimples. "Thank you. I should have looked into this debauchery business years ago."

"I'm glad you waited," said Violet, still laughing.

"I'm glad I waited for you."

The laughter's edges changed to something Maud couldn't interpret. Violet kissed her once more on the lips, friendly and soft. Then Violet slid out of bed and went into the bathroom, where Maud heard the sound of water in the basin as Violet washed up. Violet re-dressed with hands and magic both, transforming herself back into the shocking Miss Debenham. Gown on. Hair up.

"We should both get some sleep," she told Maud. "You've organised a busy day for us tomorrow."

When Violet left, Maud washed as well, then changed into her nightgown. She brushed and plaited her hair. She remade the four-poster bed, then looked at the dog's breakfast she'd made of it, sighed, and turned off the room light and climbed beneath the covers. There was nobody else in the stateroom to use it, after all. Nothing wrong with the poor cousin Miss Cutler taking the opportunity to sleep in the larger, grander bed.

The bed still smelled of bodies. Of Violet. Maud felt her mouth form a new smile.

Tomorrow, she thought, in the darkness. It was going to be busy.

18

Violet was a professional. She had once done an entire run of a show that featured an oversized velvet chaise as one of the few pieces of set dressing, and upon which chaise she had spectacularly fucked the playwright's father—who'd paid to have the theatre's seats reupholstered, and several windows fixed—on the night of the dress rehearsal. A refreshingly blunt exchange of material favours. Violet wasn't overly surprised when it turned out the man had seen one of her trouser roles and wanted her to boss him around while he frotted urgently against her tall leather riding boots. At least he'd let her ride his face afterwards, like a gentleman.

The props mistress had wearily told Violet that she liked to reserve her magic for emergency mid-show repairs and re-making the mirror that was smashed onstage every night, not removing spunk stains from velvet.

The point being: Violet could behave entirely normally in a room containing furniture where she had, not so many hours earlier, been both the deliverer and the recipient of satisfying orgasms.

Even so. Every time *Maud* glanced at the four-poster bed, Violet's cursedly vivid imagination provided a front-row seat to a memory of how Maud had looked with her dimpled thighs splayed on either side of Violet's head.

"None in this one," said Maud now, closing another hatbox with a snap. She was industriously locating every strand of Mrs. Navenby's hair that remained in the old woman's belongings, in case Ross was unsuccessful in stealing a whole lock.

Hawthorn was taking Violet over the spells needed for what Maud had dubbed the Grand Plan. His cradles had a beautiful fluidity to them despite his being fifteen years out of practice. Violet had to keep making him stop and slow down.

Violet practiced until the anchoring suffix for the Pied Piper flowed smoothly on from the rest of the charm. Then they moved on to the runes needed for an opening-spell performed in parallel on linked items—not difficult at all, thankfully. She took a break and stretched her hands, then glanced over to see how Maud was getting on.

Maud was staring at Violet's fingers. She jerked away when Violet's eyes met hers, and that irresistible blush climbed above the lace of her collar.

Violet looked back at Hawthorn. One of his eyebrows rose to a disapproving height. Too much to hope that he hadn't noticed—nor that he'd hesitate to leap to the correct conclusion.

Well. Neither Violet nor Maud was his responsibility; he'd gone to some pains to point that out. It was none of his business what they did.

Violet performed a short sentence in the cradlespeak of the Debenham household. A framing-spell for the banishing of pests, with a pointed glance at Hawthorn in place of the motion that would normally define the spell's target of mice or wasps or ants. *Stay out of it.*

Cradling without power behind it was useful for more than just practice. Cradlespeak was a common pastime of magical children, though not a standardised tongue. It depended on both a shared knowledge of the spells in question and an agreed-upon translation of their meaning.

Hawthorn obviously caught the gist. He glanced again at Maud, deep in hatboxes with the flush lingering at the visible nape of her neck. To Violet he formed the silent cradle for a spell that untangled string or rope, with a reversal prefix, and then paused on a prolonged flick-flick-flick of his index finger, which would increase the spell's potency. *You're going to make a mess of things.*

Violet, maturely, stuck her tongue out at him.

Any further reply was forestalled by the arrival of Ross. Once inside the cabin he made a show of blowing on his hands to warm them.

"Never liked damp, cold places. They always remind me of a cellar I lived in once."

"But did you get— Wait, really? A cellar?"

Ross grinned at Maud and dug in the pocket of his trousers. "Fearful place, it was," he intoned. "Full of rats. Not the ice room, Miss B—that was full of eggs and cheeses. And one very dead woman, politely covered in a sheet."

Maud leapt for the lock of hair that Ross held out. "Violet, are you ready? Can we do it now?"

Violet and Hawthorn had practiced this spell nigh to death the previous evening. It was layered and finicky, and Hawthorn had taken nearly an hour to cobble it together from both memory and Violet's experimentation.

The first sympathy clause coaxed Maud's annotated map to represent, truly, the ship itself. Violet formed it painstakingly with her hands held above the map. A new dance. A new harmony. Her magic crept outwards and outwards again, and Violet felt the size of it, the amount it was demanding from her as it built.

"Keep the radius," Hawthorn said sharply. "Remember."

Violet remembered. She'd defined the radius of the sympathy to the bounds of the ship, but that was still a long way in every direction. She lifted her hands, the spell balanced between them like a basket full of glass eggs.

She turned to the nearest wall and flung them apart.

"*Oh,*" said Maud.

"Fucking hell," said Ross.

The map of the *Lyric* glowed in pale green lines on the wall. All its decks, all its cabins, in blueprints hanging side by side. It could have been sketched there with phosphorescent paint.

"Don't *drop* it!" Hawthorn barked, and Violet brought her

hands together just in time, forcing herself to focus on the other parts of the spell.

Dangling from her fingers now was a strange cradle that reflected the lights of the room, snatching up small pieces of colour for itself, as if she'd formed it with wires made of invisible stuff. She breathed slowly, holding it. She sketched out a clause for seeking; the invisible wires shone green for a heartbeat and then faded again. Ready.

"Maud," she said. "Put the hair right in the centre."

Maud did so. It hovered in Violet's hands, a fly in a cobweb. Ross gave another bitten-back epithet as most of the map on the wall vanished, leaving only two enlarged sections, as though someone had taken a magnifying glass to them. One of the two was much brighter; the other was a thin, wispy sketch.

"That's not part of the cabin areas. That must be the ice room," said Maud, looking at the brightest map.

"Where the rest of her is," said Ross. "And the other?"

The atmosphere in the room was high and taut with excitement; *finally* they were close to the beginnings of an answer. Even Hawthorn's habitual boredom had been replaced with a bright-eyed keenness that made Violet think of foxes.

Maud touched the second map. "It's showing only a short stretch—B Deck, but I don't know which room—"

"It'll be dead centre," said Hawthorn.

Another short eternity of held breath. Maud's finger moved. "Forty-four," she said.

Ross had his notebook out, flipping. He'd copied the room directory. "B Deck, 44—got it." His voice sharpened with triumph. "Mr. A. Chapman."

"Mr. Chapman? But he's a cotton-mill owner! And he was so friendly . . . oh." Maud let out a bitter huff of a laugh. "Perhaps that's why."

"He did seem awfully keen to ask you questions about Mrs. Navenby," said Violet.

"*And,*" said Hawthorn, "someone who'd doctor a decanter

of whisky might well do the same to a glass of wine, to make you talkative."

Violet thought of Maud, swaying and giggling before she emptied her stomach over the railing; and Chapman's expression when Violet insisted on taking Maud out of the dining saloon, which she'd put down to plain disappointment at losing Maud's company.

"That's enough for me. Be careful," said Hawthorn to Maud. "We'll proceed as planned today, and if you see Chapman, for God's sake don't go running *at* him like you did with the masked man. Leave minding him to Ross."

Maud made a face at him, but promised. They coordinated pocket watches and then the conspiracy broke up for lunch. Violet tried to concentrate on the ham and cold jellies and asparagus salad with boiled eggs, but her stomach kept giving little quivers of excitement. She ate anyway. She had a lot of magic to do.

After lunch she made her way up to the sun deck and sat on a deck chair under a parasol, watching the expanse of the sea. She also continued her perusal of the Alexander the Great biography. The more time she spent with Maud Blyth, the more she felt a bemused kinship with Alexander's friends and generals.

At half past two, Hawthorn joined her, walking with a silver-topped cane as if playing at being a normal sort of gentleman. Violet stood, gave him her most flirtatious smile as he kissed her hand, then handed him both book and parasol before bending to refasten the lacing of her boot. Hawthorn held the parasol at a low angle that would hide what she was doing.

Violet cradled the charm called the Pied Piper and used the anchoring suffix to attach it to an unremarkable patch of deck, where it would lie quiescent until triggered by touch. She then tugged the deck chair sideways by a foot, to cover the charmed spot.

Hawthorn replaced her on the chair. He'd brought a newspaper, which he spread across his face, pretending to nap in what meagre sunshine managed to struggle through the clouded sky.

That was one part down. Violet made her way to the Grand Reception to meet Maud, who led the way down to the cargo hold. Somewhere else, if all was going to plan, Ross would be tracking down Mr. Chapman. His job was simply to shadow the man, to distract him if necessary, and to come and warn them if Chapman looked like heading back to his own cabin.

Now that Maud had entered the cargo hold in Hewitt's company, the bath attendant ignored them as they entered the stairwell. Maud had ascertained that the Bernard menagerie was fed at the same time every day, after which the keeper took himself off to one of the third-class saloons and played cards for beer money until it was time to clean out the cages and bed the animals down for the night.

Not that one could easily tell day from night in the cargo hold, Violet thought, as they picked their way across to the menagerie. Those dim electric lights probably shone the same at every hour.

"Not the bear, I think," said Maud. The creature in the largest cage was hunched over, paws on its stomach like a portly gentleman at the end of a good meal. "It's large enough that it could do someone damage by accident. And not the birds. If they fly off, they'll be lost entirely."

On every lock of the other cages and crates, Violet traced the linking rune and held it in her mind. She completed half the opening-spell and held it steady in her hands, awaiting the final clause.

Most of the animals, recently fed, looked sleepy. The spindly cats—*cheetahs,* Maud said—had the half-feral, half-condescending look that Violet recognised from street cats. One of them was licking the other's face.

"Time?" Violet asked. Holding the cradle for too long would cramp her fingers.

"Just on three." Maud slipped her watch away. She was bouncing on her toes, her face anxious.

Three o'clock. Anytime now the Pipes and Drums, performing by special request of the captain, would be blasting into their finest and loudest melodic form.

Here in the bowels of the ship, crouched by the menagerie, Violet couldn't hear anything but the hums and bangs and grumbling guts of the *Lyric*. And the closer noises of nearly thirty animals who were probably less than impressed at being in their fourth day at sea.

"Give it here!"

Both of them jumped at once. Violet nearly dropped the cradle as her heart shot into her throat.

"Dorian!" said Maud, recovering first. She went to the aviary. "What are you doing down here?"

"Making friends?" Violet peered into the cage.

"I suppose it is a larger space than his own cage. That was kind of Helen. Sorry, Dorian. We don't need any birds for this plan."

"There might be some wild seabirds within the charm's radius," said Violet. "Don't you love the idea of Lord Hawthorn being wooed and bombarded by gulls?"

Maud laughed. "I really thought Robin might have been mistaken about that particular vision being relevant to me. Animals loose on board a ship? But it's exactly what we need." She'd shown Violet the brief description in her brother's notebook.

"He saw this happening and wrote it down, and him writing it down is how you had the idea to do it. It's one of those snakes eating its own tail."

Both of them looked at the nearest snake. The python was a gleaming coil the colour of Violet's hair. Maud had faithfully passed on from Helen the fact that the snake was unlikely to be hungry for days. The Pied Piper charm didn't turn mild-mannered beasts into rabid ones, it simply made them extremely curious about a particular point in space.

Violet opened her mouth to comment on the irony of the antisocial Lord Hawthorn having agreed to trigger such a charm, and in that moment every animal in the menagerie picked up its head. The kangaroo's ears lifted. The cheetahs unfolded to their feet. The birds chirped and yelled, wings flapping, all of them competing for the highest perch within the aviary like a seat on a crowded tram car. If Dorian was yelling any words, they were lost in the general chatter.

The performance must have started up on deck. And Lord Hawthorn must have set his foot on the anchored charm beneath the chair, casting the Pied Piper over the ship.

"I hope there are *rats*," Violet whispered. She completed the opening-spell and cast it onto the nearest lock.

In her nerves she'd put more magic into the spell than it needed. The locks didn't click open; they *broke*. The door to every crate and cage sprang open at once.

"Violet! Up here." Maud was standing atop a pile of canvas-covered crates nearby. She helped Violet up to join her.

They needn't have bothered. The animals had no interest at all in two young women; not when magic was telling them that there was something irresistibly fascinating taking place elsewhere. An untidy exodus of spines, fur, paws, and scales erupted into the cargo hold and made its way, with varying eager gaits and exotic noises, towards the exit. Violet and Maud had left the hatch open. How the animals chose to make their way to the deck was up to them.

Violet pictured the porcupine patiently waiting for the first-class elevators. Laughter bubbled between her lips. She couldn't hear it over the frustrated aviary's impression of the Dies Irae.

"Come on!" said Maud, once the python's tail—the last sign of the last creature—had vanished from view. "We don't want to be caught down here."

They nearly were. They had barely made it out of the cargo hold and to the staircase on D Deck when a wild-eyed man in the cap and shirtsleeves of the *Lyric*'s sailors, moving at a run, nearly collided with them.

"*Oh!*" Violet screamed, and collapsed half of her weight onto Maud's shoulder. "I thought you were another of those ghastly creatures! Where are they all *coming* from? I demand that they are rounded up and—and shot! I'm sure they must be rabid!"

The man touched his cap hastily and mumbled something, then dashed past them.

"We don't want them to be *shot*," Maud said, indignant. "Don't give them ideas!"

Chaos was rising on the *Lyric*. Everywhere Maud and Violet went, people who hadn't encountered the animals heard the shouts of those who had, and paused to crane their necks and change direction and ask someone else who asked someone else—*what's happening?*

Violet cast a longing glance at the way to the sun deck, from whence bagpipes were still audible. Hawthorn was going to keep his foot firmly in place until the chaos reached him, then remove himself from the area to negate the charm. She would have paid a large amount of her new fortune to see what would happen when the Bernards' menagerie collided with the Pipes and Drums, with Lord Hawthorn in the vicinity.

But they had other things to do.

What they needed, Maud had pointed out the previous night, was something that would thoroughly occupy every security officer on board the ship, so that they were no longer watching out for jewel thieves breaking into—or emerging from—first-class cabins.

Hawthorn had said that allowing a menagerie the run of the ship was the equivalent of trying to kill an ant by dropping a grand piano upon it, but he was unable to deny the fact that it would work.

"And there you are," said Maud triumphantly, once they reached the right corridor of B-Deck staterooms. "No uniforms anywhere!"

Violet had already begun to cradle the opening-spell that worked on the cabin locks. She let them into Number 44: a single stateroom like her own, with just the bedchamber and small bathroom. The few personal items on the dresser were arranged

in rigidly neat lines. It was no reason to dislike someone—
and should have counted for nothing when set against *possible
murder*—but Violet still prickled with instinctive annoyance.
Very neat people rubbed her the wrong way.

"Keep an eye open," Maud said as they began to search.
"Not just for the silver. Anything that could tell us something
about the Last Contract and how they might use it. Even notes,
or books."

Hawthorn's magical education had finally turned up a blank
spot at the idea of a silver-fossicking-spell—"Courcey's always
known more than the rest of us," he said. Violet didn't mind.
One less thing to learn. There wasn't much cabin to search, in
any case.

"Not in there," said Maud, emerging from the bathroom.
The sound of pounding feet in the corridor outside made them
both freeze, but it must have been people running either to or
from some animal-related incident.

Violet had finished with the dresser and was cracking the lid
of a trunk when Maud—at the writing desk in the corner—gave
a stifled noise like someone hiccupping into a flute.

"Here. Here!"

Violet hurried over. "You've found them?"

"It must be—surely." Maud was crouched by the lowest
drawer. She drew out a loose and irregular bundle of folded
black velvet and stood to set it on the desk. Her hand hesitated
in an un-Maudlike way, clutching one edge. "What if it's not?"

"*Maud,*" said Violet, and Maud unwrapped the fabric.

Silver. It wasn't much, for all the fuss that had been made
over it. The bracelet was tarnished in its crevices as if the elephants had rolled in black mud. The brush and mirror were
brighter—especially the handles, polished by regular gripping.
The flask had a flat front engraved with the looping initials
R.C.N. Maud's fingers skipped gently across each piece as if
to make sure they weren't as illusory as the flowers on Violet's
hat.

The mirror lay at an angle atop the final item, shielding it from view. Maud tugged at the loop of delicate silver chain, which turned out to be broken: it slithered clear and came away in her hand.

"She always wore this," Maud said. Hushed. "He must have broken it, pulling it off her—afterwards."

Maud moved the mirror and picked up the locket beneath, which was the size of a small hen's egg.

The moment her hand closed on it, Maud's body jerked. She caught herself on the desk edge with her free hand; the other was desperately tight around the silver locket. She turned her face to Violet, and Violet choked, because Maud was—not Maud.

It was Maud's heart-shaped face and small mouth and upturned nose. It was Maud's green eyes.

But the features were folded into an expression of fierce, exhausted surprise, and her entire stance had changed. Maud held herself like a person who'd tripped on a cobblestone and righted themselves again, but for a few more seconds would be inhabiting the startled vision of themselves sprawled in the gutter. Both at home in her body and not.

The voice that emerged was sharp as fabric shears.

"That's better. By God, that's better. What on earth . . ."

Maud looked back to the mirror. Her eyes widened. Then came a short laugh as sharp as the voice had been.

Beneath her tensely hammering heart, Violet felt ill. Forget *part* of her inheritance—she'd lay down all of it, every penny, that Maud didn't have this sort of acting ability. This was something else.

"Well, well. Little Miss Blyth, the oh-so-determined girl. You didn't think it was worth mentioning that you were a medium?"

The rosebud mouth gasped and it was Maud again, trembling. Her fingers clawed around the locket, pressing it to her chest as if to hide it between her ribs.

Violet's mind and fingers were blank of all the spells she'd ever known. She was too stuffed full of questions. She could have been eight years old, sitting cold-shouldered in the bed she shared with Ellen, filling herself up with ghost stories from her father's lips.

Maud said, "I'm a *what*?"

19

At no point had Mrs. Moretti the famed spiritualist mentioned that channelling the spirits of the *dear departed* felt like dipping oneself in a lake of someone else's essence. Maud's nose kept chasing tobacco and face powder, and that pungent floral scent that lived in Mrs. Navenby's silver flask. She couldn't actually smell them. If she inhaled, they were gone. But they swam around regardless in the cavity of her mouth, which she *couldn't move*. The ghost had her lips, had her tongue, was—she could see in the mirror—carving an impatient furrow between her brows.

Don't frown like that, Maud darling, you'll give yourself wrinkles.

Maud didn't often find herself ranged on her dead mother's side of an argument. But she would have liked to tell her dead *employer* that any wrinkles Maud ended up with, she would inflict upon herself, thank you very much.

"*A medium,*" said Mrs. Navenby, impatiently answering the question that Maud had managed to blurt out before Mrs. Navenby shoved her aside again.

And it did feel like a shove. Like Maud was now a driving seat meant for one, on which two people were crammed together and engaged in a squabble over the reins.

Mrs. Navenby, currently winning, used Maud's body to look around.

"*Whose cabin is this? Who's this creature with a face like a rainy afternoon? No, settle down, I can't be forever passing back and forth,*" as Maud attempted to exert herself. "*You. Girl. Answer.*"

Violet looked mulish. "I won't tell you a thing until I'm sure Maud is all right."

"Don't talk twaddle—she's possessed, not dead. Unlike some of us."

Violet drew herself up into one of her regal, immovable looks. She said nothing.

"Very well."

And there was the relief of space: an elbow being removed from one's ribs. Maud shook herself all over.

"I'm fine," she assured Violet. "It's a very queer feeling, that's all. Er. I suppose . . . introductions?" At least she could fall back to her society manners. She had no other framework to deal with what was happening. "Mrs. Navenby, this is Miss Debenham. She's a magician, and a friend. Violet . . . this is Mrs. Elizabeth Navenby." *Deceased*, Maud nearly added.

"Charmed," said the poshest version of Violet.

"A magician. Yes, I see those rings," said Mrs. Navenby. *"Trained in America, were we? I could never see the point of them myself."*

Maud extended an experimental elbow inside her own mind. She'd had enough of sitting silent and being talked over in her life. And she had questions.

"Am I—am I possessed *forever*? Is that how this works?"

Awkward silence from both inside and out. Then Violet reached out and extricated the sunflower locket from a grasp that Maud hadn't realised was so tight. As soon as it left Maud's hands, the sensation of carriage-sharing disappeared.

"I thought so," said Violet, who was inspecting Maud closely. "It started as soon as you picked it up."

"She's possessing the locket? Not me?"

"She's *haunting* the locket," Violet said. "If that's even the right word to use."

"We could ask Mrs. Moretti." Maud giggled. It was probably an inappropriate response, but she couldn't do anything else.

The hairs on her arms rose. She was clasped suddenly in cold. It reminded her of hearing the start of a sweet, venomous dressing-down of one of the servants; running upstairs to her room and closing her door against her mother's voice, but still feeling the discontent in the house as if it were creeping fog.

She took the locket back. The sensation settled at once.

"All right," she said quickly. "So you can possess me, and only me, when I'm in contact with this necklace."

"*So it would appear,*" said Mrs. Navenby.

"Maud," said Violet, "do you think perhaps—"

The stateroom door opened, and Arthur Chapman stepped inside.

When he saw them, his hands dropped at once to the stance that Edwin took when he was holding his cradling string: no spell begun, but ready to move into whatever was needed.

Maud gathered herself to say something placating, but the other occupier of her vocal cords got there first.

"*You,*" spat Mrs. Navenby.

Chapman looked tense, but not surprised. Of course not. He knew exactly why they were there, and what they knew about him.

Why hadn't Maud *thought,* for once in her life? She was a terrible general. They should have left the cabin as soon as they had the silver, not stood around introducing ghosts to the living. Now it was the two of them against a man, a magician who was probably better trained and more ruthless, and he was between them and the door.

"It's them," Chapman said over his shoulder. "Just the girls." He stepped fully inside to make room for someone else.

Someone else closed the door behind them. The small, neat sound of it clicking shut twisted in Maud's guts. Chapman's companion was a heavyset man with close-cut fair hair and rough skin over nondescript features. Maud had seen those features before, in a split second before the illusion-mask swirled over them.

So. It was them against *two* men. Two magicians. And the second one had that awful gaze full of impersonal violence waiting to be called upon and put away.

Just the girls. Maud was so angry and so scared, she wondered there was room for a ghost inside her as well. Robin would have punched someone. What was Maud going to do—challenge them to draw a card? Play *chess*?

She dared a glance at the magician on her own side. Violet's hand was tight on the back of the desk's chair, and she was frozen. No sparkling role or dry improvisation emerged. The blankness looked odd on her, as if she were a doll in a shop waiting for her features to be painted in.

Maud opened her mouth and screamed.

She made it as hard and long and high as she could, and had the satisfaction of seeing both men wince. If nothing else, she could attract attention. As soon as there was a concerned audience, she'd figure out a story to tell.

There was a tight, ringing pause once Maud's lungs were emptied of air. She strained her hearing for any sound of help.

Another scream, as if in echo, sounded not too far away.

For the first time, Chapman smiled.

"They might think you're in here with a tiger, Miss Cutler," he said in his comfortable Northern voice. "But I don't think anyone will care to investigate."

Because the ship was full of screaming women. Because of Maud's oh-so-clever diversion plan.

"Now, the wise thing for you to do would be to leave all of those things exactly where they are," Chapman went on. "My friend here won't do anything unless you try to be foolish. And then we'll all agree to stay out of one another's way for the rest of the voyage. How does that sound?"

"That sounds like a load of horseshit," said Violet. They were the first words she'd spoken. "Stay out of one another's way? *You* started this. You stole these in the first place."

Maud could feel Mrs. Navenby stirring at that. No. The last thing Maud wanted to do now was lose what little control she still had.

"And I'm not very good at doing the wise thing." It took courage to move her gaze away from Chapman and the unnamed man, and to put the locket with the other objects and wrap them back up into a parcel of velvet.

"Miss Cutler," said Chapman. "You really aren't in a position to do anything but cooperate."

He made a small gesture to the other man, who cradled a spell with rapid ease. Violet inhaled sharply. But the man merely held the spell ready, a dense double handful of amber swirls. His eyes moved between Maud and Violet as if making a calculation. Chapman's eyes were pinned to the velvet.

Maud's pulse soared. Her hands were damp and hot, gripping the bundle. *All of those things,* Chapman had said.

"You don't know which one it is, do you?" she said. "Any more than we do."

"What?" said Chapman.

"Bluffing," said the other man, blunt as a slap.

"Honestly, I'm not." Maud had, finally, a finger curled around the reins of this confrontation. "Mrs. Navenby didn't tell me what she'd done with her piece of the contract. In case . . . well, in case something like this happened." She pulled on one of her company smiles. "And now she's dead, and she can't tell *anyone.* Isn't that inconvenient for you? Perhaps you should have thought of that before you *killed her*?"

Violet made a small noise. Maud would have liked to tread on her foot. She could only pray that Violet reached the same realisation: these people could *not* be allowed to know that Mrs. Navenby was a ghost, and that thanks to Maud she was available for questioning.

"Us? We haven't killed anyone." Chapman wasn't even bothering to sound sincere. "Do you intend to announce that we have? How many people on this ship will you unbushel in the process?"

"Chapman. Stop wasting time. Get the bloody things off them."

Chapman cast the other man a glance halfway between wariness and annoyance, as if a large dog on a leash had suddenly growled. Allies, then, but not friends.

"Maud," said Violet tightly. "Perhaps we should—"

The man holding the amber spell lifted his hands and released it. It flew like a tight cluster of hornets in their direction. Violet lifted her hands, shielding rather than cradling, a motion of bewildered instinct.

Maud shoved Violet sideways with all the force her free arm could muster.

She then flung herself backwards, still clutching the velvet. Violet went crashing into the chair. Maud felt a searing, biting warmth in her outstretched arm. She stumbled and barely kept her feet. The room spun. And kept spinning. The floor heaved; she stumbled again.

"Maud," said Violet, and then there was a crash and another voice, louder and harder.

This voice also said, "*Maud.*"

Hawthorn. That was Lord Hawthorn.

Maud stumbled to the nearest handhold, which was a post of the bed, and clung to it. It was hard to focus her eyes. She wanted to close them and stay very still. With enormous effort she made herself aware of the situation. Lord Hawthorn stood inside the stateroom's doorway; he was holding a cane tipped with silver, and the door was wide open behind him.

Violet was climbing to her feet. Maud still had Mrs. Navenby's silver, wrapped and safe.

The unnamed man was staring at Lord Hawthorn with the most emotion that Maud had seen on him yet: something stricken and close to guilt.

"Maud. Violet," said Hawthorn. "We're leaving."

Chapman reached into a pocket of his waistcoat. Whatever he took out was small and round, and glinted like glass. "I know about you," he shot at Hawthorn, lifting his hand as if in readiness to throw a dart. "You're not even—"

Hawthorn moved with a speed that made Maud's head swim with a renewed wash of giddiness. She didn't see Hawthorn's cane collide with the side of Chapman's leg, but she heard the cry of outraged pain that Chapman made.

The next moment she found herself dragged towards the door by a tight grip on her arm. Violet. Maud went, grateful for the support. She had the silver. Yes. She still had it.

"Fucking—shit—*Morris!*" cried Chapman, from somewhere around knee level. Hawthorn must have collapsed his leg beneath him entirely.

And then Maud was at the door, and Hawthorn took over supporting her, and they were out in the corridor. The effect of the amber spell had faded further, but she still felt as though the *Lyric* were rocking unevenly beneath her.

"Walk," Maud said, forcing herself to stand more upright. She kept her hand tight in the crook of Hawthorn's arm and matched action to word. "That's it. As if nothing's wrong."

"What *is* wrong?" Hawthorn demanded, low.

"They got her with a spell," said Violet, looking over her shoulder. "I—bother. That man's behind us."

"He won't do anything in public," said Hawthorn. But he looked over his shoulder too.

"Are you sure?" said Violet.

There was a very short pause.

"Run," said Hawthorn.

20

Maud looked better but still needed Hawthorn's hand under her arm as they moved. Violet couldn't stop glancing over her shoulder at where the stone-faced man addressed as Morris followed with implacable, irritated strides behind them.

"My cabin," Maud said. "Slower—please—"

Hawthorn gave a growl of frustration but slowed himself to match Maud's speed.

The corridors were emptier than Violet expected. Clearly the menagerie chaos had reached the point of passengers shutting themselves in their cabins and waiting for security to take care of it. Nobody commented on their party's speed, only eyed the space behind them as if waiting to see what creature was on their tail.

And then Maud said, "Helen! Mr. Hewitt!" and they pulled to a sharp halt.

Helen Bernard and a red-faced man knelt face-to-face with one of the cheetahs. The cat sat very upright on its haunches, ears back, staring at the new arrivals. Helen was murmuring a soothing stream of inaudible words.

"Stay where you are, sir, miss," said Hewitt. "I've a man coming with a sack so we can take her back to the hold, but Miss Helen's only just calmed her down."

"We do need to get past," said Violet. Her back burned with awareness of their pursuer.

The cheetah got to its feet and stalked with slow steps towards Maud. Its amber eyes were fixed on the velvet bundle in Maud's hands.

Fuck. The last thing they needed was for some oversized cat to *also* show interest in what they were—

Cat, Violet's brain yelled. *It's a cat.*

"Er," said Maud nervously.

Violet stepped between Maud and the cheetah. Or rather: between the haunted locket and the only sort of animal, other than human mediums, known to respond to the presence of ghosts.

"You two go ahead."

Maud and Hawthorn moved past. Robbed of its object of curiosity, the cheetah flicked out a paw and *swiped*—Violet leapt back, a little too slow. Fabric tore. There was no sting of pain, but the cheetah's claw was now caught in Violet's skirt, and it yowled with complaint as it tried to pull itself free.

"Oh, darn," said Helen. "You silly thing! Stop it!" She lunged forward and took the cheetah by the scruff of the neck. It yowled again, and twisted, but to Violet's surprise it then subsided as Helen recommenced her murmured monologue of nonsense.

Violet, dry-mouthed, yanked her skirt away. More ripping. At least they were on the other side of the animal, now, and Morris was . . .

Morris was standing within an arm's length of them, breathing hard. He looked from Hawthorn to Hewitt and back again.

"You will excuse us for now, sir," said Hawthorn, syllables dripping aristocracy like oil. "Miss Cutler is indisposed, as you can see, and we are hampering Miss Bernard in her task. You will be so good as to postpone our business until tomorrow."

It was bald-faced and risky, even for someone like Hawthorn who was never gainsaid. Morris had them all outclassed when it came to magic. Violet thought of Hawthorn's fingers pulling a card from a fanned pack.

Calculation must have been happening behind the broad forehead. Finally Morris took a step back, gave an ungracious nod, and then turned on his heel.

Violet exhaled.

They made their way without further incident to Maud's stateroom. Maud locked the door behind them, and Violet grimly cast the strongest locking charm Hawthorn knew, to reinforce it. God knew if it would help. But it was all she was good for. In Chapman's room she'd just stood there like a damned lump, unable to think of a single useful spell past the enormity of not wanting to die. She'd never had anyone direct magic at her with intent to harm. Maud, unmagical and sheltered Maud, had been the one to shove her aside.

Stepping in front of the cheetah had been an instinctive response from some ornery corner of Violet's soul determined to address the balance of favours. She'd never been prepared to risk her life in this endeavour. She wasn't supposed to risk *anything*.

Hawthorn helped Maud into a chair. Her expression was set, her colour improved. She laid the black velvet down and unwrapped the parcel.

A knock on the door made them all flinch, but the voice came at once. "It's Ross. Don't fret, that thug's retreated. All clear."

Violet recast the locking charm once they'd let Ross inside. He was full of nervous energy; he pulled off his cap, scrubbed a hand in his hair, redonned the cap, then crossed to Maud, who still had a protective arm laid across the jumbled silver objects.

"Got them in the end? Good. Sorry I couldn't give you more warning, Miss B. I was shadowing Chapman, and out of nowhere he went stiff and looked like he'd sat on a wasp. Hurried back to his room at once. I got in his way and tripped him over, but it barely slowed him, so I fetched his lordship from the deck instead."

"*Clearly* this man Chapman had set a rune-signal for intruders," said Maud, "which tipped off the both of them as soon as anyone set foot in his room."

"No need to get hoity-toity with me, you know I don't speak magic." Ross crossed his arms. "A thank-you wouldn't go amiss either."

Violet opened her mouth with a new question, but Hawthorn's sharpest tones got there first.

"How the hell do you know they had a rune-signal?"

Maud sat back in her chair. The locket was in her hand. *"And who,"* she said, *"are these extremely rude men?"*

It was the way she said *men* that slotted the realisation into place for Violet. Like she'd lifted her shoe after stepping in something sticky on the street.

Violet laughed. The look on Hawthorn's face was so angrily baffled—she wanted to frame it and keep it forever. "Do you want to do the introductions this time, Maud, or shall I?"

Maud waved a hand. So Violet explained: the items hidden in Chapman's room, Maud the medium, Maud being benignly possessed. She also filled in what had passed between the two of them and Chapman before Hawthorn's arrival.

"Jesus, Mary, and Joseph," said Ross, once the idea of *ghosts* had sunk in. He stopped himself halfway through the sign of the cross with the irritation of a man falling back into a child-ish habit.

"You look familiar," Mrs. Navenby said to Hawthorn. *"Who are your parents, young man?"*

His lordship's bafflement had given way successively to raised eyebrows, a grim frown, and now a combination of amused blue eyes and composed, cruel mouth.

"My father is Cheetham," he said. "Frederick Alston. My mother Mary was a Bastoke."

"Ah." Satisfied. *"I knew Mary Bastoke when she was first out in society. Nice girl. Tall, and all legs. Put one in mind of a colt jumping at squirrels."*

Ross burst out laughing. Unrestrained, his laugh was rich and bright as coffee poured fresh from the pot.

"Oh, this is a treat," he said. "Keep at it, ma'am. Compare his lordship's relatives to some more farmyard animals."

"No." It was definitely Maud now. "We've too many other things to discuss. Mrs. Navenby—" Her gaze skipped around the room, then landed on the locket in her hand. *"Now* I feel like a detective in a story. Only we can ask the victim directly instead of running around after clues. Did one of those two kill you?"

The transition was becoming smoother, and Violet's ear more attuned to the cadence of each voice. Mrs. Navenby said: *"Yes, it is rather satisfying to be able to solve one's own murder. It was the dark one. Chapman. He snuck into this very room not long after the voyage started. He was digging through my belongings. Of course I suspected at once he was there for my piece of the contract, after everything Miss Blyth had told me about what happened to Flora."* She looked at Maud's hands, rubbing wistful fingertips over the smooth skin of the knuckles. *"I'm not as fast with my cradles as I was. I got off a spell to knock him out, and he dodged it. He looked rather panicked, I remember that. Before I could do anything else . . ."* Her mouth firmed. *"Young people are so wasteful. He had no need to kill me. A brisk priez-vous to bind my hands and a memory charm would have sufficed."*

And he could have questioned her properly about the Last Contract instead of just taking every likely-looking silver thing in the place. But Violet knew acutely how quiet the voice of sense could be when panic was yelling inside the skull.

Mrs. Navenby hadn't been fully aware of herself as a ghost until Maud's contact with the necklace. Existing as a haunting had felt like the space between sleep and waking.

"Liminal," said Violet. Her smile was for Maud and her talk of boats, but Mrs. Navenby gave Violet a strange look: halfway between hunger and suspicion.

"Yes. Liminal."

"Maud had all but solved your murder anyway," Violet pointed out. "We wouldn't have been in Chapman's cabin if we hadn't discovered he had the silver."

And *that* led to a game of five-way verbal tag, in which Mrs. Navenby demanded to be filled in on everything that had happened since what she described as her undignified demise.

"Well," said Mrs. Navenby at the end of it. *"Bother."*

"Quite," said Hawthorn.

But Maud's head was tilted to the side as if listening for something. That pinched frown marred her brow. She looked around the stateroom and the frown deepened.

"*Miss Blyth*," she said. "*Where is Dorian?*"

"Oh, I'm sorry," said Maud. "I didn't know what I would do with a parrot, myself, and I wanted to make sure he was cared for. I gave him to the Bernards, for their menagerie, so he's down in the aviary with the other birds. Helen Bernard loves animals. She'll teach him plenty of new—"

"*The cage, girl.*" Watching the ghost interrupt the medium was a jolting experience. "*Don't babble. Where's his cage?*"

"I—I don't know."

"Arrive at your point, ma'am, if you have one," said Hawthorn. "Stop harassing her."

A dull bubble of fatalistic certainty had begun to form in Violet. It burst entirely as Mrs. Navenby lifted Maud's fierce green eyes to Hawthorn and said, "*The point, Lord Hawthorn, is that the cup of the Last Contract is none of those pieces of silver that yourselves and my murderers have been squabbling over. It is, in fact, my parrot Dorian's water bowl.*"

Violet put a hand over her mouth. Ross hissed between his teeth.

Maud's face transformed—slowly, this time, like a curtain being drawn back—into one of guilty horror.

"Fuck," squeaked Maud.

It seemed that nobody, not even magicians, knew much about ghosts.

None of them had ever met a true medium, and none of them could tell Maud anything about how her ability was supposed to work. A ghost haunting a portable item, rather than a location, was also unheard-of. Violet's stories were all of cats and theatres.

Edwin would be overcome with academic bliss. Maud wondered if she could somehow contrive to present him with this as a birthday gift. Herself, a medium, to match her brother the foreseer. A ghost in a necklace. And not just any ghost: one of the members of the Forsythia Club, whose experiments in magic Edwin had been painstakingly untangling for the past several months.

The afternoon's chaotic conference had been interrupted by the necessity of dressing for dinner. Ghost-experimentation had therefore run, hastily, to working out that Mrs. Navenby could possess Maud to the extent of using her senses—seeing and hearing what Maud saw and heard—so long as the locket was in close proximity to Maud's skin. The phantom scents and awareness of the ghost's pushy presence, which had overwhelmed Maud at first, were becoming easier to manage. It was like humming music while reading: one part of her mind kept occupied, freeing up the rest to concentrate on the task at hand.

Maud strung the locket on a chain of her own and wore it beneath a high-necked evening gown. The chain was long enough that the locket sat tucked between her breasts. She tried not to think about that.

"Please," Maud said to her dead passenger, "don't take over without asking me. Not in public. We can talk as much as you want after dinner."

Mrs. Navenby agreed. And to dinner they went.

Maud was in a whirlpool of miserable annoyance with herself. The piece of the Last Contract had been sitting safe in her room, despite Chapman's best efforts, and Maud had managed to *lose it anyway*. It didn't help that Mrs. Vaughn, the old woman whose cabin Maud had disastrously broken into, was dining on her own nearby, and kept sliding suspicious looks at Maud as if trying to catch her making off with the teaspoons.

Maud tried to sweep that aside along with everything else— ghosts, dizzying charms, Violet's distracting fingers—and focus on what mattered: extracting the present location of Dorian's cage from the Bernards.

There was a new face at their table that evening. Rose Bernard had befriended Miss Diana Yu, a serious-faced young woman whose family had founded a thriving New York fashion house. Maud was halfway through listening to the woman's plans to dazzle the new London department stores into carrying her own designs when Chapman appeared.

"I'm late," he said, "*do* forgive me," and took a decided seat next to Violet.

Cold dug its fingers into the skin over Maud's breastbone. Mrs. Navenby had clear opinions about the presence of her murderer at the dinner table.

Maud bit her tongue. Chapman was an acquaintance. There was no good excuse to cut him in public, and he knew it. She determined to keep a close eye on Violet's drinks and her own.

Helen looked more cheerful than Maud had expected, discussing the menagerie's mysterious escape. One of the main risks of the plan had been the sheer inexplicable nature of it. Cages springing open at once. A general stampede towards the upper decks. But, as Violet had pointed out, unmagical society was not looking to explain things with magic. It was more than capable of filling such gaps with guesswork and gossip.

Consensus aboard the *Lyric* had crystallised around the idea of mischievous boys sneaking down to the cargo hold and breaking all the locks as a prank, then encouraging the creatures out into the ship, where they'd been attracted by the sounds of the bagpipes.

"Which I hadn't thought would be enticing to so many *different* sorts of animals," said Helen, "but then, I can't imagine any of them had ever heard a pipe band before, so how would one know? And the poor men in the Pipes and Drums—there was one fellow who lost his drumsticks to our chimpanzee, and by the time Mr. Hewitt and myself hurried up there, the chimp had discovered someone else's abandoned drum and was banging away having a grand old time, and—oh, I shouldn't laugh, but it was *very* funny. You were there, Lord Hawthorn," she appealed to him. "Wasn't it funny?"

A pause, in which the table warily weighed the question of whether Lord Hawthorn was familiar with the concept of humour. Not many people here had seen the way his mouth deepened when arguing with Alan Ross, or heard the insouciant bark of a laugh when he was surprised by something.

Maud smiled into her water glass.

"I was not expecting to see a reproduction of the Roman arena, man against beast, on board the White Star Line's pride and joy," said his lordship. "I shall suggest they add it to the advertising copy."

"I hope none of the animals were hurt," Maud said.

"Not at all, thankfully," said Helen. "They had a wonderful time of it. I think they were glad to stretch their legs. It is hard on them to be cooped up in that horrid place for days. But poor Mr. Hewitt! Papa's promised him a week's holiday once everything is set up in England, for all his work getting them rounded up and back down into the hold."

Maud seized the opportunity to ask after Dorian. She couldn't ask outright about the cage—*damn* Chapman, anyway—but Helen readily admitted that Dorian had been excessively talkative at all hours, in their parlour suite, and she'd ended up giving him to Hewitt to be put with the other birds in the aviary.

Violet's eyes met Maud's. Mr. Hewitt. That was somewhere for them to begin tomorrow.

"You'll bore everyone, Helen," said Rose, as Helen's talk veered further into a list of interesting facts about parrots.

"I'm not bored," said Miss Yu.

"Nor am I," said Violet.

Helen beamed around the table. "You know, this *is* what I imagine university would be like. Don't you, Maud? A lot of people who find a lot of things interesting and don't mind talking about them. Miss Cutler is going to study at Cambridge," she told Rose.

"How industrious of you," said Rose. "I suppose your parents encouraged you to attend a good school?"

"We were at the Emma Willard School," put in Helen. "The teachers there were ever so strict, but *lovely*. My science mistress let me dissect as many frogs as I wished."

Miss Yu, cutlery pausing, directed an ambiguous expression down at her pork cutlet.

Maud smiled at Helen and told her about Miss Lyons, who'd been the last of her governesses, and the first not to care that Maud was dreadful at keeping her mind on things.

"She was the one who suggested I learn to play chess. I told her she'd be fighting a losing battle, but she insisted that an agile mind could see all the possibilities of a game."

Nobody had ever called Maud *agile* before that. The other governesses had preferred words like *flighty* or *wilful*.

"My brother enjoys chess." The serious Miss Yu smiled at Maud. Her hair was like black silk, setting off the glow of opals at her ears. "Have you ever played mahjong, Miss Cutler? He says it requires a similar sort of mind."

Maud had not. Over the rest of the meat course and well into the sweet, Miss Yu explained the basics of the game. Rose Bernard sighed and swirled her spoon in the cream atop her ginger syllabub. Helen ate her own dessert and then absently ate half her sister's, and looked transported with delight to be conversing on serious topics with other girls.

It was an enjoyable meal. Maud almost managed to forget, for whole minutes at a time, that they were sitting at a table with the magician who had killed Mrs. Navenby—and who would no doubt spend what little time remained of the voyage doing his very best to get his hands back on the necklace that lay, prickling her from time to time with the chill of a ghost's disapproval, over Maud's heart.

21

Violet's relatives seemed to have taken the hint that she felt more friendly towards them if they didn't try to impose their company on her. They hadn't attempted to eat with her all day, nor did they ask her to accompany them to any of the musical or theatrical performances being held that evening.

There might be other transatlantic voyages, in the future, when Violet could be a normal passenger. Take advantage of the normal entertainment.

For now, she'd chosen her diversion on the first day. Yes, it had proven both more complicated and more perilous than she'd expected. But so far—*so far,* she thought, hand creeping to the nape of her neck—she didn't regret it. And being part of Maud's quest meant retiring to Lord Hawthorn's suite after dinner, to create a plan of attack for the next day.

Maud's army kept growing. Ross, for all his protestations of being in it only for the money, had clearly found himself hooked by fascination. If you counted Mrs. Navenby, there were five of them now.

Mrs. Navenby was determined to be counted. As soon as they all sat down around the low table in Hawthorn's sitting room, Maud's spine straightened and the old woman's sharp tones emerged from her mouth.

"*Finally. There is clearly more going on than I anticipated. What on earth is Sera Hope doing aboard this ship?*"

They all exchanged glances.

"Who?" Violet asked.

"*In the dining room. I've not seen her for half our lives, but*

I'd know her anywhere. Sera—Seraphina. Hope. Though she goes by Vaughn since marrying that ghastly man."

"Mrs. Vaughn!" That was Maud. "She's the one whose cabin I broke into, when we were looking for the silver. She thought I was the jewel thief, because I ran off after Morris."

"Was she part of this business with the Last Contract as well?" asked Violet. "Does she have part of it?"

"Yes, and no," said Mrs. Navenby. *"Seraphina was a member of the Forsythia Club, but she didn't take a piece of the contract to hide."*

Ross whistled. "Do the people after this contract *know* that?"

"Stop." Hawthorn held up a hand. "There are too many things in the pot here, and I'm afraid I have more to throw in myself. One thing at a time. Mrs. Navenby—do you mean to tell us that someone *else* who knows about the existence of the Last Contract has chosen to travel from New York to England, aboard a ship that happens to contain both yourself and men who are trying to acquire the contract for themselves?"

"Yes. I didn't know Sera was in America at all."

"Sounds too fishy for coincidence," said Ross.

"Miss Blyth. If I remember correctly, from the somewhat disorganised tale of your efforts thus far, you broke into Sera's cabin because you thought someone might have hidden my stolen silver there?"

"Because I saw it there," said Ross. "Hairbrush and mirror, matching set. One of the things Miss B told me to look out for."

"A set," Mrs. Navenby said slowly. *"Yes. Flora gave one to each of us."*

"Is she in danger as well?" said Maud. "Should she be— Oh!" A hand flew to her mouth. "Morris was coming towards her room! When I was leaving it! Do you think he intended to threaten her next?"

"Sera wouldn't be able to tell anyone where the pieces are, or

what they are. We all agreed to keep that secret even from one another. It was the safest course."

"Ross is right," said Hawthorn. "It's too neat to be coincidence. Two victims conveniently trapped on the same voyage, unbeknownst to each other? How would Chapman have masterminded that?"

Violet forced herself to think. It was an unlikely scenario, but what was the alternative?

One victim. *Three* enemies.

"Maud," she said. "Morris was coming towards you, when you were leaving the cabin? But you ran into Mrs. Vaughn herself first?"

Maud began to say something, was clearly interrupted by Mrs. Navenby attempting the same, and an inelegant cough-squawk emerged instead.

"What if they were *both* coming to investigate?" said Violet. "You thought Chapman might have a rune-signal in his cabin, Maud—I mean, ma'am." There was something undeniably ma'amish about Mrs. Navenby. One imagined her at the front of a lecture hall or hammering out instructions to a palace full of staff. "Mrs. Vaughn could have one too."

"*It's . . . possible,*" said Mrs. Navenby. "*Though I would have sworn any oath, and put all my blood into the cradle, that no member of the Forsythia Club would ever turn on the others.*"

"Entertain the hypothetical," said Hawthorn. "You are not to go racing up to this woman to warn her. *Maud.*"

"And if she ends up dead as well?" Maud demanded. "And we could have prevented it? Even if she doesn't know what the items are, she'll know who, and—" Her hand went to her bodice, over the locket. "Mrs. Navenby. I know you didn't want to tell me any more than you had to, in New York, but surely now . . ."

"*No,*" said Hawthorn. "Ma'am, you will not tell us anything. Not if you think there's a chance it's still secret from the people on the other side of this, and you don't want them to know it."

"I can keep a secret," said Maud, indignant. "I've kept magic secret, haven't I?"

"Can you keep your mouth shut under torture?" Hawthorn growled. He really had begun to relax, to soften in small ways, when in this room with these people over the last few days. Exactly how much was only obvious now, when he stood: the Baron Hawthorn, taller and broader and stronger than anyone else.

Violet had a sudden memory of Chapman yelling when Hawthorn struck him with the cane. Another of Hawthorn holding a gun on Ross.

She summoned her most cut-glass accent to cover the quake of her nerves. "Sit down, Hawthorn. There's no need to go that far."

"You said you had something to throw into the pot." Maud looked up at Hawthorn like a vole to a hawk, pale and unflinching. "That man Morris *recognised* you, my lord."

Hawthorn remained standing. Violet was within a hairsbreadth of doing the same, her wariness rapidly dissolving into her usual irritation with overbearing men, but Ross got there first. The writer intercepted himself within two feet of Hawthorn, and glared.

"I'm sure we're all impressed that your parents could afford to feed you mash *and* oats as a child, your lordship, but there's no need to be such a bloody peacock about it. Pretend you're a civilised gentleman, sit down, and answer Miss Blyth's question."

Hawthorn's hands clenched as if wishing for his cane. Ross's clenched too. He had the loose, grim stance of someone who'd learned to fight for survival, not in a boxing saloon, and Violet didn't know which of them she'd back in an outright brawl.

When Hawthorn sat, abruptly, Ross looked as surprised at his own success as Violet felt.

"I recognised him," said Hawthorn. "And yes—vice versa, I expect. Morris works for the Bastokes. My mother's family.

And if you've any sense at all, Maud, you'll abandon this entire contract business now. I wasn't flinging the word *torture*
around because I enjoy the sound of it. Must I remind you
about the curse these people laid on your brother?"

Maud flinched and lost the rest of her colour.

"Your family," said Violet.

"My uncle. And my cousin George, if we're putting money
on people likely to be involved in something like this." Hawthorn assumed his usual position of arrogant lounging through
what looked like sheer bloody-minded effort. "Drop this, Maud.
George isn't Walter Courcey. Courcey's a simple bully. He likes
to find weaknesses, for the fun of watching people hurt."

"I don't—" started Maud, but Hawthorn was still going.

"George will do anything, to anyone, and feel no remorse
if he truly believes it's necessary. And for those parts that are
too distasteful for him to dirty his hands . . . he has Morris.
That man is absolutely loyal to the Bastokes, and I'd wager a
lot smarter than he looks." The lines of Hawthorn's face had
deepened. "I regret what happened to you, Mrs. Navenby. But
Miss Blyth is not a magician, and this is too dangerous for
something that isn't her business."

"It is," snapped Maud. "The Last Contract is my business—
and if not, Mrs. Navenby certainly is, and the contract is hers.
QED."

"This isn't some facile game of mathematics! This is your
safety, Maud Blyth, and if you haven't the wits to guard it
yourself, then others will have to do it for you."

Violet winced. Ross had a hand buried in his curls as he
watched Maud and Hawthorn like a man observing a cock-
fight and regretting his stake.

"*Now* you decide to be responsible for me?" Maud shot back.

"Devil take it, girl, will you *listen*? I know what George is
capable of. His—"

Hawthorn choked. On his own frustration, Violet thought
at first. His hand went to his mouth; his brow creased.

"Damn, *damn*," he said, muffled as if around a mouthful of cotton.

"Hawthorn," said Violet, with mounting horror. She crossed to where he sat and laid an assessing hand along his jaw. "Tell me what George is capable of. I know"—when his lips pressed together—"but *try*."

This time the sound was unmistakably one of pain. When Hawthorn's mouth cracked open again, sucking in air, Violet almost expected blood to spill from the corners of his lips. Instead she saw the angry glow of a symbol on his tongue.

"What is it?" asked Maud. "What's wrong?"

"That," said Violet, "is a secret-bind."

She'd never seen one. She'd gleefully passed on to her sisters the tales of magicians who'd let slip the existence of magic when they shouldn't, and the unfortunate unbusheled who'd had their tongues bound to keep it secret.

Hawthorn removed her hand from his face. His eyes were overbright. Violet's own mouth was dry with horrible sympathy. She should fetch him a drink of water, and not push.

She was going to push.

"All right," she said. "No specific details. We'll try yes or no."

"*Violet.*" Maud sounded as disapproving as Aunt Caroline.

"Is this . . . does this have something to do with what happened to Lady Elsie?"

Hawthorn's nod was convulsive. His hands were fists on his thighs. He was silent now; he'd brought his will to bear on his own pain.

"Did your cousin George place this secret-bind on you?"

A swift shake of the head.

"But George was involved."

He managed only the aborted beginning of another nod, and less than half a word, and then a kettle-steam whine of escaping breath as the bind obviously flared again.

"Stop it," said Maud. "*Stop.*"

Wishing him attacked by seagulls and rats was one thing. Having to witness Hawthorn wrestling with this agonising mark of his own history was not enjoyable in the slightest. Violet returned to her own seat and twisted her rings on her thumbs until his breathing sounded normal again. She found herself instead watching *Ross* watching Hawthorn, as if he were a mirrored shield in which to make eye contact with the Gorgon and not be turned to stone.

Ross said, "And that's what you'd do to *me,* if I blab about magic to anyone?"

"Yes," said Hawthorn. Only a hint of rawness remained in his voice. "With no hesitation at all."

Ross's lip curled.

"This is nothing," said Hawthorn. "I've seen Morris cripple a parlourmaid's hand from the inside, leaving no marks, because my aunt accused her of stealing. She couldn't cradle for days. And the way she screamed . . ."

He stopped, looking at Maud.

Tears were streaming down Maud's face, overflowing, dripping to dark dots on her bodice. She hadn't made a sound.

Violet held on to the edge of her own chair, fighting the urge to put an arm around Maud's shoulders and let her sob into Violet's chest. It was a new feeling. She'd always hated it when people cried at her. She never knew what to do when her sisters cried, except tell a story or do an impression. Make them laugh. Make them stop.

"I can't give up," said Maud. "I can't. They killed her, and I let it happen."

"Don't flatter yourself with undue influence," said Hawthorn, apparently even worse at comforting than Violet.

"*I have to agree,*" said Mrs. Navenby. But Maud shook herself back into control, wiped her face, and ignored them both.

"I'm on the *Lyric* to protect the Last Contract and to prevent these people from using it. And for Robin."

"Maud," Violet said. "Why is it so important that *you* be the one to—"

"*Because he's all I have, and I have no other way to repay him.*"

It was her, not the ghost—even so, it was the cry of a girl younger and more bewildered than Maud had ever seemed. It dug claws into Violet's ribs. Even Maud seemed shaken by what had emerged from her mouth.

She recovered though. Her voice shook only a little when she added, "So *stop* trying to scare me off."

"Why?" said Hawthorn. "It's working."

Maud glared, incredulous from red-rimmed eyes.

"Of course it's working," Violet said. "She's terrified. But can't you see it's just making her more stubborn?"

"Violet, I can have this fight myself!" said Maud. "I don't need you to do it for me. Or *you*," she added, clutching the locket.

Tension sang in the air: the solid, deafening stuff that got in the mouth and nose and tightened the airways. Violet knew this feeling. An inch in the wrong direction, a note out of tune, and everything could fall apart.

Hawthorn stood and went to the credenza. He returned with the chess set, which he laid down on the table. A piece folded in each hand, he held his fists out to Maud, who stared at him with eyes washed green as gardens after rain. Violet's chest ached.

"If you're determined to play games with your life, then we'll play," said Hawthorn. "If I win, you will hand all the damned silver to me and leave this whole business alone for the rest of the voyage."

"No," said Maud at once. "If you win, I will release *you* from helping and not bother you again. But my choices are still mine."

"It's not the worst idea, Maud," said Violet. "That man Morris seemed reluctant to hurt Hawthorn. Family loyalty might shield him. It won't shield you."

Maud tapped one of Hawthorn's hands and he opened it. White.

"Christ Almighty," muttered Ross. He smothered a yawn and exchanged a look with Violet. "Game of rummy?"

"No. I'm going to enforce timing on this game. We're not sitting here another hour because both of you are too stubborn for sense. Hawthorn, give me your watch."

The chess game was fast and irritable. Hawthorn had a beautiful case for his wristwatch that turned it into a small standing clock, silver with blue enamel and white nacre curling on either side of the watch face. Violet charmed it to flash a red light at ten-second intervals, and appropriated Hawthorn's cane so that she could enforce the time limit with prods when necessary.

She made no attempt to follow the game. Her hand stole again to the back of her neck. No itching; the rune had been quiescent that day. Perhaps it had been meant to serve some sinister purpose that was useless now that everything was out in the open, with everyone's faces revealed. Perhaps it was gone.

Violet nearly laughed at herself. She didn't believe that. The world didn't arrange itself in one's favour.

Ross played a complicated solitaire on the floor. Hawthorn didn't look up from the board. Neither did Maud; her foot tapped beneath the table, but the rest of her was entirely attuned to the game.

Perhaps a third of the chess pieces had been captured and removed when Hawthorn leaned back in his chair and finally looked his opponent in the face.

"Your brother would tell you to stop," he said.

"Possibly," Maud agreed. "But in my position, he'd keep going, and that's what I'm going to do."

The clock flashed. Hawthorn didn't make his move. It flashed again.

Violet moved to poke his lordship's leg; his hand caught the end of the stick without his eyes moving from Maud.

With his other hand, he reached out and toppled his king.

"Very well. I'll remain under your command." He inclined his head, mocking.

"Because I was going to win?" Maud frowned at the board.

"No; I was going to beat you in ten more moves."

That seemed to be all the explanation they'd get. Hawthorn didn't extend a chess metaphor in any direction. He wasn't smiling, but he was as close to it as Violet had seen when he wasn't being cruel to someone.

Maud extended her hand over the board and they shook.

"I have to tell you something," blurted Maud.

It was only three sentences into the explanation that Violet remembered: *Hawthorn* still didn't know about the notebook of Robin Blyth's visions. Maud had simply . . . kept on not-telling him.

She told him now. After the handshake, Violet noted admiringly.

Hawthorn's expression feinted in the direction of anger as Maud explained; mostly he just looked resigned, as though Maud were a stage magician's black satin hat, and he was long past being surprised at any of the bright silks or live pigeons that might emerge from it. He glanced at the chess board. He nearly touched his mouth, then made a fist of his hand and lowered it.

"Hell," he said finally. "I can't believe I didn't ask why Edwin Courcey warned you about me in the first place."

"You were being steamrollered by charm, that first night," said Violet dryly. "I know the feeling."

Maud made a face, but it wasn't very apologetic.

"Anything about me in that notebook, then?" asked Ross. He'd gathered the playing cards, and they flew between his palms in a fluid shuffle. He didn't look at all bothered by the idea of his participation being foretold. Violet's mind still shied away when she thought of that sketch of her own face.

"Nothing that I can recognise," said Maud. "Mr. Ross, *you* at least should bow out of this now, before they know you're

involved. You earned your salary in full today, fetching Hawthorn to get us out of that mess."

"And how'd I feel if *you* died and I could prevent it? No, in
for a penny, Miss B. You might need my help to get that bowl
of yours back."

So there was a scrap of conscience lurking behind the cyn-
icism. Ross yawned again, and this time Hawthorn did the
same.

Maud's jaw set. "Yes. Finding the cage and water bowl is the
priority."

"*Without* letting Chapman and Morris know that we're
looking for it," added Violet.

"*And find out what Seraphina is doing on this ship,*" said
Mrs. Navenby.

"You can't break into her cabin again, if it might be rune-
warded," said Hawthorn.

"And if nothing else," said Violet, piling another card atop
this teetering castle of potential disaster, "the locket must stay
in Maud's possession. Or we lose Mrs. Navenby as a source of
information."

"Brilliant," said Ross. "So we've to make sure that they
think the locket is this contract piece, so they don't see you
chasing the *real* contract piece, but also make sure they don't
get their hands on the decoy either. You do like to make life
hard for yourselves."

Maud's brows drew together. "Two days," she said. "We'll
manage. One day at a time. *Now.*"

Strategy might not have come naturally to Maud, but she
threw herself into it anyway, with surprisingly energetic con-
tributions from Ross. Hawthorn mercilessly pointed out flaws
in their ideas; he sometimes rubbed his leg, sometimes his
mouth, and always stopped as soon as he caught himself doing
it. Violet caught herself copying his motions, unconsciously
adding them to her repertoire of gesture.

She wasn't one for plans either. She wondered how many

great, valiant defeats had begun with a charismatic leader telling his men that they would prevail despite the odds.

Why wasn't *she* bowing out? Was it only the threat of the rune on her neck? Was it still about staving off boredom? She'd gone into this with the understanding that it would cost her nothing, and it kept sprouting sly new costs like a circus side-alley.

On the first night aboard, Hawthorn had suggested Violet had no pride. Perhaps he was right. She hadn't thought she had much left after the stripping effect of her first year in the Bowery. After Jerry had left town with the last of it in his pockets.

Whatever it was that was keeping her in this game—pride, or something else—it was proving stubborn.

"I'm going to move my luggage into Mrs. Navenby's stateroom for the rest of the voyage," she told Maud. "It may be a tight fit, but I'm the only magician we have, and we need to keep you and the locket safe. And I assume Lord Hawthorn isn't volunteering to have you share his bed."

Hawthorn raised his eyebrows at her, but just said, "It's a reasonable idea."

Ross left first. God only knew what the gossip fountains of first class thought was happening in this cabin, after the last few evenings. Violet entertained a brief, wistful thought of the pantomime absurdity they'd had with the erotica.

Hawthorn stood over Maud as she pulled her gloves back on and smoothed out her wrap. Maud turned a wary face up to him.

"I'm sorry I kept Robin's visions from you," she said. "Truly. I only . . ."

Hawthorn waved that aside. "My sister . . ." He grimaced. "She was a little like you."

"Really?"

"I would have followed her anywhere," he said. "Into any battle."

And he opened the cabin door with an air that discouraged further questions.

Violet took Maud's hand and linked it through her arm as they made their way from Hawthorn's cabin to her own. Maud smiled at her again, and Violet smiled back. She knew what she wanted to do to erase the last traces of worry from Maud's face. And now that she'd had some time to recover, she had enough magic to do it.

22

Violet layered her usual locking-spell on Maud's stateroom door with a more serious warding that Mrs. Navenby insisted on teaching her. The spell looked spitefully hot as it formed in the cradle—Violet winced, as if her fingertips smarted—but Maud felt much safer once the orange glow of it had sunk into the door.

Violet then moved things aside in the larger room so that she could set out her own belongings. She'd packed only a single valise and intended to go back for the bandboxes and trunk tomorrow.

"Careful with that!" said Mrs. Navenby, as Violet cleared room on the dressing table.

Maud had had enough mediuming for one day. She wanted to be alone in her skin. She pulled the chain of the locket over her head and went into her smaller adjoining room to discard wrap and gloves and evening purse, and hid the locket in a corner of her trunk. When she emerged, Violet had wedged her valise in a space along the wall.

"I suppose I really should sleep in the same room as you." Maud went to Violet and experimented with the upturning of her eyes. "For safety."

"For safety." Violet lowered her face: a tease, not quite a kiss. Warmth sang in Maud's body. "I want to show you something."

"Good. Yes." Maud was so fond of the tantalising dip where Violet's waist became the top of Violet's buttocks. Her hand fitted there exactly. "You should show me whatever you wish."

Violet laughed. "Something magical."

"Oh!" She couldn't feel disappointed. There was so much magic in the world, hidden in crevices and kept necessarily secret. Every small piece Maud saw, every new thing she learned, was a wonder. And she wanted *all* of it. She wanted to open her mouth and drink down the sweet and the fizz and the cream and the bitter; to poke her fingers into all the crevices she was offered.

It was the same feeling she'd had in bed with Violet. And so it was easy to take her hands back, to seat herself on the bed's edge and look forward to what Violet might offer.

Violet opened a drawstring pouch and shook out a small collection of rings. She kept the wooden ones on her thumbs and added a pair of penny-bright ones to her middle fingers.

"Copper. It helps with replication clauses. Or it doesn't, if you ask those people who think metal's too dead for rings. I think they add something."

"And the wood?"

"Illusion." Violet's fingers were moving already. The cradle seemed a complicated one. Small sparks of every colour swam between Violet's hands. "This will be better without lights."

Switching off the electric lamp plunged the room into soft darkness. The sparks danced in variegated colours. The front of Violet's dress was a cathedral dappled by its own rose window.

"Ready?"

Maud grinned in the dark. "Yes!"

Violet gave a decided flick of both hands and the sparks soared to the ceiling, where they exploded.

Maud found herself gripping the bedcovers. A gasp punched out of her throat. Each spark was a blossoming, a dandelion puff grown at zoetrope speed into tendrils of glowing colour that drooped in the air and lingered before they faded.

Faded; and were replaced. More sparks became a shower of silver and gold mingling into molten raindrops. Colour rioted in the corners of the ceiling, and the plain wallpaper of the stateroom shone green and purple and blue and the fierce red of embers as each giddying of light had its turn.

"There were fireworks at the Exhibition, last year," said
Maud. She remembered standing in a crowd with Robin, having to shout to be heard above the *bang-bang* of the gunpowder. "These are better."

"The good thing about illusion is there's no noise and no
cloud of smoke dangling in the air at the end. Though we usually added a bit of both, in the Penumbra, to make things a
little *less* magical."

Maud wanted to turn this enormous ship and sail herself back
to New York and visit this theatre where Violet had worked. But
this show was intimate. This was for *her*, alone. Violet stretched
out her fingers, when the last fireworks faded and Maud lit the
lamp again—all grey-eyed sparkle, all delight at her audience's
praise.

"Want to see more?"

"*Yes.*"

The next illusion was one that, Violet said, took five magicians working in careful harmony when they built it in a theatre. One couldn't share power or share a mind's-eye image
with another person, but with exhaustive rehearsal they could
create the effect of something enormous growing in many
places at once.

And growing it was. Uneven young grass peeked up through
the ground, dotted with stray primroses and orange poppies. A
hedge of dogroses grew along the wall and in front of the door,
its leafy tangle a barrier between them and the outside world.
Like the warding charm, it settled a feeling of safety in Maud,
even though she knew it was illusion. The eyes clamoured to be
believed. The heart clamoured to believe them.

Honeysuckle crawled up the walls as if the ceiling held the
sun. Delicate white flowers unfurled their filigree, dense and
profuse, until the plant sat heavy with their imaginary weight.

Violet's lips were parted, her brow fierce with concentration.
Illusion complete, she seesawed the cradle. Her fingertips drew
close without touching, then drew away again to let the heels
of her hands close—a rhythmic motion like the squeeze of a

beating heart. *No worse than a handful of splinters when you're spinning an orchard from twigs,* Edwin said sometimes. And here it was being spun from nothing.

"I can almost smell the flowers and hear the bees," Maud said. "Would you have someone doing those, as well, in the theatre?"

Violet nodded.

"*How* did no one guess it was magic?"

"The rules are different inside a theatre," said Violet. "Fewer questions. More trust."

Maud's fingers passed through the honeysuckle like mist, and Violet laughed. "Ah. I should have known—illusions aren't your thing. *You* like to touch." Violet's mouth curled up at the side. "It's how you know the world."

Maud's breastbone burned. She pressed a hand over it as if she could push tears down into her chest and keep them from springing to her eyes. Silly, to be overwhelmed by the fact that Violet had seen that about her. She didn't know what to say.

"I think," Violet said slowly, "I can hold it—enough—" She paused the rock of her cradle, then dropped it. The garden of illusion around them faded only a little. "Ah, good. Finishing touches, then."

The finishing touch was on Violet herself. She cradled a new spell, moving more quickly and confidently, before lifting her cupped hands above her head and letting the illusion spill down. Her features were still her own, but transformed with a man's short haircut and a vanity-thin brown moustache. She wore trousers and a tweed sports jacket over a shirt, and looked for all the world like one of Robin's school friends attending a garden party.

"Oh, *very* good," said Maud.

"This one won't hold up to touch either," Violet warned, and held out her hand.

Maud walked through intangible grass and flowers to take Violet's hand. She grinned and executed a curtsy that they were half a century too modern for. "*Mr.* Debenham."

"Miss Blyth."

Maud didn't care that there was satin and gauze beneath her palm instead of tweed. She put her other hand in Violet's and was pulled into a close hold, and they danced with more verve than grace in the meagre space between the bed and the chairs. Violet smelled exactly of herself. In those grey eyes her pupils crept outwards like wine spilled onto a napkin every time Maud pressed tighter.

When Maud released Violet's hand and shoulder it was only to slide her hands up and around Violet's neck. The nape was still bare; no necklace tonight, and her hair dressed high, nothing to contradict the evidence of the illusion.

She pulled Violet down, and this time Violet bent all the way. The kiss was dreamy as the honeysuckle over their heads. Maud wanted to melt into the magic that surrounded her, and into Violet's lips. She wanted to thank Violet for the gift of this beautiful, playful magic, created just for Maud's pleasure, as if Maud had done anything to deserve it. She swept her tongue into Violet's mouth and Violet's hands on her waist tightened convulsively.

"Ah, hell, there it goes," Violet murmured.

They drew apart. The garden had vanished and Violet's costume with it.

"You broke my concentration," said Violet, mock-severely.

"You barely need illusion. You're still holding yourself like a man," said Maud. "Exactly like when you were playing the young man who rescued the nymph. It's extraordinary."

"It's part of music-hall." Violet stepped back and spread her hands. "The audience likes seeing men dressed as women and women dressed as men, so they can laugh over it. Of course, they don't laugh so merrily when faced with someone who prefers to live in what society thinks of as the wrong clothes *all* the time." She was watching Maud as if eager to shock her, but she was a few years too late for that.

"One of Mrs. Sinclair's friends from the Women's Society is a—lady, of that nature."

Miss Hannity had been a sailor, when she was young Mr. Hannity. She told jokes that made you laugh until you creaked.

Was Maud being told something, sidelong?

"Are you . . ." Maud didn't know how to shape the question. "Would you prefer . . . ?"

"Goodness, no. I got into that sort of act because I have the build for it. And the eye for mimicry." Violet tucked her hands into the pockets of invisible trousers and swaggered. "I saw the actress Maude Adams as Peter Pan soon after I arrived in New York. This woman was thirty-four years old and still playing a young boy, and when she was onstage you utterly believed it. No magic at all, just stagecraft."

"Show me that," said Maud, daring.

Violet gave a roguish wink, flung one arm up as if brandishing a sword, and attempted to spring into a wide-legged crouch.

Unfortunately, the skirts of her gown were neither wide nor illusory. Violet overbalanced and fell onto the rug with a yelp that quickly turned into her smoky chuckle.

"Well, that's punctured my performer's dignity." She sat up and looked musingly at her evening shoes where they emerged from the frilled gem of her skirts. "I told you the theatre's a good place for people who are different. Maude Adams is another woman who prefers the company of other women."

"How do you know?"

Maud expected another wink, but Violet blushed a sudden and complete scarlet. Maud felt a tug of wistful jealousy—but also relief to think that Violet, too, had once been young and inexperienced. And she wouldn't change anything that made Violet the person she was now.

"Thank you for showing me that. All of it." She helped Violet to her feet, and Violet kept hold of her hand. The circling of her thumb on the back of Maud's hand was deliberate. Maud's body went from relaxed with laughter to pulled taut with desire as if she were hooked up to the electric and fitted with a switch. It must have shown on her face; Violet laughed and kissed the angle of her jaw.

"You undress. I need to find where I threw a few items when I was packing."

A few minutes later Maud—down to only her chemise—set eyes on the items in question and said, "*Oh!*" She reached out and picked up a large rod with a flared base. Cool ceramic kissed her fingers.

"*Not* that one," said Violet, taking it back and lifting something more modestly slender. "For your first time you don't want anything bigger than this, and we'll warm you up first."

"One of the ladies in the pamphlets fit an empty wine bottle up there," said Maud. "She *did* wail a lot during the process, though."

Violet made a choking sound and, delightfully, flushed again. "Hawthorn was right. We have corrupted you beyond repair. I am confiscating your entire collection. Where is it? In here? I shall—"

Her laugh became a small scream as Maud grabbed her around the waist and hauled her over to the bed. Violet too had undressed, down to chemise and drawers, and had taken down her hair. It spilled out like sweet yellow wine around her head as she flopped onto her back. Maud still had the smaller phallus in her hand, but lost track of it when Violet got her hands beneath Maud's chemise and moved her fingers in what was unmistakably a tickle.

Maud writhed and grabbed at Violet's wrists, trying to force them away, while her own laughter became a steady "No no *no* no—" which leapt up and down the registers of her voice.

Violet pulled away. Maud bit her tongue and studied Violet's face, anxious, too breathless to explain.

Violet was studying her in return. "No?"

"Please. Don't do that."

"No, of course," said Violet easily, and the next stroke of her hand was firm enough not to tickle in the slightest.

Affection pooled in the cracks around Maud's heart. She

was inexperienced, yes. She still knew the value of feeling safe. She let her legs fall open and reached out to slip some of that yellow-wine hair between her fingers.

Violet seemed to take the reminder of Maud's academic knowledge as a challenge to prove her greater experience. She proceeded to *warm Maud up* with lips and hands and tongue. Maud tried to commit the best tricks to memory, but her scattered attention fell even further apart when Violet lifted her head from between Maud's legs, leaned her elbows on Maud's hips, and cradled a very quick spell that left her with that illusion of a moustache again.

Maud's stomach shook with silent giggles. Along with Violet's long hair, the thin moustache made her look like a painting from the court of the French Sun King. An exceedingly lewd painting.

"It won't feel like a real one would," said Violet, "but perhaps you could pretend."

"Oh, *sir.* Do be gentle. I am but an innocent maid."

Violet bit Maud's inner thigh, hard enough for a delicious sharpness to quiver straight to Maud's clit, and muttered something that sounded suspiciously like *the hell you are.* By the time they got around to searching the crumpled sheets for the phallus, Maud was slick and warm and there was a glorious ache like a clenched fist below her navel. Two of Violet's wet fingers still felt like a stretch, but a good one.

The phallus was a different sensation again.

"*Ow,*" said Maud. And then, "No, try again! I can do it."

Violet puffed some hair out of her face, her expression halfway between laughing and exasperated. "I know you're stubborn, Maud, but this isn't some sort of heroic trial that you have to overcome. You don't have to like everything, or even try everything."

Nothing made Maud more stubborn than being reminded that she *could* back down from something. She planted her heels farther apart on the sheets. Everything else that Violet had suggested had been enjoyable thus far.

"I can do it," she said again. "I want to *know*."

"You are going to be an absolute terror at university, my girl," said Violet.

Maud was suffused with fond warmth. Not even Robin had ever spoken of her future with such casual faith.

"All right," said Violet. "Breathe. That's it."

She stroked a hand over Maud's stomach, soothing and steadying, before lining up the phallus again. She leaned down and traced a slow circle with her tongue over Maud's collarbone where the chemise had been pulled askew, and with that and the steam-bath warmth of affection, the muscles between Maud's legs forgot to tense.

The pressure inside her went right past sharp and into something new. That hot ache twisted into acute pleasure. Maud's next breath caught like wool on brambles.

"*There* you are," said Violet.

"Oh, can you—" But Maud didn't need to do more than shift her hips and leave the sentence unfinished, because Violet knew exactly what she needed. She worked Maud's clit in between slow movements of the phallus. She was gentle, and then she wasn't, and Maud bit down on the side of her hand and closed her eyes, the muscles at the backs of her legs cramping as her release came charging out of the dark.

"There," she panted afterwards, triumphant. She had sleepy midsummer winds beneath her skin. She was an entire weather system in the shape of a girl. "Oh, that was *lovely*. Thank you."

"You're welcome," said Violet, setting the phallus aside with a fastidious face.

"I did so want to try that. I can see—some of what the fuss is about."

A pause. Violet's eyes narrowed. "You've made a list, haven't you? Off the back of Ross's pornography. A list of things you want to try."

"Yes." She drew Violet down to kiss her again. Violet's leg slid firm between her own and Violet's hair smelled like sweat and flowers, and her mouth was soft and clever, and Maud could *also* see why some ingenious person had come up with a device that would allow for the phallus to be separated from, well. The rest of a man.

"You've got that thoughtful look again," said Violet, drawing back. "Are you about to ask me something alarming?"

"No," said Maud, which *now* wasn't a lie.

Violet bit Maud's lower lip, a slow drag of teeth. Maud shivered and found a tiny keening sound in her throat.

"You're gorgeous when you come. Shall we try for another?"

Maud made a face in the negative. Everything down there was sensitive from Violet's prolonged ministrations; not as bad as her ticklish sides, but certainly at a point where further attempts would be more painful than enjoyable.

Besides: "It's *your* turn," she said, sitting up. "How would you like it?" She sounded like someone proffering tea— *Milk, madam? And how many sugars?*

Violet fetched the collection of bedroom aides again. "Would you like to choose for me?"

Maud searched Violet's face for clues as she ran her fingers over the collection, and was pleased with the flicker when she picked up her selection.

"I *am* going to need slick for that one," Violet said. "There's some petroleum jelly in the dresser. We can't all carry olive oil around in a decadent little bottle like his lordship."

Maud remembered Violet imbuing the golden-green oil that they'd used to reverse the sleeping charm on Ross. It hadn't occurred to her at the time to question why Hawthorn had such a thing in his cabin in the first place.

"Perhaps they supply it to the parlour suites, like the decanters," she said. "*All* the amenities."

The petroleum jelly warmed quickly on Maud's fingers as she leaned back against the head of the bed, with Violet sitting snug between her legs. It took some wriggling to get the angle correct, but Maud quickly found a rhythm of exploration, dragging her fingers through the folds of Violet's sex. With her other hand across Violet's middle, Violet's spine pressed gloriously against Maud's front, she could feel every tense of muscle and hitch of breath. Violet hissed, encouraging, when Maud bent her fingers and pressed inside. It was so *hot*.

Violet's heart beat against her fingertips. Maud paused to wonder at it.

She paused for long enough that Violet began to direct her: one finger at a time, faster than Maud would have thought comfortable, until Maud's wrist began to ache with the angle.

"Like this?" she ventured, when Violet shifted and pressed the phallus into her hand. "Er—"

Violet used Maud's splayed legs for support as she struggled upright. "No, you're right, the angle's no good. Here."

Here was Violet lying back with one of the pillows under her hips, Maud kneeling between her legs.

"Are—are you sure?" Maud adjusted her grip on the flared base. The erotic literature's laissez-faire attitude to being penetrated by pricks—glass, human, satyr, often *multiple*—took on rather a different cast once you'd felt with your own fingers the tightness of where the thing was meant to go.

Violet grinned, sharp as a needle. There were pink splotches on the side of her neck, and her hair was untidy and her stomach creased with effort. Maud wanted to look at her forever. "I'm sure."

Maud still took it slowly, a careful half inch at a time, and stopped at once when Violet made a high, frustrated sound. When she looked anxiously up, however, Violet had slashes of colour in her cheeks and her lips were parted.

"Are you *trying* to kill me?" Violet said, ragged. "Very well—full marks for erotic torture. I'm sure the Dark Duke would be proud."

Maud flushed. "Faster?"

"For the love of God, *yes*."

Maud took a deep breath and pushed. Watching the phallus disappear inside Violet made her own cunt clench in wistful sympathy. Her breath jolted out like a carriage over cobbles.

Violet was giving a steady stream of *yes, like that*. One of her legs bent in an aborted jerk, as if she wanted to wrap it around Maud's back.

"Should have packed—a bloody harness. *Gnh*. There's something for your list. I'd love to see that on you." Violet's head had been tipped back. Now her eyes met Maud's, hot and dark. "You could fuck me on my hands and knees. Goes deeper that way. *Shit*," as Maud, losing her coordination with the sheer confused rush of arousal, shoved the phallus harder and deeper than she'd meant to.

Violet was getting closer; Maud already knew enough to translate the rapid hitches of her breath and the shake of her knees. Maud gathered up her courage and shifted herself so that she could fasten her mouth just above where Violet was stretched around the phallus. An arpeggio thrill of the new, the forbidden, danced within her. All she could smell was Violet, and salt water.

"Shit, *shit*," snarled Violet, and quivered hard under Maud's tongue as her hips bucked and shook and kept shaking.

Maud pulled back and watched her, and had never felt hungrier or more accomplished in her life.

The brown hair was a mermaid tangle as Maud laid her legs across Violet's lap, her face close enough that Violet could have counted her freckles if the light were better. Maud's smile was fond and satisfied and shy. Violet gave her a smile in return and ignored the sensation of fingerprints being laid in the soft wax of her chest.

"I really think girls should be told that bodies can do this *before* it comes up in relation to wedding nights," said Maud.

"Perhaps you should give a lecture at that Women's Society of yours. A live reading from *Mysteries of the Red Dew*."

Maud laughed. "It's so much *fun*. I can see why people do rash, ill-advised things to have it. Not that I need another excuse to make rash decisions."

"Yes," Violet agreed. "It's fun."

"Have you ever . . ." Maud rolled her temple on the head of the bed, her gaze steady on Violet's face. "Have you ever had someone that you wanted for more than just fun?"

All of Violet's sleepy enjoyment screwed itself up like newspaper: something to stain the fingers, or start a fire. She felt her face change. She pushed Maud's legs back onto Maud's side of the bed and spoke before she could catch herself.

"If you'd like another lesson in what's proper to say after fucking someone, here it is. A question like *that* is what'll show you up for a naive virgin."

Silence. Maud went red.

Violet silently cursed herself and waited for the tears, but they didn't come.

"I *beg* your pardon," said Maud, each word a chip of polished stone. "I wasn't hurling myself at you. I was asking you a *question*, which is what *friends* do. To know one another better."

"You know more than enough of me to be getting on with."

"Oh—oh, that's—nonsense." Maud climbed right off the bed, as if there wasn't space on it for the both of them and her annoyance. "That's complete nonsense, Violet."

"I beg *your* pardon?" Part of Violet tried to protest that this was still salvageable, if they took the time to calm down, but the colder and angrier part had a hand on its shoulder: *I have this. Stay back, and stay safe.*

"Do you think I haven't *noticed*, that I don't know anything about you?"

"That's not true."

"You know what I'm afraid of, and who I love, and what I want to do with my life. You know about Robin, and my parents." Maud had been counting off on fingers; now she flung that hand down as if discarding a poorly cradled spell. "I don't know anything about your family. I don't know what you want to *do* in England, with all your new wealth. I don't know what you were running from in the first place that drove you all the way to America, and why you're so determined to create further scandal on the way back. I don't know anything *real*. You talk and talk and all you've given me is—stories. Sparkle."

The words caught in Violet's throat were: *You weren't supposed to notice.*

She'd been going about this wrong. She should have been feeding Maud scraps of herself, seducing her with sweet mouthfuls of truth into believing that they were growing close—she should have done the dance of intimacy, keeping herself in the lead and safe inches of space between them.

Instead she'd been so intent on withholding, so wary of the way Maud made her feel, that she'd let them become snarled together. She'd left gaps so large they were visible.

Maud went on, "And yet you were angry when *I* withheld things about Robin's visions. That's not fair."

"Withholding information *about me* is different from keeping private things that have nothing to do with *you*."

"You think I'm too young and silly. You think you can't trust me with anything important, but I promise, you *can*."

If she wanted to manipulate a protest out of Violet, she was going to be disappointed. Violet didn't fall for self-deprecation anymore. Especially not from Maud, who could wrap the world around her fingers like a cradling string.

Violet got out of the bed and joined her. Maud looked as though she'd dearly like to have more cabin space to retreat into, but didn't. There was only a bit of empty wall, and then a pile of Mrs. Navenby's hatboxes.

Violet said, "Do you know who keeps telling you that you can trust them, over and over again? People who are going to *screw you over*."

"Is . . . is that what you think of me?"

Some of the green-eyed anger cracked, showing a river of raw distress beneath. Violet sighed and tilted Maud's face up with two fingers.

All right. All right then. Like this.

"What do I think? I like you, Maud. I think you're beautiful, and I admire your daring, and God knows if it weren't for the rest of this mess then I'd keep you in bed for the entire voyage, seeing how many different ways I can make you cry out."

A cautious hint of a dimple began to struggle into existence in Maud's flushed face. Violet leaned down and kissed it, once. She kept her voice sweet and low.

"But I only met you three days ago. I don't owe you anything, just because you're fucking me in an act of pointless rebellion against your awful dead parents, or because you're on a guilt-driven magical crusade to make yourself feel better about failing your brother."

Maud made a wordless, strangled noise and *shoved*. It was clumsy, and Violet had been expecting something like it; she went with the push, taking two controlled steps back.

Maud's hand was at her mouth. There were the tears, standing stark and yet unfallen.

Violet's mouth curled into a smile that Cleopatra would have been proud of.

"You see?" she said. "That's what happens when you show your soft parts to people you barely know. Now—don't you want the sparkling, amusing Violet back?"

"*No*," bit out Maud. "Not if she's nothing but an *act*."

The lateness of the hour, the coolness of the air against her bare skin, and her own impatience with this bull-headed naiveté rocked Violet all at once. She looked at Maud: that impossible temptation of a figure, those eyes gone huge and cold as emeralds with hurt.

"A person *is* an act, Maud. A person is a theatre. You change the set dressing depending on the season. The real parts are the parts that aren't meant to be seen."

"I don't believe you. I think that's a pretty image, but a—a load of horse droppings."

Maud was wrong. Violet's tired mind groped for a quote or a speech that would sum up how wrong she was, and came up empty except for a fairy tale that she used to tell her sisters: a lost princess who made a friend for herself out of gathered bones and her own blood. The princess stopped every person who wanted to use a tollgate and gathered from them a single secret in payment, until she had a companion whole and entire.

That's what people are, Violet wanted to scream. *Blood and bones and secrets.*

"I'm tired of talking about this," she said. "Go to bed."

She turned away. She was surprised enough by Maud's hand gripping her arm that she didn't resist when Maud pulled her close and turned her. Violet's heel slipped off the edge of the rug and her head struck the wall, hard enough to sting.

"I don't *believe* you," Maud said again. It was a plea. She was trying to fix this, trying to reverse it, to make everything fun and laughter again; it was right there on her transparent, wet-eyed face. She held Violet's arm as if she wanted to get her fingers beneath Violet's skin. As if all of Violet were an illusion-mask that could be wrenched away.

Violet tried to move. Maud's grip tightened. Signals in Violet's body, anger and closeness and the pain at the back of her head, wove themselves tight to produce a stab of abrupt, violent desire like a thorn sinking into the palm.

She managed, "Then don't believe me. That doesn't make me wrong."

"Violet Debenham, you are *infuriating*—" and Violet wondered for a strange hot moment if she were about to be shaken, or if Maud intended to rake her prim little nails across Violet's face, but the surge of Maud against her was—was Maud's mouth finding hers in a crush of lips. Violet's head hit the wall again. That hurt, but she didn't care. It was a fierce boiling kettle of a kiss.

"I'm so *angry* with you," Maud panted, "and I want you *so much.*"

Violet could have told her that there was no need to sound so bewildered—that this was a vastly common problem, in fact—but she didn't have a chance to reply. Maud had a proprietary hand in the hair behind Violet's neck, and she bit down on Violet's lip.

Violet was angry as well. Far too angry, now, to listen to

the tiny voice cautioning calm. She clenched a hand around the lace trim of Maud's chemise, where it dipped over the swell of her breasts, and yanked.

Buttons popped; fabric tore. The chemise still hung from Maud's shoulders, but it gaped open in front.

"*Oh,*" said Maud, indignant, and then made a noise that not even runes could represent, as Violet got a hand down between them and dragged her fingers demandingly through Maud's still-slick folds.

She was aware of what she was doing, and that it wasn't fair. Maud had refused to be pushed with one kind of words. Violet had reams of words, for every purpose, and now she would try another. Her free hand splayed firm over Maud's spine, keeping her in place. Maud rose onto her toes and writhed like a furious cat, but she wasn't pulling away.

"You want to know something true about me? What I *want*?" Violet twisted her fingers. "I want to work you open until I can fit my whole hand inside."

Maud choked. Her weight shifted as if her knees had actually buckled. Violet tasted satisfaction like cold wine.

"Perhaps I am rebelling," Maud managed. "Perhaps I—I like the idea that if my mother saw me right now, like *this,* she'd be horrified." She moved as she spoke, but she was only turning until her back was to Violet's front. She brought Violet's free hand to her chest, beneath the ruined chemise, and Violet took hold of what she was offered. "It's as good a reason as any."

Violet found a cry of denial in her mouth and swallowed it savagely. She'd fucked people herself on flimsier pretexts, and only sometimes regretted it. Guarding Maud's motives, Maud's heart, was none of Violet's damned business.

So Violet let the wall take most of their weight; Violet pressed that glorious breast in her hand and used the other to frig Maud in the way that she most liked it herself: hard and merciless and thorough.

This, too, was something true. If you showed someone your desires, then they could use them against you like any other soft and trembling underbelly. But if Violet didn't let any words out to trace the shape of what she was doing, perhaps she could slip it past the both of them.

Maud's second release was quieter. She soaked Violet's hand. She smelled of skin and sugar and some humid summer mixture of turned earth and wet city pavements. Her hair brushed Violet's neck as she pulled away.

Violet wiped her hand on her own chemise.

Maud's lower lip showed the dents of biting. She looked at Violet and Violet looked back. It was the place where a kiss would go: the reconciliation, the missing epilogue to a story.

Neither of them moved.

Violet tried to identify at least one of her current emotions. Somewhere in the mire was victory, and somewhere guilt, and somewhere was a black well of syrupy terror that she fastened a lid on, tight, as she breathed herself back into awareness of her heartbeat.

Fucking didn't fix anything. It never had. But it could shut people up for a while—even Maud Blyth.

Maud said, "I think I'll sleep in my own bed tonight after all. To protect the locket."

"Good idea," said Violet.

Neither of them moved.

Then Maud made a low, aggravated sound and practically stomped into the adjoining bedroom. Violet, changing into her own nightgown at last, could hear the angry slap of Maud's feet on the floor. When Maud emerged again she was brushing her hair with furious strokes, and she spoke as if continuing an argument she'd been having inside her head.

"You *knew* that would hurt me, what you said. You didn't care. Were you doing the same thing as Hawthorn and trying to scare me off?"

Violet shrugged.

"You're the one who pointed out it just made me more stubborn."

"Yes," said Violet. "I miscalculated."

Maud pointed the hairbrush at her like a gun. "It shouldn't be *about* calculation. I don't understand you. Aren't you worried that if you never give anyone anything real . . . you're going to end up entirely on your own? And I'm still talking about *friends*," she snapped.

"I don't need you to be worried!" Violet snapped back. "I am fine being alone. We don't all need to insert ourselves into other people's business to give our lives meaning."

Maud flinched. "You see? You're doing it again."

Violet wanted this to be done. She laid down each word with the diction she'd learned to toss innuendo to the highest row of the stalls. "Listen to me. I am happy not relying on anyone else. I won't be forced to be small. I won't be taken advantage of. I am *perfectly fine*."

With her long-sleeved nightgown and her hair brushed to gleaming waves, her face small and pale within it, Maud looked like a doll in a shop window. *A magical toy! Cries real tears!* thought Violet viciously.

"Do you know who I think keeps saying that they're fine? Over and over?" Maud's shoulders set. Some instinct in Violet pricked its ears and said: *You've miscalculated again.*

Maud said, "People who are desperately scared, and awfully sad, and too *small* to admit it."

And she turned around and left Violet in the larger room, with the larger bed, and with a feeling like a metal spike between her ribs.

23

There were two nights and just over two days remaining before they came into Southampton. Maud's liminal ship was proving double-edged. The contract piece had to be somewhere aboard, and their enemies couldn't disappear into the mist and the waves; but Maud's people were stuck aboard, too, in a place packed full of non-magicians. No magic could be done unless it was private or invisible.

Which was why Maud was currently attending the *Lyric*'s main entertainment and was *not* allowed to spend the day screaming into her pillows or lying despairingly in her bath until her fingers wrinkled.

A carnival had been erected on the sun deck. Bunting of coloured flags hung between anything vertical and anything hook-shaped, and small stalls sold food or crafts or games of chance. A man did sketches for a few shillings apiece. The string quartet played lively tunes, and the cellist scowled whenever the wind tried to fling his pegged sheet music off the stand.

It was extraordinarily gusty. Stall canvas bulged between securely fastened corners and the flags snapped and danced on their strings. Clouds scudded as if pursued, and the grey ocean fretted with foam atop every swell. Men and women paused to clutch at their hats or adjust the pins that held them in place, and at least one young girl had already burst into tears when her parasol leapt from her hands and spun away lost, high and quick as a kite.

It seemed the worst possible weather for the sport of badminton.

But a Tournament of Badminton had been on the posted schedule of attractions, and clearly nobody had engaged the initiative that would have been required to move it into one of the enclosed promenades. So Maud and Violet stood on the deck—close but not touching, prominently idle—and waited their turn.

Today, Lord Hawthorn would create a small diversion by going to the master-at-arms and asking to have a precious personal item transferred to the ship's safe. It could muddy the waters, at least. Help preserve the illusion that they did know what the cup was, and had it safe in their possession.

Ross, as the only one who could still act without being potentially watched by Chapman and Morris and anyone else on their side, had been charged with tracking down Dorian's water bowl.

Maud had wanted allies. She hadn't wanted covert troops who would do all the interesting things while she stood around and tried to keep her best yes-I-*am*-enjoying-the-party smile from slipping off her face. How did real military generals stand it without churning their nerves into restless butter?

And most generals probably weren't stuck with a bodyguard-companion in the form of someone they'd fucked, argued ferociously with, fucked *again,* and now existed with in a tense, insulted silence.

Not that Violet looked tense. Violet was performing the scandalous Miss Debenham as beautifully as ever. She flirted with any man who came close, from the swaggering groups of youths to the elderly men promenading with stately wives on their arms.

A sparsely bearded blond boy stopped in response to Violet's smiles and, after greeting them in accented English, regaled the two of them with an earnest, incomprehensible monologue in a language that sounded like German and French muddled together and spoken through silk. He pressed Violet's hand, practically clipped his heels as he bowed over it, and wandered off in the direction of the stall selling fruit punch.

"Goodness," murmured Violet, "do you think I just passed up the opportunity to become a tsarina?"

She turned to Maud, but Maud hadn't been ready for her cue to play along. The sparkling look in Violet's eyes, inviting her in on the joke, was quenched in the length of Maud's hesitation and died above Violet's smile, which remained pinned in place.

Maud, belatedly, forced herself to smile in return. She could do this. She wrenched together memories of every interminable evening she'd ever spent in a room full of too many people, watching Lady Blyth fool them all into believing that she was a warm-hearted fountain of charity and generosity and social conscience instead of a gorgeous, selfish creature who wore whatever face suited her at the time.

"*What*," said Mrs. Navenby, "*is the* matter *with you girls today?*"

Maud managed not to reach up to where the sunflower locket lay beneath her shirtwaist. Panic slid its hand into hers. She didn't know the rules of being a medium. The ghost inhabited her body, her mouth—could it *see her thoughts*?

No. Mrs. Navenby wasn't the sort to ask a question if she already knew the answer.

Maud and Violet exchanged a semi-truce of a look, containing their complete agreement that there were certain things not to be discussed in front of the necklace.

"We had a disagreement," said Maud.

"I'd say we're still having it, wouldn't you, Maud, my dear?"

To disagree would be to lie. Maud neither stuck out her tongue nor told Violet to go jump over the side. She turned to the current game of badminton and applauded a point instead. Rose Bernard and Diana Yu were demolishing their opposition: an elegant redheaded woman and a young man with an untidy moustache, who were far too busy gazing besottedly at each other to have their attention on the game. The word *honeymooners* seemed designed expressly for them.

Maud's lips tingled, but the ghost decided not to comment further on Maud and Violet's tension.

The hell with it. They couldn't afford to be at odds; there
was too much at stake. Both of them had made a mess of things
last night, but Violet was clearly too bloody-minded to admit
it and apologise. Maud would have to bend first. The very necessity of it made her more annoyed.

"I'm sorry," she said stiffly. "I'm sorry for—*telling* you what
you wanted and felt, instead of listening to you. I know how it
feels to have someone trample over you when you're trying to
tell them what you want. And yet . . . it seems I'm a naturally
trampling sort of person."

There was nothing in that to specify exactly what kind of argument was had, or how few items of clothing were being worn
during said argument. Violet gave her a startled look, as though
an apology were akin to Maud having handed her a small rabbit
or a spiked plant in a pot.

"Thank you," Violet said eventually.

"Your motivations have always been self-centred, and you've
never lied to me about that. You've never pretended to be in
this for anything more than intrigue and boredom."

Hmm. The apology had leapt a hedge and was racing off
cross-country. Before Maud could yanks on its reins, Violet narrowed her eyes.

"You have a real trick for beating people around the head
with the truth like it's an umbrella, did you know that?"

Maud nodded.

A matching apology failed to materialise. But frustration was
bleeding through Violet's mask now. Violet's cruelty last night
had hurt, yes. Maud was still certain that she preferred this
narrow-eyed, snappish, *honest* version of Violet Debenham.

"The most annoying thing," said Violet, low under the noise of
the wind and crowd, "is not actually the trampling. It's that you
act as though you occupy some enormous moral high ground,
when you're just as self-centred as I am. Britain's magicians don't
need you to be their champion. It's not *your* fight. And you're
going on about the misuse of power and acting all self-righteous,

but you're in this to prove yourself to your brother. And to have an adventure."

Heat gathered in Maud's nose. But—Violet might *not* be causing deliberate harm this time. Violet might be giving her the truth she wanted.

She let Violet's words settle into her, and breathed past their sharp corners.

"Can't it be both?" she said. "No—I do—I think you're right. About me. Robin's always been the unselfish one, he's always let me think only of what *I* want, and that's why . . . it's my turn to try, for him." Truth. No matter its awkward shape. "He's the only person who loves me. Maybe the only person who ever has."

Half of Violet's mouth pulled into a small, amused expression. "Oh, I absolutely refuse to believe that."

There. When the sparkle slipped there was a wall behind it, and when *that* slipped, there was this: a glimpse of a bright, funny, affectionate person who was just as real as the sharp-tongued Violet, only disguised more heavily. Maud was sure of it. It was tugging her in two directions like ropes at her wrists. Part of her still swam with horror that she was so attracted to someone who was what she'd always sworn to avoid: a two-faced, beautiful liar.

The opposite-tugging part of Maud knew she couldn't control how she felt; it wasn't in her nature. As a girl she'd been happy to give all of her love to her brother. Then delighted, when her last and best governess, Miss Lyons, arrived in her life, to find that she had a whole new armful of love to give, as though it had been waiting patiently under dustcloths in an attic somewhere. And she'd loved Liza Sinclair the same: each helping of love just as huge and easy as the last.

We've known each other three days, Violet had said. It was true. And they'd only just begun to learn where they kept the ugly corners of their personalities. Violet wanted Maud to stay at a safe distance. Maud should be worldly and carefree about it all.

But everyone Maud had loved, she'd loved at once, on instinct. Greedily. Violet Debenham was selfish and secretive
and difficult to know, and vibrant and artistic and bold, and
Maud was *allowed* to tumble into unwise love as long as she
stared clear-eyed at the finish line.

Six days on a ship wasn't nothing. So it might hurt at the
end. Maud would drink her fill for now.

"It's us," said Violet, stepping forward.

The Misses Yu and Bernard were taking a breather; they retreated in triumph to the refreshment stalls. Maud and Violet
were handed their racquets and installed behind the net, and a
pair of young men installed opposite them.

"Miss Cutler," said one of their opponents. "Miss Debenham."

The locket around Maud's neck shuddered and burned over
her ribs.

"Mr. Chapman." Violet tapped the racquet against her
palm. "What an unexpected pleasure. If you were hoping to
have things all your own way, I'm afraid we will disappoint
you."

Chapman smiled at them through the net. There was nothing sinister about him, even now, but Maud remembered the
way he'd sneered at Hawthorn and addressed Maud and Violet
as if they were foolish children. There was more than one way
to treat people like things.

"There's no place for chivalry in sports of this nature," he
said. "I intend to win. And I don't believe you'll pose me any
real difficulties in the end."

"I say," said his partner disapprovingly. "No need to get
bloodthirsty over a bit of fun, is there? Name's Simmons," he
added to Maud and Violet. "Didn't realise everyone else was
already acquainted."

Simmons had a bony face and the sort of lanky frame that
one mentally dressed in cricket whites. Maud dimpled at him
out of sheer gratitude that he didn't appear to be another horrible magician, and introduced herself and Violet.

The match seemed likely to fall in favour of the gentlemen, at first. Simmons's reach compensated for his awkwardness, and Chapman played with sharp focus. Violet was tall enough to lunge for tricky shots. Maud was the weakest player, and had to keep reminding herself that this was just something to pass the time and keep Chapman occupied and guessing, not a metaphor for their more figurative fight. She could lose a match to him. It wouldn't mean anything.

Maud *hated* losing.

So did Violet, it seemed. Poor Simmons looked steadily more discomfited at the violence with which Violet and Chapman attacked the shuttlecock.

The first game was at fifteen-twenty when Maud finally got off a rather good shot, scooped up from low and aimed squarely at the net's far corner. The shuttlecock sailed in a promising arc—and then gave a hiccup, as if poked midair with a finger, and hit the tape. It fell to the deck.

"Rotten luck—that was going to make it. Blast this wind." Simmons offered Maud an encouraging smile.

"Yes, indeed," said Chapman.

Violet retrieved the shuttlecock. When she handed it to Maud to serve, the feathers had bent with the force of her grip, and her smile was rigid as she directed it through the net at Chapman. She'd shifted her racquet grip to free up most of her fingers.

"Violet," hissed Maud, before Violet could move back to her own position.

"He's *cheating*," Violet hissed back.

"He's trying to make you cause a scene."

Violet laughed loudly, as if Maud had said something witty, and patted her on the arm. She kept her voice low. "I've used magic for eighteen of my twenty-three years, Maud. I can pull off a few spells in front of the unbusheled and leave them none the wiser."

The small flame of caution in Maud was roundly outvoted by the part of her that wanted to see Arthur Chapman *trampled,* and a girlish part that pointed out that Violet was seeking vengeance in a tournament on Maud's behalf, like a medieval knight.

Yet another part thought, startled: she's only four years older than I am.

Violet tucked the racquet under her arm and bent as if adjusting her bootlaces, her hands hidden by the curtain of her skirt.

"Are your fingers cramping, Miss Debenham? Perhaps you should forfeit the game."

"How thoughtful of you, Mr. Chapman," said Violet, honey-dripping. "Maud, my dear, why don't you serve?"

God only knew what any weather-watchers would have thought was going on in this corner of the deck, if they tried to track the effect of the wind. Shots went high, wide, too fast, and too slow. Violet and Chapman found any excuse to free their hands: dropping things, adjusting clothing, claiming that their fingers *were* cramping with the effort, and they'd just take a moment to stretch them. Even so: unless one knew what cradling was and how it looked, it would just appear to be a bafflingly chaotic match.

A game went to the ladies; a game to the gentlemen. The final game nearly went to twenty-all, but Maud found herself tripping over nothing as she lunged, and took a tumble that cost them the match. She climbed to her feet with a sigh.

"Well played," announced the steward in tones that suggested he wasn't sure it had been. "Victors to play on."

Maud exchanged an apologetic look with Simmons as they shook hands beneath the net. She offered her palm gamely to Chapman.

Pain like a cluster of needles sank deep into the flesh of her hand as he shook.

Maud bit her gasp in half as it emerged. She tried to pull away. Chapman's hand was tight around hers. What was she going to do, his taunting eyebrows asked—make a *scene*?

She felt cold all over when he released her. She linked her arm through Violet's before Violet could be subjected to anything

similar, and chattered inanely about the food stalls, tugging
Violet across the deck. Maud's skin didn't stop crawling until
she'd tugged off her glove and assured herself that her palm
was free of blood or black marks promising further pain. Just
a warning, then. Just to bring home the message that Chapman
had power and Maud did not.

Violet bought them cones of shaved ice with fruit syrups
ladled over. Maud stared at the large white block as the man
chipped away at it and thought, with a whirl of unreality, of
Mrs. Navenby's corpse.

Whatever was in the ice room wasn't Mrs. Navenby, really.
Mrs. Navenby was the voice and the anger and the will, haunting the sunflower locket and dwelling unseen within the animated creature that was Maud. She had no idea how to think
about a *soul*. She'd have to ask Edwin about it.

"Chapman's—oh, he's still in the tournament," she said, as
they stood with spoons and cones and watched the occasional
soar of white feathers and red rubber above the heads of the
intervening crowd.

"Yes, the bastard didn't think that one through," said Violet
with satisfaction. "He's stuck there for another match at least.
Unless he plays at rolling his ankle and limping off, but I'd say
he's the wrong sort of man to think of that. Wouldn't want to
look weak."

"*You* made me trip to lose the match. Not him."

Violet smiled beatifically. "I haven't been in a charm-flinging
quarrel since—" She closed her mouth. Looked down at her
ice. Then looked at Maud, with something between defiance
and caution.

Maud held her breath. Would she finally hear something
about Violet's family life? Much as she longed to hear about the
games that magical siblings might play, she'd have settled for
even an anecdote about playing badminton in the garden. Anything that was true.

But Violet said, abruptly, "You're scared of failure."

Maud lowered the spoonful of ice before it met her lips. "I'm

not afraid to lose a *badminton* match, Violet, and I can see it
was—"

"No, listen. You said that I know what you fear. I do. And I
can see that it makes things—unbalanced." Violet's chest rose
and fell, once. Decisive. "I'm scared of the sight of blood. I hate
it. Even a small cut makes me queasy, and in larger amounts . . ."
She made a face.

"Oh." It was a small offering, but it was something. Maud
managed not to blurt out *What about your monthlies?* "I suppose that's not uncommon."

"Why did I choose lemon? This looks like street-side snow
that someone's pissed in," said Violet, wandering New York–
ward in tone. She took a spoonful of her yellowish ice and
swallowed it pensively. "I didn't mind blood for most of my
life, really. But then I killed someone."

Maud fumbled her cone and it fell to the deck.

Rather unfortunately, she'd chosen raspberry syrup. The
resultant mess resembled, well, a gruesome amount of blood.

But Violet laughed and bought her another, then asked a
steward to send someone with a mop. She and Maud retreated
to a pair of deck chairs. Chapman would be able to watch them
all he wanted, once he was done with his game. Treats in hand,
they sat.

"*Killed someone?*" said Maud at once. The roof of her mouth
felt odd, like a sea cave throwing back echoes. Either it was
the numbing effect of the ice, or Mrs. Navenby had decided to
chime in with the exact same question.

Violet spooned a larger amount of lemon ice into her mouth.
Robin did that at meals when he didn't want to answer questions.
Maud waited, murmuring over the spattering of raspberry-blood
on the hem of her own skirt. "Don't even think about it," she
said, when Violet tried for a second spoonful. "Talk."

Violet talked. She told Maud about the night when a man had
followed her home from the theatre, in the cool small hours of
the night, and she'd slipped into an alley to get rid of him and
ended up trapped there when he drew a knife and came at her.

"The thing about a *real* knife," said Violet, "is you can use it to threaten people, to see if they'll back off. But a knife-spell's only purpose is to cut. I only had time to cradle one spell. If I'd gambled on an illusion, I'd have been helpless if he called my bluff. So." She looked as if she might be about to say something else, but swallowed, hard. Her eyes had gone distant, her cheeks ashen.

"It's all right," said Maud quickly. "You don't have to tell me the details. It sounds like it was awful."

"For a moment it felt *good*. Bright and good." Violet made a fist over her lower sternum. "Like the part of me that's just anger was finally allowed *out*, was allowed to *be*. And then I realised I had killed a man and he could have been anyone, and I didn't have my family and my birth to protect me. I was just another music-hall girl. Standing in a stinking alley, covered in blood." Her voice faltered. "I had to magic the stuff out of my clothes. It took half the night because my hands wouldn't stop shaking and ruining the cradles."

Her brittle tone hit Maud like the crack of a cane. This wasn't a penny dreadful or a grisly tale from the *Illustrated Police News*. This had actually happened, to the person sitting next to Maud right now. Violet had sounded so cheerful about her life in New York—among magician-artists! On the stage! Creating beautiful illusions and sleeping with whomever she pleased!

Sparkle. Distraction.

Maud had asked her for something true. She wasn't going to prove herself too naive to handle it.

"Anyhow. It's hardly a tragedy for the ages. I don't like blood. That's why."

Maud opened her mouth to thank Violet for telling her, then closed it. She'd been owed something. Violet had paid.

She finally ate more of her raspberry ice, letting the sweetness spill over her tongue. She kept eating, spoon after spoon, until she'd forced the question *And why are you so scared of telling the truth?* back down her throat.

"Will you tell me more about Lady Enid?" she asked instead. There: the midlands between intimate secrets and impersonal stories. "She sounded like a true character."

"She was." Violet smiled sidelong. "You should visit, once everything's sorted out with the estate, and I'll show you some of the musical instruments in the house. She and Mr. Taverner created a viola that produced taste-illusions, though they could never get it to do anything but apricots or Stilton."

That was the first time Violet had expressed any kind of desire to continue their friendship past the voyage. A warm sensation fuzzed between Maud's ribs.

Oh. That was the sensation of the ghost rising.

"Lady Enid? Taverner? Are you talking of Enid Blackwood?"

"That's right, ma'am," said Violet. "She was a cousin of mine. Did you know her?"

"Did? Was?" A ringing pause. *"Do you mean to tell me that Enid is deceased?"*

"Yes," said Violet slowly. "Lady Enid's death is the reason I'm on this ship."

"Enid Blackwood," said Mrs. Navenby, *"is—was—oh, damnation."* The word splintered in Maud's mouth. *"She was the third keeper of the Last Contract. Which means that all three of us are now dead."*

24

It was just Violet's luck that Chapman extricated himself from the badminton tournament as Maud and her phantom passenger were having a pair of clashing conniptions. Maud's face was contorted as if she'd taken a gulp of rotten milk.

Violet patted Maud on the back and glanced again at Chapman. He was leaning on the railing some way away, lighting a cigarette and casting them the occasional glance. Fine.

"All right?" she asked Maud.

"Yes," wheezed Maud. The rotten-milk expression had given way to one of guilty misery, as if Maud were now blaming herself not only for Mrs. Navenby's death but for the death of Lady Enid. Even though there wasn't the slightest thing she could have done to prevent—the *murder* of Violet's cousin?

Honestly, of the three of them, Violet had the most right to a conniption.

"*How did Enid die?*" Mrs. Navenby asked. "*And when?*"

"I don't know how," said Violet. "But I'm sure my inheritance would have been even more contested if there was a suspicion of foul play."

"*Your inheritance . . . ? Don't tell me that son of hers was off creating by-blows before he died. He was barely a grown man.*"

"Her father's brother was my great-grandfather, on my mother's side. As for *when*—it was in March. Nearly two months ago. There was some extensive argument over the will before Aunt Caroline and Clarence dispatched themselves to bring me back to England."

"*And Flora was killed in September last year.*"

"Yes," said Maud. "She was the first one they found, because of her great-nephew. Reginald."

"A long gap, and then two in close succession," said Violet. "Seems like someone finally learned how to track down these bits of silver."

"Part of the point of moving to America with my piece was that Flora was certain it would disrupt any attempt to do what we Forsythians had done in the first place, which was find them due to the effect that they have on British ley lines."

And now they were on an ocean. Liminal space, indeed.

"Perhaps they followed *me* to New York, and to Mrs. Navenby," said Maud in a small voice. "They may have known who I am all along."

"But you never had any contact with Lady Enid, and she died first. And your brother and Edwin never uncovered her name, in their investigations?"

Maud shook her head. Brightened a little. "And Chapman has called me Miss Cutler, every time."

"So these people—Chapman and Morris—came to America expressly to find you, Mrs. Navenby, just as Maud did." It was an obvious conclusion, but an unpleasant one. "Bastoke and his friends know about all of you. They got their hands on the full list."

"Four of us is hardly a list," said Mrs. Navenby, and stopped. *"Seraphina."*

"Mrs. Vaughn *must* be in danger too," said Maud.

"Or she's the one with the list," said Violet grimly. "It's too much of a coincidence that she's on board the same ship as yourself, ma'am."

"And the same ship as the heir to Lady Enid's estate," said Maud, wide-eyed.

"Estate?" said Mrs. Navenby sharply. *"Or fortune?"*

"Everything," said Violet. "As far as property goes, there's only Spinet House. James Taverner built and bought everything he had. If he left it all to his widow when he died, and they had no living children, then she could leave it to anyone she wanted."

"Which means," Maud said slowly, "that whatever and wherever the knife is, Violet . . . it's *yours* now."

Violet nearly asked *knife?* before she remembered. Coin, cup, knife. The Last Contract.

"If it hasn't been stolen already," she said.

"*Nobody would know how Enid disguised it*," said Mrs. Navenby. "*Not Sera, not even Flora or myself.*"

The back of Violet's neck itched, hard and sudden.

"Maud," she said urgently. "Adjust my collar."

Maud obeyed, and Violet heard her intake of breath. "It's glowing again. And—oh, blast. It fades so quickly."

Violet looked at Chapman, as the most likely suspect, but he had his hands full. An enterprising stallholder was wandering around with small cups of punch, and Chapman held one in his cigarette hand while fishing for coins in his pocket. Unless he could activate the rune without cradling, perhaps it was Morris. And they still had no bloody idea what it *did*. Violet felt no different.

Not quite correct. She felt overfull, overstimulated, which was unusual for her. The revelation about Lady Enid had been one stone too many dropped into the whirlpool of her feelings. Violet didn't want to be on this crowded deck full of wind and noise. She needed a few minutes to think.

"We'll let Hawthorn know about this at lunch," she said. "I still need to move the rest of my luggage to your cabin, Maud."

Maud passed her the cabin key. "I can see the Bernards. I'll stay on deck and keep Helen company until lunchtime."

"Promise you won't go approaching Mrs. Vaughn or doing anything else impulsive on your own."

"I'm not on my own," Maud said innocently, patting her hand over the centre of her chest.

"*Promise.*" Violet was not letting Maud wriggle out of this, no matter how adorable her dimples were. At least she could trust Maud to keep her word.

Maud sighed. "I promise."

Violet sent Chapman one more brilliant smile before leaving

the deck. She moved fast, taking a circuitous route; she did know how to lose a man who wanted to follow her. Most of the time.

She swallowed down an abrupt and lemon-sweet rise of bile, thinking again of that night when she'd realised that she'd miscounted alleys and entered a dead end. The footsteps behind her, heavy and confident. Moonlight kissing the exposed blade of the man's knife when she turned.

It had been dark. She hadn't seen clearly. The wound had been monstrous, neck to groin torn open like a black gash in the earth. Most of all she remembered the abrupt splash of hot liquid across her neck and chin, drenching her front and her gloves. And the smell. The smell woke her from sleep for a month after.

She'd given Maud her fear of blood because she'd never given it to anyone else. Thom and Claudette knew about the attack itself; nobody knew how blood had made her flinch ever since.

She'd given Maud her fear because it was the closest her craven tongue could come to apology. The previous night she'd lain in that four-poster bed aching with both the distance and the closeness of Maud, asleep in the next room. She hadn't slept much. She kept hearing Maud saying of Robin, *He's all I have,* and realising all over again that Maud Blyth was a desperately lonely girl.

Maud had reached out in friendship. And Violet had shrunk away, instead of letting Maud's knowing fingers sink past any of her illusion.

Back at her own cabin, Violet thought at first she'd opened the wrong door by mistake. Doors and drawers and her large trunk were open, with clothes scattered on the bed. Tasteless fizzing sherbet tingled the back of Violet's mouth when she inhaled: a sign of heavy magic recently performed in a small space.

And her cousin Clarence was rubbing his forehead, frowning down at a pile of Violet's clean stockings and petticoats.

When Violet entered the cabin, Clarence turned. Surprise

warred with guilt on his face, which reddened as he glanced around as if in search of some excuse.

"Where *is* it?" he burst out.

Normally Violet prided herself on having the right cutting comeback. Especially for someone like Clarence, whose entire manner begged to be verbally pruned. In that moment, however, fear wiped her clean of words.

Clarence? *Clarence* was part of this?

She'd sworn, after freezing like a prey creature when facing Morris and Chapman, that she wouldn't be caught without magic at her fingertips again. As she'd told Maud, she had been a magician for eighteen years. She had no idea how to cradle the priez-vous that the Coopers favoured, but there was more than one way to bind a man's hands.

The spell was a fierce, hungry indigo in Violet's cradle. Clarence said, "What the devil are you—" and it leapt across the space between them like a rope carved from the night sky and sailor-tossed from deck to dock.

Clarence made a dismayed noise and flung up his arms to shield his face. The magic wrapped around him lovingly: binding forearm to forearm, hand to hand, then looping down to wrap around his legs. Clarence's eyes bulged as he fell, managing to twist awkwardly and get himself onto the bed rather than the floor. He lay on his side. The spell dripped starlight and moved in gentle coils like snakes.

From time to time, the Penumbra's magicians pretended at the more mundane sort of stage magic. Violet and Inez had spent two seasons as magician's assistants: disappearing, reappearing, being sliced in half. Tying each other up. They'd developed this spell to look titillating on a body otherwise scantily adorned. Clarence, in his respectable brown walking-suit and tie, looked only silly.

Silly . . . helped. Violet released her breath.

"Take it off!" Clarence said.

"Stop whining." This spell wasn't tight enough to be painful, only secure.

Clarence subsided. "There's no need for this. I know it's not the thing to be going through your effects, Vi, but you wouldn't *show* us."

"Show you what?"

"The *letter.*"

Violet rubbed a hand over her eyes as if that would turn the world the right way up again.

"The letter?"

"From Lady Enid. You've been so darned secretive about it, there must be *something.*"

Violet had refused to show Aunt Caroline and Clarence the letter because it had annoyed them so much. And because it was *hers.* They were words meant for her.

Did this have nothing to do with the Last Contract at all?

"Why do you care? You know what it says. She left everything to me."

"Everything? She didn't mention anything in particular?"

"No, Clarence. There is no line in Lady Enid's letter specifically mentioning a giant pile of gold that she wants me to hand over to *you,* or—wait." Her skin prickled. "What do you mean, in particular?"

Clarence's eyes cut sideways. "I don't know. Any items of particular sentimental value."

"You *do* know. You *are* talking about the Last Contract. You're working with the people behind this conspiracy."

Clarence had the gall to look hurt. "It's not a *conspiracy.* They're just trying to recover stolen property."

"Is that what Chapman told you? Or are you working for that man back in England—Bastoke?"

"What? Who?" Clarence's brow furrowed.

Violet opened and closed her mouth. She dragged a chair out and sat down. She thrust out her legs, wide as her skirts allowed, a mannish pose that Aunt Caroline detested. One of them was coming at this from the wrong angle, or Clarence was lying, and Violet was an expert in lies. She drew her fingers together idly. Clarence's gaze followed them.

"Tell me how you got mixed up in this," she said.

"A chap from the Assembly. One of their advisors. He came calling one day, not long before we left England, and said he'd heard about Lady Enid's passing and—the circumstances of your inheritance, Vi."

"What was his name?"

Another pause. Another meaningful feint towards a cradle by Violet.

"Walter Courcey."

Edwin's brother. The one who'd tried to hunt down Edwin and Robin.

Clarence went on, more easily now he'd decided to speak. "He said that Lady Enid had stolen a powerful magical item and hidden it somewhere, and that for the good of the Empire it needs to be returned to the Assembly. He said he was trusting me with a special job." His face darkened at Violet's snort. "It's the Assembly, Violet. They work for the safety and betterment of all the magicians in Britain."

"Bollocks they do," said Violet. "So he trusted you to . . . what, exactly? Irritate me to death so that you could find this object yourself? Congratulations. You're doing a bang-up job."

"Stay close to you," said Clarence, with as much enthusiasm as one would use to say *clean the privies*. "Perhaps even . . ."

"Marry me, and make my inheritance yours. Which is what Aunt Caroline wants from you as well. How very neat."

"It didn't need to go that far. It would be enough to be on friendlier terms with you, so that I could bring people to visit the house. Let them search it properly. But Courcey said that Lady Enid had changed this object's appearance, so I needed to find out if she'd left any hints. If she'd told you if there was anything she particularly didn't want you to sell."

"And as far as you know, there's nobody else involved in this on board the *Lyric*?" Violet asked.

"Why would there be?"

Violet stared at him. She knew Clarence enough to have little faith in his intelligence or resourcefulness, and he'd never struck her as hungry for more magic than he already had. He was gullible enough to take a story of a villainous, thieving woman at face value, but his only real value to this conspiracy was his proximity to . . . Violet.

Whatever the knife is, it's yours now.

This wasn't a diversion that Violet had been tugged into by chance. This had been her fight all along—far more hers than Maud's, in fact. No wonder she played a recurring role in Robin Blyth's visions. She was in this up to her neck.

For a moment she entertained a vivid thought of discarding her finery and going down to third class. Becoming someone with a working-class accent and a different name. Stepping off the *Lyric* in Southampton and losing herself in the crowd. Not letting this touch her.

No. If she wanted to be Lady Enid's heir—if she wanted to be Lady Enid's revenge—then she had to be Violet Debenham, whose name was on the will. She had to be herself.

"I can't trust you, Clarence," she said finally.

"What does that mean?" His tone went high. He gave an experimental wriggle within the ropes. "Vi?"

Violet permitted herself one slow and evil smile, enjoyed Clarence's resultant whimper, and cradled a silence-spell. The only one she knew was actually a finicky one for altering the loudness of a sound while maintaining a pure tone. Lady Enid had taught it to Violet, long ago in one of those wonder-stuffed visits, showing her how it could be adjusted to imbue the materials of an instrument.

It gave Violet great pleasure to use the charm on Clarence.

She left the cabin to go to Maud's, where she negated the warding and let herself in with the key. Maud kept the truth-candle in plain view, sitting on a gold-rimmed lily-pad saucer. Violet pocketed it and left again, hurrying, struck with a niggle of worry that the rope-spell would wear off faster than she'd hoped.

She steeled herself and used a hatpin to prick Clarence's

finger for the blood—only a drop, she could manage it—and propped the lit candle awkwardly between rope coils. She negated the silence-spell but wasn't removing the other until she had her questions answered.

Had Clarence ever heard of the Last Contract? No.

Was he aware of anyone else on board who knew anything about Lady Enid's mysterious item? No.

Green flame on both. Violet extinguished it. She'd done some thinking, on her excursion to fetch the candle.

"Here's what will happen, Clarence. You're going to forget that this—oh, shush, I'm not going to use lethe-mint on you." Even if she wiped his memory of the past few hours, he'd remember his mission from Courcey and keep bothering her about it. "You will tell Walter Courcey that I'm just as contrary and horrible as you remember, and impossible to engage in civil conversation. And that you snuck a look at the letter and it contains only Lady Enid's hope that I use the money to live an enjoyable life. Which is true."

Clarence glared at her. Violet smiled.

"I am never going to marry you, Clarence," she informed him. "And I do not intend to let hordes of government magicians loose in Lady Enid's house. But if you don't tell Courcey that I know about his plan, then I'll give you and Aunt Caroline a gift. *Money*," she said, in the face of continued glaring.

That made Clarence lift his head from where it lay. Then he dropped it again. He looked more worried than Violet had expected, now that she'd offered him exactly what she'd spent the past week delightedly intending to withhold.

"I don't know if I could hide things from him, Vi. Courcey . . . he's powerful."

"And you're a toad," snapped Violet. "Do I have to secret-bind you?"

Clarence blanched. Violet struggled with her temper; with that part of her carved out of anger, which always wanted an excuse to lash out. At the same time, it was as if Maud were there in the room with her, laying a hand on her arm. The memory of Hawthorn choking around his own secret-bind flashed across her mind.

Damn it.

Violet's thoughts cleared. Even if Clarence told Walter Courcey that Violet had been asking questions about the Last Contract, it was no more than Chapman and Morris already knew.

"All right," Violet said. "Tell him everything. Tell him I've no idea what this bloody item is, but he and the Assembly have no right to come rummaging through my property."

She cradled a negation and the spell fell away. Clarence's glare returned as he climbed off the bed, rubbing at his wrists. The cleanness of his dislike was refreshing compared to Jerry's habit of laughing at Violet's anger and Maud's stubborn refusal to stop liking her, no matter what. Clarence had never fallen for Violet's stories. Clearly they were about the wrong things— about her, and not about *him*. He'd fallen right into the arms of a story painting him as an important agent on a secret mission.

For all that her cousin was an obnoxious parsnip of a man, Violet didn't want him hurt. Well. Not much.

"Go away now, Clarence."

"Do you know, Violet, you're going to end up exactly like Lady Enid," Clarence shot at her. "Alone with all your money, unable to tell if anyone truly likes you or is just toadying up to you because you're rich. You probably won't even *do* anything with it. Just sit on it like a dragon, feeling smug about the fact that you've ruined the family's reputation."

It landed hard on the bruise Maud had left. Violet *should* have fed him mint, should have branded his tongue, should have left him silenced forever. It wasn't as though anything Clarence said was improving the world; and she very much doubted that giving him money would improve anything either, except to reduce the whining.

"How wrong you are, Clarence," Violet said brightly. "I'll spend it all on scandalous parties, where I invite only the most dissolute and radical guests, and we all walk around in the nude. Though perhaps I *shall* have a pile of gold in the corner for me to lie on. What a helpful suggestion."

Clarence, purple-faced, had given up around the word *nude*. He slammed the cabin door as he left.

Violet arrived in the Café Marseille and joined Maud and Hawthorn for lunch. Maud was engrossed in telling Hawthorn what Mrs. Navenby had said about Lady Enid and Seraphina Vaughn.

At one point Hawthorn coughed into his napkin and indicated with his eyes: Ross had entered the café and was doing some lively notepad-wielding at a distant table. Maud had pointed out that meeting him in public, during daylight hours, was likely to attract less suspicion than sneaking off to meet in secret.

In between bites of her own ham and stealing forkfuls from Maud's eggy, curry-fragrant dish of spinach and minced lamb and almonds, Violet told them about Clarence.

"So, Walter Courcey still has his fingers in this." Hawthorn drawled the name as if scraping it from his shoe. "Damn. And you think Morris and Chapman know about Lady Enid as well, Violet, and your cousin doesn't know about *them*?"

"I don't know," said Violet. "Neither of them seemed much interested in *me*, during the first days aboard, but I suppose Mrs. Navenby and her contract piece were the more urgent issue. None of us can do anything about the knife until we're back in London." Though she remembered the rune again, with the now-familiar prickle of fear that ran all the way down her spine.

"And then I sat next to you at dinner on the first night." Maud made a rueful face. "It really must have looked as though we were in cahoots."

"We *are* in cahoots."

"Cahoots of circumstance," said Maud solemnly.

"Either way. It appears that I'm well and truly in this for self-interested reasons now."

Maud started to say something, then stopped. Not wanting to start up their argument again in front of Hawthorn, no doubt.

They ate and drank in silence for a while. The sweet course was blackberry pudding draped in a delicate milky custard. Tart berry melting on her tongue hurtled Violet back to a childhood summer, a dining table loud with girls talking over one another. She tried instantly to put the memory down and walk away from it.

Then she stopped, and forced herself to sit with it instead. Remembering her old life gave her the same off-balance sensation as Maud's aggressive openness, Maud's questing eyes, which reached past the polished versions of Violet and demanded whatever was beneath.

What *was* beneath? Nobody Violet recognised. A girl with a berry-purple tongue who'd grown too tall for yet another of Meg's old skirts. A girl full of stories, who didn't know *anything* about the world.

Nobody at the Penumbra had ever asked to meet that girl. It was one of the unspoken rules. You were allowed to reinvent yourself as many times as necessary. The *Lyric*, and Violet's flight back to England, was supposed to play by the same rules.

She hadn't anticipated Maud Blyth. She didn't know how anyone ever could.

Violet turned the maple ring on her thumb, drew her spoon through a streak of custard, and exhaled.

"My sister Alice was wild for blackberries," she said. "She would come home with an apron full of them as soon as the hedges were full."

"You don't talk about your sisters," Maud said after a cautious pause.

Violet glanced at Hawthorn. He looked back, blue eyes sardonic as ever. Nothing Violet could say would move him. And after the last few days she knew more than he'd ever wanted her to, she was sure, about Lady Elsie and his cousin Bastoke and a secret-bind that Hawthorn had been carrying for years.

This, too, felt like something owed.

"I don't talk about them because I abandoned them," she said.

The story sounded small and petty when she told it. She didn't have a well-crafted set of words with which to convey her father's ever-growing disappointment with each year that failed to deliver a son; her mother's fretful nature similarly worsening with time, until she could tighten the strings of Violet's body just by entering a room.

The expectation that the Debenham girls would all marry, as soon and as advantageously as possible, and live good, small lives and never learn more magic than was proper for a gentleman magician's daughter—never do anything that could cause society to talk—never seek change, or adventure, or wilder, larger magics.

She told them about Ellen, who never had much magic or care to use it, and didn't mind hiding it forever when she married an unmagical parson. Meg, who took their mother's worries to heart and married a rich and unpleasant man. Alice, the truly beautiful one and the family's hope, who to their mother's horror fell in passionate love with a poor soldier when she was barely seventeen. Julia, the bookish youngest, who swore steely-eyed she'd *never* marry.

And Violet, stuck between her sisters like a double set of parentheses. Too tall and too prone to talking back; too prone to putting fairy-tale dreams in her sisters' heads or doing devastating impressions of their suitors or using unladylike amounts of magic. Violet, the one who ran.

"You didn't tell me any of this, when you came to me asking to be ruined," said Hawthorn.

"Would you have cared?"

"No," he said calmly.

"I told myself I was making the others look like angels in comparison, by running off and turning myself into the most scandalous of all," said Violet. "But I am selfish. If I'd stayed, I could have been there for them, like your brother was for you."

"And married when you didn't want to?" said Maud.

"No, I—wait." Violet pointed a spoon at her. "Why are you on my side now?"

"It was a hard situation. I can see why you did what you did. And I still think it was awfully brave of you to even think of it."

"You're too good a person, Maud Blyth," said Violet, because she needed to tease. Teasing was easier. "There must be a catch."

"I'm not *naturally* good," said Maud. "I'm selfish too. And I know how to unravel someone with gossip. How to pick at anyone's faults. But I decided that there were enough people like that in our house already. I wanted to be different." There was a weariness behind her words. That wax-sensation gentled its fingers in Violet's chest again. "Perhaps I did shove myself in where it wasn't my business, wasn't my fight, *because* my parents wouldn't lift a finger for other people. Oh, they were great philanthropists. But they wouldn't give a beggar on the street a single penny if nobody was around to see them do it."

"And you would," said Violet. Of course Maud would. She'd probably start a petition on the spot for more shelter houses too.

"Mrs. Sinclair says you look at the world and decide you can live with it or decide you can't. And if you can't, you decide what you're prepared to do about it."

"Did you get that down, Mr. Ross," said Hawthorn, "or would you like her to repeat it?"

Ross stood at Maud's shoulder. "Moral philosophy doesn't go down well in the society papers."

"Whereas advertising is well known for it."

Ross looked down at Maud. "Reporting in, Miss B. Bad news, I'm afraid."

Maud's face fell. "You can't find it?"

"Your bird's been put in the larger cage with the others, so they didn't need the small cage anymore. I talked to that Mr. Hewitt, the keeper—he said he gave it to one of the first-class undercooks. Wasn't sure why the man wanted it but didn't mind getting it off his hands in exchange for a drink or two, once he'd checked Miss Helen didn't want the thing back."

"That's your idea of *bad* news?" said Violet. "You move fast."

Ross gave an impatient waggle of his notepad. Yes. Tracking down information wasn't new work to him. "That's as far as I managed. I'd have headed to the kitchens after that. But one of the thugs from security said the master-at-arms wanted to see me."

"About . . ." Maud lowered her voice. "The jewels?"

"I wouldn't be standing here if that was the case, would I? No, he wanted to point out that I'd been spending a *lot* of time in first class. And wasn't I meant to be speaking to *all* the passengers? And this wasn't a pleasure cruise for scribblers, young man—and a lot of similar folderol."

"I don't understand," said Maud.

"Means someone's seen me leaving *someone's* cabin late at night and made a complaint about the White Star Line's moral standards," said Ross bluntly, looking at Hawthorn. "His lordship's entertaining floozies. Everyone knows that."

Maud made a small choking sound.

"They can't ask *you* lot to leave the party when we're in the middle of the ocean. But they can disapprove of *me* being invited to partake."

"Perhaps they're envious," said Violet.

Ross shot her a startled look, then broke into a grin. She hadn't really been joking. Alanzo Rossi, with his curls and

coffee-dark eyes and insolent tongue, could have walked off
the pages of fantasy for plenty of rich women who watched
their driver bend over the hood of the motorcar to polish
it, and dreamed scalding little dreams in their cold marital
beds.

"That's as may be. Either way. I'm not to have my run of
first class after dark any longer."

"If someone's noticed enough to complain, then Morris
or Chapman might notice you next," said Hawthorn. "You
shouldn't meet with us again."

"Well, woe the fucking day." Ross flipped a showy page in
his notebook. "How *will* I live without the nightly orgies in his
lordship's suite?"

"Violet, that illusion you did, changing your hair, and . . ."
Maud gestured to her face. "Could you do one on someone
else?"

"Yes?"

"We'll make you a disguise," Maud said to Ross.

His eyebrows went up. "A magical one?"

"Partly. We'll get it to you before tonight, so you can attend
all the orgies you want." She raised her sunny smile to him.
"What's your cabin number?"

"I'm worried that Chapman seems to have given up on us," said
Violet. "And we haven't seen Morris since yesterday."

"Perhaps they've decided to wait until we're off the ship,"
said Maud dubiously.

"*You're right to worry about silence*," said Mrs. Navenby.
"*It's when you don't hear a peep out of children for an hour that
you discover they've dug a moat in your rhododendron patch
or decided to render the Bayeux Tapestry in wax crayon on the
wall.*"

They'd returned to Violet's cabin after lunch, packed up

some more of her belongings, and taken them to Maud's, where they faithfully checked the hairlock and Violet applied Mrs. Navenby's warding. The atmosphere between Maud and Violet had thawed. Violet swung between resentment and relief that all it had taken was the peeling-back of her sleeve to show the vulnerable course of her veins. Figuratively speaking.

"I wouldn't classify Chapman and Morris as children," said Violet now. "Clarence, possibly yes."

"You mentioned Lady Enid had a son," said Maud. "Do you have children, Mrs. Navenby? Goodness, I should have asked earlier. I shall have to telegraph *someone* that you're dead."

"No children of my own, but Ralph's sister in Boston had plenty, and we visited enough to witness the carnage. Now, what was your plan to disguise that young man, Miss Blyth? Do you fancy yourself a magician now?"

"No," said Maud. "But you know how it is when two ideas that have been living on different shelves in your head knock against each other, and suddenly there's a *new* idea there." She was flitting around the cabin again, touching things absently. Maud was thinking and so needed to move.

Violet did not need to move. Violet rather fancied a nap, if she was honest. She contented herself with sitting down.

"I can cast a costume illusion on anyone you like, Maud, but I've never done it unless they're in front of me, and it takes more concentration to sustain on someone else. We used them for quick changes and tricks. Nothing that needed to last on-stage. I could probably get Ross up here looking like someone else, but I'd need to be close to him the whole way, and that'd defeat the purpose."

"Yes," said Maud. A touch of the curving frame of a mirror; a touch of the bed-post. "You said you could anchor illusion to an object? Like the flowers on your hat?"

"I don't know if it'd work for something that large," Violet said. "Something that'd need to shift and move with a person."

"What if it was just the head?" said Maud. "New hair, new

face. Not an entire outfit. And what if I could show you a new way to anchor it, so it'd last? Mrs. Navenby can sew magic into clothes. You can create illusions to turn a person into someone else." Her fists lifted one after the other, then knocked together. Two ideas on a shelf.

"Your faith is touching," said Violet. "What do you mean, sew into clothes?"

"*The green coat, girl,*" said Mrs. Navenby. "*That's the easiest to explain.*"

Maud fetched a coat from one of the trunks. It was an old style, full-skirted and with puffed upper sleeves, made of a green fabric showing rub and wear at the cuffs and elbows. There were only so many times you could patch and repair something, even with magic.

Maud exposed the inside of the coat's collar. Instead of a tailor's mark there was a row of yellow embroidery, which looked for all the world like—

"Runes?"

"*A similar principle. This one's an imbuement for warmth. One imbues the thread with the spell, then the pattern anchors it to the garment. It can last for years, if you put enough power into both steps.*"

Violet traced the yellow characters. "Where did you learn this technique? It seems so useful, I'd have thought it would be passed down in families."

"*I invented it,*" said Mrs. Navenby carelessly. "*Now, you'll need thread. It works with cotton or silk, but the cradles for the imbuement differ for each.*"

It was a one-handed cradle. Something else that Violet had never seen. It made her hand cramp, the first time she tried it, but Mrs. Navenby had none of Hawthorn's patience with teaching—she just said, "*Practice,*" and then, "*To what, pray tell, were you thinking of attaching this spell? I'm not sure any of my shawls will suit that boy.*"

"I've an idea for that as well." Maud moved to the dresser.

"Mrs. Navenby, which of these would you say is your *least* favourite jewel?"

A minute later Maud left the cabin, leaving Violet to her work. Most two-handed cradles contained the sense of string within their patterns. Violet hadn't used string since she was twelve. She had enough power that most things fell out well enough, with a little practice.

She built a quick face-illusion of Thom, fast and comfortable as if she were backstage at the Penumbra. They'd done an absurd, risqué, vaguely Shakespearean show centred on identical twins, and one of Violet's roles had been to stroll across upstage wearing Thom's face a few moments after he'd dashed through the audience and vanished. It was easier to hold an illusion if it was a face you knew. She made a couple of tweaks— thicker eyebrows, a skin tone closer to Ross's olive—then let it dissolve into nothing.

She went back to practising the one-handed cradle that was Mrs. Navenby's imbuement clause, and was singing to her leather rings when Maud returned to the cabin.

"That's a lively tune," said Maud. "What is it?"

It was a Newfoundland shanty that Jerry had taught her, and which had a tendency to rise up and tangle in Violet's mind at inconvenient moments. Rings don't care *what* you sing to them, Claudette used to say, just that you make them feel welcome in the magic. Make them your own.

Violet had left a lot of her life behind in New York, sacrificed on the altar of her gullibility, but she refused to abandon music. She'd sing this song as many times as it took to lose the sting; to make it as much a part of herself as her rings.

Violet said none of that. Telling Maud the truth felt like a dangerous habit to have begun. Stories and secrets were surfacing in Violet like an ocean stirred up by a storm. She would let them out as she chose, and no sooner.

She said, "What have you got there?"

Maud proudly unfolded the bundle beneath her arm: a White Star Line steward's uniform of trousers and trimmed jacket.

"Bribery accomplished, I take it."

"Yes. I found Jamison—the one who blabbed on me to the master-at-arms after I was caught leaving Mrs. Vaughn's cabin. No doubt he thinks I *am* a jewel thief, now, but a thief who's happy to share her gains to keep him quiet. And I already knew he takes bribes."

"A productive friendship," said Violet dryly. "Now, how is this going to work?"

"*How's your embroidery?*" asked Mrs. Navenby.

"Poor. I've always used magic for mending, and not done anything decorative for years."

"Mine's not bad," said Maud. "Miss Lyons and I discovered that it helped me to do something with my hands when she was teaching me history and French."

"*It hardly matters how good yours is, girl—it won't do us a whit of good, because you've no magic.*"

"So the act of stitching is like the act of cradling?" asked Violet.

"*If it helps to think of it that way.*"

Violet decided on her maple ring on her left thumb and leather on the right: this was going to be illusion and imbuement mingled. Maud found the yellow cotton thread in Mrs. Navenby's sewing kit and cut off a long length of it, threaded through a needle and doubled. She held it taut, and Violet built her illusion of not-quite-Thom, finishing off with the one-handed imbuement clause. The illusion began to spin and then to thin out, until it was no more than a murky, dark length like ink smudged in the air. This flowed down and wrapped itself around the thread, back and forth several times, winding and tangling, tighter and tighter, sinking in.

When there was only yellow visible once more, Violet took the needle and thread from Maud and sat down to do her best to replicate the anchoring runes from the green coat. It didn't feel like cursing over her embroidery hoop in the parlour while Julia snuck pages of her book between rows of knitting and their mother spun catastrophes out of nothing. It felt like *power*. The spell steamed from the thread in small wisps of darkness that slipped between Violet's fingers.

Half of illusion work was holding the desired effect in your mind. Violet imagined that she was attaching a hood to the jacket collar. She could almost feel it taking shape, like velvet made of shadow.

Her rings warmed on her thumbs. She was humming the shanty again. Maud told her to add the words; Violet laughed and taught Maud the chorus. It had a rhythm of larger actions than this, of bending backs and straining arms. A sea pulse. Maud improvised a sweet alto harmony beneath Violet's melody.

"There," Violet said when she'd tied off the final knot and cut the ends. "Maud, will you do the honours?"

Maud donned the jacket with aplomb. The illusion swallowed her as soon as the top button was fastened. Thom's short brown hair, wide-set eyes, and broad, broken nose looked somewhat absurd atop Maud's skirts, but the illusion was crisp and detailed.

"That's perfect," said Maud, inspecting herself in the mirror. "Violet, you're an *artist*." She turned jerkily, as if to catch the illusion out. Hearing her voice emerging from Thom's mouth was even odder than hearing Mrs. Navenby's out of hers.

"It should hang even more neatly on Ross, given it's closer to his appearance," said Violet. "I'll sew a different face into a scarf for you, shall I?"

Maud unfastened the jacket and was herself again. She turned, delighted. "Will you?"

"We've been looking for a way to move around the ship without attracting suspicious eyes. Wouldn't it be useful to have a disguise like this in your bag or your pocket, so that you could slip it on in a quiet corner and emerge as someone new?"

"Oh, *yes*! And it would be so much more elegant than those horrid fog masks. You should make me a redhead with an enormous boil beside her nose," said Maud with relish. "A redhead called Imogen. As a girl I always wished my name was Imogen.

Could you make it now, so I can take this down to second class for Mr. Ross?"

"I haven't enough magic now." Violet felt threadbare and her stomach was growling for food. "But as soon as I can, yes. And don't worry about the delivery. I'll take care of that."

They transferred the pornography from the battered suitcase to a large bandbox, and the steward's uniform into the suitcase. Then Violet, suitcase in hand, went to knock on Lord Albert's cabin door. At least his lordship's valet made no attempt to shoo her away this time.

"Hullo, Miss Debenham," said Lord Albert. "Have you been up to the carnival? That wind nearly had me overboard, but there's a frightfully clever chap doing caricatures, look—d'you think it'll make Elle laugh? It's all r-right, Carter. Miss Debenham knows what's what. We can trust her with our deepest, darkest secrets."

The valet refrained from commenting on that assertion. So did Violet. She murmured politely over the sketch Lord Albert was showing her and asked, "Are you still making trips down to second class to see her?" She nearly wanted to offer *him* a magical disguise, or at least something better than the hat she'd seen him wearing.

Lord Albert nodded. "Staff don't ask questions," he said. "Not if you're generous with the tips."

"Good," said Violet. "Go pay her a visit, and while you're there, deliver this to the gentleman in this cabin." She handed over the suitcase and a slip of notepaper with Ross's cabin number.

Lord Albert took the suitcase without a murmur. He was too well bred to ask her what it contained, though he looked desperately curious.

"It's a man's clothes," said Violet, obliging him with the truth. She sent her most strumpetly look through her eyelashes at Carter, who was pretending to brush down a dinner jacket while listening intently.

Lord Albert blinked at her, then at the suitcase.

"Of course," he said. "Anything to oblige. Don't suppose you'd oblige *me* with your company in the bar before dinner? Sip a few cocktails, hang off my arm, the usual?"

"I'd be delighted," said Violet, and leaned in to kiss his cheek for the satisfaction of seeing Carter twitch in her periphery.

26

"Good Lord," said Hawthorn. "Your stitches must be coming loose, Violet. He looks like he's been left in the rain until his colours ran."

The door to Hawthorn's cabin was firmly closed and warded, now that they'd all gathered here for the nightly war council. In the centre of the parlour, the uneven illusion atop Alan Ross's body scowled. That made things even worse.

What on Maud had been a convincing illusion of a young man's head was on Ross an unfortunately lopsided collection of features, which *slid* when one stared at them hard. Maud was put in mind of a Victoria sandwich cake of which the upper half was slowly attempting to divorce itself from the lower.

She was relieved when Ross removed the jacket, solidifying into himself.

"It was perfectly fine on Maud." Violet sounded annoyed.

Ross wordlessly passed the jacket to Maud. It *did* still work on her. It worked on Violet. It even worked on Hawthorn, who could barely fasten a single button as the garment strained over his shoulders.

"Is it that I'm not magical?" Ross asked.

"I am not a magician, and neither is Miss Blyth, medium or no." Hawthorn looked hard at Ross. "You don't appear in foresight, and you wreak havoc with an illusion. What *are* you, Master Cesare, beyond a damned inconvenience?"

Ross's expression shouted *Try me and find out*. Maud didn't want to waste good strategy time watching men snipe at each other.

"It got you up here, at least," she said hastily.

"Most toffs don't bother to look closely at the staff."

"I doubt it'd have held up if anyone stopped you," said Hawthorn. "This may not be the solution you're looking for if you want him bowl-hunting tomorrow, Maud."

"I could wear it!" Maud's spirits rose at the prospect.

"Maud, darling," said Violet. "Not even the most short-sighted of *toffs* would miss that you're the wrong shape entirely for that uniform. I doubt we'd get the trousers on at all."

Maud inspected her hips and chest and had to admit Violet was right. Violet might have fared better, except that she was far too long-limbed for it. Her wrists had stuck out of the jacket cuffs like a child wearing something outgrown two seasons ago.

"I'll make you one of your own," added Violet. "First thing tomorrow."

"I'm here now, at least." Ross made himself at home on one end of the sofa. "Make the most of me. And tell me everything you couldn't at lunch."

Violet told him about Clarence, Walter Courcey, and Lady Enid. Hawthorn poured drinks for Violet and for himself, and—after a pause of deliberate and needling rudeness—for Ross. He'd disposed of the tainted whisky and acquired a new decanter from the private store of luxuries that seemed to make itself instantly available in any space frequented by nobility. There was probably a cellar on this ship full of wine and brandy and port that would have made Maud's father, Sir Robert, gasp with envy. She almost wanted to go looking for it, just for how smug she'd feel standing there. *Look at me now. Look what I'm doing.*

"Did he threaten your cousin, this Courcey, do you think?"

Maud dragged her attention back to the conversation. The question had come from Ross.

Violet frowned. "Perhaps? Clarence did seem nervous at the prospect of crossing him. But then, Clarence likes society to be orderly. To have lines drawn that tell him where to stand and who to talk to, and who he should respect and who he shouldn't. I rather scuffed those lines, by daring to inherit his family's fortune when I'd tossed all my respectability out the window." She grinned. "If Courcey's a senior advisor to the Assembly, then Clarence wouldn't blink at obeying. He really swallowed that line about the Good of the Empire, and didn't ask questions about why this mysterious object was so important."

"Nice to know you magicians don't content yourself with the normal sort of toffs and gutter classes and everything in between," said Ross, with a resigned sort of sarcasm. "You have to throw in a handful more hierarchies on top. More magic sits you at the top, does it?"

"It's more complicated than that," said Hawthorn.

Maud thought of Chapman sneering at him. *I've heard of you.* More magic might not be everything, but *losing* magic had clearly sunk Lord Hawthorn, future earl, into contempt.

"The search for the Last Contract is all about greed for power," said Maud. "We've always known that."

"And not just more power," said Mrs. Navenby. *"Power you're not entitled to. That you haven't earned."*

"Most power's unearned." Ross was sitting forward, tense. "What did Lord Arsehole over there ever do but be born to the right parents? What did he do to earn all those stewards tugging at their forelocks, or being a *lordship* instead of a simple *sir,* or any of this luxury we're parking our arses on and pouring down our throats?"

"Quite the radical you've recruited here," said Mrs. Navenby, amused.

Ross saluted Maud with his glass, black-eyed and keen. "Up yours, ma'am."

Mrs. Navenby's crack of a laugh felt abrasive on the way out. *"Well, Hawthorn? Are you going to give the little Robespierre an answer?"*

Hawthorn didn't look angry. *His* posture was relaxed. Maud wondered what it took to grow that shell, that impermeability to the emotions of others, and how much of it was true.

"He's quite right," he said calmly. "I did nothing at all. And we could sit here drafting seditious pamphlets all evening, but it's beside the point, because we're not speaking of titles and wealth at present. Nobody has to earn magic. Magicians are born. Magic exists in its own right and cannot be given or taken away—"

Nobody spoke into the abruptness of his pause.

Hawthorn drained his glass.

"Edwin's tried to explain it," said Maud. "The Last Contract *was* a contract, a—a *witnessed* inheritance, when it began. The magicians of Britain were given the magic of the fae, in return for accepting responsibility for the land. He thinks that the tendency of houses and estates to become entwined with the magic of their owners is something similar, but working by different rules. Because inheritance doesn't *have* to be about bloodline. He inherited Sutton, after all."

"It can't work that way everywhere, can it?" asked Ross. "Handshakes with elves? Or are you telling me there isn't a single magician in Italy or China?"

"Of course there is." Violet sat up. "It can't be all about where you live. English magicians come to America and still have magic—and their children still have magic. And use it by cradling. It'd never occurred to me that it might be done differently elsewhere, but . . ." She lifted her ringed thumbs and wiggled them. "A friend of mine once told me that New York City is an argument of magicians. She said that her ancestors did magic entirely by song, but her family's lost most of the secrets of it."

"*Careless,*" said Mrs. Navenby.

"I suspect the abduction into the slave trade was somewhat to blame there," said Violet. "The point is, nobody knows what the damned rules are, really. If you'd told me three days ago that you could anchor an illusion with single-handed cradling . . ."

"Mrs. Sutton did that too," said Maud. "Edwin's been learning it from her notes."

"*Flora always was one for keeping notes,*" said Mrs. Navenby. "*And laughing at the idea of rules.*"

Unlike Edwin, for whom any inconsistency against assumed rules was both a puzzle to be worried at, like a dog with a bone, and a matter of deep personal affront.

"It sounds as though you and your friends did great things, ma'am," said Violet. There was a wistfulness to her that made sense now that Maud knew more about her past, and the fears that had driven her across the Atlantic in the first place. "Producing new magic on your own—discovering the Last Contract and then keeping it hidden—didn't you want to share any of your accomplishments with the world?"

"*Perhaps we would have,*" said Mrs. Navenby, dry, "*if they'd cared at all to listen to a group of silly women.*"

"We're listening now."

It was Hawthorn. Maud stared at him. His lordship had settled back into his chair. He made a startlingly elegant gesture of invitation. "The other side knows exactly who you and your friends are—or *were*—so my point about keeping things from George and Morris no longer applies. And we're all deep enough in this business now that I'd rather like to hear where it started."

Maud felt the wavering flow of Mrs. Navenby's indecision. The locket sat warm against her skin.

"So would I," said Violet. "You've been alone with these secrets for a long time, ma'am. I imagine part of you has been bursting to have a safe place to air them."

Maud's heart thudded. If she was to learn anything more about the Last Contract to share with Edwin and Robin, Mrs. Navenby's ghost was the best source she would ever find.

"Please," she said softly.

Even Ross nodded encouragement, curling his feet up onto his seat as if settling in for a long evening in front of a fire.

"*Hmm,*" said Mrs. Navenby. "*Let's wet this throat I'm using, shall we? Lord Hawthorn, I'll have a glass of that, if you please.*"

"Can you taste what I'm eating and drinking?" Maud asked, startled.

"*Not exactly. But there's a— I hate to make the obvious comparison, but a ghost of a sensation. Perhaps it's just memory. I'll take it, either way.*"

Maud had never tried whisky. She took a cautious sniff from the glass, hesitated, and decided to plunge in. The amber liquid was like opening one's lips to the kiss of a dragon: eye-watering fumes, smoke, and heat.

"*Thank you,*" said Mrs. Navenby when Maud was done coughing. Then another long pause. Maud did her best to settle herself out of the way in her own mind; it was an odd sensation. She felt her face move through a moue of embarrassment. "*You were right, Miss Debenham. It's been such a secret, for so long, that I don't know how to begin.*"

"Tell it like a story in a book," said Violet. "Tell it like a monologue. Ignore us. We're on the other side of the footlights. We won't interrupt."

All very well for *her* to say. Although it would be harder for Maud to thoughtlessly interrupt when it was her mouth that was telling the story in the first place.

"*A story,*" said Mrs. Navenby. She took another sip of the whisky. This time it went down more smoothly, even as it burned. "*Very well.*"

THE STORY OF THE FORSYTHIA CLUB

If you asked Flora, she'd tell you that it started many years before. But as far as I'm concerned everything started on a summer evening in 1850, at a dinner party being held in a good house in a good corner of London.

A scare had gone around the magicians of London the previous year, due to a number of things—most notably a book purporting to expose a secret underworld of witches and Satanists, and an unfortunate mass unbusheling in Brighton af-

ter a deadly public disagreement between two members of the
Assembly.

The remainder of the Assembly had decreed a dampening.
Magicians were to conduct themselves with more circumspec-
tion, blending their edges more smoothly with the unmagical
society of Britain in which we all had to exist, until the rum-
blings had died down and the Coopers had quietly discovered
all the smouldering embers of true suspicion. And, where
necessary, stifled them.

One unexpected side effect of this affair was that my anxious parents had kept my brothers home from school for several terms, wanting them to learn better control, and had them
tutored in the English tradition of magic at home. Little mas-
tery was expected of me. Magic in the female was to be turned
towards the betterment of the home. But I was bored, and my
brothers were restless boys, and I was considered a good example for them in the schoolroom.

All of which is to say: on this particular summer night, at
this particular party, I was eighteen years old and had spent
several months having my mind and my magic pried open
like the lid of a box, allowing through a chink of that marvellous light which is the birthright of all magicians. I was
hungry, where I had never thought to have appetite. I wanted
more.

It was a large and busy gathering. Dinner was not due to be
served until dark fell, but that would not be for another hour. I
left my parents deep in renewing social ties and slipped away
to explore the house, which was one I'd never visited before.
It was old and deeply magical—far more so than our own residence. I was careful to pause on thresholds and touch door-
frames with respect, trusting that the house would tell me if
I was venturing into spaces where I was unwelcome. So far, it
had given me nothing but a slow, strange sensation in the pit of
my stomach, like the knot of nerves that preceded performing
on the piano.

I came out into the courtyard just as the light was changing, pouring a golden syrup of illumination down the rosy stones of the building, turning the neat trees in their pots and the bushes in their beds to clusters of ink. A woman was crouched inspecting a bed of flowers. The folds of her silver gown had gone lavender in that dusk light.

I stopped, and thought about retreating. Before I could move the woman glanced over her shoulder and saw me.

"There's something wrong with the magic in this place," she said in lieu of greeting. "Have you noticed?"

"Er," I said, with great intelligence.

"Look at this."

I hesitated, thinking of creases and mud on my gown; but she sounded so assured, so certain that I would find this interesting, that I found my body hastening over to join her.

"You're the Godwin girl," she said as I knelt.

"Beth," I affirmed. "Forgive me, have we met, ah—" She was old enough for a *madam*, could well have been a decade my senior, but there was no ring on the hand gently turning leaves aside.

"Miss," she said, dry, as if she knew what I was thinking. "Flora Gatling. We have met, but you would have been a child then."

"Of course." My parents did know the Gatlings. And their eldest daughter had spent some time living in Scotland, I remembered now, with another branch of the family. "I'm delighted to make your acquaintance. Again."

Miss Gatling showed me the garden. Or rather, she showed me what was wrong with it, which was a great many things. Nothing that was obvious to a cursory glance, but clear if you took time and had a naturalist's eye. Ugly mustard-yellow specks covered an otherwise flourishing bed of pansies, and a lemon tree's trunk was beginning to twist and blacken. A substance like ash coated Miss Gatling's fingertips when she touched the darkest streak.

"Perhaps they've a lazy gardener," I suggested.

"There's too much wrongness. Some of these are diseases of overwatering; some of drought. Some aren't natural conditions of plants at all. And it feels wrong." She took my hand and pressed it flat at the tree's base, on the soil above its roots. A taste like sluggish mornings filled my mouth. My own magic tried to shrink back from my skin like a fox kit seeking refuge in its burrow.

I recoiled.

"Yes," said Miss Gatling. "There's a *rot*."

"It's in the house too," said a frank voice from behind us.

We stood. I clumsily executed something between a nod and a curtsy. "Lady Enid."

The Blackwoods were better society than we usually mixed with. Lady Enid's father was probably the loftiest gentleman present. Though even in this light I could tell that her gown had been reworked several times, and that her adornments tended more towards flowers than jewels.

"What have you noticed, Flora?" Lady Enid asked. "The mirrors in this place keep shifting their positions on the walls. A box of dried rose petals in the powder room tried to nip at my fingers. And have you noticed that nobody's sitting down for long? You can't remain in a single room without feeling that the place would rather you were *elsewhere*. Everything's out of kilter. Something's horridly wrong here."

"I could have told you that. Without any need to go scrabbling in the dirt or fondling the furnishings."

We all turned. And now there were four of us; or rather, there had been four all along, but one of our number had been seated on a bench tucked behind a hedge, listening, unmoving and invisible in the fading light. Now she stood and joined us.

I didn't know Miss Seraphina Hope well. I was not a naturally gregarious or amiable person, not someone who made friends easily, and Miss Hope had a skittish air that didn't encourage closeness, despite her pretty, open face. She always made me think of blackbirds.

We were in her house. Or her father's house, at least. The Hopes were magicians stretching back untold generations, like the Gatlings; Mr. Hope was a pillar of the community and ex-Secretary of the Magical Assembly.

Had I come outside, seeking quiet in the garden, of my own volition? Or had the Hope house made me as restless as all the other guests?

I wondered if Lady Enid or Miss Gatling would apologise for the insult to their hosts. Instead Miss Gatling said, "Do you know what it is that's wrong, Sera?"

Miss Hope looked around the walls of the courtyard as if suspecting spying ears. She gave a low laugh. "Where would you like me to start?"

That was how it began. The four of us, girl magicians with curious minds and the ability to recognise a kindred spirit, standing in the garden of a house where the contract between magicians and residence had been corrupted to the point of disaster by the sheer intensity of unhappiness spun within the walls through the actions of one man. Even when we became close friends, Sera never told us everything. Or even most things, I suspect.

Two months later, Mr. and Mrs. Hope disappeared.

First her, and then him. The Coopers searched for them, but not very hard—not once the servants began to speak out. The Assembly cleared their collective throats and moved on.

There are some things that no blood-pact will forgive was all Sera ever said.

Her eldest brother inherited, of course. None of the Hope sons had any interest in the potion shop of Whistlethropp & Hope, so they sold their father's share in the business to Hamilton Whistlethropp, despite Sera's protests that *she* could keep up the development side of the business. I don't think any of them were as bad as their father, but they'd learned contempt from him. They would never have taken their little sister seriously.

Sera didn't wish to remain in that house. She married quickly, taking what she could get, as women often did and still do. An unmagical man, Mr. Vaughn. I didn't understand until she pointed out that he knew less, and so was less likely to see what she was doing, if she *was* to be forced to learn all of her magic in secret.

And secretly was how we learned, and taught ourselves and one another, and flourished into new knowledge. Flora was the eldest and the natural leader: nine years older than myself and Sera, and seven years older than Enid. She was the one who named us the Forsythia Club. In the language of flowers, which was much in fashion at that time, it meant *anticipation*. By which she meant the patience to wait, and work, for a future goal.

Which was Flora Gatling all over. Anyone would have called her beautiful, and it didn't take long in her company to recognise she was brilliantly clever, but the word I would have stitched into the collar of her soul was *strategic*. Another might have been *cautious*.

She'd had plenty of offers of marriage; to her parents' despair, she had turned them all down. She was well past the verge of spinsterhood when she set her sights firmly on Gerald Sutton. He was her elder by some fifteen years, unremarkable in looks—I used to make fun of his red-brown beard with Sera when I was feeling catty—and not well known to London magical society. He spent much of his time abroad, and when in England he preferred his estate in Cambridgeshire.

But Flora wanted to marry him, and so he married her and agreed to teach her everything he knew. Flora left London and moved to Sutton Cottage.

Somewhere around this time Enid married as well, after falling in love with the young thaumoluthier who delivered her sister's harpsichord, and so plunged beneath the notice of her appalled family. She was the happiest of all of us, I think. James was as understanding as Gerald, and their marriage was a partnership in the deepest sense of the word.

The four of us travelled often between our houses to visit one another, and slowly we developed individual interests in our pursuit of the magic that nobody thought we should be pursuing.

Flora had a passion for botany. From her love of living things grew tendrils of curiosity about the land itself, and stories fallen out of fashion—including the ley lines of legend, the channels by which magic flowed through the land and renewed itself as it went. Flora was convinced that all truly interesting magic existed in the liminal spaces, where different *sorts* of power met and mingled, and that living things were the key to it.

Enid had a mind that enjoyed solving and creating puzzles. And she was musical. She became as keen and creative an artisan as her husband, and I'm sure no little portion of his eventual financial success can be laid at her own feet.

Sera had an uneasy relationship with her own passion for imbuement, given the man she'd inherited it from, but it never stopped her from honing her craft. She would give us new creams to soothe sun-scalded skin, and denude Flora's garden of herbs in search of the ingredients that would best hold a wakefulness charm. She was too proud to approach the shop now only known as Whistlethropp's to offer them her findings; like the rest of us, she worked only for love of the work itself.

As for me—Miss Beth Godwin, the only unmarried member of the Forsythia Club—I honed my needlework, but I wanted to know *everything,* and could never narrow it down for fear there was something more exciting lurking around the next corner. Flora would tell me that I was the most invaluable of the Forsythians, because a long conversation with me was worth a week in a library. I knew how to ask the right questions, to make an idea appear from a different perspective. And given my tutoring with my brothers I had the most comprehensive knowledge of what English magic *thought* it could do.

Which was useful to know as we went about proving it wrong.

Flora was the one who realised that the Last Contract might be real, and who studied the ley lines until we found it. She believed first and believed hardest; I don't know if the rest of us truly thought we'd find anything when we took that trip to North Yorkshire, until we put our hands into the ancient cubbyhole in that ancient church and touched silver.

It was me who realised that the nature of the Last Contract would allow it to be used to transfer power from one magician to another. That was my real gift, I think. Finding new ways of doing old things; or old, old ways of doing something terribly new.

We disagreed as to whether we should keep working at it. We *argued*. Though we were friends, united in our desire to pursue knowledge and power, we were still different kinds of women. And we could disagree fundamentally, we discovered, on how much we were willing to risk and where the lines of decency lay.

In the end, caution won. We made the Last Contract more difficult to find, for anyone who might come after us. Three of us took a piece each, to disguise and keep hidden.

After that Flora had a habit of giving us silver objects as gifts. It was a kind of joke. That mirror-and-brush set of mine was from her; she gave one to both Enid and Sera, too, each with a slightly different design.

And this sunflower locket was a secret gift for me, alone, to match the silver rose pendant Flora had worn since she was married. I had to consult a book to remind myself of the symbolic meaning of sunflowers, because Flora never did anything that wasn't layered in symbols.

Gratitude, and loyalty, and adoration.

Whatever question you're thinking of asking here, the answer is probably *yes*.

Flora was the most important person in my life, and I know she felt the same way about me. She and Gerald were an intellectual match, they respected each other deeply, and she'd singled him out as her best chance of learning strong magic from a sympathetic teacher. I assumed he'd fallen for her immediately, because who could help doing so? Who wouldn't know her and love her helplessly, without surcease?

But Gerald had never married before Flora, and spent months travelling to dusty corners of Europe with one of his lifelong friends: a bachelor who studied fossils and old rocks. And he and Flora never had children. I always wondered . . . but could never, quite, gather the courage to ask.

Without a household of my own, I visited Sutton Cottage far more often than Enid or Sera. Gerald was often away with his friend. So it was the two of us, Flora and me, in that beautiful house Flora had made so entirely her own, bound so sturdily to her will and her magic. I could pretend that I lived there, too, twined thick along the fences and walls of Flora's heart like any other bramble rose or holly hedge. I could pretend that Sutton was *ours*.

Again—did I say it outright? Did I push? Did I ever touch her with anything more than friendly affection? No. Flora was no more religious than the average magician, but whatever unusual shape her marriage took, she respected the vows she'd spoken to create it. She believed in contracts once she'd made them.

And I was as happy as I imagined I could be, because in this area of my life and no other, I put deliberate shackles on my imagination.

After many years, a friend of my brother's called Ralph Navenby, who'd drifted quietly in and out of my awareness since childhood, asked me to marry him. It was a surprise. I surprised myself further by accepting. Ralph was a widower by then—a kind man who desired companionship but placed few demands on me—and we were past the years where children would be possible. He took me to America, where he had family. Flora and I wrote letters—still fond, but less frequent with every year that passed.

It was easier to let go with an ocean between us. Easier to wear my sunflowers, and to think of her surrounded by her wonderful gardens, and be content that she existed at all.

"And now," said Mrs. Navenby, her tone shifting, *"we are both of us dead. I am just a voice and a bit of silver that came to me from her hands. And if I can do* anything *to bring hurt to the men who murdered her, then I will."*

It took Maud some effort to take control of her own body again. During Mrs. Navenby's story she'd curled herself up, like Ross in the chair, in a corner of her own mind. She'd almost forgotten that she was a body at all. She was simply an audience.

Now, silence. Now the dryness of her throat and the lingering taste of the whisky—now the warmth of the locket beneath her clothes, the stiffness of her legs from sitting so long unmoving. She almost wanted to ask for more time, to sort through all the things that she was feeling. But she stretched and wriggled her toes and focused her eyes.

There was a rosebush growing out of the table.

Ross uncurled enough to lean forward and brush his fingers against the half-opened yellow blooms closest to him. His fingers passed through the illusion like smoke. Now that Maud looked more closely, it was *two* rosebushes, twinned and twining trunks wrapped tight around each other—and then growing apart as the higher branches rose, like a picture Maud had seen once of a snake born with two heads. One of the rosebush's heads grew yellow flowers; the other, red.

All of it was the creation of Violet, wooden rings gleaming on her thumbs, grey eyes narrowed in concentration.

"You've a real gift for illusion, Miss Debenham," said Mrs.

Navenby. Maud's voice croaked. She said, "I could do with some water, I think."

Violet let the rosebushes dissolve into nothing, but Hawthorn was already standing. He fetched her a glass of water, and Maud drank gratefully.

Hawthorn stayed close. Maud couldn't read his expression. She remembered, suddenly, that he, too, had loved someone who had died, and that his twin sister's death might possibly have had something to do with the Last Contract. Maud *would* find all three pieces of this blasted thing, and then do whatever it took so that people would stop having to die.

Hawthorn said, "Do you think that's why your spirit anchored onto the locket when you died, ma'am? Because it had strong personal meaning for you?"

"I was thinking of her in the moment, certainly. I was so angry that she was dead and I hadn't been there, and I was about to die as well—that what we'd worked for, together, was to be erased by entitled men."

"Anger's a powerful force," said Ross. "It's what they say of ghosts, isn't it? Unfinished business."

"Nevertheless. I don't think people are supposed to go on existing in the world, after death." Mrs. Navenby managed a sniff. *"It's not proper."*

"You mean you wouldn't want to stay a ghost?" Maud ventured. "You wouldn't want to—always have a medium, in order to live longer?"

"It isn't living." Said with conviction. *"As I said: I appreciate the opportunity to have a hand in this business, in order to avenge myself and my friends. But you can't wear me around your neck forever, Miss Blyth."*

"Forgive me," said Hawthorn. "But would you prefer to be stuck to a piece of cold metal forever instead, with *no* medium to give you the option of expressing your will?"

A sickly sensation slid down Maud's chest. What a horrid prospect.

"It wasn't unpleasant," said Mrs. Navenby, as if in answer

to Maud's thought. *"The haunting without being drawn to a living body. Between asleep and awake—there are worse states. And to be a ghost in the presence of a medium is the opposite of restful. There is a constant itch to be in motion, without any flesh of my own to truly feel the itch. I am finding it . . . wearying."*

And she sounded it. For the first time, fatigue dragged at that impatient voice. Maud's hand settled over the locket in unthinking fellowship. There were days when she felt like that: body and mind tired and impossibly restless, both at once. At least *she* had the option of exhausting herself with a long walk.

"Would you want to be banished, then?" Ross asked. "Exorcised, if that's the word to use?"

"I'm sure we can come up with some solution," Maud said hastily. This was all becoming distressingly morbid, and they still had the bowl to find. "When we're back in England, Edwin will read twenty books and find the answer. I'm sure of it."

"Regardless of what happens, I owe you a debt, Miss Blyth. You did me a service in coming to America to warn me and you're doing me another now, and I know you never volunteered for the latter."

A lump formed in Maud's throat. It tasted like the guilt that she'd been carrying around since the moment she saw the old woman's body motionless on the stateroom floor. Of course she'd never asked to be a medium—but if offered the chance to give voice and vengeance to someone wronged, someone with no other possible champion, who *wouldn't* volunteer?

"I suppose," Mrs. Navenby went on, more animated, *"that given this Courcey boy was worthy of Sutton, and Enid particularly wanted Miss Debenham here to inherit, I should be leaving my own fortune to you. It would be nicely symmetrical, if nothing else."*

Maud choked. "You hardly know me! And I'm sure you have relatives of your own!"

"Oh, yes, they're the ones in the will," said Mrs. Navenby, as if Maud had pointed out some window spots that the cleaners had missed. *"Nieces and nephews and the like, all grown. I*

doubt they've been waiting to pounce, as the Blackwoods were for Enid. It's not a true fortune by any measure of the word. Most of it went to my own upkeep after Ralph died. What's left is the house in New York, I suppose. Or the proceeds from its sale."

"I heard a story once," said Violet, "about a ghost who haunted a writing desk in her own house, and so saw exactly how her relatives behaved and squabbled after her death. When the executors arrived it turned out that one of the law clerks was a medium, and through him the ghost overturned her own will and left everything instead to one of the under-gardeners, who'd always brought her fresh flowers and told her how the gardens were looking when she was too ill to go outdoors."

Silence, as they digested that.

"It's not exactly precedent," said Hawthorn. "But there are aspects of magical law that work oddly. You could consult someone in the legal offices at the Barrel."

"Edwin doesn't trust the Assembly or the Coopers. But," Maud said, "I could ask Kitty Kaur if she knows anyone suitable. She used to work there." As if this were a real thing that was actually going to happen. Maud felt breathless. She allowed herself to imagine it: coming home to Robin with enough money to ease things, to erase the worry from his brow.

"Fascinating as it is to discuss the transfer of wealth from the filthily rich to the only grubbily rich," said Ross, "how do you want to handle tomorrow, Miss B, if I can't wear that jacket for longer than it takes me to dash up here for after-dinner orgies and storytelling?"

Once again they needed *plans*. Maud chewed her lip and tried to think. Nothing swirled in her mind except thoughts of Flora Sutton, and Beth Navenby, and Violet. An ache had lodged itself in her heart: a shrapnel piece of all the histories of women who'd been *important* to one another, stretching back through time.

"Violet will make me my own illusion disguise," she said finally. "If you can tell me which of the under-cooks had the cage off Mr. Hewitt, I'll take it from there."

"And hearing about the Forsythia Club has given me an idea," said Violet. "If we still want to find out what Mrs. Vaughn's doing on this ship but don't want to risk being alone with her—I know how we can go information-digging in public. Though I may need some bribery money, Hawthorn."

"You're an heiress," said Hawthorn. "Provide your own bribes."

"Heiress-to-be," said Violet sweetly. "You'll give Maud a loan to buy a bushel of pornography, but you won't extend one to me in the name of the greater good? Pay up, my lord. I promise you'll be very entertained tomorrow, one way or another."

Hawthorn looked at her. Possibly calculating, as Maud was, whether Violet had ever been less than entertaining for more than a few minutes at a time. Or possibly calculating the interest he intended to charge on the loan.

Eventually he sighed, hard, through his nose. "Money, cheque, or jewels?"

One of the guiding principles of Violet's life, since she'd slipped out the kitchen door at midnight three years ago, was this: don't ask *what if,* unless to compare yourself favourably. When lying awake debating whether to use the sparks of your magic to kill cockroaches or drive back the damp, think deliberately about the ways in which life could be *worse.*

A cruel husband, say, or a dull one, or one determined to keep redrafting the lines around his wife—smaller and smaller each time. Magic used only to hide faded spots on curtains or add lustre to the guidelights dotted across a dinner table.

All the stories, all the wonder, slowly stifling for lack of air—until all that was left was a tall blond woman with lines on her brow, an illusion of Violet within which dwelled the anxious spirit of her mother.

Those thoughts made Violet's reckless decision to run shine all the brighter in her personal history. There was no point in dwelling on the other sorts of *what-ifs*. They didn't warm her toes or bring audiences flocking to the theatre.

And yet.

Violet and Maud made their way back to Maud's cabin without talking. Maud tugged restlessly at the fingers of her evening gloves. Violet wished for a spell that would render Maud's skull transparent, her thoughts visible. Was Maud, too, dwelling on the members of the Forsythia Club?

Like Violet, those women hadn't consented to be small. So, half a century before Violet ever packed her midnight bag, they'd taken action. Instead of running they'd planted themselves in their own soil and gone their own way in secret. And in fellowship.

What if. If Violet had been open with her sisters, if she'd allowed Julia or Alice or even Ellen into the darkest fears of her heart, what might have happened?

If she'd had any close friends, girl magicians like herself, what then?

In the cabin Maud pulled the locket's chain over her neck as Violet warded the door. She took it into the smaller room. Violet heard a low murmur, as if Maud were confiding something in the ghost, and experienced an absurd bolt of jealousy. Maud Blyth's caring was not *hers*. It was wide enough to encompass the world.

And it was hard to feel jealous when Maud emerged, neck bare, and came straight to stand in front of Violet with a little sigh. Her finger thoughtfully traced the beaded neckline of Violet's gown. Both of them, Violet thought, had fallen into Beth and Flora's story and were still in it up to their waists: a fast-flowing river of regret and loyalty and the years of a life rushing past you.

Violet wouldn't let herself die regretting a moment on this ship.

"What's next on that list of yours, O honoured general?" She spread her arms, laughing, inviting. "I'm yours to command."

Maud didn't laugh in return. She inhaled sharply, and a sliver of space appeared between her lips. "Are you?"

Maud's eyes were ravenous. The room shrank around them. Violet's skin became a size too tight as she registered the question. Not for a fortune could she have done anything but nod.

"You have to say no," said Maud, a tumbled rush. "If it's something you don't want, you have to *tell* me . . ."

Violet opened her mouth to dryly say, *Of course.* But—it would be easy, wouldn't it, to perform the cool and experienced Violet Debenham? The girl who would strive to be as scandalous as possible, even for an audience of one?

Violet had let several people take that version of herself to bed. If she ran her fingers through those memories, it might take her some time to untangle how much of it she'd actually, truly *wanted*.

"Yes. I'll tell you."

Maud's smile was a burst of light that Violet could nearly feel on her lips. She licked them. Their bodies swayed, untouching but hotly aware. The kiss that was surely coming swam in the air between them.

Maud said, "Undress, please?"

Violet smiled. "Shall I make a show of it?"

"No," said Maud. "No. I don't want you to perform at all."

Maud's body thrummed with fine movement: the rapid tap of her fingers against her own leg. The tension made little sense, but it was bleeding into Violet, and finally Maud's words settled home.

No performance at all.

No wonder Maud had insisted on Violet being able to say no. By agreeing to this, Violet was agreeing to be herself, Violet, alone. To set down her characters and mannerisms, her illusions and voices.

Undress.

Yes, quite.

"I know it's not a small thing. For you." Maud spoke into Violet's hesitation. "But *I* need it. I need to be sure that I—that this is what you want. I couldn't bear it if this was only pretend."

"I've never had to pretend to want you, Maud Blyth."

It sounded like a contract, spoken and witnessed. Violet reached for the first of the buttons in the small of her back.

It took effort. It was *hard* not to make it playful or deliberately attractive. Violet had done striptease on the stage; she'd done it in the office of the producer she approached, hollow-bellied, before she found the Penumbra; she'd done it for lovers, in private. The attention of one's audience was a ray of light. Performance was both protection and reward.

This, now, was the undressing of being so comfortable with someone that protection was unnecessary. It was more intimate than the roll of a stocking down one's leg.

Maud sat on the edge of the bed and watched. Violet didn't look at her directly, but those small movements were still there in the periphery, making Maud's presence impossible to forget. Fiddling with her skirts. Air-tapping the foot of one leg crossed over the other.

"Stop," Maud said finally.

Violet was down to chemise and drawers, and had taken down her hair. Her drawers were a longer style than Maud's, airy angles of fabric that brushed the knees.

She stopped.

"Come here."

Soft, and not harsh, but it wasn't a question and she'd not said *please*. Violet went, flush with awareness and wanting. Even the act of walking felt awkward without performance. How did Violet Debenham move her arms, her legs?

"Maud?"

"I'm thinking."

Maud's voice was cool as shadowed grass. Violet remembered Maud saying, *I'm not naturally good.*

Saying, *I know how to unravel someone.*

Violet wanted, with a sudden thrill of desire, to know what happened when Maud Blyth allowed herself to be a little *mean*.

"Now undress me." Maud slid off the bed and turned her back. A curl of brown hair wilted down the side of her neck. Some of the gauze overskirt had caught on its own embroidery, puckering into a fold. Maud had a small scab on one elbow. Violet noted detail after detail as she unwrapped the gorgeous trappings of Miss Cutler, laying the garments over a chair, to reveal the soft body of Maud beneath.

She undid the garter clips that hung from Maud's corset and attached to the stockings. Maud sat back on the bed so that Violet could kneel and remove her shoes. They were black and pink, with two small pearl buttons securing the strap.

"It's not that I don't love watching you perform," Maud said all at once, as if the words had been straining at a leash. "I *do*. I love watching you more than anything. I can't stop thinking about the first night, when you frigged yourself in front of me, and—and what might have happened even before that, if I hadn't burst in and interrupted you and Lord Hawthorn. What it would be like to watch you come apart on someone else's fingers, or—or prick."

And how was Violet meant to keep calmly tugging a stocking free of Maud's toes when Maud was saying things like that? For the sake of her composure, she didn't look up, but she raised her eyebrows pointedly. Maud hadn't told her to keep quiet, but Violet didn't want to discourage Maud from speaking. Though she'd been enjoying the silence too—the better to hear the betraying catch of Maud's breath when Violet's fingers lingered against her skin.

Or now, when Violet set the stocking aside and brushed her thumbs up and down the front of Maud's shins. Something about the sight of Maud's bared feet, the blue veins there, made tenderness mingle with the tightening knot of need in Violet's belly.

Violet shuddered with the first touch of Maud's hand in her hair. It was neither hesitant nor soft. Maud's fingers slid against her scalp like the wide teeth of a comb, and Violet closed her eyes. Her cunt ached with demand. She wanted so badly to touch herself, and from what Maud had said—

But when she reached for the folds of her drawers, meaning to delve beneath, Maud's hand tightened in her hair. Violet stopped and looked up.

Kneeling. It was rather an obvious position. And Maud had a list; Maud had read a *lot*. Including those purple Roman pamphlets, which, for all that they only featured men, played very obviously with restraints and power.

But Maud said, "Show me something magical."

With the word *restraint* echoing in her mind, the spell came easily to Violet's fingers. It felt right to use it this time in a place of joy and pleasure. She cradled the night-sky rope she'd used on Clarence and sent it climbing Maud's beautiful bare legs.

"Oh," breathed Maud, and "*oh*," more guttural, as Violet tightened the rope's grip. She wanted it firm enough not to tickle at all. She wanted Maud to feel it like Violet's own hands.

Up, and a curl around Maud's waist; and higher, until it could wrap lovingly down her arms as well. Not binding limbs together but decorating Maud's body like ivy coaxed around a lamppost.

"Yes?" said Violet.

"*Please.*" Maud lay back on the bed. She was breathing in tight little gasps. Her legs were splayed. The ropes curled lazily and lushly slow around her.

Maud had given Violet permission to perform in this small way, but it didn't feel like performance. Violet was inhabiting her own magic with the same pure, greedy joy that she'd felt as a girl, even if there was nothing childish about the slide of sparkling shadow around Maud's plump thighs and up beneath the white fabric. Heat clenched in Violet's cunt at the sight.

Violet let her hands ease apart. The ropes parted Maud's legs farther and wrapped around her wrists.

"Tell me to hold you down like this," said Violet. "Maud. Tell me to keep you pinned and make you scream."

Maud made a sound like she'd tried to swallow a whine. The stretch of her neck gleamed with sweat. Violet would be ruined for written erotica for the rest of her life. No lurid fantasy would ever hold a candle to the way Maud looked now and the power humming hot in Violet's hands.

"I want . . ." Maud managed to lift her head. Her eyes were green fire. "I want . . ."

"Yes?"

"Far too many things. But I want to touch you most of all. Always."

It's how you know the world. Violet cast a quick negation, and the ropes vanished. She'd been doing this from her knees; they clicked as she stood.

"Let's get the rest of these clothes off you." She helped Maud to stand again and divested her of corset and drawers. Only the chemise was left, a body-warm promise as Violet took hold of its hem.

"Stop," said Maud.

Violet had never been so aware of two thin layers of fabric separated by a single inch of space. She wanted to rub against something. She was *ablaze.* Maud laid her palm on Violet's chest, fingertips on Violet's collarbone as if reminding herself of landmarks.

"Kiss me. Now, kiss me now, I—"

Violet interrupted her with selfish obedience. She slid her own fingers into Maud's hair and drew their bodies together hard. It was a kiss fresh and overwhelming as rain, rough at the edges with desperation. Maud clung to her, dug fingers into her flesh, for a small and glorious eternity. Then pulled back with a little jolt.

"Fuck me." The word fell over Maud's lower lip with defiance, as if she'd had to give it a shove.

"I can fetch—" Violet started, but Maud shook her head.

"No. No. Just you."

Violet bent and kissed Maud's shoulder. Opened her mouth, glorying in the sugar-salt of skin. Scraped her teeth. "All right."

Violet guided Maud onto the bed, then knelt in front of her. She helped Maud bend and lift one leg, her lower body angled a little to the side, chemise rucked up to her waist, exposing her sex so that Violet could shift forward and slot her own against it. This took a few bitten-off curses as Violet shoved the layers of her own drawers aside, trying to get the garment's opening lined up. Maud began to laugh, but didn't suggest that Violet remove them, and Violet was by now a line of gunpowder awaiting a flame; a spell anchored to one spot, awaiting the clause that would trigger it.

Both of them gasped when flesh met flesh. One or both of them was already wet enough to make the grinding motion easy and slick. Violet hooked the pale weight of Maud's leg over her own hip.

"Mm." Maud closed her eyes. Her fingers flexed on the bedclothes. "*Oh*. I could do this for hours."

"That might be a tad—ambitious," Violet managed.

A smile widened Maud's mouth. "Are you surprised, by now?"

"Not in the slightest."

Heat lay over Violet's shoulders like a cloak with the sun sewn into it. She ran a flat palm up Maud's belly, pausing to circle her navel with a single finger, then farther up to rest beneath Maud's breasts.

"All right?" Violet said, soft.

This time the *mm* was syrupy, satisfied, further from words. Maud's stomach rose and fell beneath Violet's arm.

Violet drew her hand down Maud's body again, exerting more pressure, and at the same time moved her hips in a savage circle. The air was loud with their breathing, each inhalation a rasp of sweet frustration. The folds of Maud's cunt were too soft, too yielding, against the part of Violet that demanded something firm. She lost patience and shoved her hand down between them.

"Oh, yes, please, you can—inside me—please," Maud panted, and Violet slid two fingers straight into the throbbing heat, angling her thumb where she could push against it herself.

Maud's leg clenched tight over Violet's hip, the other suddenly curling in too as if to keep Violet pinned tight against
her. The tear-bright look on Maud's face as she shook her way
into orgasm was enough to haul Violet along with her a few
moments later, frantically riding the heel of her own hand to
drag out the waves of pleasure.

After that, Violet assumed they were done for the night.
Maud, practically glowing with satisfaction, proved her wrong.
She sat up and gestured impatiently for Violet to lie down, and
Violet hissed at the first touch of Maud's fingers down where
she was sensitive and soaked. Her hips twitched of their own
volition.

Maud said, "Show me something magical, Violet."

The note in her voice—God, *God,* Violet had cast this all
wrong from the beginning. In this moment Maud was Cleopatra. Alexander. She could have pulled armies to their knees.

Violet said, hoarse, "Tell me what you want."

Maud smiled like a catastrophe. "Illusion. I want to see if
you can hold it."

There were illusions that the magicians of the Penumbra
created and regretfully had to put aside. Illusions that would
stretch even the bounds of a theatre audience's credulity. Violet
brought her pleasure-weak fingers together and summoned all
the magic she had left, and began to work.

Scarlet fish the size of plane leaves swam in the air around
Maud's head, their scales glittering in scattered flecks of silver
and bronze and green. Maud scrunched up her nose when one
flicked its tail near her face. But her delighted eyes returned
to Violet's face, and her fingers moved with deadly care and
intent.

I want to see if you can hold it.

Maud watched people. Noticed things. Maud had learned
that Violet unravelled for firm hard strokes delivered right in
the wake of release, pleasure so sharp it crossed into pain.

One fish wavered as if seen through rain. Violet wanted
more than anything to screw her eyes shut and simply feel her

own tightening need, but she'd lose the illusion entirely if she did. She'd lose the game.

"They *are* lovely," said Maud, all earnestness now. Her thumb moved in brisk circles. The unbearable need to move trickled like hot candle wax down Violet's legs.

Power could take the place of precision. Falling apart, Violet forced the illusion to live by pouring magic from the heart of her, more and more—a school of brilliant glimmering colour moving faster and faster around Maud's head and shoulders—until even that gave out, and Violet's skin seized, and the fish vanished as Violet sobbed and cursed, dropping the cradles in favour of clutching at the bedcovers. Too much. Too much for one body. She'd have to be as wide as the horizon to hold it all.

When her breaths were the size of a rib cage, not an ocean, she lifted her head. Maud was curled up with her folded arms resting on Violet's pelvis. Her gaze was wild and certain and full of fireworks. Her heartbeat was palpable through the places they touched. Her fingers tapped on the side of Violet's hip.

Pipes and drums, Violet thought. She felt stripped away and exhausted. She felt new.

Thank you, said Maud. Soundless, just her lips moving.

Then she dropped her head, as if the strings of her own masterful act had been cut, and buried her face in Violet's bare stomach.

No matter what happens between us, Violet thought numbly, I will never be rid of this moment. I will carry it always.

If she'd told herself a year ago that she'd find herself here, she might have smiled to hear about some of it. But she wouldn't have known what to do with this part. This stirring of a drowsy thing in her chest made of soft wax and the smell of honey. The utter strangeness of yearning for something that she'd *had*—and had thoroughly, at that. Of being in a bed with a beautiful girl and still feeling her heart ache like a muscle long unstretched. She wanted to tell Maud stories and have her laugh at them, to flirt with her over coffee and watch her wander around rooms, thinking with the roaming of her fingertips.

And maybe Violet would again be easy to abandon, and maybe she'd end up with yet more rings on her hands to remind her of it.

Maud straightened and lifted a hand to smother a yawn. Brown hair billowed around her shoulders like the densest London fog, and she absently touched the top of her breast-bone, as if aware of the locket's absence.

Better thumb rings, surely, than jewellery worn as a re-minder that every day you ached and loved and settled for less than what you wanted.

"What is it?" Maud said.

Nothing was on Violet's tongue, but Maud had requested truth from her, tonight.

So Violet reached for Maud's hand, lifted the inner wrist to her mouth, and kissed it. It wasn't an answer. It was truth, withheld. Maud smiled, and in her smile was the fact that she'd noticed and let it go.

28

"Maud," said Violet. "This is possibly the ugliest garment I've ever seen, and I worked in a *theatre*."

Maud lifted the jacket by one sleeve. It was a garish shade of burnt orange trimmed with blue piping and fussy rosettes of crimson ribbon, and had been the height of fashion for approximately five minutes last season.

"I know," she said. "But I've never worn it on the *Lyric*, so it'll help the illusion that I'm someone other than myself."

The new illusion that Violet had created—the head of a red-haired woman with a boil beside the nose, as instructed—wavered in the air. Violet had based it on her eldest sister, Ellen, she'd said, and Maud had bitten her tongue on anything more than an encouraging nod. Violet was pulling back the curtains of her performance bit by bit. Maud was so heavy with gratitude, at the courage Violet had shown last night, and was showing still, that she didn't know how to express it. She didn't want to scare the true, laughing girl into stepping back behind the sophisticated facade.

"Thread, if you please," said Violet.

Maud stretched out the red cotton thread and Violet cradled the imbuement clause. The red-haired woman dissolved into smudges of kelp-shadow, smothered the thread, and vanished. Violet cradled a thimble of glowing silver with a spell that her fingers flowed through with unthinking grace, took the needle and thread, and began stitching. Again she'd written the embroidery runes down, for reference.

"Whatever possessed you to buy it in the first place?" Violet asked after a while, shaking the offensive jacket into a new position.

"My mother would have hated it," said Maud. "I do a lot of things because my mother would have hated them."

Violet didn't look up, but her mouth quirked as if she could feel Maud's gaze and knew that she was thinking about the previous night.

One of Maud's quiet, buried-deep fears was this: What if she *had* no personality, no taste, no true core of her own? She'd formed herself, from the age she knew how to choose things, by setting herself opposite what her parents wanted in the hope of making them disapprove. Making them *notice*. When she'd bought that jacket, her mother had been three months dead already, and Maud hadn't questioned her impulsive satisfaction until her maid Teresa had unwrapped the parcel and conveyed her scepticism with a raise of her brows.

There was no point in irritating Lady Blyth now. Maud had won all the arguments, all the provocations, forever. And also lost them, because she could become the most depraved and disreputable woman in all of England—could waltz down High Holborn in the nude, playing the bagpipes as she went—and her mother would never again stir a single hair in reply.

Maud squeezed her hands tight enough to hurt. Won. Lost. Against a dead woman. What kind of daughter had thoughts like that?

When the illusion was sewn into the jacket, Maud tried it on. The unfamiliar features wrinkled and widened delightfully in the mirror as she moved her face through a series of expressions.

"I could try an accent. Perhaps Imogen is from Cardiff, or the daughter of a Scottish laird. Och, aye, I'm longing to be home with my family—"

"*Please* do not try an accent."

Imogen's lips pouted. It was true that Violet would be the better choice for skulking around pretending to be someone else. But Violet had other things to do this morning and wanted to preserve as much of her magic as possible, in case she needed it for what they had planned for the afternoon.

Violet signalled when the corridor was empty. Maud—illusion intact—slipped out. Ross had given her the name of the under-cook who'd acquired Dorian's cage from Hewitt. Maud presented herself at the galley entrance; a kitchen maid bobbed a curtsy but also gave the orange jacket a look that said she suspected its wearer of having come to complain about breakfast.

Maud parried with a convenient piece of half-truth: she'd heard this man Andrews might have won something at cards that her elderly aunt had given away to one of the servants in a temper, and had now changed her mind about.

"And it'll be hell to pay, forgive my language, if I don't get it back."

The girl looked over her shoulder. "Lunch prep's waiting on the bell and Cook's gone for a smoke. Give us a moment, then."

Andrews proved to be a fat man with the sheen of kitchen grease holding his black hair in place, eyes a similar bright green to Maud's, and a spattered apron lovingly cradling the sag of his stomach. He nodded along when Maud explained the situation and tentatively asked why he'd wanted the parrot cage.

"My sweetheart's one of the ship musicians. Plays piano for the singers. The musical director's got a real bee in his bonnet about this ball tonight, so everyone's scrambling around for ways to make it fancier. That Miss Broadley's singing some soppy thing about a nightingale in a cage and wanting *out* of its cage, and my Betty was hoping to beg a stuffed bird off of someone's hat. I thought the empty cage might be nicer. A metaphor, like. They could hang it from the piano with the door open."

Having delivered this piece of dramaturgy, Andrews shifted his weight to his other foot.

Maud cast around for an excuse, then remembered that she was Imogen and didn't need one.

"If you wanted it as a prop, did you empty the cage? Take out anything from inside?"

"You mean the swing? The little bowls for food and drink? Nah, left 'em. Makes it more poignant, if it looks like the bird was there and now it's gone."

"I quite see your point," said Maud faintly. "Thank you, Mr. Andrews. I'll try to find Betty a stuffed bird in exchange, even if it won't be as—poignant. Do you know where she'd be at this hour?"

An attempt to venture into the *Lyric*'s rehearsal spaces, however, was less successful. Maud was turned back by a young man with the red eyes of the sleepless and sheet music falling out of his arms, who was quite adamant that rehearsal was not to be interrupted by *anyone* for *anything,* and Mr. Kingsmill would have Betty Cohen's head if she left her seat at the piano to chat to a passenger. Sorry, miss. Good day, miss.

Perhaps Maud should have made Imogen a laird's daughter after all. She was sure that Lord Hawthorn would not have been turned away, though perhaps Betty Cohen would have paid the price for it afterwards.

Maud moved from this to imagining Imogen an entire family, and from there to a surprisingly vehement mental version of herself, as Imogen, refuting a sinister viscount who had come to demand her hand and had designs on her father's estate. This took up enough of Maud's thoughts that she turned into the corridor containing her cabin and was a good two yards along before she realised that Morris was kneeling in front of her cabin door.

She faltered. For a moment.

Then she recommenced walking, at a slower pace. There was a leather pouch of tools by Morris's knee and a hint of red light adorning his fingertips, and he jerked one hand back from the door lock as if stung.

Maud forced herself not to smile. Mrs. Navenby's warding charm was working.

She'd been waiting for Morris to appear. Chapman had been keeping an intermittent eye on them—and an overt one at meals, forcing them to engage in light conversation until they appeared to be on friendly terms with the horrid, murdering rat. It had been making all of them uneasy that Chapman hadn't made any obvious attempts to find the silver items and steal them back. And Morris had been nowhere to be seen. Until now.

Morris glanced up sharply at Maud's approach. Their eyes met.

Should she smile at him? No—he was dressed as a workman, and disguised as one, with those tools. Imogen might have no taste in fashion, but she was still a first-class passenger, and Ross had been right: most toffs didn't notice the staff. Morris might have been counting on that fact.

So Maud pretended to be a mixture of her mother and Mrs. Navenby. She flicked her eyes down to Morris's scuffed boots, then up to his cap, and allowed herself to arch her brows and barely sniff: dubious that such a specimen was in the right place. With a hint of I-heard-there-was-a-jewel-thief-aboard. But not caring *enough* to pry into someone else's business.

It was a complicated look. Imagining all its nuances kept Maud calm as she drew level with her own door—Morris touched his cap to her as she passed—and her tread remained steady, even as the point between her shoulder blades stung with awareness and tension as she walked to the other end of the corridor and around the corner. Thank God it wasn't a blind end.

She scurried to the café and ordered a cup of coffee, which she drank without tasting it, and to her relief Morris was gone on her return. The faint mark of the warding on the doorframe was untouched. It had held.

"*Of course it held,*" said Mrs. Navenby when they were inside. She gave exactly the kind of dismissive sniff that Maud had been aiming for with Morris. "*That was one of Flora's spells. She was very keen on secrets and security.*"

Yes—Flora Sutton, who'd managed to ward her entire property against any magician not granted explicit permission to cross its borders, and hidden the coin of the contract in a murderous maze.

"You kept *your* piece of the contract right out in the open,

as if it were nothing of consequence." Maud unbuttoned the
orange jacket and shrugged it off. "I think that's brilliant."

"*I had not foreseen that someone might make a* gift *of my
parrot and his cage.*"

"You didn't foresee that you'd die either, ma'am. Or that I'd
be a medium." And neither had Robin. He *would* have mentioned either of those.

The old woman's hard laughter filled her mouth. "*True enough.
Life makes fools of all our plans, Miss Blyth.*"

Violet returned to the cabin soon after, humming a bright
tune and agleam with satisfaction.

"Hawthorn's money well spent," she said. "Mrs. Moretti was
determined to bluff it out at first—she's a tough old boot—but
I appealed to her, one fraud to another, and she swung around
nicely once she heard I'd make it worth her while. I told her I'd
done some fake mediumship of my own, and I'd be employing
some tricks that she mightn't have seen before."

Maud laughed. "Will she ask to be shown your secret con-
traptions?"

"Very likely," said Violet cheerfully. "She's busy studying
the script for now."

Maud explained her own morning's mingled success and
failure.

"Leave that to me," said Violet, on hearing of the obstacle of
Mr. Kingsmill. "I'm sure Lord Albert will be able to speak to
his wife in between rehearsals. I'll see you at lunch."

Maud was left to twiddle her thumbs until the lunch service.
She embroidered her mental fantasy of Imogen some more, then
busied herself refolding and repacking clothes, and then wandered down a side road of that task by asking Mrs. Navenby to
point out and explain all the charmed pieces of clothing. Maud
made a careful list in Robin's notebook, for Edwin.

"Is there a charm for good luck?" she wondered aloud, fold-
ing shirtwaists back into a trunk between layers of tissue paper. "One could sew it into a pair of gloves and be unbeatable
at the card tables."

"Luck's in the same basket as time and death, girl," said Mrs. Navenby. *"Many magicians have tried, but none have ever mastered it."*

Lunch was in the main dining saloon. Violet appeared by Maud's side and caught her arm before they could take their seats, speaking in a low voice.

"I'm beginning to feel as though we're in a fairy tale and we've been set tasks by an evil imp. Miss Broadley says that Betty did show her the cage, and suggested it for her nightingale song, but this morning Mr. Bernard's keeper came and took it back again. The bloody parrot's to be a prize in the lottery tonight."

They took their seats at what had become their usual table: Hawthorn, Chapman, the Bernards, and a handful of rotating others. Today, Mrs. Moretti was among them. She had a distracted air and sighed heavily as she shook her head in response to an offer of wine.

So the cage had moved hands again. Maud stared down into her plate of salad and curling slices of pink roast beef, wondering if their enemies could, somehow, be ahead of them.

Well—Chapman was sitting right there. Either he knew about the bowl and had it already, or he didn't, and Maud was just talking to her new friend about her ex-employer's parrot.

"I heard Dorian's to be a lottery prize tonight?" she asked Helen.

"Oh, yes!" Helen made an apologetic face. "It was kind of you to think of me, Maud, but I think he's too used to being a *human* bird. He didn't get along with the other birds in the aviary. He was teaching them horrible words and pecking at them. Papa says we can have an African Grey when we're in England, but Mama's put her foot down and says it won't be *this* one. Of course you may have him back if you wish, but Papa assumed you didn't want him. And the head steward was *so* pleased to have such a novel prize for the lottery."

"Oh, no, of course he should be a prize," said Maud's mouth before her brain could catch up. She was acutely aware of Chapman watching her. *Don't act as if you care. This is just luncheon chatter about nothing important.* "My brother would scold me terribly if I brought home a parrot prone to yelling rude words."

"Are you looking forward to the ball, Miss Cutler?" asked Chapman. No doubt wanting to know if she'd be out of her cabin, so they could have another try at breaking into it.

"*Very* much," said Maud, arming herself with dimples.

They'd have to find some way to win Dorian back, cage and all. And there was no such thing as magical luck.

Mrs. Moretti cleared her throat. "I'm sure the ball will be enjoyable, as these things go," she said. "But we mustn't forget that this ship has already borne witness to matters of life and death. Indeed, I have been given to understand that the dearly departed woman—Mrs. Elizabeth Navenby—has some messages she *urgently* wishes passed on to the living souls aboard."

A fascinated silence fell over the table.

Mrs. Moretti preened. "I plan to hold a gathering at three o'clock this afternoon, in one of the private card rooms, in order to contact her spirit and question it more closely."

"How thrilling," said Violet. "May anyone attend?"

"I'm afraid the presence of certain persons would make it impossible. Sceptical hearts—negative auras. But the poor dead woman has already reached out to me, in my dreams, and her spirit messengers indicate that there are some whose auras are *ideal* for our purpose. You in particular, Mr. Chapman. I must insist on your presence."

Head turned. You could have heard a raspberry drop onto the carpet.

"Er," said Chapman.

Professional that she was, Mrs. Moretti barrelled on before he could refuse. "Yes, yes, and you must bring with you some of those whose fortunes are tied to yours." She screwed up her face. Her eyes rolled. "Morris?" the woman ventured. "Do you know a Morris? Or Horace, perhaps? Forgive me, the spirit voices are so faint . . ."

Chapman's face had gone wooden. He shot a look at Maud, who deepened her dimples.

"Goodness," she said. "How *exciting*, Mr. Chapman, to be so personally requested. Would the spirit of the dear departed object to my presence, ma'am? Do I have the correct sort of aura?"

"It is *imperative* that you be present, Miss Cutler," said Mrs. Moretti. "You were closest to her before she passed. Your own spirit will act as a flame to a moth. You must be present as well, Miss Debenham. And you, Lord Hawthorn."

Helen Bernard looked nakedly envious. But even she joined the rest of the table in turning an inquiring look onto Hawthorn. He'd barely spoken at meals except to be sardonic and off-putting, and altogether the kind of man who would squelch an invitation to a séance beneath the heel of his shoe.

Hawthorn blinked like a cat.

"Why not?" he drawled. "You're quite right, ma'am. The lack of entertainment on this ship is enough to make one welcome even the prospect of ghosts."

29

Violet still disliked Mrs. Anna-Maria Moretti, but had to admit that the woman knew how to set a scene. They'd secured a card room on A Deck at short notice through Maud's mercenary relationship with the steward Jamison. Mrs. Moretti had hung a piece of red gauze over the porthole, plunging the room into a close, warm redness like swimming through watered-down wine. The white tablecloth laid over the pushed-together card tables took on a pink tinge. A modern electric lamp glowed like a small sunset in the centre of the table, an elegant brass stalk mushroom-topped with a dome of etched glass. A hint of old cigar smoke clung to the air.

"Please be seated," said Mrs. Moretti. The con woman wore a fox-fur-trimmed hat and an eye-wateringly glittering brooch in the shape of a peacock. Her voice was vaguer than usual, as if part of her had already split off to dwell on the spirit plane.

There were ten of them in total. As well as Violet, Maud, and Hawthorn, the Bernard sisters had been issued invitations more or less as camouflage, and Diana Yu had brought herself along out of pure curiosity.

Mrs. Moretti had frowned at this transgression against her spiritual authority, but Violet gave a tiny shrug, so Miss Yu's aura was deemed acceptable.

"Does it matter where we sit?" asked Helen.

It mattered to Violet, who had already manoeuvred herself to Mrs. Moretti's left hand. Mrs. Moretti assured the group that success would be due more to the combined force of their auras than any specific placement.

"Miss" came flatly from Violet's other side.

The skin of her cheeks crawled as Morris touched his cap and nodded down at her. There were ways and ways for men to look at women, and Violet knew most of them. This malice-tinged disinterest was both new and unnerving.

Unlike Morris, who looked out of place among the first-class finery, Chapman held himself like a man who had the right to be wherever he was. He took a seat next to Maud and dropped a gauntlet of a smile. Maud's smile in return was impeccably po-lite, but she shifted an inch away from him and towards Haw-thorn, who'd already claimed the seat on her other side.

"Shan't we need candles, or a letter board?" asked Rose Ber-nard.

"Perhaps a *charlatan* would." Mrs. Moretti dripped disdain. "A true medium needs only her own gifts, and a strong and open mind. Now, I'll ask you all to concentrate quietly. The conditions on this plane must be perfect for Mrs. Navenby's spirit to draw close to the veil. We must all join hands and cre-ate a circle of invitation and trust."

Violet steeled herself as Morris's fingers closed around hers. She'd asked Mrs. Moretti to insist on the circle; she wanted everyone's hands where she could see them.

Silence fell.

A circle of trust. It was a lie so full it was bursting at the seams. Three curious spectators, four people in on the sting, and two-possibly-three members of a murderous conspiracy.

At least Violet's hunch had paid off. Even if they suspected a trap, neither Chapman nor Morris had been able to resist turn-ing up; Maud and her allies had the contract piece, as far as they knew. And despite being thwarted once, Chapman and Morris still had them outclassed in terms of magic.

Thus the Bernard sisters, and Miss Yu, and the two ship's stewards who stood inside the door: Jamison and a pimply younger boy who looked outright nervous at the idea of ghosts. They were witnesses. Nothing too violent, too truly magical, or too revealing could take place in this room.

Mrs. Moretti had approached Seraphina Vaughn personally and reported that the woman had seemed uncertain but flattered to be included. Mrs. Vaughn's brow was furrowed now, where she sat draped in a grey shawl between Hawthorn and Miss Yu.

"I cannot hear the dear departed clearly yet," said Mrs. Moretti in that distant voice. "I can sense—I can barely glimpse—a vision. A large garden. Flowers, everywhere. This place was important to her. Roses, lots of roses."

Violet snuck a glance through her lashes at Mrs. Vaughn, whose eyes were abruptly wide in her sweet, moon-round face. Mrs. Vaughn's mouth half opened, as if to speak, then she reconsidered and closed it again.

Violet had given Mrs. Moretti enough information to be both vague and tantalisingly specific. Now she tapped Mrs. Moretti's ankle with the toe of her boot, encouraging. They'd laid a hook. Time to create some slack in the line.

"Ahh," said Mrs. Moretti obligingly. Her eyes snapped open. "She has arrived! Can you feel her presence? Welcome her! Let her know this is a place of safety!"

Maud gave a stifled little gasp, as if someone had dropped ice down her back, and looked at the ceiling. "I felt a breath against my cheek. Could that have been her?"

Mrs. Moretti rained approval on Miss Cutler, *clearly* a girl of unusual psychic sensitivity. Rose Bernard ventured that she, too, had felt a change in the temperature of the air.

"Mrs. Navenby did not meet most of you in life," said Mrs. Moretti, "but she can feel your belief, your *need* to know that she's close. It's strong. Very strong indeed. Perhaps she's drawn to some of you because you have lost people in your own life. Who have you lost, my dear?"

This last was addressed to Miss Yu, two chairs to her right. Miss Yu blinked and, after a moment, volunteered that she had indeed lost her dear Charlie, just last winter.

"Ah." Mrs. Moretti adopted a look of limpid sympathy. "There are no certainties beyond the veil. But if Mrs. Navenby were to encounter your Charlie's spirit, are there any messages you would wish her to pass on?"

Miss Yu considered this. "She could throw a spirit-ball for him to chase, I suppose. Charlie was a spaniel."

Helen gave a stifled giggle.

Mrs. Moretti's sympathetic look gained an irritated edge. "It might amuse you to play games with the forces of mystery," she said, "but I cannot see the humour in it. We are dealing in the weighty matters of life and death."

Violet squeezed the woman's hand firmly. They didn't need Mrs. Moretti to turn diva. The woman had wanted to use her usual approach: clients expected a spirit guide, she insisted. Violet had pointed out that *she* was the only paying client in this scenario. The lack of real knowledge about how mediums worked was going to play in their favour here, but things had to look semi-plausible to the other magicians at the table.

Mrs. Moretti sighed and turned to Maud. "For you, Miss Cutler, her voice rings clear. She wants you to know that she doesn't blame you for her death. She knows you would have done everything you could, if you'd been there. But . . . she's glad you weren't. Oh, she's distressed, remembering it. Mrs. Navenby! Elizabeth! Stay with us! You must let yourself inhabit it without pain!"

Maud looked somewhere between touched and distraught. Morris's hand tightened around Violet's.

"What does she mean? What pain?" asked Maud, taking up her cue. "Oh, I hate to think of her death being painful!"

"No, not the moment of death. There is something she's trying to show me . . . some shadow hanging over this memory . . . a sense of danger."

Chapman had the sense not to react to that, but he and Morris exchanged a glance. Chapman's mouth was a firm line.

Another single ankle-tap from Violet. Time to move on to the main event.

"Sarah?" said Mrs. Moretti suddenly. "Is there a Sarah at the table?"

A long, careful sigh like the creak of wood came from Mrs. Vaughn. "My name is Sera."

Mrs. Moretti drew herself up. Violet's hand was tugged an inch towards her. "Sera. There is a sense of grave danger that surrounds you as well. That is why you're here. Be careful. She says . . ."

Absolute silence. The room hung on Mrs. Moretti's next words, uttered as if she were translating them from an ancient language.

". . . she says, *All the rest of us have proven disposable, and you may too.* Does that mean anything to you?"

"I . . ." Mrs. Vaughn shrank back.

"It's all right, ma'am," said Rose encouragingly. "The spirit clearly wishes to help you."

Morris's hand was a vise. Violet gritted her teeth against it.

Mrs. Moretti's tone sharpened. "She says— *Why* are *you on this ship, Seraphina Hope?*"

Mrs. Vaughn dragged her hands back from Hawthorn and Miss Yu. She set palms on the table as if she might rise, but stayed, pinned to her seat, staring at Mrs. Moretti.

"She doesn't want to think the worst of you," Mrs. Moretti continued, "but she says it's terrible to think of the alternative. To think of you betraying a trust in that way, when you—"

"*What trust, Beth?*" hissed Seraphina Vaughn, sudden as the strike of an asp. "You didn't trust *me* with a piece of the thing."

Everyone else rocked back in their seats. It was as if the sunset lamp had exploded invisibly and they'd felt the blow. Violet's pulse thundered in her ears. They'd done it. They'd actually done it.

"Ma'am . . ." said Chapman urgently, but clearly had no idea what to say next.

Fury rouged Mrs. Vaughn's pale face. Her attention swung between Mrs. Moretti and the ceiling, as if she wasn't sure where to direct her tirade against the ghost of her friend. "What do you want me to say? It was never going to stay hidden. I told you someone else would work it out eventually, and they *did.*"

Violet went to tap at Mrs. Moretti's ankle again, willing her to keep the woman talking, but there was no need for it. Mrs. Vaughn's quavering voice strengthened as it continued.

"And if Flora had been an inch less stubborn—less certain that *she* knew best, that *she* should make decisions on behalf of all of us, of all—" Violet heard the gap where the woman managed not to say the word *magicians*. Mrs. Vaughn sucked in an uneven breath and finished: "Well. If that was the case, perhaps she'd still be alive today."

"Get her name out of your mouth, you traitor."

Violet's elation turned like the flip of a card to fear. It was Maud standing, Maud's chin held with that particular arrogant angle that wasn't her own mannerism at all. And it was Mrs. Navenby's voice steaming out.

"Don't you dare *speak of her. You turned us in, didn't you? Enid, and then me. You gave our names to these* men"—nearly spitting the word, with a wave of her arm that encompassed Chapman and Morris—*"and they killed her, and they killed me, and now you're the only one left to be listened to. Just as you always wanted."*

The silence was wine-coloured, blood-coloured.

". . . Beth?" said Mrs. Vaughn.

Everyone stared at Maud. Violet couldn't feel anything past her knees or elbows. She had no idea if Morris or Mrs. Moretti still held her fingers.

"A . . . a truly impressive sensitivity, Miss Cutler," said Mrs. Moretti. "Have you ever felt the psychic vibrations before now?"

"Beth?" Mrs. Vaughn said again. "It is—oh, Lord—"

"*What* is going on?" asked Rose.

"Ladies, gentlemen," said one of the stewards. "If I might remind you—"

"Perhaps," said Chapman loudly, "Miss Cutler would like—"

"I don't think Miss Cutler—" began Hawthorn, even more loudly.

"*The cup,*" said Mrs. Vaughn.

It was uttered low and sharp and clear to Chapman. The words would not have meant anything to the unmagical people in the room. They might not even have heard Mrs. Vaughn speak. Panic spiralled high into Violet's gut, where it twisted.

"The cup. Beth knows what it is. And *this girl* is the medium."

Oh God, Violet thought—oh *fuck*.

She shot an appalled glance at Maud—and it was Maud again, swaying on her feet with a hand to her mouth as if to cram the betraying voice of the dead back into her lungs.

"*Quiet.*" Chapman was standing, too, all the musicality of his voice vanishing in the kind of bellow that would quell a street fight. "This farce has gone far enough. Miss Cutler, I'm afraid I'm placing you under arrest."

At least five people spoke at once. Violet might have been one of them; she could barely hear herself within the chorus of alarm.

"You'll do no such thing," Hawthorn growled. "Who do you think you are?"

"Special Branch," said Chapman.

"Special Branch of *what*?" snapped Violet. She was ignored. Chapman had the flow of the scene, and he knew how to use it.

"I've been on the trail of this young woman for some time. I suspect her of being not only a thief, but also a con artist. Such a low, immoral thing, staging a séance to throw suspicion off herself after her supposed relative died— Oh," he went on, triumphant over Maud's furious gasp, "do you think I didn't notice that you were at such pains to establish you weren't present at the time of death? Do you deny that this entire gathering was masterminded by yourself, under false pretences?"

If there was ever a time for Maud to lie, this was it. She was red-faced with anger, and to Violet's horror there were tears standing in her eyes.

Maud managed, "How—how dare—this is—"

Chapman raised his eyebrows and smirked. He looked around the table, letting his gaze linger on Mrs. Vaughn, Violet, and Mrs. Moretti.

"A pretty performance, ladies, but the game is up. And believe me, the law won't look kindly on anyone who helped her."

"It was her," blurted Mrs. Moretti, shooting out a finger to point at Violet. "She paid me! She told me exactly what to say!"

The only experienced fraud at the table, she'd clearly not been expecting the voice of the law to appear. She was trying to save her skin. Violet nearly bit her tongue with the effort of not lashing back. What good would denying it do? Why was the truth so damning, and how had she lost control of the script? God, why couldn't she *think*?

Chapman's smirk widened at this unexpected gift of testimony.

"Well. We all know that Miss Debenham is an accomplished actress." His tone coated the noun with grime.

"Maud?" said Helen, in a small voice.

Chapman reached into a pocket of his jacket and pulled out—

"Are those *handcuffs*?" said Rose, sounding close to hysterics.

"I didn't do a thing!" screeched Mrs. Moretti, not much better.

"You're a damned Cooper." Hawthorn didn't raise his voice, but the low drawl of it carried. "Aren't you? You work for my cousin."

Nearly everyone was on their feet now. Violet didn't know when she'd stood, or when Morris's grip had moved from her hand to her forearm.

"He oversees my branch of the government, yes," said Chapman.

Wording that would sound unremarkable to non-magicians, and yet a horrible chill joined the rest of Violet's fear. George Bastoke, Hawthorn's cousin and likely the most senior member of the conspiracy to use the Last Contract, also oversaw the magical police. Wonderful.

"Lord Hawthorn," Chapman went on. "It's kind of you to extend your protection to this dissolute pair of women, but it'd be best if you stayed out of this."

Maud was by now nearly hyperventilating, a hand to her chest where beneath her clothes the locket—

The *locket*. If a magician got Maud alone and helpless in a room, determined to get Mrs. Navenby's truth out of her . . . Even if Hawthorn and Violet could talk the ship's actual authorities into forcing Chapman to release her, it might be too late. The Coopers extracted information and extinguished problems. That was their function.

The dark core of Violet's anger welled up like a boiling pot, and she cursed the well-meaning planning that had landed them here with non-magicians on all sides.

Chapman turned and took hold of Maud's arm. His fingers pressed cruelly deep into flesh as he brought the first cuff to her wrist.

Violet snatched up the table-lamp in her free hand and threw it at him.

It was yanked back by its thick electrical cord like a dog on a leash, but she'd thrown brass-end-first, and with force; Chapman shouted and threw up his hands before the lamp stopped midair and fell back onto the table. The glass shade cracked but didn't shatter.

"Maud," Violet said, "run. Run *now*."

Maud dodged around Chapman with the speed of panic and made for the door. Morris started after her, dragging Violet with him, and Violet twisted and flailed. When Morris turned on her, his face ugly with annoyance, she stepped close and drove her knee up as hard as she could into his groin.

That was the plan, at least.

Her bloody narrow skirt hampered the force of it, and Morris had good reflexes. Violet managed only a glancing blow between his legs—not what she'd intended, which was to drive his fucking bollocks so far up his arse his *ancestors* would be singing soprano.

It was enough for him to grunt, and for his grip to loosen. Violet twisted again, pain worming through her shoulder at the awkward angle, and snatched herself free of him.

"You meddling bitch," said Morris, and reached for her again. His hand had just tangled in Violet's hair—she yelped with the flare of sharp pain across her scalp—when he let out another, louder grunt and released her with equal suddenness.

Miss Yu stood at his shoulder. In her hand was a hatpin, wickedly sharp and long.

"Mind your language," Miss Yu said coldly.

Violet took a few stumbling steps towards the door, where Maud—oh, the little *fool*—was hovering anxiously, waiting for her. The stewards had vanished some time ago, probably to fetch ship security. Violet exchanged a frantic look with Hawthorn.

He lifted his hands and cradlespoke speed. *Go.*

Then he grabbed Chapman's arm, dragging the man back.

That was enough for Violet. She opened the card-room door with one hand, took hold of Maud's arm with the other, and they ran.

As ignoble attempts to escape pursuers by dashing through the ship went, this was Maud's least favourite of her attempts thus far. Last time had involved a cheetah, and she'd been unsteady from the effects of a flung curse. She'd also had Hawthorn at her side, and the knowledge that she'd be relatively safe in crowded spaces and *very* safe once they reached her cabin.

This time, none of that applied.

"Where to?" Violet asked as they ran past a young woman who, wide-eyed, gathered two toddling boys into her skirts.

Maud wanted to snap at Violet, and also to burst into tears. Had letting Maud make the decisions ended in anything except more and more disastrous chaos, up to this point? Couldn't someone *else* do it?

"Cargo hold," she heard herself say. At least there'd be plenty of dark, poky places to hide and take a breath, and plan their next move.

"Slow down," Violet hissed as they emerged into the Grand Reception. She enforced this by grabbing Maud's hand. "People will remember which direction we went, if we're running like hellions."

It was crowded beneath the glass dome, a well-dressed mill of people emerging at a sedate, chattering amble from the main artery of corridors. Perhaps there'd been a performance, or some other activity that Maud could have attended if she hadn't been so busy falsifying a séance—though was it false if there was a real ghost involved?—and being denounced as a *career criminal,* and if she hadn't spluttered like a beached cod instead of defending herself—oh, God, what would Robin do if she went to *prison*?

"Maud," said Violet sharply. She squeezed two of Maud's fingers together hard enough for the flare of pain to puncture Maud's spiralling thoughts. "Breathe slower, walk faster."

Maud shook her head to clear it. Her chest felt overfull of air. "Sorry."

Violet was looking over her shoulder. Her head whipped back to face the elevators, her brow clouded. "Damn and fuck. And he saw me too."

"Who?"

"Morris. Hopefully Hawthorn's keeping Chapman distracted. Come on."

They pushed their way towards the closest elevator. Maud ignored the grunt of outrage from a monocled man as she ducked beneath his elbow, pulling Violet with her, and slithered inside the half-full elevator just as the attendant pulled the cage closed.

A series of gasps and the monocle's withering "I *say*, sir" heralded Morris doing his level best to reach the elevator.

"Going down," said the attendant.

"Open the door," snarled Morris, finally in front of them.

"Elevator's full, sir."

It was not. But the cage was closed.

Maud clung to Violet's arm. Morris, breathing hard, stared at them from a yard away. Murmurs of shocked displeasure came from the others in the elevator. Maud contemplated swooning. If he reached through the gaps and grabbed her—if he tried to force the cage open again—

Lord Hawthorn would have done it without thinking twice. Even Chapman might have made a pompous fuss and demanded the elevator be halted so he could remove the pair of criminals.

But Maud saw, clear as if written, the moment when Morris's habit of working in the shadows combined with his awareness that he was a servant in a space full of first-class passengers who were about to ask him his business.

The hesitation was enough. With a jolt, the elevator slid downwards.

Morris swore and looked around. Maud's eyes were at the level of his waist, then his knees, and then his shoes moved and he began to run again.

"Are you all right, miss?" asked someone from behind them. "Is that chap causing trouble?"

"Oh, it's awful," said Violet, a masterful throb of tears in her voice. "He won't leave her alone."

This time the murmuring was supportive.

"I'll call ship security at once if I see him again, miss," said the attendant. Maud sent him a tremulous smile.

They took the elevator down two decks to the Grand Foyer. Morris was nowhere to be seen when they stepped off. From there they plunged down the staircase that led to the cargo hold, and Maud only took a conscious, rib-expanding breath when they'd stepped through the hatch into the familiar grey-gold dark.

"Don't just stand there." Violet tugged her between piles of crates and canvas-draped trunks. Maud stubbed her toe on an errant protrusion and yelped, then clapped her hand over her mouth. She listened hard but heard only the ship's engines and the complaints of parrots from the menagerie corner. Perhaps if Morris appeared they could set the cheetahs on him.

Violet stopped next to a hulking shape tethered to the floor with ropes. "Hm. It's not a dark street, but I suppose it'd look like one in a vision."

"What?"

Violet was already opening the door. "*Harriet, on a dark street, climbs into a motorcar.*"

The notebook. Robin's vision. "Are—are you sure?"

"It gets us out of the open, in any case."

"Can't you hide us by magic?"

"I'd rather hide us by magic *and* by actual hiding," said Violet shortly. She hauled and squeezed herself into the car's cabin, and Maud followed, tugging the door closed behind her.

Violet sat on the floor with her knees tucked up and her back to the opposite door. Maud lay on the backseat, just beneath eyeline if someone were to glance at the windows. Inside the car, the smell of the cargo hold gave way to a richer one of new leather. Maud could only just make out Violet's face, her hair gleaming like green-rotted copper in the meagre light, her pale gloves moving through a cradle.

"A curtain-spell? Good. Make it fast."

Maud startled. Mrs. Navenby had been silent, her presence undetectable, since they'd left the séance. She'd entirely forgotten she was wearing the locket.

"I *am*," muttered Violet. "I'm trying to keep it confined to the car, that's all."

A pearly shimmer expanded from Violet's hands and vanished.

"There. Nobody will be able to hear us, or see anything out of the ordinary, unless they come within the spell's radius."

They sat in a fraught breathing silence. Maud broke it as a thought elbowed its way into her mind. "Actually, this is my third time running from pursuers. If you count the time I ran away from Mrs. Vaughn's cabin, when she caught me in there. And I was the one following Morris then, but it only made things worse. It made me look awfully guilty." She looked down at Violet, a bubble of dread and anger rising within her. "Why did you tell me to run *this* time? Why did I do what you said?"

"Thank you, Violet. You're welcome, Maud," snapped Violet. "Would you rather have stayed there and let Chapman handcuff you?"

"Running makes it look like we have something to hide! Like we *are* jewel thieves and con artists. If Chapman and Morris go to the master-at-arms with the story of being secret policemen, then they'll go straight to my cabin! Are we supposed to stay hidden down here for the rest of the voyage?"

"We've less than a full day at sea left. I know it's not the conditions you're accustomed to, *Miss* Blyth, but do you have any better ideas?"

Maud didn't. Perhaps if she calmed down she could think of one, but her mind was going even faster than her heart, skipping back and forth, picking up threads of thought and shaking them into nothing. Neither of them was at their best with their nerves being shredded like this.

She opened her mouth with an apology in it. What came out was: "Violet. The rune on your neck."

The red glow was like the burning end of a cigarette glimpsed at night, faintly illuminating the space behind Violet's head. Violet put her hand to it. "It was itching before, too, I didn't think . . ."

"That can't be a good sign, can it?"

"Maud," Violet said abruptly. "Get out of the car. Get away from me."

"But . . . the curtain-spell."

"*Yes*, but I think—"

Footsteps sounded somewhere in the cargo bay.

Maud flattened herself to the cushioned seat, propping her head at a low angle for the comfort of being able to meet Violet's eyes. She trusted Violet's curtain-spell. Even so, she hardly dared to breathe.

Was it a crew member on some innocent errand? Hewitt come to see to the animals? Even if Maud lifted her head to peer through the window, she'd see only the nearest pile of crates.

The rune gave another red throb.

"*Tracking*," said Mrs. Navenby.

"It must be," said Violet in a grim whisper.

"A tracking clause to a rune-curse overrules a warding," Maud blurted.

Violet stared at her. Maud stared back. Edwin would be so proud of her if she survived this; sometimes she did manage to retain the things he talked about, after all.

She ventured, "Could it . . . overrule a curtain-spell?"

"Shitting Christ," said Violet weakly. "I—"

"Good afternoon, ladies," said Chapman.

Maud, through the drenching crash of fear, had never

wanted so badly to be someone else. If she were Robin, she could land a solid blow or two in Violet's defence. If she were a magician, she could do some magic. What could she do, being only herself?

Nothing.

Chapman opened the car door a crack on Violet's side. Violet was scrambling upright, a cradle of green light already coming to life in her hands, but Chapman said, "*No* you don't," and tossed something through the gap. A small round thing bounced off Violet's skirts and landed on the floor of the car. It gleamed like glass. Its contents were a swirl of grey smoke.

And then the glass ball fell apart, that grey smoke rushed thickly out to fill the car, and Maud choked. It was worse than fog. It was like sticking one's head in a chimney, only without the heat.

Violet swore and turned to the half-open door. Chapman made a motion as if tossing a glass of wine down her front. Violet's hands clapped together, clasped, and stayed there.

"Out you come, Miss Debenham," said Chapman, taking her by the wrists.

Violet spat in his face and called him a name that Maud didn't think she'd manage to bring herself to speak even if she lived to be a hundred, but she climbed out of the car.

Maud coughed. Her eyes were streaming with the smoke, her chest on fire. Her hands scrambled to open the door on her own side even as her mind howled protest.

Morris was there. Maud kicked out with her boots, but Morris ignored her as he would wave away a wasp. He reached in, took hold of one of her hands, and slipped a glowing piece of string around it.

Maud's entire body went soft and useless at once. She could do nothing but follow, pliant and dull as a doll, as Morris tugged on the other end of the string and directed her to come out and be quiet and behave.

The Goblin's Bridle. Robin had told her about this spell. Both he and Edwin had been subjected to it at various points during their own adventure; Bastoke's people were clearly fond of it.

It was horrible. It was worse than horrible. It was sickeningly close to sitting aside in herself while Mrs. Navenby spoke, and yet worse, because she had no chance of seizing control again. Maud yearned to scream, but she couldn't. She could do nothing but stand there at Morris's side as they joined Chapman and Violet at the rear end of the car, the four of them awkwardly cramped in the space.

Behave. It had been said to Maud hundreds of times and never, *never* had she ever been left with no choice but to obey. She'd always been safe enough to misbehave and lash out and provoke. Now she stood in acute, trembling awareness of how much larger than her Morris was; of how much power he had over her; and that nobody would stop him if he decided to use it.

"Maud?" Violet sounded guttural with horror. "What have you— You leave her *alone.* I will slit your *fucking* throat."

"So dramatic. I don't think you will." Chapman had the calmness of victory. "And she's the one we're interested in, Miss Debenham. You're no more than a nuisance. Morris, give me the medium, and get rid of—"

The crack of Violet's laughter echoed, wild as breaking stone, in the cargo hold. Maud would have jumped if she were able.

"You know even less than you think you do, young man."

It didn't sound like Violet. It didn't look like Violet; her lips were drawn sneering back, her posture stiff with age. It was Mrs. Navenby.

"What the fucking hell," muttered Morris. "Shut her up, Chapman."

"You already tried that. Killing me was a fair effort, I will allow you that much, but I'm still talking. And I will continue to do so."

Chapman looked from Violet to Maud and back again. Bewildered anger began to creep into his expression. "What—"

"Has my dear old friend Seraphina been keeping secrets from

*you? The Forsythia Club was doing magic beyond your compre-
hension before you were a spark in your father's eye, my boy. Do
you think a magician of my calibre would be limited, in death,
to the use of mediums? There are barely any of them, after all.*"

Maud, even as her heart skipped in slow realisation of what
Violet was doing, wished savagely that she could turn her head
to see Morris's face. Still. Watching Chapman's was satisfying.

"*This girl?*" Violet gestured with her magically bound hands
towards Maud. "*She was only the closest useful mouthpiece. A
prettier instrument than many I could have chosen, but not a
special one.*"

"We're wasting time and we're in the open," said Morris.
"Bring them both along. Sort it out later."

Chapman didn't look pleased to be given orders, but he
nodded.

Maud didn't know if both of them being captured was better or worse, but at least Violet hadn't been *gotten rid of*. And,
selfishly, no matter what happened next, she was glad to have
Violet with her. It would be easier to be brave.

Violet managed a quick wink down at Maud as the men directed them towards the hatch. Chapman was already building
a spell that he said would discourage attention.

Maud hoped the wink meant that Violet had anything approaching a plan to get them out of this. Because Maud certainly
didn't.

The last time Maud had been inside Cabin 44, B Deck, it had been with exactly this group of people: Violet, Chapman, and Morris. They needed only the arrival of Lord Hawthorn to complete the party.

This time, she and Violet were deposited in chairs. Chapman rapidly cradled a spell that held Maud's feet flat on the ground, her legs pressed back against the legs of the chair. The same for Violet. It didn't hurt; nor did it give in the slightest. And it was far, far from the sparkling and spine-tingling spell that Violet had wrapped around Maud the previous night.

Morris removed the Goblin's Bridle from Maud's wrist. On their way through the ship she'd rehearsed a number of increasingly violent options for what she could do once she had the use of her hands, but her nerve failed her. All her instincts screamed that it would be a bad idea to make Morris angry.

"Now then," said Chapman. "Mrs. Navenby, I assume you're able to hear me, one way or another. Who's going to answer my questions?"

"*Wouldn't you like to know?*" Violet's hands were still clasped, but the angle of her chin was entirely arrogant.

Clasped hands. Priez-vous. Maud remembered, horribly, another vision recorded in Robin's notebook. *Harriet, tied to a chair.* A fair-haired man striking her across the face. Possibilities and probabilities. Maud had the warning, set down in ink, and she still couldn't prevent this.

Chapman's lips curved into the smile of a man who had the situation under control now, and so considered himself untouchable. "I'm afraid I don't believe you, now that I've thought about it. Mrs. Navenby's ghost could simply have used that Moretti woman, if she has the ability to use any mouthpiece at all."

Morris made an impatient sound. "Doesn't matter which one talks, as long as one of them does."

"It was truly a great performance, Miss Debenham," Chapman assured her. "A pity. You should have stayed on that New York stage."

"And you should have stayed in England and not let this Bastoke send you off on a wild goose chase for bits of silver," said Violet. "Though perhaps you *enjoy* threatening girls. You can't get any female company unless you're forcibly restraining them, is that it?"

Maud bit her tongue as Chapman took an aborted step towards Violet's chair, annoyance hardening his face. *Violet* clearly had no qualms about making them angry. Or was this part of a plan?

"There's certainly been enough goose-chasing on this voyage." Chapman stood in front of Maud. "It ends now. The ghost will tell us exactly what her piece of the contract is, and *where* it is, and Miss Cutler will pay the price for any further games or time-wasting."

"My name isn't Cutler," said Maud at once. If there were ever a time to play her trump card, this was it. "It's Blyth. My brother is Sir Robert Blyth, baronet, and he's expecting my safe return. And"—her tongue slipping with haste—"he's also the only foreseer the Magical Assembly has access to."

Chapman snorted, clearly about to dismiss this as yet more playacting, but Morris put a hand on his arm.

"Bugger. No, Chapman, hold it. She's right about Blyth." Those incurious eyes sharpened with recognition. "She looks enough like him too."

"The Assembly has a *foreseer*?" said Chapman. "Why didn't I know that?"

Maud managed to meet Violet's eyes in a sliver of space between the two men. Violet raised her eyebrows.

"You didn't need to," said Morris.

"*And,*" Maud plunged on, "Walter Courcey is under blood-oath not to cause me any harm, or else the Assembly loses Robin's cooperation for good."

She had no idea if this would work. It did, at least, make Morris frown. Chapman waved an impatient hand.

"Walter Courcey isn't here, is he? Besides, I don't intend to leave you with any injuries, Miss—whatever you call yourself. I'm hardly an amateur." He reached out and delivered a teasing flick to one of the small buttons of Maud's waistcoat. His fingertip stayed in place, resting gently just over Maud's heart. "I can heal anything Morris inflicts."

The implications of that wrapped Maud in clammy flannel. She flinched away, then wished she hadn't when his expression only grew more pleased. Was his enjoyment the only reason he intended to get answers through fear and pain? There was such a thing as a truth-spell, and Walter Courcey had learned it from Edwin, its inventor. Edwin had used it to imbue the truth-candle's wax.

But there didn't appear to be much love lost between these conspirators. Perhaps Walter had kept the truth-spell's existence from his allies, in case it was used against *him* one day.

"Mr. Bastoke wants the contract, end of story," said Morris. "If it gets the information, I say we risk it. Lethe-mint when we're done."

"There, you see?" said Chapman to Maud. "You won't even remember it afterwards. It'll be like it never happened. Of course, it'd be a lot easier if you just told me what I wanted to know now, and then we wouldn't be arguing about nasty things like *injuries.*"

What would the late Lady Blyth have said in this situation, tied up and threatened by a self-congratulating policeman from the North with no society clout at all? Probably she would have *laughed.* Maud didn't manage it. She straightened her spine, pulled as much of her mother's metallic uncaring around herself as she could, and looked Chapman right in the eyes.

"I think you're a horrid, pathetic little man. And you can go *fuck* yourself."

Chapman hit her.

Violet yelped. Maud only heard it muffled, beneath the pain erupting over her cheekbone and mouth and in the base of her neck as her head snapped to the side. It wasn't worse than a cane across the palms. Perhaps exactly as bad. Her head swam with brown stars and brassy bells. She tasted a hint of blood, as if the satisfying obscenity had scoured her on its way out.

When she focused on him again, Chapman looked startled—but it melted at once into satisfaction, as if he'd gotten away with something unexpected. He had a temper. He lashed out when things didn't go to plan. It was why Mrs. Navenby had died in the first place. Maud should use it. She should think of some way to use it. *God,* her face hurt.

And then she was nudged aside in her own body.

"*I am sorry for the girl, of course,*" said Mrs. Navenby. "*She's only doing her best to help. But this one is right*"—with a nod to Morris. "*The contract is the most important thing. Keeping it from you and people like you was the task of my life, and it remains the task of my death. Miss Blyth doesn't know what you're looking for. I do, and you can't kill me twice. So I won't be telling you anything.*"

Morris shook his head. "It might take longer, is all. But you will."

The toe of Morris's boot found the front of Maud's leg as if her skirt and petticoat were invisible, and connected with the force of a cricket-bat. Maud let out a cry that was half surprise, and this time didn't manage to stifle it before it turned into a wet, whimpering breath. *That* was definitely worse than a cane. Her leg throbbed with red fire.

"Stop it!" yelled Violet.

"Shut it," Morris said. "If you screech one more time, I'll break her arm."

Violet's mouth moved, her glare turning sharp, but she said nothing else.

Maud clutched her arms to herself. He sounded implacable. That was the awful part. Chapman swung between nervy and smug; Morris, now that he'd decided what had to happen in the service of his employer's goal, was almost *bored.* As if he'd clean the blood off his trousers—Maud's blood—and then have a calm pint of beer with his dinner and sleep the sound sleep of the just.

"Get on with it, then," said Chapman. "She'll snap fast, ghost or no. Women always do."

Morris didn't spare him a look. He looked hard at Maud, as if measuring her for a new suit, and cradled a spell. Maud tried not to watch the fluid, rapid dance of his fingers.

She flinched when he released it, but nothing happened. The spell, soft as pale syrup, flew outwards like the curtain-spell that Violet had cast in the cargo hold.

"Muffling-spell on the room," Morris said flatly. "It might hasten matters if you scream, miss. Don't be stupid and stubborn like your brother was."

"You put the curse on Robin?"

Morris tilted his head, scornful. "He writhed around like a damn fish."

It was possibly the worst thing—or the best—that he could have said in the circumstances. Violet had talked about the knife-spell coming from a part of her that was only anger. Maud felt a dark flicker, deep in her belly, thinking of Robin. She couldn't transform the anger into magic. But *oh,* she wanted to, in order to hurt this person in return. She wanted to take his skin off inch by inch. She wanted to watch *him* writhe.

But she couldn't. She was the one who was going to hurt.

Maud set her teeth and dug her fingertips tight into the crooks of her own arms. Even if she did scream, and sob, and empty her guts onto the rug, she would endure for as long as possible before she admitted what and where the Last Contract was. Then at least she could hold her head high when she told Robin she was sorry for failing him.

"I think you'll find," she said, "I can be very stupid indeed."

Morris lifted his hands to cradle again. Maud wanted to screw her eyes shut; she didn't want to see it coming, whatever it was, except that the alternative was even more unbearable—

"Wait," said Violet. "I think I can help. *Without* anyone being injured."

Morris paused. Maud exhaled.

"Do you know where the cup is, then?" Chapman demanded of Violet.

"I'm almost certain I do. And"—before either of the men could interrupt her—"I have something else I can offer you into the bargain."

Chapman looked her up and down, lip curling. "Your charms aren't as universal as you think they are, Miss Debenham."

"No, I suppose not," Violet said with equanimity. "You don't think much of me at all, do you, Mr. Chapman? You told Morris here to get *rid* of me."

"You've nothing to do with this business," he said shortly. "You've just stuck your nose in where it isn't wanted, and you're paying for it."

Realisation began to creep over Maud. Now she held her breath for an entirely different reason.

"Hm." Violet smiled. The attention of the room had begun to recentre on her, and Maud could see Chapman wavering; he didn't know *why*. Violet looking this pleased with herself didn't fit his idea of the script. "How did you find us in the cargo hold?"

"Tracking rune," said Chapman. "Morris had the sense to get that onto one of you, at least."

"Here's the thing." Violet leaned back in her chair. "I don't think Morris *did*. When would he have had the chance to get close enough? Perhaps at the end of the séance. But that rune's been there for days now." She shifted her gaze to Morris, who looked stolidly back at her. "It was my cousin Clarence, wasn't it? He put it on me sometime in New York. It glowed for the first time when he was looking for me and didn't know I was in the Turkish baths. And then again when he needed to know I wasn't in my cabin, so he could go and search it for Lady Enid's letter."

"What the devil are you nattering about?" said Chapman, angrily. "You're stalling."

"I'm elucidating," said Violet. "Try to keep up. So Clarence laid the rune, but *Morris* could activate it, because he knew that it was there. Morris knew what Walter Courcey had instructed Clarence to do. Morris has tried to stop me, but I don't think he'd ever have killed me. Because your dear friend Morris here knows that the late Lady Enid Blackwood left me all her worldly belongings when she died. Including the knife of the Last Contract, whatever and wherever it might be." She beamed at Morris as if he were a chivalrous protector. "Maud's brother might be useful to your cause, but I'm *vital*."

Chapman's face, during this recital, had moved through irritation to an irate shade of puce.

"*What*," he growled. "Morris? Is any of this true?"

"Did Mr. Bastoke not trust you with that part of the scheme?" said Maud. She widened her eyes up at Chapman. "Perhaps it was something else you didn't need to know?"

"*Morris*." A snap.

Morris shrugged. Nothing could have more perfectly communicated his disdain. Maud, despite everything, nearly burst into a choke of laughter.

"It's not much fun being a tool, is it, Mr. Chapman?" said Violet. "Just pulled out of the box when you're needed and kept in the dark otherwise."

Chapman looked as though he wanted to hit all three of them, and even lifted his hands as if to start a cradle. Then he thought better of it. He said, bullish, "Mr. Bastoke knows my worth. He'll let me in on the larger picture once I've done my job and delivered the cup."

"Exactly my point." Violet swept on. "If you'd shut up for a moment, you'd realise I'm *surrendering*, Chapman. I'm not a ghost and I don't intend to become one, and I *don't* believe in prizing mythical objects over people's lives. I'm prepared to buy our freedom and our safety. When we get back to England you can bring your pals over to search Lady Enid's estate. Or I'll sign all her knickknacks over to Clarence, and he can deal with them. Whatever you wish. *If* you let myself and Maud go, now, unharmed."

"*Violet!*" came out of Maud, ringing with alarm. She didn't know if it was herself or Mrs. Navenby who'd said it.

"And as a sign of good faith," Violet went on, lifting her clasped hands, "if you take this bloody spell off me, I'll tell you where Mrs. Navenby's cup is. I'd appreciate it if you'd hurry. I've already lost feeling in two of my fingers."

"How do I know you're not pretending again?" said Chapman. "Tell me first. Then . . . yes. You'll both be free to go."

Violet sighed. "You're terrible negotiators. Don't you understand what good faith is? It's what you still have, *barely,* because the worst you've done so far is kick Maud in the shins like a schoolboy. Here's the thing: Maud and I both know where the cup is. But if you torture her, Mrs. Navenby will just use her mouth to spout gibberish. Whereas I"—grandly—"will tell you, with no fuss. If you let me go."

"I don't like it," said Morris.

"I'm still making the decisions here," snapped Chapman, another part of his composure fraying. He frowned at Violet. "I don't trust you."

"And I don't trust you not to take out your temper on me just for the fun of it as soon as you have what you want. I want to be on my own feet, with my hands free. Give me that and I'll keep Lord Hawthorn off your back." Violet shot a look at Maud. "I'll tell a story of why we all disappeared for an hour, and why Maud has a split lip, that *doesn't* end up with you having to answer a lot of uncomfortable questions from his lordship and ship security."

Chapman was a man coming to the end of his rope. Maud didn't blame him. Watching Violet at her most obnoxiously needling was a marvel, when it was turned on someone else.

Chapman frowned one more time and then cradled a negation, which he flung at Violet.

She stood, making a show out of stretching.

"Just in case you get any ideas." Morris's hands throbbed with a green spell; the equivalent of keeping a gun pointed at Violet's head, Maud supposed. "Hands apart. Now talk."

"*You self-interested, conniving little hussy!*" Mrs. Navenby shouted. "*Is this how you repay Enid's generosity?*"

"Ah. I thought you'd weigh in sooner or later, ma'am." Violet, moving slowly with an eye on Morris, crossed to stand in front of Maud. She leaned down until their faces were close enough to kiss. "I don't like the way you talk to me. And I don't like the way you use my friend as an *instrument,* either."

Violet gave another wink. This one was a measured, deliberate twitch of her eye, delivered with a flicker of a smile. Maud hesitated, and felt the ghost's speechlessness as well.

Violet said, "I'm sick of running errands and putting myself in danger for the sake of the dead, when there are living people here I actually care about. And if I told you that I want to keep Maud safe more than I want anything else—well, ma'am, you of all people should understand that."

Her fingertips alighted on Maud's lower lip. Traced a path down Maud's chin, her neck. Those grey eyes were sparkling again, a mixture of tension and affection holding her expression taut. When she reached the uppermost buttons of Maud's shirtwaist, she undid them. Then the ones below.

Maud kept her arms by her sides, but couldn't help the curl of her hands into fists. Did she trust Violet?

Yes. Just enough.

"What are you doing?" said Chapman.

"I'm holding up my end of the bargain," said Violet.

Beneath Violet's fingers, Maud's heart began to pound. The sides of her shirt folded back, revealing the lump of the locket beneath the neck of her chemise.

The plan fell into place.

"Don't," Maud pleaded, as tearfully as she knew how. She

took frantic hold of Violet's wrists as if to halt her. "Violet, I don't want you to do this for me. Not after everything we've done to keep it safe."

Violet kissed Maud's cheek. Her fingers were gentle, clever, as they hooked beneath the chain of the locket and tugged it into the light.

"Maud, darling," she said, very soft. "You're worth more than this quest. I've told you that all along."

"*Don't you dare!*" Mrs. Navenby said. Shrill, but there was a theatrical note to it. Maud would have grinned, if her mouth were her own. "*Miss Blyth! Stop her!*"

"Mrs. Navenby," said Violet. "I truly am sorry. But this is for the best."

And she yanked the sunflower locket away from Maud's neck. The thin chain snapped.

Violet turned with the locket in her grip.

"Gentlemen," she said. "I present to you—Elizabeth Navenby's piece of the Last Contract. Here—catch."

32

Morris caught it.

"There," said Violet. "You're clearly the brains of this outfit as well as the muscle."

Partly, that was to keep chipping away at the grudging alliance between their enemies. The other part was just to annoy Arthur Chapman, who was now neck and neck with Jerry in the stakes of men whose corpses Violet would cheerfully walk over for a cup of tea.

Sure enough, Chapman scowled.

"*No!*" burst out of Maud. "*Miss Debenham, I shall* never *forgive you!*"

Violet tingled with the momentum of being with someone who was prepared to meet her improvisation, to keep step with her, to harmonise without fear. She still wasn't sure if Mrs. Navenby had caught on in time, but she *knew* that Maud had.

"I'm not interested in your forgiveness, ma'am. I am interested in keeping our skins intact—those of us who still have them."

"*You will have no further help from me on that score. Or any other,*" said Maud, furious and frosty, and then her jaw clacked shut.

It wasn't altogether convincing, if you'd spent the last few nights hearing the difference between the ghost's voice and the medium's. But it didn't have to be. Chapman and Morris had what they wanted now. All that mattered was that they had no reason to think, even for a moment, that Mrs. Navenby's ghost had left Maud along with the locket.

Catching the thrown locket had forced Morris to drop

whatever nasty trick he'd been cradling, and removed his focus from Violet's fingers. Casually, she moved through the first
few motions of a general negation, then held it half-finished
between her hands.

Chapman looked on the verge of demanding Morris hand
over the locket, but victory had calmed him again. "If the other
one's still useful, so be it. But now the old woman's served her
purpose, the medium is nothing but a liability. Will you kill
her, or shall I?"

"That wasn't the bargain!" Violet managed, barely, not to
drop the half-completed negation. "You were to let us both go,
unharmed!"

"Did I put my blood into any oath?" Chapman smiled nastily.
"Be grateful you've escaped with your own skin, Miss Debenham. And this will stand as a reminder to you, as to what might
happen if you later decide to double-cross us out of the knife."

Violet opened her mouth to retort that he had no business
double-crossing her and warning her against it in the same
breath, but Morris got there first.

"Don't be a bloody fool, Chapman. The last thing we need
is ship security up our arse because a dead woman's relative has
also shown up dead. And Mr. Bastoke won't be happy if the
foreseer takes against us because we've killed his sister. Just use
lethe-mint and be done. It's been less than a week."

"Miss Debenham might fill her in on the details afterwards,"
said Chapman. "It'll have to be both of them. And—blast, Lord
Hawthorn might still shove his oar in. A secret-bind would be
neater."

Maud's eyes went huge and her hand covered her mouth.
Violet cursed silently—*damn*, she'd hoped it wouldn't come
down to this—and finished the negation. She shoved power
into the cradle, too much, too hard, and the negation burst like
an overfilled skin before she could gather the control to direct
it. It flew wide as the room. Still, it did the job. Maud's legs
jerked abruptly away from where they'd been held against the
chair.

Violet was already cradling her next spell as she got herself between Maud and Chapman. "Maud, stay out of the way."

They couldn't kill her. They couldn't kill Maud. Violet just had to get them *out* of here.

"Forget Chapman! Get the locket!" cried Maud, in a stroke of creative genius, as she obediently scurried to press herself against the bureau.

Chapman was a fast cradler, but Violet had started first, and finished first as well: a fire-spell, with a clause to encourage it to catch hold even on difficult material, and another to turn it into an arrow. The spell flew into one of his thighs and began at once to burn through his trousers.

"*Fucking—shit.*" Chapman dropped his half-formed cradle. Violet jerked her head urgently at Maud and then at the exit.

"Morris!" panted Chapman. He batted at the smouldering patch on his leg. "Don't just stand there! Help me!"

Morris had his palm protectively over his pocket. He was close to the door. Having acquired the item that Mr. Bastoke wanted, he was visibly loath to put it at further risk. He was considering leaving Chapman in the lurch.

Chapman saw it and cursed. His teeth were bared as he spun back towards Violet. A reddish patch of raw skin peeked through the ashy edges of fabric. He began to build a cradle that frothed and billowed in his hands, mustard-yellow smoke glinting green where the light hit it.

Violet couldn't identify the spell, but Chapman had formed it in fury and there was nothing but thwarted anger in his eyes as he advanced. Fear wiped Violet's mind clear. Maud was shouting something that turned to cotton wool in her ears. She took an unmeaning step back and collided with the chair.

When you can't think, cherie, let your hands think for you.

It was Claudette's voice. Claudette sitting on a prop table in the green room, smoking cigarette after cigarette—Claudette nodding at Thom, who was playing a more sinister role than his usual, advancing on Violet from every angle. From behind, from the side, with a knife, with a handgun. The weapons were illusions, but lackadaisical Thom was a consummate actor when he wanted to be. Violet's nerves recognised only threat, and turned that threat into a bucket with which to reach down into the well of her anger.

Claudette saying *Again,* and *Again,* until Violet's fingers could fly through the cradles of the knife-spell without conscious thought. They didn't practice finesse. They only practiced speed, and the ability to pull this to the surface when the rest of the body was singing panic.

Violet lifted her hands, barely seeing the pink light that limned them.

She took a step forward, closed her eyes, and slashed.

All of her was braced for the hot splash of blood on her face. It didn't come.

She heard the muffled shriek from Maud. She smelled something new and coppery and fierce. She heard a gurgle like water running beneath a grate, and then a small, unimportant crumpling sound, not far from where she stood. She couldn't get enough air in, though she fought her lungs for it. In the end, she opened her eyes because it was that or fall over.

There was blood, after all. There was a lot of it: all down Chapman's front, and wet on his hand where he'd grabbed the wound, and on the floor, where it seeped and clashed with the green and yellow of the rug.

A few scarlet spots adorned Violet's bodice and sleeves, as if painted there with a delicate brush.

She should be shaking. Instead she was hollowed out. She felt as though she had spent an hour in the ice room, like Mrs. Navenby's corpse, and walked out chilly and calm. An unpleasant and yet necessary chore had sprung up in her path and been completed.

She looked at the body of the man she'd sliced open.

"I told you I'd slit your throat." Her voice should have hung visible in the air. "I did tell you."

The rest of the world rushed in at the edges: colour, sound, warmth. Now the smell of blood did curdle Violet's stomach.

Morris, inches from the door, had frozen in surprise. He looked from Chapman's body to Violet, and back.

None of them moved. Violet's breathing seemed the loudest thing in the world.

A bang on the cabin door proved her wrong.

Maud gave a little leap. Even Morris flinched and looked at the door as if it would fling itself open. It did not. Another brisk knocking followed the first. A few interminable seconds went by before Morris cleared his throat. "Who. Who is it?"

The muffling-spell he'd cast must have gone down with Violet's overzealous negation, because the reply came almost at once.

"Ah, Morris," said Lord Hawthorn's sternest tones. "Excellent. Open the bloody door."

"We're in here!" shouted Maud at once. "We're both fine!" Which was a generous twisting of the word *fine* and also showed a touching assumption of what Hawthorn's priorities would be.

Morris looked at Maud. Then at Violet.

"Open it or I fetch the master-at-arms and a large axe," said Hawthorn.

"He knows we're in here," said Maud to Morris, low and quick, "and so far the only one who's killed anyone is Violet. Do you want Lord Hawthorn to open the door and find *our* corpses as well?"

Morris's hand strayed over his pocket again. His expression was unreadable, but uncertainty bled in at its edges.

He turned the key in the cabin door and opened it.

"Morris," said Hawthorn.

"M'lord."

Hawthorn stepped briskly inside and shut the door behind him before Morris could gather his wits to escape. His lordship's eyes flicked over Maud and the blood-sprinkled Violet and then landed on Chapman—after which they closed, briefly. Then opened in resignation.

Maud and Morris spoke at once.

"He was—"

"It was—"

"*I don't care.*" The Baron Hawthorn was in full force. He spun to look at Morris with military precision. "As far as I'm concerned, I walked into this room when you were standing over him with a bloody knife, and I will swear that on my name and my title in front of the master-at-arms and any magistrate it takes."

Morris paled. He actually looked offended, as if he'd expected his retainer-loyalty to be respected and returned by his employer's cousin.

"Right," Morris growled. "Don't suppose your name's worth any more to you than your magic was, *my lord*."

It was a reasonable jab, but it might as well have been a blown kiss. Hawthorn didn't blink.

"Remove yourself, Morris. And given that you're soon to become a wanted man, you might want to lie *very* low for the rest of the voyage. I'm sure you're a capable enough magician to manage it."

"The necklace! He has the necklace!"

"*Maud*," Hawthorn barked. "There is a corpse in the corner and the two of you will be lucky not to be arrested for murder on top of thieving and fraud, at this rate."

"No, she's right!" said Violet, earnestly polishing this gem of misdirection. "We can't let him escape with it! Not after everything that's happened!"

Finally, Morris saw sense. In one abrupt move he lunged at the cabin door, let himself out, and was gone. In his haste he slammed the door so hard it bounced ajar.

Hawthorn, after a moment, went over and closed it again.

"Do you think he bought it?" Maud asked, breathless.

"I hope so," said Violet.

"Why," muttered Hawthorn, "did I ever set foot on this accursed ship?" He stalked across the room—narrowly avoiding Chapman and the furniture—and turned Maud's face in his hands, somewhere between clinical and avuncular, frowning down at the split lip. "Maud Blyth. You are a terror and you should not be allowed to run loose in the world."

Maud's smile looked shaky. "Robin always says that."

"He has more sense than I thought." Hawthorn released her and turned inquiringly to Violet, who had managed to drag some composure together.

"As rescues go, this one was belated, Hawthorn. We had things in hand."

"My apologies—were you about to dispatch Morris as well? Did I interrupt?"

"We were about to do what we just did, which was let him go, believing he had the contract piece in hand."

She explained how the scene had played out. In return Hawthorn explained that Chapman had managed to charm him unconscious in the séance room. He'd woken sometime later to the sight of Mrs. Moretti having professional hysterics at the master-at-arms; the spiritualist claimed not to remember anything from the moment they'd all joined hands around the table.

"I," said Hawthorn dryly, "claimed to have been overcome by a malicious spirit. Then I made my escape and came to Chapman's cabin. I thought there might be a mess of some sort to clean up, and that it would be best not to bring along an audience of security officers."

As one, they looked at Chapman, then away again. Nausea rose in Violet's throat and her knees weakened at the sight of the blood. No. She was *not* going to faint, or empty her guts, or apologise.

"We'll have to come up with a good story for why this is Morris's fault," she said. "And what we were all doing here."

Maud made a long, soft sound and collapsed at the knees.

"Maud!" Violet knelt.

Maud hadn't swooned. She had simply wilted, to sit on the floor white-faced. Tears brimmed in her eyes. "I'm *sorry*. Goodness. I should be made of better stuff than this, shouldn't I? This all began with one dead body. I don't know why I didn't think to prepare myself for more of them."

Violet moved without thinking, reaching out to gather Maud up in one arm. Maud made a sniffling noise and collapsed against her. Hawthorn dangled a clean handkerchief at them; Violet handed it to Maud, who gave a gurgling sound as she cleaned her face.

"It's not— Oh, I'm crying about Mrs. Navenby, I think. I *hate* to think that she didn't get to tell us goodbye."

"She was thankful to have your voice for a while. She said so," said Violet. "And you know she'd have wanted you to protect the real cup, above everything."

Maud blew her nose, loud and unladylike in Hawthorn's kerchief, and looked marginally brighter when she was done. "It was very clever of you, Violet, making them think the locket was the piece they were looking for."

"We all thought it, when we first found the silver. I was just showing them what they wanted to be true. And performing the selfish bitch was easy enough." Her smile felt tense. Her rings sat heavy on her hands. "Most men stop looking closely when you start being the person they expect you to be."

At that, Maud lifted her eyes to Violet, a hint of reckless fire kindling in the grassy depths. "You know, I have an idea of what the story can be. Of what happened at the séance, and why it was Morris who killed Chapman." Her gaze shifted to Hawthorn. "Did you bring your chequebook on this rescue mission, my lord?"

A resigned pause. "And how much will this cost me?"

Maud removed her weight from Violet entirely. She folded the damp handkerchief into quarters, then eighths, and dabbed beneath her eyes with the freshest corner. "That depends on how much our Mr. Ross likes you," she said, apologetic. "But having watched you two bargain over pornography, I'd say . . . quite a lot."

The master-at-arms leaned back heavily in his chair and inspected the bounty spread across his desk as though he expected it to vanish at any moment.

"My word," he said, for the third time.

Violet and Maud sat across from him; Hawthorn stood near the door, as unobtrusive as such a man could be, which wasn't very. Mr. Berry looked at all of them in turn, then back at the jewels and valuables. The pile contained every item removed from first-class cabins by the elusive jewel thief operating aboard the *Lyric*. It had—supposedly—been recovered from the bottom drawer of Cabin 44, B Deck.

Maud had, in fact, insisted on searching Chapman's cabin thoroughly before they left, in case they turned up any clues in regards to the Last Contract. Violet had muddled Chapman's over-neat arrangement of toiletries into vindictive disorder but hadn't found anything interesting or incriminating.

"How did you first come to suspect Mr. Chapman?" asked Mr. Berry.

"He stole some things of Mrs. Navenby's," said Maud, wielding her lethal honesty. "He was careless, and I saw him with them, and I—I liked the idea of playing detective, to see if I could get everyone's jewels back. I thought it would be an adventure." She hung her head. Hawthorn's handkerchief was still clutched in her hand. "I truly didn't think it would be so dangerous."

"It was a foolish thing to do, Miss Cutler." Mr. Berry was aiming for stern, but it was wilting in the face of Maud's sniffles. "You should have come straight to the proper authorities."

"I know that now." Sniffle. "I realised it when he tried to accuse Miss Debenham and me of being the thieves. He'd heard about the misunderstanding with Mrs. Vaughn's cabin." Her face shone with rueful, innocent appeal. "He—he *threatened* us. He was going to force me to admit that I stole the jewels, and I *didn't*!"

"I've known men like that before," said Violet. "Miss Cutler—forgive me, dear, but you know it's true—is still naive in the ways of the world. I told her to run. We didn't realise he had an accomplice."

"Mr. Joseph Morris?"

Violet gave a shudder. "They tied us up, and they were

arguing. Morris wasn't happy that things had escalated from theft to *abduction*." This really was easier, when you sprinkled in truth with a generous hand. "And then . . . I think matters flew out of control."

A domestic spell to remove spots from clothes had left Violet unspattered by blood. Hawthorn had, indeed, given a vivid description of catching Morris—red-handed, as it were. Heavily implied was that his lordship had heroically rescued and untied the helpless girls, which made Violet feel spiky with irritation.

"Morris is nowhere to be found now," Mr. Berry said. "You have my word, Miss Cutler, that we will search tirelessly for him until the *Lyric* puts in to port."

"Suspect the man's spooked," said Hawthorn. "He knows he's nowhere to run. He might even have leapt overboard, to cheat the hangman."

Maud gave another snifflet. Mr. Berry directed a disapproving frown at his lordship for this grisly suggestion. "Jamison and Rogers told me there was a matter of . . . being possessed by ghosts, my lord." It didn't quite gather the courage to be a question.

"It was a chilling experience, sir," said Hawthorn. "I do not recommend it."

"It's such a pity everything went wrong. The séance did make me feel closer to Mrs. Navenby's spirit," said Maud wistfully. "I do so wish she were still here with us!"

Violet couldn't resist. "Yes—before Chapman took control for his own purposes, it was quite thrilling, I thought. You should engage Mrs. Moretti to do them on every voyage," she told Mr. Berry, "as an attraction."

Maud kicked the side of Violet's ankle beneath the desk.

Mr. Berry gave her an uncertain smile, then glanced back at the jewels. He was transparently overcome with relief that he'd be able to return them all to the passengers and salvage the White Star Line's reputation.

They'd handed him a story he could swallow, and they'd made it sparkle.

"Very well. Thank you again, my lord, for your—efforts. And I hope you've learned a lesson, Miss Cutler."

"Oh, *many* lessons," said Maud. "I do think this has been the most educational week of my life."

Violet went to return the kick, but Maud had tucked her feet beneath the chair, out of the way.

"Now, we've the ball to prepare for," said the master-at-arms. "Though I suppose you'd like to rest quietly, after your ordeal. The stewards could . . . bring you dinner in your cabin . . ."

He and Maud shared an awkward moment that Violet didn't understand. Maud looked like she was overcoming laughter.

"We've *so* been looking forward to the ball," said Maud. "Miss Broadley's performing, isn't she? And the lottery? We wouldn't miss it."

Christ. The bowl. They still weren't done. Violet had actually managed to forget the existence of Dorian the bloody Grey's water bowl.

"Wouldn't miss it," she echoed.

The four-poster bed seemed to taunt Violet as she and Maud dressed. Not for sexual reasons, this time. She remembered how soft and inviting its pillows were. Nerve-racking events made Violet want to *nap*.

No. They had to get hold of the bloody bowl, or all of this would have been for nothing.

Both of them picked out the dresses they'd worn on the very first night aboard. The indigo blue was Violet's finest; and though Violet preferred the silver-grey, she couldn't deny that the sunset pink set off Maud's complexion gorgeously.

They helped each other with buttons and laces, Violet formed braids back from Maud's temples and looped them into the pinned pile of her hair, and they threw ideas back and forth. Dorian and his cage might be on display during the dinner that preceded the dancing, or they might not. The lottery would involve small bits of paper. They had Violet's magic—what else could they use? The Pipes and Drums? Lord Albert? A kangaroo?

Violet slid her entire collection of rings into her evening bag.

"This is your last night to create scandal, Miss Debenham," said Maud. "Are you sure you don't wish to attend with short hair and a moustache?"

Violet, tugging on her gloves, laughed. "We are Lord Hawthorn's strumpets, and we were abducted by murderous jewel thieves. We're already going to have enough attention to make getting our hands on this bowl a trial. Here, look at me. Should we cover up those battle wounds of yours?"

She cupped Maud's face, lifting it to her own. The split in Maud's lower lip had scabbed over. The memory of Chapman's blood kept trying to climb into Violet's throat, but she shoved it down.

"I don't know much healing," added Violet. "I'm better at greasepaint."

"We could ask Mrs.—" Maud's hand faltered, reaching for the sunflower locket that wasn't there. Her face fell. Violet let her hands drop.

"I really am sorry," Violet said quietly.

"I know." Maud chewed her lip. She was going to reopen the cut. "Violet, if you hadn't thought of the locket—if it really was a choice between giving up the contract and letting them hurt me, what would you have done?"

Violet had no idea what answer Maud wanted. She had even less idea of what the truth was.

Maud went on, "I didn't tell you all the details of how Walter Courcey ended up with the coin, did I? Edwin made the bargain, for Robin's safety—and mine—and gambled that it was better to be safe and free, and able to plan for the next battle." Her fingers hovered over her bruised cheek, then fell. "I don't know if I'd be able to do that. If it would have occurred to me. It certainly didn't occur to *Robin*." A self-deprecating flicker. "We're not great thinkers, we Blyths."

"If I'd done the same . . ."

"I could hardly have blamed you," said Maud. "It would have made the next few battles harder, but I would have understood. And probably been grateful, once I'd stopped shouting at you, that you'd consider me worth it."

Violet said with absolute honesty, "I don't know what I'd have done."

Now it was Maud looking at the bed. She didn't look tired. Violet had never seen *tired* on Maud Blyth; she looked entirely alert until she slept, when she looked as though she might never wake.

"When we . . ." A slight blush. "Last night, I thought, *I could tell her to do anything, and she would.* Anything." Her eyes cut to Violet with undoing speed. "Because the more outlandish it was, the more outrageous my request, the better a shield you'd have for the truth."

"But you didn't," said Violet, careful.

"No. I told you to put the shield down."

"You told me I could say no."

Maud chewed her lip again. Violet curled her hands to stop them from reaching out to stop her.

Violet said, "Is this an apology?"

A moment's hesitation, and Maud shook her head.

"Do you wish you'd asked for something else?"

"No," said Maud. "But now I can't stop thinking about how far I could push you."

Maud, with her *lists.* Only Maud had ever looked at Violet with this hunger that veiled itself in nothing at all, unashamed and ceaselessly questioning. Violet smoothed her gloves for the fourth time, and her skin cried out for more.

They were fully dressed. They should be leaving. They would be late for dinner.

Violet said, "Give me an example."

Maud's face was florid pink, like the first time she'd stepped out from Hawthorn's bedchamber with her eyes screwed shut. As if, even now, she was picturing something that she was too well-bred to put words to.

Maud said, "You mentioned tying me down and making me scream. I'd like to see you try that. And I liked watching you do magic, and *especially* liked making you unable to hold it. I think . . . I could ask you to stay silent, and then see how loud I could convince you to be."

Now *Violet* was picturing it. Maud had learned a lot in a few days. And if it were a competition—if she were again doing her determined best to make Violet lose control—

"Fuck," Violet said. "You *shouldn't* be allowed loose in the world."

"And then—"

"No. Stop talking now, or I *will* tie you to the bed and fuck you in the ruin of that dress, balls and bowls be damned."

Maud looked delighted that Violet had met her ante and raised it. Her smile was a promise and her posture loosened.

Violet's need loosened too. Now it was a yearning only partly to do with Maud's skin and Maud's laugh and the way Maud's upper lip looked as though someone had dented its centre with the press of a finger. Violet wanted to curl up in a window-seat and just *talk*. She wanted to ask Maud, who was frequently terrified but never defeated, what she thought happened after death. Whether she feared it, or saw it as another quest, or a boat suspended on the world with no land in sight.

"Shall we be going?" said Maud.

"We don't have a plan yet," Violet pointed out.

"I know." Maud's collarbones rose and fell as she shrugged, shifting her necklace of golden lilies set with tiny seed pearls. "Let's start by getting ourselves into the room with Dorian's cage, and go from there. Between us, we're not bad at thinking on our feet." A sudden grin. "If all else fails, I'll go and weep all over Lord Hawthorn until he's forced to help. Or trade all of Mr. Ross's pornography back in exchange for him stealing Dorian from the winner."

"*All* of it?" Violet said, mock-appalled.

"I can make sacrifices too. Besides"—with a wicked fleeting dimple as Maud turned to the door, which made Violet's entire chest seize like corset laces—"I've read most of it by now."

The tables in the dining saloon were crammed along the sides of the room like timid wallflowers, allowing for dancing in the centre. No pattern-dances were possible because of the pillars, and it was a far cry from the lofty-ceilinged ballrooms that Maud had set foot in before; but the air was gilded with chandelier light and someone had opened a hatch leading out to the narrow strip of deck, so that the evening air could breathe coolly into the body-press heat. An aviary of gorgeously plumed passengers chattered and laughed as they ate and drank and moved around the room.

Maud took her lottery ticket from the steward at the entrance and gave it to Violet, who committed both numbers to memory before stowing them in her bag.

Even more than usual, eyes followed them from the doorway. They left a churned-up wake of murmuring as they went. Maud had expected it, but her skin still felt sensitive to the force of so many glances. She'd never been so grateful for the granite-solid nature of Violet's act. Violet kept her chin high and didn't modulate her laughter, and allowed herself to be drawn into a breathless and only slightly fabricated version of their *terrifying* chase and abduction.

Maud drank water, and ate poached sole in butter sauce, and thought about the fact she still hadn't asked how Violet was feeling; Violet, who'd killed her second man with a spell that opened throats, and who'd looked frighteningly blank afterwards.

She didn't think Violet would lie to her. And Maud had only now realised, far too late, how much power she had demanded by asking Violet to lay down her shield. It was undeserved. It was more than she'd bargained for. More than a contract should allow one person to steal.

Violet might wear her sparkling recklessness well, but beneath it she was careful, careful, careful. Maud was not; but she would learn to be. She would *choose* to be, as she chose every day to be generous and kind and all the other things that defied the coiled snake of her inherited nature.

After the meal they strolled out onto the deck. There were fewer people outside than Maud had expected, explaining the crush of the saloon. Light spatters of rain were whipped against them by the wind. No stars. A grudging glow from the shrouded moon.

"Ugh," said Violet. "So much for fresh air."

Maud dragged in another lungful anyway. "I rather like it."

"I don't think inspiration is going to strike us out here," said Violet. "And they're setting up for the lottery."

Back inside, Maud's eyes leapt from person to person. One of the Boston sisters was fanning the other, both of them talking at once. Maud had to gather her skirts to inch around the possible honeymooners, who'd pulled their chairs close and were giggling together. The red-haired woman wore a gown with gorgeous lace ruffles, and the man's moustache was more lopsided than ever. What would *they* do if they won an African Grey with an unfortunate vocabulary?

Maud was wondering with some bemusement whether the best strategy mightn't be marching up to the winner, whomever they turned out to be, and asking outright to *buy* Dorian back—in memory of her poor dead aunt, et cetera—when Violet's hand closed on her arm.

"*Look,*" said Violet.

Maud followed her gaze. There were a lot of people in that direction.

"It's worth a try," Violet murmured before Maud could ask. "Give me a moment."

The man she approached had a short blond beard and a scarlet coat—almost a military style, trimmed in black and gold. Violet's manner was at its most flirtatious, commanding his attention. It wasn't until he kissed Violet's proffered hand that Maud recognised him as the young man who'd approached them during the carnival and spoken in another language.

Violet fished in her bag. The man fished inside the front of his wonderful red coat. The two of them shook hands, as if closing a business deal.

Maud almost laughed, as another of Robin's visions fell into place. She could feel the humour on her mouth as Violet took her leave and returned to Maud.

"Oh, well *done,* Harriet."

"It may come to nothing. It might be as disastrous as following the motorcar vision was. But one doesn't see a red coat on a man very often."

"Climbing into the motorcar was a perfectly sound idea," Maud protested. "It wasn't Robin's fault that they put a tracking rune on you."

"Yes." Violet made a face and looked around. "I'll find Clarence and have him remove the rune tonight. Even if Morris is lying low, I don't enjoy knowing that he could follow me around whenever he fancies."

The bearded man now bowed in their direction, and Violet kissed her fingers to him. "Nice boy," she said. "I hope my ticket wins him a lovely bottle of port."

"What did you tell him? I hope you didn't promise to become a tsarina after all."

"I told him," said Violet solemnly, "that during Mrs. Moretti's séance, a spirit informed me it was *vastly* important we should trade tickets. I think his English stretched that far. He seemed rather tickled by the idea, in any case."

Sadly, Violet's ticket didn't win the gentleman anything. A case of wine, a season ticket to the Royal Opera and another to a Broadway theatre, a pretty standing clock, and several White Star Line souvenirs were handed out to men and women who waved their tickets triumphantly in the air.

Finally came the late addition to the list of prizes—*"An amusing and lively creature, ladies and gentlemen, generously donated by Mr. Frank Bernard!"*—and Maud stifled a leap of delight when Violet lifted ticket number 172 and strode to the area in front of the fidgeting orchestra to collect her prize.

She brought Dorian, cage and all, back to where Maud stood. All of Maud's effort went into looking merely amused that her friend had serendipitously won the parrot that had once been hers, instead of allowing any of her elation to creep onto her face.

It was there. The cup of the Last Contract was right there. Maud was past carelessness: that bowl was going to be on her person from now until the moment she could put it into Edwin's hands.

"Oh!" she said, as if it had just occurred to her. "Miss Broadley can use it for her nightingale song after all! Here, Violet, let me . . ."

Maud opened the cage door and extracted first the food bowl—full of nuts and fresh grapes, she was glad to see—and then the water bowl. Then Dorian, who hopped onto Maud's gloved fingers with as much condescension as a duchess accepting a footman's assistance down from a carriage.

Violet hoisted the empty cage and swept her way back to the performance area, where she made a production of offering Miss Broadley the prop. She held the eyes of the room effortlessly, and the singer—radiant in a white gown with opalescent beading—accepted it with a deep, ironic curtsy. There was a smattering of applause—mostly, Maud thought, because the crowd was in the mood to applaud.

"I'd offer to duet with you, Miss Broadley," said Violet, projecting her smokiest tones, "but you *may* have heard that the kind of songs I'm used to aren't exactly of the *classical* calibre."

Laughter as well as applause, this time. Nobody had attention to spare for Maud emptying the silver water bowl into the pot of the nearest standing fern and then slipping it into the deep pocket that was the main reason she'd chosen this evening gown over all the others.

"Maud?"

"Helen! Good evening."

"Good evening." There was a stubborn angle to Helen's chin. Maud braced herself for yet more questions about the séance—Helen deserved to ask, if anyone did—but Helen simply looked at Dorian, face softening. "I *am* sorry we couldn't take him. If Miss Debenham doesn't have room for him, *please* do ask her to write to me before she sells him to a collector. I'm sure I could wriggle around Mama somehow."

"We'd better hope Violet doesn't teach him any music-hall songs in the meantime," said Maud.

Helen giggled and reached out a finger to scratch the side of Dorian's neck. The parrot gave a chirrup of approval and stretched his head towards her.

"You could write to me too," said Helen. "I'd love to show you the menagerie when they're properly settled in and happy, not shut up in crates."

Or racing around the ship under the direction of a Pied Piper charm. Maud felt a glow of affection for the girl, who could have decided that their tentative friendship was too much bother now that Maud had turned into even more of a flypaper for scandal.

"Here," said Maud. "Would you hold him for me, during the singing? I have the start of a headache. I think I'll duck out and get some air."

"Isn't it raining?" Helen asked, though she was already reaching out, her smile widening. Dorian followed his food bowl, stepping from Maud's wrist to Helen's, and even closed his eyes in avian pleasure when Helen scratched his neck again.

"I'm sure the rain's stopped by now," said Maud.

She was surprised to find that it actually had. The night air hung heavy and cleanly damp. Miss Broadley had begun to sing, and the caramel-smooth notes followed Maud out through the hatch. She stood on deck a while, listening, shivering with pleasure at the music.

She didn't have a headache, but she did want to be alone with the fact that she'd done what Robin needed her to do. She touched the bowl, solid and real in her pocket. She tipped her head back and counted the few stars that dared to peek through the clearing clouds.

Footsteps sounded behind her, and Maud turned to see Violet holding two glasses of champagne, one of which she handed to Maud with an arch smile. Violet touched a finger to her lips as if they were schoolgirls getting away with something at a grand adult party.

They toasted, the clink of glasses dissolving into the throb of opera and engine and water against the side of the ship. The champagne was lukewarm, sweeter than any Maud had tasted before, but the bubbles tickled teasingly at her lips as she drank two good swallows.

"I left Dorian with Helen," she told Violet. "Did she find you? I—"

The deck rose and fell beneath Maud's feet with sudden insistence. She reached out to steady herself, found nothing, and fumbled the half-empty glass. It fell to the deck and shattered with a *ting* that sent splinters of white sound into Maud's temples.

"Oh, dear." The voice was not any of Violet's many voices. It was soft, it was sweet, and it quavered with age. "You're not used to drinking, are you, Miss Blyth? You don't look well at all."

Maud couldn't focus her eyes. The blurred column in front of her still looked like Violet. Maud smelled musty roses. It was all wrong. Her entire body tried to pull away and again she stumbled over her shoe, over the hem of her skirt. This time she almost fell.

She was prevented by a grip beneath her arm, supporting and inescapable. Papery skin. Maud shuddered. Above her head the few brave stars spun in sickening circles.

"Now, now," said that sweet voice. "Can't have you taking a tumble, can we? Let's find you somewhere to sit down."

34

Applause from the dining saloon spattered into the opening notes played by the orchestra. The piece was familiar, but the breeze snatched the quivering melody of the strings away before Maud's ears could catch proper hold.

A curtain-spell, thought Maud fuzzily, *can be used solely for concealment of what lies inside its radius, or can have its clauses adjusted so that those within cannot see or hear what takes place without.* One day she would find herself sitting exams at Cambridge, trying to dredge up facts about history or philosophy or art, and instead would be able to recall nothing but Edwin Courcey's voice as he explained magic to her entirely unmagical self.

With effort, she hauled her thoughts back to the present moment.

The effect of the imbued champagne was already lessening. Maud clung to that, along with the fact that she had not been tied to any more chairs. She had simply been led, gently but firmly, to sit in the corner of the deck farthest from the hatches leading back into the saloon.

The illusion of Violet had vanished when Mrs. Vaughn cast the curtain-spell around them. It had served its purpose.

How had Maud been so stupid? She would never, *ever* drink champagne again. She'd fallen twice for the same trick. She'd dropped her guard, too wrapped up in self-congratulation at having finally put her hands on the bowl.

The bowl.

Maud's throat closed. She laced her hands together instantly and squeezed tight enough to hurt. She would not touch it. She would not *think* of it. It wasn't there.

The items of the Last Contract are undetectable by seeking spells, said the dry, comforting voice of her inner Edwin.

Seraphina Vaughn cradled a spell that solidified into a folding-stool. She seated herself with the slowness of the elderly, rescuing the fringed ends of her shawl from where they were slipping down her elbows. Maud couldn't make out the colour of the embroidery at the shawl's edges, though Mrs. Vaughn sat with her back to the railing, and golden light spilled out of the closest porthole, illuminating her face well enough.

Some more of the sick giddiness receded. Maud felt well enough to tuck her legs to one side, take a deep breath of the bracing air, and look Mrs. Vaughn in the face.

"You weren't there when I told Chapman and Morris who I am, and why you don't want to do me any harm."

Though Mrs. Vaughn had called Maud by her real name, Maud remembered with a lurch.

"No. Joe Morris filled me in on the details. A *foreseer*—fancy that." Mrs. Vaughn looked tired. A frown pinched the wrinkles of her face like a finger pushed down in the skin atop heated milk. "I don't know if that whimpering wide-eyed look is for show, girl, but you can set it aside, if so. I won't hurt you. I only want to have a conversation."

"And if—if I get up and walk away, right this moment?" Maud had no idea if her legs would hold her.

Another fretful petting of the shawl. "I suppose I would try to stop you. I am a magician, Miss Blyth, and you are not." It was spoken with such calm resignation that it almost didn't register as a threat. "Though you *are* something interesting."

Yes. This woman had to believe, as Morris believed, that Mrs. Navenby was still haunting Maud; that the locket had nothing to do with it at all. And this woman was one of Mrs. Navenby's oldest friends, even if they hadn't spoken for decades. Maud couldn't hope to fool her for long with a simple impression.

"Mrs. Navenby won't tell you anything," said Maud. "She— she has nothing to say to you."

"I know."

Maud blinked. "You know?"

A twinkling, Christmas-card sort of smile, with malice dusted faintly at the edges. "Beth would fling you overboard herself before she'd betray any more secrets that Flora wanted her to keep. Has she already given that actress a scalding earful for giving up the cup?"

"No," said Maud. "She's . . . been quiet." Truth. It tasted dangerous on her tongue.

"Sulking." Mrs Vaughn snorted. "She was never a graceful loser."

Maud's head was entirely clear now. She thought again about the contents of her skirt pocket. She was almost certain she'd be able to run. But Mrs. Vaughn, for all her showy infirmity and twinkling roundness, had cradled with the nimble speed that Maud had seen in old women knitting quilt-squares for charity.

And . . . a conversation meant information flowing in both directions. Chapman was dead and Morris in hiding. This might be the best chance Maud had.

She looped her clasped hands around her knees, stretching out her back.

"If you know Mrs. Navenby won't talk to you," she said frankly, "then why do you want to talk to *me*?"

"Why you, instead of Enid's heir?"

That was a revealing assumption. Maud nodded. Mrs. Vaughn's silver brows rose.

"The one who surrendered the cup when she realised this was a more deadly game than she'd bargained for? No, no— she sounds like a practical, self-interested girl. I've no doubt she has her price, and we've plenty of time to discover what it is. But you, Miss Blyth, strike me as less easily bought. And less likely to do anything rash like slitting the throat of an old woman."

Maud was struck speechless: both by the casual, insidious *we,* and by the fact that someone could be so sharp and yet so utterly wrong. Then she wondered at her own surprise. After all, Violet had been performing selfishness from the moment she set foot on board, and Maud . . . Maud was the *nice* one. Everyone knew that.

"I wondered," Mrs. Vaughn went on, "if you might listen to reason."

"Reason? Your friends magicked me to a chair and tried to pummel information out of me!"

"Friends? Indeed. Mr. Chapman was a Cooper." Mrs. Vaughn shook her head like a disappointed grandmother. "The Coopers are bullies to a man, Miss Blyth. They're in love with their own power and will eat from anyone's hand if they think it'll get them more. Chapman had all the worst of that with no strength of character to offset it."

Maud, off-balance, barely managed to bite back her whole-hearted agreement. *Don't interrupt,* she told herself savagely. *For once in your life, Maud Blyth, don't open your mouth.*

"Morris is a far better trained dog. He's a blunt instrument in his master's hand, and he can't be turned. And these men tolerate me because I know things they need to know, but they still think there's something *grubby* about their reliance on a woman. An old woman, at that. You call them my *friends*?"

Mrs. Vaughn laughed. It was a comfortable chuckle, so warm and soft that you wanted to cut off a slice and spread it with butter. "You have no idea how angry these men are that they've been forced to look at old women and take them seriously. That idiot Chapman probably killed Beth out of sheer affront that she'd lifted her hands to do magic against him."

"Then why work with them at all?" asked Maud. Should she

be trying to reason with Mrs. Vaughn in return? Talk her out of it? All of Maud's instincts still told her she was in danger, but Mrs. Vaughn was talking with the steady, slightly defensive fluency of someone who'd not been listened to and now had an audience. And Maud was so *curious*. She wanted to hear what kind of person Seraphina Hope was, outside of the story that Mrs. Navenby had told.

"Because their larger goals are laudable," said Mrs. Vaughn simply.

"Stealing power?"

"Pooling power." She frowned. "The fundamental limitation of magic is that it's individual. We magicians only keep ourselves hidden because we're vastly outnumbered, and working large spells needs difficult coordination."

"You think magicians shouldn't be secret?" said Maud. That was a new piece in this puzzle. "You think everyone should be—unbusheled."

"I think the Forsythia Club didn't go far enough," said Mrs. Vaughn. "The world would have tried to stop us because we were women, and instead of laughing in their faces and proving them wrong, Flora made us stop *ourselves*." A bitter, salt-soaked lash of a word. "We could have done things that no man ever could. We could have pushed magic further. We almost had more power than anyone, and we *gave it up*."

"It sounds like you did do more than most men," said Maud. "Incredible things. Wasn't that enough?" But she thought of Violet, running across an ocean in order to live a life more magical than the one she'd been allotted.

"It's a weak kind of ambition that recognises *enough*. I thought I'd found my true friends. I thought we were in agreement that we would change the world. Flora and her ley lines— she could have rerouted rivers, she could have uprooted every forest in England, and instead she scrabbled around in the dirt and grew roses. Beth was always flitting from one thing to the next, content to be a dabbler. And *Lady* Enid, who began on a higher footing than any of us, was happy to work with her husband for no more than *music.*"

There was so much disgust there that Maud pushed down her instinctive response. She thought of roses climbing the walls, and lights exploding in the sky, and glittering scarlet fish. She thought of Miss Broadley's voice. She thought: *Nothing is wasted that's beautiful.*

She chewed her lip as if in doubt. She took some truth and twisted it.

"I . . . I've always hated how little is expected of women. My brother didn't take me seriously when I told him I wanted to study at university."

"There, you see?" Mrs. Vaughn snorted.

"And you, ma'am?" Maud asked respectfully. "What was your speciality of magic?"

"Ah, well. There are still some ways for a small amount of magic to have a large effect," said Mrs. Vaughn with a smile. "I could have poured one of my imbuements into the soup served at dinner, or into the freshwater tanks, and made this entire ship sleep for a hundred years. As though you, Miss Blyth, or some other princess, had pricked your finger on a spindle and cursed them."

A chill passed through Maud at the thought of the ship floating forever, silent, too far from land to even overgrow with ivy and thorns.

"You imbued Lord Hawthorn's whisky," she blurted as the thought slotted home.

"He picked up on that, did he? I thought he must have, given he's still walking around. Even a sip would have put an elephant into the depths of unconsciousness for a week. In a man, it'd have appeared almost like death."

She sounded wistful that she hadn't had the chance to see the success of her creation. Maud thought of Alan Ross, on whom magic never quite worked as it should, slumped on Hawthorn's rug in a shallow and easily negated sleep.

"Regardless," said Mrs. Vaughn. It took Maud a moment

to remember what they'd been speaking of. The Forsythia Club and its goals—yes. "The others said that they wished to push at the boundaries of magic, to rewrite what *men* had assumed, but they all turned squeamish at the cost. And I was outvoted."

And not trusted with a piece of the Last Contract. And had carried her bitterness beneath her tongue like an unswallowed pill all the years that followed.

They were close, *so* close, to the answers that Robin and Edwin had been seeking. Was the fragile kinship Maud had woven between them enough for her to dig further?

"What was the cost?"

Mrs. Vaughn's gaze was distant, as if fixed far beyond the *Lyric* and all the souls aboard. "Oh, blood," she said. "It always is, for real power."

Maud drew breath to prod further, but the woman's attention sharpened. Her eyes returned to Maud and a curtain drew over her expression.

"So yes, Miss Blyth. I considered it worth the tedium of dealing with men. Necessity makes strange bedfellows. If the contract can be put to its obvious purpose, *every* magician will benefit. Men and women alike."

"And you honestly think these men will share their power with you when they have it?" It flared out of Maud before she could snatch it back.

Mrs. Vaughn's face hardened. "I think I will live long enough to fix my mistakes. I have no intention of dying with regrets."

"No—just making sure that your friends are murdered with theirs."

"They made their choices," Mrs. Vaughn snapped. "Flora was dead before I ever knew what was afoot."

Maud bit her tongue on any further accusations. So—Mrs. Vaughn had told Bastoke's conspirators where to find Lady Enid, who'd died just as Flora Sutton had, rather than betray the contract to them. And then—

"Did you come to America to try and talk Mrs. Navenby around to your side?" Maud asked.

A small, half-amused nod. The last knot of guilt in Maud, at the prospect that *she* might have led them to Mrs. Navenby and so caused her death, slipped gratefully free.

"They didn't want a repeat of what happened with Enid. If nothing else, I knew Beth well enough that I might be able to discover what she'd done with the cup. But Morris had barely time to—what was that dreadful term?—*scope out the joint*, when *you* arrived, and Beth was suddenly making plans to move back to England." A genteel shrug. "It's all turned out for the best. We have the cup now. And we'll have the knife, too, though that will go easier if someone sympathetic has Miss Debenham's trust."

It was an obvious prompt, seeking an obvious answer. Maud looked over at the well-lit portholes where the party carried on without her. Had Violet missed her yet? Had she come to the hatch and seen nothing but sky and the empty deck?

"You can't let the dead rule your life, girl," said Mrs. Vaughn. "Take my advice on that. You can only reach out and take what's best for *you*."

It echoed unpleasantly what Violet had said when Maud was tied to the chair; and Violet had been acting, but not quite acting.

And Maud was in the same fix, and it was going to have the same outcome. It was all so stupid. She was starting to tremble with cold.

"I'm sorry," she said; the only lie she could muster. "I can't help you. I won't. Mrs. Navenby and I are in agreement on this point."

"Why?" It sounded like a genuine question. "You don't owe anything to the magicians of Britain."

Hawthorn had said that. Violet had said that. All the usual answers—Robin, revenge for Mrs. Navenby, the inherent wrongness of taking from another without asking—brimmed on Maud's tongue.

But she touched her mouth with the side of her thumb. And told the truth.

"No, I don't. But if I have to create myself every day, with every choice I make, then I want to make the choices *I* won't regret when I look back on my life at its end."

There was a sigh from Mrs. Vaughn. "A pity. Life's not kind to idealists, girl, when you haven't the power to go with the ideas."

She cradled. Maud barely had time to tense before the spell was done, a dense white light that Mrs. Vaughn turned on herself and rubbed into both of her forearms like cold cream. Then the old woman stood, creakingly, and offered Maud a hand up from the deck.

Maud, drilled in society manners and entirely unsure what was happening, took her hand.

The yank that brought her upright made Maud yelp with pain. She'd been braced for a gentle tug, not a pull like she'd been roped to a motorcar. Now Mrs. Vaughn held both of Maud's arms snug against her sides, just above the elbows. Maud might have been wedged in a crevice of stone.

"Unlike the men with whom I find myself working," said Mrs. Vaughn calmly, "I have no qualms about disappointing George Bastoke. It doesn't matter who or what your brother is. If Elizabeth Navenby wants to stand between me and the power I've worked for, *again,* and if you will do nothing to prevent it, then I must act for myself."

"What—"

Mrs. Vaughn's spell-strengthened arms lifted Maud clear off her feet and then higher, as if she were no more than a hollow toy sewn from leaves and feathers. Maud let out a shriek, and then a louder one, and tried to kick for all she was worth, but her aim was wild with panic and her toes kept glancing off the vast softness and slipperiness of Mrs. Vaughn's skirts.

She was two feet off the ground. The breeze off the sea, swift and sly and suddenly hungry, dragged cold fingers over the bare skin of Maud's neck and arms. And Maud realised what was about to happen.

As Mrs. Vaughn lifted her clear over the railing at the edge of the deck, Maud found an icy point right in the centre of her fear. It said: *This, or nothing.*

Survive, or nothing.

She lashed out one last time with her foot and connected with a crunch.

Mrs. Vaughn made a grunt of pain and fumbled her grip. Maud scrabbled in midair. Her stomach formed a stone as she realised it was too late—she was too far out over the edge. Nothing but magic could save her from falling now.

For a single, awful moment she was facing straight down, into the distant black expanse of the sea: a foam-tipped mouth waiting to swallow her cold.

But she had the use of her arms back.

Mrs. Vaughn was still cursing behind her, and the skirts of Maud's lovely dress slithered against the damp metal of the rail as she tipped over, and she twisted her body in a movement that felt like it came from that smouldering wordless place of anger deep inside her chest. Her hands moved frantically. They wanted to *grab*. The railing was just there, and her only option.

She missed the top rail. One finger erupted in new pain from jarring at an angle, and she slid down—grabbed for the lower rail, hearing a sound like a snarling fox come from her mouth— and she had it with one hand, which began at once to slide free—and then the other.

Another yank. Her shoulder throbbed. Something tore in the bodice of her dress.

But it was the yank of a body's weight coming to a stop.

It had taken—how many heartbeats? Time had turned slow and cold, and fire-hot and fast, both at once. And now Maud and her layers and layers of clothes, Maud who'd never learned to swim, dangled high above the night-darkened ocean, from ten gloved fingers holding cold damp metal with no magic to strengthen their grip.

Mrs. Vaughn appeared at the railing. Her nose bled an inky streak down the blur of her face. She glanced down at Maud, made a tutting sound, and fished something from a sleeve to dab at her nose. They were farther from the light. Maud couldn't see the woman's expression, just the white flag of her handkerchief.

Any moment now, Mrs. Vaughn would take hold of Maud's hands and pry them loose.

Lifting one of her own hands from the rail was the hardest thing Maud had done in her life. She slid her freed hand into her pocket.

First she touched the bowl. The cause of all of this. For a wild tantrum of a moment she pictured herself tossing the bloody thing into the sea. But no: Maud could fight for Britain's magicians, but it wasn't up to her to make choices of that size on their behalf. She was done trampling on people's lives and powers without thought.

The other object in Maud's pocket was something she'd found in Chapman's room.

Maud had searched Chapman's luggage, looking for clues about the contract, while Violet took the desk and dresser. The hinged wooden box had been tucked into a travelling bag. Inside it were nestled a cluster of glass baubles the size of a nutmeg, each one filled with smoke of a different hue.

Chapman had flung one into the motorcar to make Maud and Violet climb out. And before that, when they first found the stolen silver, Maud remembered Chapman beginning to toss one at Hawthorn before his lordship got him in the knees with a stick. A neat little box of nasty tricks. Perhaps, like the priez-vous, all the Coopers used them.

Maud had quietly transferred the baubles into her own possession. She hadn't told Hawthorn; he'd likely try to take them off her, for her own good. She hadn't even told Violet. After the

Goblin's Bridle, after being hit and kicked and threatened with worse, Maud had gratefully seized the prospect of having some secret magic defences of her own. She'd brought a jade-green bauble in her pocket tonight, much as Violet had brought her collection of rings.

Now she closed her fingers carefully around it and pulled her hand free.

A curtain-spell, like an illusion, requires sustained focus.

"Now then," said Mrs. Vaughn, rather nasally. "Let's—"

Maud lifted the bauble with her aching arm and tossed it right into the woman's face.

Only the edge of the smell caught Maud, but it was still enough for her to retch: a solid, horrific stench of rot. She turned her face away, shoved her free hand over her mouth and nose, and took a huge breath through the damp dirty palm of her glove.

Then she opened her mouth and screamed—a shrill, high sound as loud as she could make it. With the next breath she yelled, *"Help! Someone help!"* for good measure, before screaming again.

Mrs. Vaughn was coughing into her hands. She stumbled away. Now all Maud could see was the white rail and her own gloves, gripping it with shaking fingers—she latched on her second hand, feeling the muscles of her forearms stretch painfully— and the side of the ship above the deck, stretching up and up to where plumes of smoke from the vast chimneys cast a blurred shadow on the night sky.

Maud sucked in another breath for the next scream. The jade-green stench was thinning with the wind. Her arms burned and she felt frantically for toeholds. Her shoes scrabbled against metal panels dotted with cruelly small bolts and irregularities. The top railing would take so much strength to reach, it might as well have been yards above her head.

Could she hear voices? She couldn't hear music any longer, but the wind and her own pulse were exchanging breathless cries in her ears.

Her left hand spasmed and slipped free, and the next scream was entirely involuntary, short and sharp. *Robin, Robin, I'm so sorry.* She gritted her jaw so hard with anger that her face ached.

"*Maud!*"

It was Violet, her voice harsh and thin with fear as she leaned over the rail. Maud almost sobbed. "Careful!" she gasped, as Violet's clumsy grab nearly dislodged her fingers.

"Vi, get out of the way" came another voice, just as harsh.

A second pair of hands—these ones ungloved, thin fingers brimming with a murky-gold spell—descended in her direction. She strained, flailing up with her free left hand—missed once, missed again—and was caught fast.

Clarence Blackwood's grip lacked the iron strength that Mrs. Vaughn had used, but something about it felt utterly unshakable, as if he'd welded his palms to her wrist. Maud's right hand slipped from the rail. She barely budged an inch, dangling from the single arm in Clarence's grasp.

"Can—grab Vi with the other," Clarence panted. "Might take both of us."

Violet took fresh hold of Maud's hand and leaned perilously far down to grab Maud's dress at the shoulder. Fabric strained and tore as she and Clarence heaved, but Maud was held steady, and she let out her breath in a wheezy sob as her waist passed over the railing and she half slid, half fell in an awkward heap on the deck.

"I'm fine," she found herself saying, over and over. "I'm fine, I'm fine. Really. I'm fine."

She was mostly trying to convince herself. She would sort out the truth of it later.

She struggled to her feet with Violet's help and looked around. People were trickling out onto the deck and pressing their noses to the portholes, trying to see what the commotion was about. She saw the top of Lord Hawthorn's head where he was using his cane and his sharpest manner to part the thicket of people in the hatchway.

And there. Off to the side and half-shadowed was Mrs. Vaughn, her face now clear of blood, her hands folded in front of her—a harmless, currant-bun woman with a will as large as the moon.

She smiled as she met Maud's eyes and cradled something, then disappeared entirely.

Violet shook hands with Lady Albert before heading back to the first-class areas. The woman had no doubt marked Violet down as a determined eccentric, but all theatre folk knew you took the money from eccentrics when it was offered.

The Bartons had been helpful. And Violet had to start deciding what she wanted to do with her inheritance, if she wasn't to be a dragon atop a hoard. Becoming an official patron of London's first coloured opera company seemed like something that Lady Enid would have approved of.

Dissolute naked parties weren't entirely off the table either.

The May morning was hazy with blue heat, as if the rain had swept everything clear for summer to step onto the stage. The *Lyric* was less than an hour from arrival in Southampton, and the ship was alive with packing and porters and parasols.

Violet and Maud had done their packing after breakfast. Dorian's cage now bore a tag that marked him as part of Miss Violet Debenham's baggage. A rude and talkative parrot, Violet reflected, was practically a required accessory when one was embarking on becoming a rich and eccentric old woman.

Maud and Hawthorn were currently in conference with the master-at-arms and the senior ship's clerk, arranging for a message to be sent to Mrs. Navenby's solicitors in New York. For her luggage to be stored awaiting word from her relatives. And, one assumed, for something to be done with the corpse in the ice room.

Maud had stroked a wistful hand over the rune-sewn garments but had packed them all up without a murmur, saying stoutly that they weren't hers to take.

Violet had retrieved the heat-charmed coat and packed it between two of her own skirts when Maud was in the bathroom. She was sure Mrs. Navenby would want Maud to have something to remember her by.

She'd wait a while before giving it back to Maud, though. Perhaps until the winter.

"Took your sweet time," said Alan Ross, when Violet knocked on Hawthorn's cabin door. "So we *are* meeting. I was half expecting ship security, ready to accuse me of stealing the candlesticks."

"Didn't you hear? Our thief was murdered by an accomplice," said Violet. She closed the door behind her. No point asking how Ross had made his way inside, given his facility with lockpicks. "Maud and Hawthorn will be along shortly, I'm sure."

They were. Ross looked up from where he was shuffling a deck of cards in preparation for a game. He nodded at Maud, but his gaze rested, hostile and unsettled, on Hawthorn.

"You *summoned* me, your lordship? Is now the time when you put one of those magical things on my tongue, to keep me quiet?"

"If you thought that was going to happen, you wouldn't have come." Hawthorn dropped a small leather box in Ross's lap on his way to sprawl in the largest armchair.

Curious, Violet sat next to Ross on the sofa. The light caught on the box's contents as he cracked the lid.

Ross sucked in a breath. Gingerly he prodded one of the diamond cufflinks, then the other. His fingers hovered over the third object as if afraid to be burned. It was a fob watch, the case gleaming with the warmth of gold and set with an intricate spiral of tiny glittering stones.

"What's this?" Wariness swam in his voice.

"Compensation for damages," said Hawthorn. "You didn't ask for enough from me. One of those brooches you stole is worth half as much as my townhouse; I don't know why the woman didn't have it in the ship's safe. I didn't realise you were an *amateur* jewel thief."

"Oh, *fuck* you." Ross looked almost ill.

"Ignorance like that, you would have been cheated by any fence you went to. Stick to pornography from now on."

Ross's head rose sharply and he glared, narrow-eyed. But he couldn't keep his gaze off the glitter of the watch for long.

"Where'd this spring from?" he demanded. "It wasn't here when I searched the place and found the cufflinks."

"No. It was in the ship's safe," said Hawthorn, in his driest drawl.

Maud peered down and gave a low murmur of admiration. Ross closed the box. He stood in a sudden jerk and went to hold it, stiff-armed, in Hawthorn's face.

"*No.* I don't know what this is—if you're trying to soothe your own conscience, if it even exists. But I don't need protecting from my mistakes. So I let you take my winnings off me for a song. More fool me. I'll know better next time."

"Ha!" Hawthorn sounded pleased. "*There's* that pride. What is it that keeps you swallowing it, I wonder? Family fallen on hard times? Saving up to marry your sweetheart?"

"Shut up, you patronising prick." Ross's hand shook.

"No. Take it." Hawthorn pushed the box back towards Ross's chest. "You won't have any trouble selling it; I can even suggest some reputable places. The value of it's negligible to me, as you so kindly pointed out, and I *do* have some idea of what it would mean to you."

Ross let his arm drop, defeated. He nearly hummed with anger. "You really are a right bastard, aren't you? Even for a lord. You're putting *effort* into it."

Hawthorn gave a small smile. "There's still a chance Morris or Mrs. Vaughn realises you were involved in this, and you could be in real danger if so. Any doubts, anything that seems off—come to me."

"I wouldn't come to you if I were on fire. I'll go to her."

Ross nodded at Maud. "Knock me up if you need someone to go snooping for a fee, Miss B. Ask for me at the *Morning Post*."

Hawthorn's eyebrows rose. "A conservative rag, Robespierre?"

"As you say, my lord." Ross gave a deep bow, nearly from the waist. "It's amazing how much the lower orders can *swallow*, for a wage."

Ross let himself out. Hawthorn gave Maud and Violet his London addresses: townhouse and clubs.

"*You* won't be stubborn enough not to come to me for help. In fact, I am resigned to the inevitability that you'll come banging on the door in the middle of the night, Maud, requesting the loan of my valet and two hundred pounds."

"Our deal was for assistance during the voyage only, my lord. Is this compensation for damages as well?" Maud's dimples danced.

"Leave before I regret it," Hawthorn told her, and Maud laughed and pulled Violet towards the door.

From there they went up to the sun deck. It was already crowded with passengers eager to catch sight of friends or family as the *Lyric* pulled in. Or simply hungry for the sight of dry land, Violet supposed. She found them an empty stretch of railing angled away from the harbour, where it was quieter. Violet leaned her arms on the railing. Maud—gripped it, but stood half a foot farther back.

Of course. Maud wouldn't exactly be feeling friendly towards the edge of a deck at the moment. A chill echo of panic squeezed Violet with the memory.

"Shall we go back down?" Violet asked.

"No." Maud, who clutched her fear and did things anyway, took a firm step forward to stand beside her. "I'm going to miss this view. I want to enjoy it while I can."

The sky was unclouded and the high sun warmed their backs. Gulls called and swooped excitedly. Their arms were only just touching. They'd stood in a silence like this just before Maud asked Violet what she'd meant by *fucking other women*. This one had a similar feel, of things crowding unsaid, building and building like a cup held beneath an endlessly pouring jug.

It brimmed, unbearably. Violet turned the ring on her thumb. Violet opened her mouth to speak.

"It's hard for me," said Maud, low, "to know there are parts of someone that I can't see."

"I—"

"Because in my experience, the face you can't see is mocking you."

Violet had realised that much. Just because Maud had defied her upbringing to be a naked blade of *good,* it didn't mean the damage wasn't there, slipped in between all the stories about governesses and the strange, bleak, hostile fog that was the way she talked about her mother.

Violet said, "Most people aren't mocking you."

"I *know* that." Frustrated. "You can't let me trample on you while I'm learning it. And I—I trust the parts of you that you've let me see. So whatever it is that you're not telling me, *don't.* Not until you actually want to."

Violet turned to her. Maud kept looking out at the horizon. Her eyes today were an indeterminate sea green that paled beneath the vividness of the sky.

"You really do have a sense for people's weaknesses," Violet said, shaken.

Maud looked uncomfortable. "I know there's something— large, and fresh. It's lodged in you like a haunting."

"You're right. I don't want to talk about it."

Yet. It was too much of a promise to say aloud.

"Perhaps," said Maud carefully, "you could think of it as taking time to rehearse it properly first."

If Violet's immediate past was a monologue, what would it be? Defiant; ironic. Acknowledging the audience but not aiming at them. Delivered not from the centre of the stage—too bare, too exposed—but perhaps a stool or a dressing-chair set off to one side. Turning from the mirror, body only half-committed to the motion at first.

The character says, *You want to know why I'm scared to be myself.*

Shall we start with my marriage?

I fell in love with a man who could charm the world into knots. He talked me into investing all the money I had—he used my trust to get money from my friends, and they forgave me for it, and that was worse.

He might have loved me. I don't know.

I do know he gave me rings of wood, for illusion, and I didn't take the hint.

I ran away from the expectation that I would marry, and I got married anyway, because I mistook the person he expected me to be for a person I wanted to be. I am still married. The only reason my husband is still alive is because he disappeared, taking everything I had, before I could realise that he's a far better actor than I am.

I'm not ashamed at all of killing one man, or two.

I'm ashamed of the Violet who let a man dupe her and humiliate her, so that she fled the city where she'd clawed a place for herself as soon as the prospect of comfort was dangled. I'm so furious with her it makes me sick. I needed not to be her for a while. And so I ran onto this ship and found you, and you want me to be—myself.

The person I could be with you is a person I still barely recognise. There are no layers to her, and that scares me.

Even though I trust you—even though it feels like coming home, like setting down a weight—it scares me.

It was like having an audience after all, standing at the railing with the vast stretch of the sea like rows of seats invisible beyond the footlights. Saying nothing, but imagining it all exhaled and heading away on the wind.

It had been a long pause. Violet smiled sidelong at Maud. "It's awfully rough yet. It'll need to be in rehearsals for a long time."

"I don't mind. As long as it takes."

"I'll tell you this, without the price of a ticket: I don't know how Lady Enid put up with it all. I want to see my family, but I don't know how *much* of them I want to see. Especially now there's a good chance they'll only care about my inheritance."

"Nonsense. I'm sure your sisters love you for yourself," said Maud.

"You haven't met them. They could all be monsters."

A quirk of Maud's mouth. She seemed to have picked it up from Hawthorn. "Are they?"

"Maud," said Violet thoughtfully, "how would you react if I tried to give you some of my inheritance?"

"*What?*"

"There's no chance of Mrs. Navenby declaring you her heir in front of witnesses now. And I *am* going to have more wealth than I know what to do with."

To her surprise, Maud burst out laughing. "Violet. We've spent three nights in the same bed. If you now hand me an enormous sum of money, I'll be an even more successful trollop than if I really had become Hawthorn's mistress."

Violet caught the dimples and realised she was being teased. She smiled.

"I'm the one who gave away the locket. It would be—compensation for damages."

Maud sobered. Violet waited, arching a brow to let Maud know she hadn't actually been joking.

"For your brother?" she suggested.

"Oh, damn you," said Maud. "I should tell Mr. Ross I know exactly how he feels."

"This is what happens when you show people your weaknesses," said Violet. "They take advantage."

"Yes, how *dastardly* of you." Maud leaned her shoulder against Violet's. "I—I don't know. Let me talk to Robin."

"Of course."

"Violet . . ." It seemed like even Maud's courage was having trouble with the next part. She started again, then stopped. Finally—"We've had six days in very odd circumstances. Liminal space." A smile. "I'll understand if you say that this"—waving her hand between them—"is something that can't follow us onto dry land."

It was an easy escape, if Violet wanted one. But Maud had sidestepped another piece of the truth.

"What do *you* want, Maud?"

Maud's expression wavered and went luminous. It only occurred to Violet after several heartbeats to wonder if anyone but her brother had ever asked Maud that question before.

"I *want* us to keep on . . . um."

"Fucking," said Violet. It won her a scandalised look from an elderly couple who'd been ambling closer. She beamed at them and they hurried away again.

"I—yes. Though—I'd still want to spend time with you, even if you never touched me again."

I couldn't, Violet wanted to say. *One of us would have to move across an ocean.*

She breathed. She considered. She forced herself to think unselfishly, instead of grabbing at what she was being offered.

"Maud, you said it yourself. It's only been six days. You shouldn't leap into anything. And besides—you deserve someone like your brother's Edwin. Someone calm and clever and certain."

"But I'm not my brother," said Maud, "and that's not what I want." She met Violet's eyes. Waiting to be told no, and asking anyway. "I want someone who delights me. Nobody has ever taken me seriously the way you have, or made me feel so alive. I want to touch every part of you until I know you inside out."

"Christ," said Violet. "I almost want to let you."

She wanted to cradle a spell larger than anything she'd ever done before: a magic that could stop the ship so she could stand there for hours, warmed by the sun and by the breathtakingly honest force of Maud's affection. She wanted to say more. *I've never met anyone so deliberate about being good. I want to follow you forever, to see what you do to the world.*

She said, "Though I'm sure when your brother meets me, he'll agree that I'm a terrible influence."

"Not at all. He'll draw you aside and warn you not to let me use you as a chimney sweep."

"I haven't heard it called *that* before."

"No—oh. You're joking."

Violet surrendered all in a rush. She leaned in and kissed Maud's reddened cheek. There were more people around now, even on this side of the ship, but they were women. Companions. There was nothing scandalous about it at all.

Not that you'd have known it, by the way Maud's gaze dropped for a longing moment to Violet's mouth.

"Robin wants me to be happy," Maud said. "And being with you—when you're not *enraging*—makes me happy."

Violet was rescued from responding aloud when they were jostled by two young boys, both attempting to climb onto the railing and squabble for space as their parents scolded. They were coming into harbour; the horizon was cut up with buildings now, and the noise of civilisation filled the voyage's last minutes. Liminal space was where the magic was done, but you couldn't hide in it forever. Sooner or later you set foot on dry land.

The smile growing helplessly on Violet's face was one that she didn't recognise from her repertoire. It might have been lopsided. She couldn't tell. It felt young, and it felt true.

EPILOGUE

"Sir Robert's not home yet, Miss Maud," said Mrs. Hathaway. "He'll be sorry to have missed your arrival, I'm sure."

Maud had been missing her brother with a pang that grew sharper and sharper as the train swallowed up the miles between Southampton and London, but she sagged in unexpected relief. She could do with some time on her own, settling back into being Miss Maud Blyth.

"He knows you're expected—he'll be in before dinnertime," the housekeeper hastened to assure her, perhaps mistaking the softening of Maud's shoulders for disappointment. "And he's bringing Mr. Courcey as well."

Maud stepped to the side of the narrow entrance hall to allow the footmen to pass with her luggage, carried up from the cab. "I'm so glad. I've been longing to see them both."

"I'm sure they'll want to hear all about America," said Mrs. Hathaway, in tones that meant *and so do the rest of us.*

Maud laughed. "You know I won't be able to stop talking once Robin is home. I'll go and wash off the dust in the meantime."

The Blyths had sold their family townhouse earlier that year. This new house was smaller, and Maud loved how empty of memory it was; how much easier it was to breathe in every space. Visitors assumed it was her touch on the decorating, but most of it had been Robin's choices. The best of their parents' art collection crowded walls that were cheerfully papered in the newest styles, among which their old sedate furniture sat like elderly patrons in a butterfly-house.

It felt like walking through Robin's affection even when he was absent. Maud touched the corner of a picture-frame, straightening it against the red wallpaper with its pattern of honeysuckle and tulips.

She waved away the offer of help from one of the upstairs maids, then sponged down and changed out of her travelling-suit. Her lady's maid, Teresa, had taken a temporary position at her aunt's millinery shop, but Mrs. Hathaway would no doubt send word for her that very day. In the meantime, Maud could do for herself.

She paused for a moment with her fingers on the lace that edged her chemise, feeling her cheeks heat with memory.

Before they'd parted at the station, Maud had turned to Violet and said, *Don't let me ruin this.*

She'd expected a flippant reply about how Violet had ruined herself first. But Violet had looked at her, eyes grey and steady as rainless clouds.

And said, *You're doing a good job, Maud. I'll tell you when you aren't.*

Maud was putting the final touches to her dinner-dress when she heard voices downstairs. She flung down the bracelet she'd been failing to fasten around her wrist and went out into the upstairs hall to peer over the banister.

Robin and Edwin didn't hear her footsteps, muffled as they were by the thick hall rug. Neither did they look up. Robin was talking animatedly about what appeared to be a boxing match as the footman accepted their hats and briefcases and carried them away, leaving the two of them alone.

Edwin picked up one of Robin's hands as Robin talked, and examined the knuckles with a critical air. Then carried it to his lips for a brief, absent moment that made Robin's voice trail off entirely. Robin took his hand back. He looked at Edwin as though this slim, unremarkable man was everything he could imagine wanting.

Wistful heat slid through Maud's veins. She did want that sort of assured devotion, one day. And she wanted university.

And adventure. And to set the world right, both magical and unmagical.

"Standing around like a lump instead of taking your guest into the sitting room, Sir Robert?" she called down. "Anyone would think you'd been badly brought up."

Delight spread over Robin's face. "Maud!"

Maud dashed down the stairs, tripped on the edge of the rug, righted herself, and flung herself into her brother's arms. Something small inside her that had been tensed and afraid finally relaxed with the warmth of his grip and the familiar smell of his clothes.

She sent a beaming smile around Robin's arm to Edwin, who returned it with a small one of his own. She'd have flung herself at *him*, too, but Edwin was fussier about when and how he was touched.

"Oh, it's *so* good to see you both." She squeezed Robin, then released him.

"Your telegram from Southampton was singularly uninformative," said Edwin. "Robin had to go and exercise his nerves on an unfortunate viscount's face."

"Maudie, what happened?" said Robin. "Tell us everything."

Everything. Maud bit her lip. What was she supposed to say?

She was now the supposed mistress of the Baron Hawthorn, a shameless trollop, and still half-suspected of being a jewel thief.

She'd recruited three people to the cause. She'd had a chance at an inheritance, and lost it, and might have been offered part of another. She'd learned to say *fuck,* and to perform the verb; and to have it performed upon her, thoroughly, by a music-hall magician with a hundred smiles and one high-walled heart.

She could speak in the voices of the dead, and had only a fraction of an understanding of what that meant. She was the same Maud Blyth and yet she was someone different: more knowing, more cautious. More aware of her power.

She'd failed, and failed, and succeeded. She'd brought them

the cup of the Last Contract and knew where the knife was likely to be, even if their enemies knew it as well.

One on each side, and one to find, and a battle of some sort ahead.

"It is rather a lot to tell," she said. "But I suppose I should start with the parrot."

ACKNOWLEDGMENTS

I wrote this book during the latter half of 2020, which didn't look anything like we thought it would. All I wanted was to create something that would be *fun*. And, preferably, involve travel. Apologies and thanks to my editor, Ruoxi, for letting me follow an English manor house book about vulnerability and wallpaper with a bubbly Wodehousian romp.

Publishing in particular has had a dreadful slog of it these past few years, and I want to thank everyone in the industry who has worked so hard to continue bringing books to life.

In particular, the team at Tom Doherty Associates in the US: Irene Gallo, Ruoxi Chen, Sanaa Ali-Virani, Caroline Perny, Jocelyn Bright, Renata Sweeney, Megan Barnard, Samantha Friedlander, Lauren Hougen, Steven Bucsok, and Megan Kiddoo. And the people responsible for making this book look just as gorgeous as the first one: Christine Foltzer, Jess Kiley, Will Staehle, and Heather Saunders.

And the wonderful Tor UK folks: Bella Pagan, Georgia Summers, Jamie-Lee Nardone, Becky Lushey, Neil Lang, Stuart Dwyer, Leanne Williams, Rebecca Needes, and Holly Sheldrake.

We did it, team! Through viral variants untold and supply chain issues unnumbered we have fought our way here to the castle! And now we can cradle stubbornly in our arms the screaming child that is this book.

Thanks go as ever to my agent, Diana Fox (even though she made me take out the ghost threesome), as well as Ari and Isabel from Fox Literary, for their hilarious support and keen editorial eyes.

To Alexandra Rowland and Jennifer Mace, for their stalwart friendship, and for bashing out the plot with me and making me think harder and more deeply about the magical system.

To Jenn Lyons, for naming Dorian the Grey and introducing me to the history of Black opera companies in New York.

To Magali Ferare, for being the first pair of eyes and knowing exactly which bits to scream over.

To Kelsey, Alyshondra Meacham, Emily Tesh, Em Liu, Lex Croucher, Alix Harrow, and Grace Li, who all read versions of this book and provided enthusiasm at points when I most needed it.

To Tegan and Stuart for connection and laughter in a time of disconnection, and for dragging me groaning in the direction of productivity every Tuesday afternoon. And for all the wine.

To my family—Mum, Dad, Rob, Jess, and Lauren—I owe you more than I can say for your unstinting love and support. Particular thanks to my mother, for reading an early draft and telling me how to fix the exposition, always being up for an in-depth discussion of historical research (I'll put smugglers in the *next* trilogy, shall I?), and making sure I spelled Southampton correctly.

To the booksellers, reviewers, and fellow authors who welcomed my first steps into professional publishing with enthusiasm and generosity.

And finally, to every reader of my first book: those who preordered, those who picked it up on a whim, those who reached out to me with their glee at seeing queer joy on the page, and those who informed me that the elderly members of their book club had *not* expected the sexy bits but enjoyed them anyway. My debut year was nothing like I expected. You all still made it marvellous. Thank you.